A LION IN THE GRASS

MARK ZVONKOVIC

DOS PERRO PRESS

PART 1

1942 to 1964

OH SO SECRET

A FEW INCHES OF SNOW had fallen overnight and his boots made oval indentations in its clean, white surface during his early morning walk up Summit Avenue to Snelling. He bought a newspaper in the drugstore on the corner and walked through the Macalester campus to a diner on Grand Avenue. The waitress wasn't beautiful but he thought she was pretty because her face was full of character. And he liked the way she leaned against the end of the counter in front of the big opening to the kitchen where the cook put up the orders when they were ready. She appeared lost in thought but he knew she was vigilant because she would be in motion toward a plate on the counter before the cook rang the bell to announce it was ready.

Today was the anniversary of the Japanese attack of Pearl Harbor. He'd come to the diner before morning classes since the fall of 1940. It was his routine to display the inside cover of a textbook on the table so she could see his name printed there: Raymond Hatcher. Perhaps she would take the initiative of telling him her name. But the strategy had failed. So far she hadn't even acknowledged that he was a regular, as he'd observed her do with certain other customers. What was it that made her be distant? Raymond was young, only seventeen, which was why the clear explanation did not occur to him: that he was so much younger than the other customers, who were all at least the age of his parents. In Saint Paul, students didn't go to the diner for breakfast. They went to the dining hall on campus. Even if one had stopped at the diner, he would always be accompanied by at least one friend. Raymond was always alone and three years younger than his classmates.

Raymond watched the waitress serve another table. She wore a similar outfit every day. It wasn't a uniform; the diner wasn't a place that would require one. Each of the three outfits he'd seen was a dress, fitted nicely on the top, belted at the waist and extending loosely over the hips and just covering the knees. The sleeves went halfway from the shoulder to the elbow and buttons ran down the front. There was a collar around the neck and borders on the ends of the sleeves, both the same color and different from the dress. With the light blue dress, which she wore today, the collar and sleeve ends were tan. She also had an apron the color of the dress with a border matching the collar. There wasn't a hat, but if there was Raymond was sure that it, like the apron, would have the same color scheme. The other waitresses he'd seen from time to time were older and wore only drab, baggy outfits and hairnets.

Maybe she writes poetry and she'll let me read some of it, he thought. It was silly and hopeless. So he returned to reading his newspaper. The news was bad, as it always was. There was a letter to the editor that was clearly written by an isolationist. Saint Paul was infested with them. It made him angry. He resolved, as he did every day, that he would lie about his age and enlist in the army. His thoughts caused him to lose track of her and he was startled when she stood next to his table, so close that her hip touched its edge. Sitting straight up in his chair, he looked into her eyes for the first time.

"Sorry," she said. "I startled you."

He was so flustered, he couldn't speak. His mouth opened and then closed without a sound. He'd waited for years for this moment. All he could do was blush.

"You're Raymond Hatcher. Is that right?"

He found his composure. "Yes. But I don't think we've met."

"Every day you have a text book open with you name on it." She smiled in a way that made him think she knew what he'd been doing all along. "But we've met."

"I'm sorry," he said, blushing again. "I've forgotten."

She laughed. "We were very young and I only know because my mother reminded me last night. We met at a Christmas party at your grandparents. You were visiting from Europe. My mother and your mother are old friends from school."

"Oh," he said, not knowing what to say. There had been several Christmas parties and many children. His parents were in the foreign service and he'd lived in Europe his whole life. When it had been possible, which wasn't often, they'd traveled back for holidays.

She laughed again. This time it was closer to a giggle. Her hair was parted in the middle and held back behind her ears by barrettes. It was just long enough to slide across the tops of her shoulders when she moved.

"My parents were talking last night at dinner about the Hatchers being detained for five months in Germany after war was declared. I asked them, 'Would they be related to Raymond Hatcher?' And they said, 'Of course. He's their son.' Then I told them how I saw you almost every day here at the diner, and they thought it was such a coincidence. And that it was funny."

Her eyes were a deep blue, accented by the dark hair that was so curly it was like a picture frame around her face. His heart felt like it was being squeezed by a hand inside his chest.

"Would you like to sit down?" he asked.

"Oh no. That's against the rules."

"Maybe later, after work."

"I go right to school after my shift. I'm still in high school, even though we're the same age. My parents told me you were already in college, that you started when you were fifteen. They said you were some kind of prodigy."

Again, he was tongue-tied. Having spent so much time in ex-pat communities and embassies, he was very good at carrying on conversations with adults. And friends from the ex-pat schools had been easy to talk to as they were all thrown together in identical circumstances. But this was new territory. She tilted her head to the left and brushed back the hair that settled on that shoulder. He suspected she was showing him she was waiting for him to speak, in the same way raising her eyebrows would have suggested she was impatient.

"It's not so," he said. "The schools where we lived in Europe were advanced. And I went to school twelve months a year. They had to keep me busy."

The cook rang the bell at the counter and she had to go retrieve an order. As the time approached 8:00 a.m. the diner became busy as it always did, and their interactions were limited to eye contact and smiles. When he stood to leave for his first class, she came by and suggested he come an hour earlier the next day. She came to work at the diner's opening at 5:00 a.m., and business did not pick up until 7:00 a.m.

Raymond was a quick study when it came to social and cultural interactions, and in only a couple of days he was conversing easily with the girl. He thought her mysterious because she told him she lived in an affluent neighborhood on Grand Avenue, not far from his grandparents, and he wondered why she was working in a diner in the early mornings before school. It was hard to get his questions answered because their conversations were sporadic, in between taking orders and delivering food. Then, just before Christmas, she came with her parents to his grandparents for a Christmas party and they sat on two chairs pulled close to the fireplace, talking as intensely as the snow flew back and forth outside the window near them. After three hours and almost as many feet of snow, he had many questions answered, but the mystery remained unsolved. She was as independent as a cat, which explained why she worked and why she had not accepted the overtures he had made with the open flap of his text book until she had discovered on her own who he was. He learned she would attend Macalester in the fall of 1943. What he couldn't figure out was the source of her motivation, the force that propelled her to work, to achieve academic honors and, yes, to write poetry.

They became close friends, although not in the romantic sense. Raymond frequently thought that he loved her, but he worried that a declaration of love would push her away from him. He wasn't sure whether it was practicality or independence but he believed she would not be receptive to romance. His instincts told him that their friendship would flourish if romance wasn't involved, but he was too young to understand why that was the case. He felt he could tell her anything about himself, and he soon told her his plan to lie about his age and join the army.

"It's just stupid," she said. His face must have shown that the comment hurt him. "I don't mean you're stupid, Raymond. I mean you have not given much thought to the idea. Why not add a course in the spring and graduate early?"

He'd told her that he had enough credits to graduate in three years if he took one more course. But he hadn't thought much more about it because he intended to quit school and join the army. "I could do that," he said, although not convinced.

"Think about it Raymond," she said. "You will turn eighteen next June, so you won't have to lie. And, you'll have a degree, which will let you get a commission and have more say in how you will serve. I know you believe the war is necessary, but you can't be so foolish as to think you should fight in the trenches."

"I suppose that makes sense, but, officer or not, I want to go where I can be of the most use."

"Right," she said and laughed. "They really need a brain like yours in the infantry. Besides, you're going to get caught in your lie. Your grandfather is on the local draft board. Do you think he won't find out?" She shook her head, which caused a riot to break out among her curly hair. When not at work, it was never restrained by barrettes. She was right. And her face was beautiful when she was triumphant.

He took the extra course. She also convinced him to inform his father of his plans. A frantic correspondence between Raymond and his father ensued. His father assured him he could get him a deferral of service or at least a position that would result in his remaining in the United States for the duration of the war. Raymond refused all such overtures, but finally agreed that before he enlisted he would go to Washington to meet a friend of his father's, a Mr. Kennan, for advice on which military branch he might best serve.

Raymond met Kennan in a townhouse in Georgetown. Kennan was in a comfortable chair, his long legs on an ottoman covered with a quilt. His hands were never still. To Raymond it looked like he was in a constant struggle to keep them from grasping one of the many books piled on end tables on either side of him. They spoke for two hours before the next visitor, Kennan's doctor, was announced. Raymond was instructed to return the next day. When he ran through their conversation in his mind that evening he struggled to understand the relevance of Kennan's comment that American institutions were dysfunctional and bureaucratic, and, according to Kennan, the question for Raymond was where he would best triumph over the mountain of incompetence he would face. Who cares? Raymond asked himself. I'm just going to fight an enemy, not a bureaucracy. Kennan had also suggested that Raymond's young mind had not yet mastered the application of the fine intellect he exhibited, so Raymond could confidently discuss the theories of Clausewitz, but had no clue as to their application. That comment Raymond understood, and had to agree with. But he didn't like it.

When Raymond returned to the townhouse the next day, he found that Kennan had two other guests, whom he introduced as David Bruce and referred to as "Bruce," and an older gentleman, clearly an Englishman, whom Kennan called "Woolley." Although they were dressed as civilians, they sat and spoke with a military presence. There was much small talk, which finally strained Raymond's patience. His obligation to his father was met, he decided, and he was on the verge of standing to leave when David Bruce leaned forward and addressed him.

"Can you swim?" he asked.

Raymond was unnerved. "Of course I can swim."

"Right," Woolley chimed in. "But can you swim or just keep from drowning?"

"What?"

"There's a difference. If I threw you off a boat, would you swim the mile to shore or just tread water until someone rescued you?"

Raymond saw that Woolley controlled his demeanor perfectly, as only the English can do. Raymond was familiar with that, and he could have been comforted, but the vague questions aggravated him.

"I played water polo when I spent a summer in England a few years ago," he said. He sounded to himself like a querulous boy defending himself from an insult. They said nothing. "I had to swim laps to train," he added.

"Young man," said Woolley, "we understand from Mr. Kennan that you plan to enlist in the army, but we're looking for a few candidates for assignments in the Pacific. We'll have to give you some tests, but you may possess the skills we have in mind."

"I hadn't thought of the navy. Where would I be stationed? Would I serve on a ship?"

"Actually, you'll be stationed on the East Coast at first, at a special facility."

Raymond laughed and shook his head. When he saw that neither Bruce nor Woolley changed his expression, he thought perhaps he'd misunderstood. They looked at each other silently for a few moments.

"That's not my plan," he said. "I don't want to spend a lot of time training, and then be deployed as an adviser. You probably think my academic credentials warrant that kind of job."

Both Woolley and Bruce smiled. Raymond wondered if they understood what he was feeling.

"You would not be staying home," Woolley replied. "If you're accepted, you will be commissioned as an officer in the navy and then immediately loaned to another organization. You–"

"Loaned? How does that work?"

Raymond looked at Kennan, who had picked up a book and was paying no attention to them. The two men were not making sense to Raymond. He regretted that he had come to see Keenan rather than proceed with his original plan.

"We can't tell you much until we do a background check and get you a security clearance," Woolley continued. "But I can assure you that you'll have a combat assignment. It will be one where you'll need your intellect as much as physical prowess. You would be a part of a small team, not a platoon. You would be deployed in the Pacific. That's all I can tell you now."

Raymond sat for a while looking at the two men, neither of whom seemed uncomfortable with the silence. He did not view himself as an impetuous person, but for some reason he wanted to make a decision now, get it over with, whatever it was. He thought about how meticulous his father always seemed when making a decision. But he had a hunch, suddenly, that what these guys were talking about, even if he didn't understand it, would be much more exciting than the army.

Raymond hadn't said anything, so Woolley added, "If you're accepted, you'll have to depart immediately and the training will be intense. You'll more than likely take part in an operation before the end of the year. Going through boot camp in the army, if you went that route, would not put you in action until next spring."

Raymond jumped to his feet. "Where do I go to apply?"

2

AFTER HIS SECURITY CLEARANCE WAS confirmed and he signed up, Raymond discovered that Woolley had bent the truth somewhat. The Office of Strategic Services–the OSS, which was what he'd joined–was a freewheeling organization, and no matter what the plan was at any time, William Donovan, its head, could change it at will. OSS operations required agents with intellect and creativity. As a young man with knowledge of European geography and fluency in four languages, Raymond was a prize. He understood that the OSS would probably deploy him in Algiers. The Pacific story had been bait. But it was okay with him.

In June, he reported to a secret facility in Maryland where he undertook OSS basic training. Due to the dearth of intelligence professionals in their ranks, the OSS condensed the typical three-month military training into three weeks. That made the training insanely rigorous–the recruits were up before dawn and trained until late at night. Weekends were no different from weekdays. Several members of the class dropped out, but Raymond, already in good shape at the start, excelled both physically and mentally. Every night, his muscles aching, he fell asleep quickly, filled with the satisfaction that comes from achieving a milestone toward an aspiration, like passing the first mile marker in a footrace. At the end of the period, the instructors, including several OSS officers from Washington, who were actually psychologists from the Morale Operations

Group, threw them a party, which actually turned out to be a final exam on their abilities to maintain secrecy and a sense of mission at times when ostensibly their guard was down. A few more recruits were eliminated the next day.

Specialized training occurred over the next six weeks, which included sabotage and celestial navigation. There were lessons in close combat from an older Englishman known as Fearless Dan, who spoke with perfect diction and rarely smiled. Raymond always volunteered to be the one on whom Fearless Dan demonstrated his moves. In the evenings he studied the precise location of the black-and-blue marks on his body as a way of committing those moves to memory.

After three weeks, Raymond and three others moved to another facility, where they engaged with Fearless Dan in more intense hand-to-hand combat training, including offensive and defensive moves that involved knives. Fearless Dan called this combat "gutter fighting," in which there was no sense of fair play. "There is no sportsmanship involved in what you will face," he told them. "Be a sportsman and you will die." It was a strange premise, Raymond thought one evening after he'd finished a survey of his bruises. You gave no benefit of the doubt before you killed. And it's perverted, he mused, that the ideal spy is one who kills without remorse. Can achievement of an ideal be iniquitous? The more accomplished he became with Fearless Dan the more he felt a darkness seeping into him. But he'd worry about it later, he decided.

When the Fearless Dan exercises ended, Raymond was granted a five-day pass. He thought his training was going well and he didn't particularly want a break. But he felt an obligation to visit his aunt and uncle with whom he had lived during his college years in Saint Paul.

In Saint Paul, Raymond walked the length of Summit Avenue. At the west end, he stood on a bluff overlooking the Mississippi River and gazed toward Minneapolis. At the other end, where Summit intersected Selby Avenue, he climbed the stairs in front of the Cathedral. From there he looked down at the city buildings clustered along the ninety-degree bend in the river. He imagined he was looking at the same segment of river water he had seen from the Minneapolis view, having kept pace with the flow of the river during his walk down Summit. It was silly, he thought, but it was comforting to think he could match the pace of the river. He believed the river's greatest power came from its steadfastness, and it was exhilarating to think he could imitate it.

While sitting on the Cathedral steps, he considered walking back up Summit and over to the diner. But he decided he wouldn't. He had changed dramatically on account of his training and he was afraid she, a pacifist, would see it and be disappointed. It wasn't that he didn't like the person he'd become. But the rules of secrecy imposed by OSS would make it impossible to answer the very sharp questions he knew she would ask. It would be awkward. He would write her a letter at some point.

When he got back to his aunt's house on Summit, he saw his reflection in the glass on the door. His reflection bothered him because he appeared so conventional. They'd cut off his wavy brown hair. He hadn't thought he was handsome, but he'd thought his general appearance was young and appealing. He knew he should get over it, that it was better for an officer to look older, particularly for one as young as he was. The ensign in the reflection was someone Raymond was supposed to be, and he was skeptical he could pull it off. Inside the house, his aunt was waiting for him to assure her he was going to be okay, that no harm could possibly come to him. He was going to lie to her, and he wasn't happy about it. On account of what he'd learned so far at OSS, he feared it would be the first of a great many lies he would tell.

When Raymond returned to Washington on Sunday afternoon to pick up his gear, he found a marine waiting for him at his barracks.

"Your orders have changed," the man told him. "Get your things and come with me."

Raymond had heard a rumor that a new maritime base was being established in the Bahamas, and he guessed he was being sent there. As a foreign-service child who had been relocated frequently, he was accustomed to last-minute changes, and he thought this one a good thing because swimming in the Potomac had never sounded appealing. When the marine took the car over a bridge into downtown Washington, Raymond figured he would be put on a train for Florida.

"Train station," he said, not really expecting a reply.

"No, sir."

"Oh, of course. Then to a suite at the Hay-Adams."

The marine glanced over at Raymond for a moment and said, "Headquarters, sir."

After he arrived at a cluster of buildings on E Street, Raymond was ushered into a conference room where David Bruce and a tall, husky man were looking at a map. He saw that it was a map of the Adriatic, scaled to show the coasts of Italy and Yugoslavia. He had lived in Dubrovnik for a time and liked it.

Soon, General Donovan walked into the room, followed by another tall man. Raymond sprang to his feet and pushed back his shoulders. But before his arm started the arc to a salute, Donovan gestured that it was unnecessary.

"This is the OSS, young man. We dispense with that saluting nonsense."

The other men had stood as well. One of the tall men greeted the other tall man, saying something that David laughed at but Raymond did not catch. Following Donovan's lead, they all sat down.

"So, Ensign Hatcher, Colonel Bruce tells me you're one very smart swimmer."

"Sir?"

Raymond was confused for a moment. He had not yet done any swimming and in fact had forgotten about the questions months ago from Woolley and David. Donovan was quietly looking him over with no expression on his face.

"And it seems you spent some time with your family when you were younger in Dubrovnik and in Belgrade. And you have Croatian-language skills."

"My father is a foreign-service officer and we were posted there for several years. I'm not sure about the language skills. There are many dialects in the region." He didn't want to boast, but he did have a knack for languages. After a couple of days in a country he could speak a language well enough to get around and order dinner. In a week he could have a conversation on the street with a resident. His mind took in idiomatic expressions the same way his lungs inhaled the air.

Donovan laughed. "Right. You don't suspect that I know what he does in the foreign service?"

"He's a foreign-service officer in the State Department. What exactly he does, sir, I couldn't say."

Raymond's father, Leland Hatcher, began his career in 1904 as a young lawyer in Watertown, Connecticut, where he worked for Robert Lansing, specializing in international affairs. After the Germans sank the Lusitania, Lansing was appointed secretary of state and created the Bureau of Secret Intelligence, to which Leland was assigned. In 1918, Leland became a special aide to Lansing and lived in Versailles during the treaty negotiations.

Donovan took a moment to read some papers in a folder and then looked at Colonel David Bruce. "He's had all his basic training, I see."

"Yes," Bruce answered. "He's scheduled to start training with the Maritime Unit tomorrow. We have him slated for the Operational Swimmers Group."

"We're going to delay that," Donovan said authoritatively, after perusing a few more papers.

He pulled another folder from the stack and began to look through it. Raymond thought the man bore no resemblance to the character called "Wild Bill Donovan" by so many. Dressed in a three-piece suit with a white handkerchief emerging like a pyramid from the chest pocket, he appeared to be reviewing papers for a banking transaction. His hair, combed neatly, was parted high up on the right side of his head and was almost white; he had turned sixty at the beginning of the year. He could have been on his way to a casting call for a movie involving Roman senators, although when his face was at rest his demeanor was inviting, and not stern.

Raymond sat tranquilly, wondering what would come next but feeling no impatience. He thought about the river flowing by Saint Paul. It had been a good trip. After a minute, Donovan looked around the table. His gaze stopped at Raymond.

"You've been introduced?"

"No, sir."

"These two gentlemen on either side of me are army types. Major Farish on my left and Lieutenant Colonel Seitz on my right. And you already know Colonel Bruce."

"Yes, sir."

"Next week, we're going to drop Farish and Seitz into Yugoslavia," Donovan stated. "We'll give them each a parachute to make it easier." Donovan kept his deadpan expression. Farish and Seitz grimaced.

"General, if we sent you, you could just walk across the Adriatic from Italy," Bruce said.

Donovan smiled at that. "Farish is going to see Tito right up here." He stabbed his finger at an area of the map near Jajce. Then he moved his hand across to the mountainous region of Ravna Gora, south of Belgrade. "Seitz will jump here. Of course, they'll be accompanied by our English cousins."

Raymond knew Yugoslavia's geography. He guessed that was why he was at the table. The terrain would make the mission perilous, he knew.

"I've had jump training," he said.

"Oh yes," Donovan said, leaning back in his chair. "But you won't be needing that. You know your way around a sailboat, I understand."

Raymond was astonished. He looked around the table at the composed faces of the others and saw he was the only one who didn't know what Donovan had in mind. If they were not all looking so serious, it might have been comical, he thought.

"These gentlemen are jumping into Yugoslavia with British intelligence to try to get a handle on who's doing what to whom there, the problem being that the resistance leaders seem to be more focused on fighting each other than the Germans," Donovan said. "The Brits have already sent in a couple of teams and come up with nothing. They're spending entirely too much effort trying to decide who should be the captain of the resistance. We've no time for that. We don't give a damn who the captain is. What we want is to put arms and supplies in their hands and point them at the Germans. It's easy. Whoever does it best, gets the most."

There were some nods but no one spoke. They waited. Was this how OSS made all its plans? Raymond wondered. Four guys in a room with a couple of maps, waiting for a visionary to speak?

"While the Brits go clodhopping around the country," Donovan continued, "we're going to sail right in with some goods and get things cracking. We're not going to tell them. Farish and Seitz here will keep them mollified, and will give us a heads-up if we need to adjust our plans in any way."

Donovan paused. He appeared to be awaiting a question or a reaction. None came, and Raymond thought he looked irritated. When he continued, he looked directly at Raymond. "I do mean sail. To get things started, I want you to take a sailboat across the Adriatic to Yugoslavia from here." He drew a line from Bari, on the Italian coast, to the Dalmatian coast. "You've sailed in these waters. You know the harbors, the people, the customs. If you do it right, we don't think the Germans will be suspicious."

Raymond was dumbfounded. Donovan was overestimating his sailing experience on the Yugoslavian coast. Did he have good information? He had been a kid. He was still a kid. And then it dawned on him.

"You've spoken to my father?"

Donovan shrugged, and a tiny grin curved up the sides of his mouth. "Now and then. We go way back."

"I was a boy when we sailed there." And I'm still a boy.

"It makes no difference. You captained that boat into a harbor at night without a bump."

The memory of the incident, not to mention that Donovan had the details, made Raymond nervous. He had been thirteen. The winds that day had been fickle and they had not made port by dark. There was no moon, and they could see no lights on an island not far off the coast they thought they were near. They'd not even been sure they were at the harbor entrance they saw on their charts and not just off another part of the rocky shoreline. His father had made him take the helm. "Take it slow, son, and we'll feel our way in," he'd said. As they inched forward, listening for surf on rocks and indications of the harbor, like a dog barking or a bell from a marker buoy, his father had occasionally said, "It feels like we should move a touch to the starboard. What do you think?" In the end, they were guided by a lone, dim candle in a window of a small house on a tiny bay just to the west of the main harbor shown on their chart. The chart had no indication of the bay. After they'd dropped anchor, Raymond had shaken for an hour.

"My father was with me."

"And you passed the test. That's good enough for me."

"What kind of boat is it?"

Donovan waved his hand in dismissal. "I'm sure you'll find something when you get there." He paused for a moment. "And I assume you've heard that the Italian forces agreed yesterday to lay down their arms."

Raymond and the other men were shocked. Their faces showed it. No one had to speak.

Donovan chuckled. "We're very good at keeping secrets from each other. In any case, the army plans to keep it quiet in case the Germans don't know about it yet. They want to get our boys up the boot before the Germans regroup. They're not sure either whether the Italian forces in Yugoslavia are part of the deal, or even if they know about it. So we've got to move fast."

And that was that. Donovan launched into deployment information for each of them. Raymond was to find transport as soon as possible to Cairo, where he was to report to Major Dutton, who was planning the shipment of arms and supplies to the coast of Yugoslavia. After Donovan left, Farish and Seitz reviewed with Raymond the routes into Yugoslavia from the Dalmatian coast and arranged a tentative rendezvous for the end of the following month. Colonel Bruce returned with written orders for each of them, which they would need for their transport.

Raymond thought he should keep his thoughts to himself, but he couldn't. "I'm not sure I entirely understood General Donovan," he said, hoping he had put it as tactfully as possible.

The men laughed. "No one really understands Donovan," Bruce said. "Depending on your point of view, he's either unconventional or just plain crazy." He added that Donovan was more creative than methodical and would propose schemes that astounded everyone around him. His strategies sometimes led to missions that were outside the conventional military wisdom. Although he'd had his share of failures, his results made the tactics he employed look prescient.

As they were about to leave the room, Raymond looked at his orders. "There's a mistake in my rank, sir. I'm an ensign," he said to Bruce.

Bruce shook his head. "No mistake, Lieutenant Hatcher. You've been promoted. He does that sometimes. You're probably the youngest lieutenant JG ever to serve in the navy."

3

IN THE SPRING OF 1940, Georges Piquart, fifteen years old, glanced anxiously over his shoulder, back toward Île de la Cité. It was a crystal-clear day and the midafternoon sunshine sparkled on the surface of the river Seine. He was strolling along the pedestrian way of the Quai des Tuileries with his friend Bernard de Lattre, who was twelve. A minute earlier, the two boys had been holding hands when they entered the shadow beneath the Pont Royal. They had not seen the gentleman approaching them, an officer in the French Fourteenth Infantry Division, of which Bernard's father was the commander. Georges had released Bernard's hand immediately, but too late, for the officer had glared at them as they went by. Without having to ask, Georges knew Bernard was unperturbed. For him, holding Georges's hand was no more than a demonstration of friendship. But Georges's father would hear of the incident from Commander de Lattre, and Georges would be spoken to harshly, reminded that he was an older boy who could be thought to be exploiting young Bernard's affections.

Bernard soon resumed their conversation, as if nothing had intervened. Georges was having difficulty paying attention to Bernard. A few moments earlier, Bernard had said something that caused Georges to remember the past summer, when he and Bernard had spent a week at the Piquart family's country chateau at Honfleur. There, they'd stood on a quay to look at the water flowing from the mouth of the Seine into the English Channel.

"Well, do you think we could beat them?" Bernard asked, stopping suddenly and walking to a point just above the river. The move jolted Georges back to the present.

"Beat who?"

"You haven't been listening to me, Georges."

The boys looked at each other for a moment. Bernard took Georges by the hand and the two of them faced the river. To Georges it felt like a bolt of electricity had traveled up his arm and then down into his groin.

"The liters of water now passing us in the river, Georges. Do you think we could beat them to Honfleur?"

Georges thought for a moment. "Perhaps if we were in a boat and there were no obstructions. The roads meander through the countryside too much—we couldn't go fast enough in a car."

Bernard shook his head slowly. Georges felt his hand being released. It fell to his side, a limp vestige, cold and lifeless.

"You will never be a poet, Georges. The answer is no. No matter how fast we went we would not beat them. The river is both constant and inconstant. It is transformed by everything it passes, and the liters are never the same. Yet, at Honfleur it possesses its same greatness, because it hasn't lost its connection to Paris. It's a comfort to me. To see the river water pass in front of us and know the very same thing is occurring at Honfleur."

Georges didn't know what to say. Bernard could be obtuse. It was remarkable that a twelve-year-old boy could think in such metaphysical terms. Perhaps it came from his being an only child. Georges could rarely make sense of it. He was patient with Bernard only for the chance of holding his hand again.

"Yes. Yes. I see what you mean. Of course," Georges said.

Bernard laughed, then took Georges's hand. "Come," he said, and moved toward the Tuileries Garden. They would sit on a bench and wager on the date the buds on the trees would blossom.

Those blooms were hardly off the trees when the Germans arrived in Paris. The Reich soldiers goose-stepped down the Champs-Élysées daily. Walking in the Tuileries Garden was impossible, particularly in the vicinity of the Jeu de Paume, where the Germans were collecting confiscated works of art. Two boys who sat on a bench holding hands would be risking their lives.

It was a moot issue. Bernard matured rapidly during the occupation, as if the invasion had triggered this biological change. Over the next two years, his voice deepened and his manner became surly at times. He bristled when Georges displayed affection; he was too consumed by books concerning the art of war to bother with their old pastimes. Bernard hated the Nazi's and often said he would fight them with the resistance as soon as he was old enough to leave school. His father, Jean de Lattre, had fought with the resistance against the Vichy government. Then the Vichy regime was pushed aside and Germany occupied southern France. Bernard's father was arrested and sent to prison at Riom. In September 1943, Georges accompanied Bernard to Riom, where they aided the underground in bringing about the elder de Lattre's escape to Algiers.

When they went into hiding in the Pyrenees soon after, Bernard was as tall as Georges, and as physically fit as Georges was soft and gentle. Georges had a delicate, almost porcelain countenance. His nose and chin were sharp but not pointed, and his mouth and eyebrows seemed to flow across his face. He had diminutive shoulders and a chest that was hard to detect beneath his shirt, which made his neck appear twice as long as it was. In Paris he had often worn a beret, which he'd positioned toward the left side of his face at a rakish angle. In the Pyrenees, emulating Bernard, he wore a hat with a brim all around, although he used its chin strap to curl the brim on the left side, while Bernard's hat sat squarely on his head, the strap hanging against his collarbone.

One evening Georges overheard one of their small band of partisans refer to him as "pretty George." He knew then that he had to change himself or he would lose Bernard's friendship completely. Hope for a requited love was already lost. Bernard had begun to fraternize with the other men. Georges was tolerated, not embraced. So he set about making himself into one of them.

A few days after Georges turned nineteen, he and Bernard made their way across the Pyrenees to Spain. There were four of them traveling together. When they reached the small mountain passage through which they would cross into Spain, they split into twos, Georges going with a man named Felix and Bernard with the other. Georges and Felix came upon a German soldier having his way with a girl on a bed of pine needles. Without warning, Felix moved rapidly toward them, motioning for Georges to follow him. They surprised the couple and Georges found himself struggling with the soldier. "Your blade, your blade," Felix hissed, as he grappled with the girl, holding his hand over her mouth to stifle her screams. Georges and the soldier were in a tight struggle, but Georges had the advantage because the soldier's pants were around his ankles; he hadn't had time to get them buttoned or to retrieve his weapon. The physical contact with the man suddenly exhilarated Georges. Energy flowed through him. In a wild release of passion pent-up for more than a year, he plunged his knife into the soldier's chest.

He was reunited with Bernard soon after they crossed the border. They traversed Spain over the course of several nights. On the Mediterranean coast, they sat in a small café, waiting for the boat that would take them to North Africa.

"You haven't told me what happened back at the border, Georges," Bernard said casually. "Felix told me you had to kill a border guard."

Georges glanced at Bernard, who was gazing off into the distance. No doubt, Felix had also said something about the struggle, yet Bernard appeared indifferent. Georges did not like the way Bernard had become insouciant about all things. If a bomb had exploded just outside the café, Georges would have jumped to his feet, while Bernard would have maintained his composure, at most turning his head in the direction of the smoke.

"It was nothing," Georges said.

"Georges, killing a man is something. It didn't bother you?"

"It was nothing," Georges repeated.

How much did Felix tell? Georges wondered. He suspected that Felix had seen the passion on his face after the soldier had crumpled to the ground. And then the girl. Georges had fallen upon her in a craze, ripping away her remaining clothing and pinning her to the ground with his hips, and his arms, straight, holding his upper torso aloft. He had barely heard her cries, so loud was the rush of blood through his veins. At his climax he had thrown back his head and roared. When he'd regained his senses and stood above his whimpering conquest, buttoning his pants, he'd seen Felix leaning against a tree, one ankle crossed over the other, arms folded across his chest, a wide smile on his face. But nothing had been spoken between them. They'd simply picked up their gear and gone to meet Bernard.

In Algiers, Bernard was welcomed as a hero, while hardly any notice was given to Georges. Only Bernard was given credit for General de Lattre's escape from Riom the prior year. General de Gaulle granted a special dispensation to allow Bernard to join the Free French Army, as he was only sixteen years old at the time. Georges joined the Free French as well, but he knew that Bernard's father would make certain the two were separated immediately. Bernard was to be a part of Operation Dragoon, commanded by his father. Georges was given orders to go to Italy to serve under General Juin, whose Moroccan Goumiers were about to attack the Gustav Line.

They sat in a bar the evening before they would muster for their transports. Bernard's enthusiasm had been infectious at first. But the more Bernard talked about his orders, the clearer it became to Georges that his mission to Italy was an inferior assignment. He began to think Bernard's pronouncements were expressions of self-importance. This attitude aggravated Georges and made him fear that Bernard had no strong feelings for him.

"We shall restore the glory of France," Bernard repeated for the tenth time. "The enemy will be chased across the Maginot. Paris will be free."

"I am happy for you," Georges said. "You'll be taking part in history."

"But you also, Georges. We will be moving forth together, to Germany."

Georges held his tongue. Bernard had evidently not paid close attention in geography class when they were students together in Paris. An immense mountain range separated Italy from France and Germany. He wouldn't be marching in the same direction as Bernard. If he ever moved beyond Italy, it would be to the east.

Finally, the two stood outside, on their way to their separate barracks. Bernard remained flushed with excitement. Georges was pale, his skin cold.

"My friend!" Bernard exclaimed. He hugged Georges, delivering several hardy slaps to the back. "We shall next meet in Paris. Yes?"

They were an arm's length apart; Bernard's hands were on George's shoulders. Georges's eyes flashed. Deep inside, he felt his emotions stirring. He looked at Bernard's lips. He thought to put his mouth to them. But he was suddenly filled with disgust, a caustic taste on his tongue. He pulled himself away.

"Yes, Bernard," he said, and looked beyond the boy into a dark alley, at the end of which, he knew, was a brothel. "We shall meet again in Paris."

4

AROUND THE TIME OF GENERAL de Lattre's escape from prison, Raymond reached Cairo. There he found a line of officers waiting outside the door to Major Dutton's office. One of the officers told Raymond they were waiting to volunteer for Dutton's mission. As this was the OSS, no facts about the mission were available. There wasn't even confirmation that there really was a mission. But anything was better than sitting around Cairo watching the sand blow down the streets, the man told Raymond. Dutton was in a rage at the moment, so no one dared to enter his office. Raymond made his way past them and closed the door behind him.

"Goddamn Royal Navy," Dutton yelled, as he threw a handful of papers into a trash can. Then he saw Raymond standing by the closed door. "And who the hell are you?"

"Lieutenant Hatcher."

Raymond tried to appear confident. It was hard, because he was tired. It had taken him almost a week to get to Cairo, flying in broken-down transport planes from one airfield to another. He handed his orders to Dutton.

"Just what I need, another baby lieutenant," Dutton said, throwing Raymond's orders onto the desk. "Go wait in line."

"No, sir," Raymond said, and stood as straight as possible when Dutton turned on him with a fierce look. "General Donovan instructed me not to leave your office until you brought me in on the operation. So I can't wait in line."

It was true. General Donovan knew Dutton, so he had expected this scene. "Hold your ground, even if he says he's going to shoot you," he had said. "He'll come around."

Dutton ripped up the orders and threw the pieces at Raymond. "I don't care if Jesus Christ himself sent you. Get the hell out of here."

"I've sailed in the Adriatic around Dubrovnik," Raymond said quickly. "I know all the smaller harbors around there."

Donovan had told him to exaggerate. The look that came across Dutton's face showed Raymond it had worked. Dutton spread out a map on his desk and beckoned Raymond to approach.

"Where are you from?"

"General Donovan sent me."

"Where were you born?"

"Saint Paul, Minnesota. But I've lived in Belgrade and Dubrovnik."

"Well, I'll be damned! Sit down, son."

It was Minnesota, not Yugoslavia, that made the difference. Dutton was from Duluth, Raymond learned. Dutton tried to piece the orders back together. After a minute he said, "Whatever," and threw them into the trash can.

Dutton explained to Raymond that he'd thought the most difficult part of his mission to Yugoslavia would be obtaining supplies. But that had been easy–so easy, in fact, that he was having difficulty finding storage for the stuff. His plan all along had been to load the supplies onto naval vessels in Bari and haul them across the Adriatic to the coast near Dubrovnik. Evidently, Donovan had not suggested a sailboat to him. Now, Allied command in Algiers had just informed him that Germans had moved down the Yugoslavian coast to replace the withdrawing Italians. The larger ports were mined and heavily fortified. He would use smaller ships to access the smaller harbors, he'd told them. Their response had been alarmingly vague, a statement to the effect that they would have to see what was available. Worse, they had told him he'd have to coordinate with the Royal Navy; the coast of Yugoslavia was their turf. He didn't care for the British, he told Raymond. They had too many rules, and they'd sent him an inch-thick stack of papers to fill out.

"You say you know some small harbors," Dutton said. "Would they be mined?"

"I don't know. But if we could get to Bari, we might find some sailors in the harbor who would know."

The idea improved Dutton's mood. "We can worry about the goddamn British later," he said.

The next day, Raymond and Dutton went to Algiers. Dutton's mood was positive; he had several ideas for how to get the navy to give them transport ships once he could tell them he'd located some harbors without mines. But Raymond watched his optimism slip away after a few days of waiting for one bureaucrat or another, who would eventually say he couldn't help them.

"Maybe we should go camp out in Ike's waiting room," Raymond said after a couple of days of failures. Algiers was where Eisenhower had his headquarters. Dutton looked at him the way one looks when he's just heard something too dumb to believe he's just heard it. Then he laughed.

"Raymond, if we do that, we'll be on the next plane back to Cairo."

They kept looking for an angle. It was apparent that no one on the American side wanted to deal with England's military chief in Italy, who preferred an invasion of Yugoslavia over supporting the partisans. The Americans wanted only to keep moving up the boot of Italy until they pushed the Germans north of Rome. Eisenhower and Roosevelt favored an invasion of Germany from the west; the Balkans would be too much trouble. Everyone they talked to agreed that sending aid, not troops, to Yugoslavia would be a good thing. But they needed British concurrence.

Finally they caught a break. At a special-operations office, Raymond sat in a waiting room next to a man who looked as frustrated as Raymond felt. Raymond thought he was an Italian resistance fighter because in his lap was a cap with a single star on its front. Then the man muttered to himself about how long he'd been waiting. Raymond recognized the language.

"Zdravo," Raymond said to the man.

The man was startled. For a moment he looked at Raymond suspiciously, but then he began speaking rapidly in Serbo-Croatian. Raymond had to stop him.

"My apologies," he said in the formal Croatian he knew, "but you're speaking too fast for me."

The man laughed. "It's okay," he said in English. "I can talk like you."

Josep Stegineo was one of Tito's partisans. He explained to Raymond that he'd brought a boatload of wounded men to Bari from the Dalmatian coast. The U.S. naval officer in charge–the NOIC–at Bari had not known what to do with him, so he'd sent him to Brindisi to see the admiral in charge of Italian operations. The admiral had passed him to Allied headquarters at Algiers, where he'd been explaining over and over again that all he wanted was to fill his boat with fuel and supplies so he and his crew could go back across the Adriatic. But Churchill had not decided whether to support Mihailovic or Tito. So, no one wanted to stick his neck out by sending the partisans back.

Dutton told the U.S. command staff that he would take the man back to Bari, fill his boat with the supplies he already had, and send him on his way. Eisenhower's staff officer jumped at the chance to get rid of all three men. If someone made a stink about it later, he could say it was an OSS operation; then the

British would be Donovan's problem. He issued travel orders to Bari for them.

When they got to Bari, more trouble surfaced. Dutton had a lot of supplies sitting on the dock. He needed more than Stegineo's single boat.

"You're crazy," the NOIC said. "I'm not giving you any boats. That coast is mined. The Germans patrol it. You think you can just tool over there loaded up with stuff for Tito?"

"With all due respect," Dutton said, "the man you sent to Brindisi made it to Bari in his boat."

"I don't give a rat's ass whether he slipped through," the NOIC responded. "His boat is an old washtub and he looks like a fisherman. You're asking me to redeploy cargo transports now servicing Naples, and I can't afford to have one of those damaged or sunk."

Ever resourceful, Dutton found an empty Italian supply ship in the harbor and went back to the NOIC for a crew. The NOIC, who had not slept for two days, was belligerent.

"Get the hell out of my office!" he shouted. "Where do you think I'm going to get a crew? Call them back from vacation?" Raymond managed to get Dutton out of the room before he said something that would get them court-martialed. But before they got down the hallway, the NOIC emerged to yell after them, "And your team is taking up precious space down there. Get those goddamn supplies off my dock by the end of the month or I'll throw them in the harbor!"

Raymond went to see Stegineo's boat, the Brbavica, and meet his crew. While standing on deck, Stegineo pointed out all the schooners and other sailboats that had sought refuge at Bari when the Allies had arrived. General Donovan had said a sailboat could be used to cross over to Yugoslavia, and Raymond mentioned this plan to Dutton. One sailboat alone wouldn't do, but there were enough of them in the harbor to do the job if they all made the trip. He got Dutton's permission to try to recruit some of them for the crossing.

The next day, he and Stegineo set off in a dinghy to recruit men and boats to ferry the supplies. It proved difficult. Many of the crews were Aegean itinerants who wanted only food and protection. They claimed to be refugees who had escaped from German or Ustase authorities in Yugoslavia. Raymond knew it wasn't true, because they were no more Yugoslavian than he was. More likely, they feared being conscripted or arrested if they admitted their real nationalities. The last thing they wanted was to attract attention to themselves. Yet, Raymond found a couple of boats with crews intrigued by his smuggling operation. Once he judged a crew trustworthy, he had them bring their boat to the dock and load up as much supplies as they could get aboard. It was a risk: the men could disappear with the stuff. But Raymond figured that was better than the NOIC's hauling it all away.

After the first day of recruiting, Raymond could tell without even boarding a vessel whether its crew would participate. He passed by the boats that had trash strewn about their decks and went aboard those with their lines in orderly piles, clean decks, and shined railings. His questions to the skippers he interviewed were meant to gauge whether the man and his crew possessed the skills to ghost their ship into a cove in the middle of the night. Raymond had ghosted a sailboat out of a harbor only once, but that had been in broad daylight. So, it was guesswork on his part.

They were about to pass by one boat, a ketch that looked to be about sixty feet, when Raymond made a wide arc to see Plava Guska painted on its stern. He thought he had been aboard that boat during a weekend outing with several expat families from Trieste, when he was thirteen; the owner had been a foreign-service officer in Rome. The current captain was tall, with sun-bleached hair that swept back over his ears. He was inhospitable and answered Raymond's inquiries curtly. The young boat skipper Raymond remembered had been so handsome and gregarious that the teenage girls in the party had hardly left his side. Still, Raymond saw a resemblance. But he couldn't remember the skipper's name. Then he noticed a small skull-and-bones amulet hanging on a hook at the helm. The man had gone to Yale. It came back to him.

"Mr. Sanders," Raymond said, more of an observation than a question.

The man's eyes reacted, and Raymond's recollections began to sharpen, the way the topography of a shoreline becomes recognizable as the distance to the land becomes smaller. It was the same man. The name of the boat then had been Blue Goose.

"My name is Reed Sanderson, actually," the man said. "Have we met?"

"Trieste, 1938. My father and I were on a vacation. I think this boat belonged to my father's friend, who was with the U.S. consulate general."

Sanderson looked at Stegineo. Raymond guessed his hesitation was caused by suspicion and said, "He's okay. He's a Croatian partisan and we're working together. I'm with an American intelligence outfit trying to help him get supplies back to his people. They're fighting Germans over there."

"Your father's friend was my father. He never told anyone I was his son because he wasn't happy I was living on his boat instead of using my education back in the States. He was killed by the Germans and I slipped away with the boat because they thought I was only a hired skipper, not his son. Now, I'm a refugee from Trieste. That's my official position, anyway."

"I'm sorry about your father, Mr. Sanderson," Raymond said.

"It's water under the bridge. And you can call me Sanders. Many people do."

After a minute, Raymond said, "Our official position is that we're looking for friends to go sailing with. Maybe you'd like to join us?"

That night, Sanders brought Plava Guska to the dock and they loaded medical supplies aboard. He had qualms about taking on weapons, so Raymond didn't push it. In the days that followed, Sanders helped with the recruiting. No one noticed, or perhaps no one cared, that the mound of supplies on the dock dwindled and several boats in the harbor rode low in the water.

The NOIC became more belligerent. He wasn't buying their story that they had nothing but medical supplies and were going across solely to look for refugees. But he hadn't inspected what was on the dock. It was how the navy operated, Raymond thought: what the NOIC didn't know about, he wouldn't have to fix. The British were in charge of the east side of the Adriatic, the NOIC had told them; his responsibilities stopped at Bari. "If you want to go across, go talk to the limeys," he'd said.

Sanders told Raymond he had recently sailed up and down the Dalmatian coast on Plava Guska. The small harbors weren't mined. He had fed himself by fishing and a few days' work in the smaller villages now and then in exchange for food. The Germans had boarded Plava Guska on several occasions, but Sanders had rigged the engine so it didn't work well—it would exhale huge plumes of smoke. The Germans hadn't found any smuggled goods and had thought the boat not worth the trouble to seize.

Since smuggling was what they were planning, Raymond and Sanders went to a few cafés to see if they could find a smuggler. It was dumb, Raymond soon realized. No smuggler was going to talk to them. But they ran into an Englishman named Martin Belvedere, whom Sanders remembered had been a teaching assistant at Yale. He was wearing an old sweatshirt and didn't look to Raymond like a professor. When Sanders asked him what he was doing in Bari, he showed them papers identifying him as a lieutenant in the Royal Navy. Raymond was suspicious.

"Don't you have uniforms in the Royal Navy?" Raymond asked.

"If I wore a uniform, no one would talk to me," Martin replied.

"And you're out looking for friends?"

"Actually, I was looking for you. I want to get a look at the Yugoslavian coast. I heard a rumor you might be going there and thought you might give me a ride when you go."

Raymond was disturbed that Martin knew about their plans. Since they had not told even the NOIC what they were trying to do, it was mysterious that this man had the information. But a Royal Navy officer might be helpful to them. So Raymond brought Martin to the Brbavica to see Dutton, who was using the boat as his headquarters.

"Can you get us out of the harbor if we take you along?" Dutton asked.

"Oh, I can take care of that straightaway," Martin said breezily.

Raymond laughed. Does Martin take us for a bunch of fools? he wondered. But he guessed Dutton might play along on the off chance that Martin could do what he said he could. It would otherwise be difficult, working through proper channels, to get the Royal Navy to approve their trip.

Dutton welcomed Martin to the crew, and Stegineo grabbed a handful of cups and a bottle of rakija. Stegineo and Dutton obviously thought they'd finally made some progress. But it's insane, Raymond thought. Nothing is this easy.

"Ziveli," Stegineo said. When Martin made a face after a sip, Stegineo added, "So it's not slivovitz! We drink that after the crossing!"

After the celebration ended, Raymond went with Martin to his lodgings. It was about a ten-minute walk. He thought he'd try to get more information out of Martin.

"You said earlier that you were looking for me. How did you really hear about us? It's hard to believe it was a rumor."

"It wasn't a rumor. Sorry to be circumspect, chap. I know you're OSS because I'm SOE–Special Operations Executive. So we're brothers-in-arms and all that. The SOE has been at the intelligence thing a long time, and the OSS is a bit new at the game. We know you and the major are scheming to take supplies over to the coast. My superiors think it's a bloody stupid plan, to tell you the truth."

"And you've been assigned to keep an eye on us?"

"They're expecting you to fail. When I tell them you're ready to pull up anchor, they'll be bloody surprised, to be sure. I was surprised. You chaps are very industrious."

"So we won't get exit papers after all?"

"Oh no. I'll get them for you, but only for one boat. I'll say we're going up the coast to Vieste to look for a few more crews and to check out Mr. Sanderson's boat. You'll have to back me up on that, if you're asked later."

"Why would you do this? You'll be sticking your neck out, no?"

"Maybe, but it's bloody boring hanging around Bari. And I very much liked Mr. Sanderson when he was at Yale. He's top notch, by the way. Good you found him."

"Yes. Still, you think we'll fail, don't you?"

"Sorry to say, but I think you will. You'll never make it over there without being spotted, probably from the air. The krauts patrol it constantly. They're looking for Tito's men. Don't know if you know what's going on there. You have a man named Farish with some of our people in country now. Seen a report from him?"

"No."

"Tito and Mihailovic are enemies. They don't collaborate. Mihailovic has been favored back in London because he's a royalist. Tito is a communist. That's why you won't get help from the English command. They only want to use air drops to supply Mihailovic."

"You know, I'm sure, that Dutton will want to go across once we're up the coast."

Martin was quiet for a moment. "That's occurred to me, of course. But I don't know that for certain. My orders are to report immediately if I find out you're going to try a crossing. You'd not make it out of the harbor after that. And you've not told me that's the plan. So I'm perfectly fine to go along when you're ready. But, as you know, every day is a new day in this bloody war. We can go out to see how fast Mr. Sanderson's boat sails and how far we get before we spot a plane. Perhaps another idea will bubble up once we're under way."

They came to Martin's hotel. Raymond was billeted just down the street. He couldn't decide whether Martin was being straight with him. Many in the OSS were circumspect about the SOE's cooperation. "I appreciate your candidness, Martin," he said when he shook his hand. "Let's see what happens in the morning." It's a cat-and-mouse game, Raymond thought. Maybe no orders will come through. The SOE could be playing them—the minute they turned to the east, a British patrol boat could come after them.

Raymond spent several hours sorting through what he knew. Stegineo was desperate to get home and would try anything. Dutton thought this was their only shot and he'd been planning too long to give up now, even if the odds were against him.

It was why he'd joined the OSS, he'd told Raymond on several occasions, to take crazy chances like this. He'd be upset to find out that they were just going for a practice sail. Sanders was a wild card. He'd told Raymond that he had stayed with the boat in order to avoid repatriating himself, because he knew he would be drafted. His family, in Connecticut, thought he'd been killed with his father. He had faded away into the Adriatic woodwork. It was unclear how much risk Sanders would agree to take in the end. And as for himself? This was what he'd signed up for. He'd wanted action. Here it was.

Raymond made a plan for how to play it. He would tell Dutton that making the first run with only one boat made a lot of sense. They didn't need to risk all their supplies at first. He was confident Dutton would be okay. It was Martin and Sanders who were the wild cards.

The next morning, when they reconvened aboard Brbavica, Raymond suggested they attempt to cross with only the Plava Guska to the island of Vis, which had a good harbor. It turned out that Stegineo knew Vis well. He and his crew had stopped there for the night on the way over to Bari. The Germans had not occupied the island, and the residents frequently traveled back and forth to mainland Yugoslavia. Sanders thought Plava Guska could make it to Vis in a single night after they crossed out of Allied-protected waters, which would mitigate the risk of being spotted by the Luftwaffe. Dutton liked the idea. He proposed that they go immediately.

"I can get the exit permit by tomorrow," Martin said.

When the others were busy with preparations for the trip, Raymond pulled Martin aside and asked, "Should I be planning a way to manage their disappointment?"

"Not at all. Somehow I've reconciled myself that a trip to Vis is not a trip to the coast. As I said last night, I'm going to tell my people we're just making a test run up to the north and back. I won't specify Vis, but it is north of here, isn't it? I'll say I'm going along so as to keep in your confidence. Part of the job, of course. If we all get bloody killed, then I won't be worrying about a court-martial. If we make it back, I can report that we got off course, a problem with the rigging or something, and we had to put in at Vis for a couple of days. I'll report that you've told me you've decided to give up the idea because the passage was so difficult. Then I'll be on my way to another assignment, and you can do whatever you do."

"Thank you."

"You'll remember that last part, I hope. About telling me you're giving up."

Plava Guska left the harbor early the next morning. Her crew was composed of Sanders, Dutton, Raymond, Martin, Stegineo, and Stegineo's sister, Vera. A strong wind pushed against their beam, and by nightfall Vieste was to their port side.

The plan had been to put into a small harbor at Peschici for a day. But the wind was steady, so they turned to the northwest. They stayed just inside Italian coastal waters until the next night, when they turned east to make a dash for Vis. The crew settled in for the evening.

Raymond studied Vera as inconspicuously as he could. He had been doing so off and on since he had met her the first time he'd gone to Stegineo's boat. She was not at all glamorous. She wore a work shirt and loose-fitting overalls. Her brown hair was tied back and hidden beneath a scarf, which Raymond thought was an effort to disguise the fact that it was dirty. Despite the baggy clothes and her diminutive height–just a bit over five feet–she was strong and agile. She could hoist a crate of supplies up from the dock as well as any of the men. She was also smart. Raymond saw that she understood most of the conversations among the men, regardless of the language being spoken.

Vera had green eyes and sharp features. She had recently turned seventeen, which was not much younger than Raymond, although he had told everyone he was twenty-two. Dutton had torn up his papers back in Cairo, so he thought he wouldn't be called on the lie.

Sanders, Vera, and Raymond were the only crew members with sailing experience, and one would take the helm while the other two slept. Vera had the first watch of the crossing to Vis. Raymond didn't want to sleep; he wanted to sit aft and watch Vera at the helm. But Sanders insisted, so Raymond went to the forward deck. A full moon made the mainsail glow, and at first he anxiously scanned the sky for the Luftwaffe, even though Stegineo had said the German patrols didn't fly at night because the airfields in Yugoslavia didn't have lights.

As he lay on the deck, Raymond was sure he was in love with Vera. Although it always seemed brand-new, Raymond was an old hand at falling in love. He'd been smitten countless times by shining eyes and delicate features, or by character in a face, like the waitress's in the diner. But his normal confidence failed him when it came to making an overture of romance, not to mention sexual relations. It was too confusing and mysterious, and he'd hidden it by talking to girls he liked about books and art and other grand things. They liked him for this, and because he wasn't always trying to get his hand up their skirts. He'd often been frustrated.

Not long after Raymond finally fell asleep, a crash of thunder caused him to spring to a sitting position. It was very dark and he had to orient himself during flashes of lightning. His clothes were wet and there was a line tied to his belt. He made his way back to the cockpit. Vera, still at the helm, was as wet as he was. Sanders stood beside her.

"You were sleeping like the dead," Sanders said. "We had to tie a line on you so you wouldn't be washed overboard."

Raymond thought he saw a smile flicker on Vera's lips. She expertly kept the vessel moving diagonally into what looked like rolling mountains of water. The wind was blowing from the northeast and their tack was a close haul. Sanders had lowered the mainsail and winched in the main jib. Only the sail on the mizzen was up.

"The wind is too gusty and the seas too high to take us about for additional speed," Sanders explained. "We'll try to make a little headway while we wait it out."

Vera went below to sleep and Sanders stayed with Raymond. They took turns at the helm. The gusting wind made steering difficult. By dawn the wind gusts had abated and the clouds were scattered. Sanders consulted the chart and changed their course to the north. They raised the mainsail and let out the jib. When the sun was above the horizon, the water droplets covering the deck and the sails glittered. The air was clean and brisk. But Raymond could see that Sanders wasn't happy. "We were pushed southwest during the night by the storm. We're out in the middle of the Adriatic and we won't make Vis until late afternoon," he said.

By noon the sky was completely clear and the swells had lengthened. Plava Guska sliced through the sea at a good pace, like the relaxed canter of a Thoroughbred horse, and the warm sun had hoodwinked the crew, except for Sanders. He insisted that Raymond make regular scans of the horizon with the binoculars, looking for a Luftwaffe patrol plane.

For a while, Raymond enjoyed the cloud of danger hanging over them. Then he made himself be serious. He hadn't experienced an actual life-threatening episode before, and he thought it was immature not to accord the situation respect. Plava Guska was a ketch, much bigger than a sloop that pleasure sailors would use. And she was low in the water on account of the supplies in her hold. A smart German pilot who knew his boats would be suspicious.

About an hour out from Vis, Raymond spotted an airplane. It was flying northbound a good distance to the east of them. For a while he thought the pilot hadn't seen them, but then the plane banked left and headed directly for the boat. With her sails up, Plava Guska was hard to miss. Sanders yelled a warning to the crew to get below and barked an order to Raymond: "Just lean back and act like a diplomat's son who doesn't have a care in the world."

"I should be able to do that," Raymond responded.

The pilot took a westerly course that brought him about a quarter of a mile south of Plava Guska before making a wide turn to the north. Raymond guessed that gave him a good view of the boat from a safe distance. The plane passed them about a quarter mile off their port side. Raymond thought they were clear until he saw, through the binoculars, the aircraft make a sharp turn back to the south and head straight for them.

"He's coming back directly on our bow," he said grimly.

"Everyone get on the floor under something," Sanders yelled. "You too, Raymond."

At that moment, Vera came charging up the companionway with two cushions under her arm. She sprinted along the port side of the boat toward the bow until she was on the open deck between the mainmast and the jib, where she put down the cushions. With a single easy motion she took off her overalls and her shirt. Clad only in a red brassiere and panties, she reclined on the cushions in a sunbathing position.

Raymond felt paralyzed, not caring at all that he might soon be gunned down where he stood. Sanders adjusted course a bit to the east and let out a small length of the jib to broaden the viewing area for the pilot. That tipped Raymond off to what was happening. With her red garments, Vera shone up from the deck like a beacon.

"Close your mouth and sit down," Sanders said to Raymond.

When the noise of the aircraft's engine came, Vera raised herself on her elbow and used her hand to shade her eyes. The plane was lower now, probably at strafing altitude. Vera waved casually. The aircraft went by with a roar, no bullets fired.

Sanders held his course. Raymond had not waved at the plane, lest the pilot think the scene was being staged. Vera had made it appear that they had nothing to hide. But Raymond figured the pilot would probably come back for another look; he certainly would if he were the pilot. He stretched out near the stern on the port side, his back propped against a railing stanchion, a book in his hand: Mein Kampf. He pictured how they looked from above. It was so absurd, he laughed.

"You're a bit overboard with your reading choice, no?" Sanders remarked.

"Perhaps," Raymond said, his gaze fixed on Vera, who had gone back to reclining with her hands behind her head. He was perspiring, and he knew it was on account of her, and not the danger from the plane. A cool jump into the ocean sounded pretty good.

The plane's engine, straining behind them, became audible again. The pilot had flown about a half mile south before turning back. Raymond watched him slow his speed, decrease his altitude, and head for the port gunwale of the sailboat. When the plane was just behind them, Raymond held his breath. He was sure Vera knew that the pilot's attention was centered on her. She sat up in a cross-legged position, with one hand on a hip and the other waving at the plane, which banked slightly to enhance the pilot's view as it roared by them. When he was just past the bow, the airman swiveled his wings right and left several times, banked to the northeast, and headed for Yugoslavia.

Raymond expected a cheer from the crew, but none came. Everyone was now on deck, quiet and completely mesmerized by Vera. When she saw them all looking at her rather than the retreating plane, her composure fell away and she blushed as red as her underwear. She deftly slid her arms into her shirt and her legs into her overalls.

"Really, Vera. Red!" Raymond quipped in Croatian when she approached the companionway. He wanted her green eyes to look at him.

She stopped to stand tall and direct a commanding look first at him and then at the rest of the crew. How can she be so poised? She reached behind her head and flipped her curls with her fingers.

"I am a communist. What did you expect?" she said in perfect English, then disappeared below.

The rest of the trip to Vis was uneventful, although as they entered the harbor a volley of bullets churned the water around the boat. It was a test, Stegineo told them, before he went bravely to the bow and stood holding the forestay. When he was recognized, a brief cheer arose from the dock and a bell clanged. By the end of the afternoon, many of the townspeople had gathered and more cheers rang out as the supplies were brought up from below. One of the doctors, when he saw the cases of drugs and bandages being piled on the dock, fell to his knees, crossed himself, and said a prayer. A town banquet was prepared and much rakija was consumed, which in turn led to the embellishment of many stories. The best tale of the evening was, inevitably, the story of Vera and her red underwear.

The next day dawned upon a red brassiere hanging from one of the shrouds of the mizzen mast. Raymond guessed it wasn't Vera's. He'd learned the night before that most of the women wore red underwear. They had once been white, but were dyed red, or sometimes blue, to disguise how worn they'd become; when cloth was available, it was used for uniforms.

After dark on the second evening, Dutton, Martin, and Stegineo went off in a small craft to the mainland, where, Dutton told Raymond, they hoped to rendezvous with partisan forces and establish a plan for transporting supplies from Vis to the coast. How Martin rationalized his participation in the excursion, Raymond couldn't guess. Raymond remained on Vis to work with Vera on a staging area for future supplies.

Vera became Vruć Vera, which translated to "Hot Vera." She blushed whenever she heard it and the men would promptly fan themselves with their hats. Raymond wished they would stop. It made him jealous to think the men were imagining her nude, even though he was doing the same thing.

Raymond looked for opportunities to engage Vera in personal conversation. He'd become confident in his Croatian and thought he could pull it off. But she didn't make it easy. In the evenings she retreated to her lodgings in the home of a young couple. The couple had three small children. Raymond considered tagging along with her, but, as an only child, he felt intimidated by the children. They followed Vera around the town like she was the Pied Piper. So Raymond spent his free time talking to Sanders or lying on the deck of Plava Guska. The night sky was full of stars. He imagined Vera was there with him. If she asked, he thought, he would gladly spend the rest of his life there on the island with her.

Dutton returned in a euphoric mood. He told Raymond that he'd been introduced to Tito in the coastal mountains. He'd also met, and returned with, Major Farish, who was gaunt and willowy, a contrast to the robust officer Raymond remembered.

They left for Bari that same night. Vera stayed behind and Raymond awkwardly hugged her on the dock. She'd offered only her cheek, and appeared dispassionate. He was unhappy with himself for not getting up the nerve to tell her how he felt about her. All kinds of possibilities flew through his mind. Perhaps she feels strongly for me but is too shy to say so?

The wind from the northwest provided them a broad reach all the way. Dutton and Farish talked energetically about a report on Tito that Farish was to submit. By the time Sanders had the boat tied up to the Bari dock, Dutton was making plans to launch an armada to Vis.

Farish departed for Washington to brief Donovan, and Martin left for Algiers to brief the SOE. Raymond made sure to tell Martin before he left that he thought they'd give up on their plans because the passage had been so difficult. But, two days later, Raymond and Dutton dispatched two boats to Vis, their holds full of provisions. The NOIC and the Royal Navy weren't paying attention to sailboats crewed by itinerants.

Raymond wanted to go back to Vis, but Dutton wouldn't let him. He was fielding a lot of questions from Algiers. As they watched additional boats depart the next day, he said to Raymond, "It appears I stepped on some English toes by going to see Tito. They're quite upset about it. Why I was there doesn't seem to make any difference to them. They're sticklers for the whole chain-of-command thing, evidently."

Several days later, a couple of MPs approached Dutton and Raymond when they were having breakfast in their hotel's dining room.

"Major Dutton and Lieutenant Hatcher," they said.

"The very ones," Dutton said flippantly.

"You two are confined to quarters. The kitchen will bring your meals up from now on."

"What's this about?" Raymond asked. He'd recently thought more about Vera than about their trip to Vis. Maybe Martin's report had been turned over to the NOIC, whom they hadn't told about the trip. He hoped Martin wasn't in trouble. Whatever it was, he worried that it would prevent him from going back to Vis.

"That's none of our business," the MP told him. "We were told only to keep you here."

The next day, the NOIC showed up with a British general. The NOIC looked sheepish. The general was turned out in a perfectly pressed uniform with a variety of medals. "We have requested that you gentlemen be court-martialed for the flagrant failure to obey orders," he stated curtly.

"What are you talking about?" Dutton demanded. "What orders?"

"There are standing orders that no one go into Yugoslavia without prior authorization from British command," the general continued. "Your visit to Yugoslavia was not authorized and endangered our operations there."

Raymond was about to point out that a British officer had gone with them, but Dutton grasped his arm to keep him quiet. "General," he said, "you have your head up your ass. We're not in your damn army. You can't court-martial us."

The general turned red. "We will see about that!" he exclaimed, and then, turning to the NOIC, who was attempting without much success to suppress a smile, he sputtered, "We are done here."

A week of confinement later, the NOIC returned and presented them each with new orders. Dutton was to go to London and report to the OSS station chief. Raymond was to return to Washington, report to OSS headquarters, and then travel to a secret base on an island off the coast of California. The orders had been signed by General Eisenhower.

5

THE TRIP BACK TO THE United States was a long ordeal of waiting for broken airplanes and weather delays. Raymond was sure he would spend Thanksgiving eating beans in a makeshift barracks next to an airstrip in the middle of nowhere. But he got lucky finally and was granted a short stay in St. Paul for the holiday, after which he boarded a train to Los Angeles. He didn't mind the slow pace to the west; he'd had all he could stand of airplanes. From Los Angeles he was driven down to Pendleton, and then, in the middle of the night, a boat took him to the secret base on Catalina Island.

In the mornings, the OSS trainees on Catalina Island ran up the mountain above Toyon Bay and then down its west side to Hell Beach, so called because it had no sand, only a plain of jagged rocks leading to waves crashing in from the Pacific. The swimmers ran over the rocks and into the surf. Once beyond the breakers, they spent thirty minutes treading water before they were whistled back to the beach. Then, they ran back over the mountain.

During their run on the second day of 1944, Raymond saw the spot when he ran by. It was set on a level patch of rock at the ridge of the mountain above Toyon Bay. He was sure he'd be able to see the Pacific Ocean to the west and the San Pedro Channel to the east.

Right after evening chow, while the others collapsed into their bunks, he slipped away and climbed up to the ridge. He was right about the spot. The setting sun was a huge orange orb at the end of a bright, shining path that stretched back to Toyon Bay, below. The sky was pastel blue, and the setting sun made several lines of clouds glow red. This is why life is precious, he thought. He didn't want to miss a second of the sunset. It would mean going back down the mountain in the dark, but he didn't mind that.

The descent to Toyon Bay at night provided a good opportunity for Raymond to practice the scouting skills he'd been taught recently by a Native American named Jimmy Nearwell. He was careful to make each step quiet and deliberate and, as Jimmy had instructed, to follow his inner sense of direction. About halfway down, Raymond paused in a space between a manzanita thicket and an ironwood tree. The expanse of sky out over the ocean glittered with starlight. It was too beautiful not to spend a little more time there, so he decided to attempt another technique Jimmy had shown him: to synchronize himself with the rhythm of nature around him. Theoretically, when he became completely harmonized with the hillside he would be invisible to an enemy.

He stood for a while with his eyes closed, trying to feel the landscape. When nothing happened, he decided it might be easier if he was seated. But when he leaned against the trunk of the ironwood tree, it moved. He scrambled to his feet in alarm, which started a small avalanche of loose rocks.

"What the hell!" He immediately crouched into a defensive position.

"Easy, boy," a voice said softly.

Raymond stayed in his crouch. His heart pounded and his mind raced. Maybe the grunting of a wild island boar had sounded like a person speaking, or the rustling of the tree's leaves had sounded like a voice. The moment was gripping at first, but then it seemed ridiculous. He felt like a boy looking under the bed for the monster. The voice returned. "Let's sit down on those rocks a little farther down the path," it said.

Raymond could see nothing down the path, it was so dark. The rocks could be on the edge of one of the gullies that pierced the mountainside. They were steep and narrow. He pictured himself being pushed when he reached the rocks, his skull cracked and his bones broken. A hand touched his shoulder and he spun around. He looked desperately for its owner. The voice laughed.

"Raymond, you're as touchy as a cat," Jimmy said. "Take a deep breath. Look at the horizon."

Raymond recognized the voice now. He followed Jimmy's instructions and his heartbeat slowed. The two of them moved down the path to some rocks.

Raymond remembered the story about Jimmy Nearwell. He was the descendant of an Apache scout named Dead Shot, who had been a part of the Sixth Cavalry in Arizona during the early 1900s. In 1942, General Donovan had gone to Fort Huachuca to meet the Apache scouts who lived there and had found Jimmy living in a hut near a well on the perimeter of the fort. Donovan had heard that Jimmy could move undetected across any terrain and track any quarry. Such skills, Donovan had believed, would be extremely useful for the missions he hoped to undertake with the OSS. The newly enlisted Private Nearwell had left the fort with Donovan.

"So much for my scouting expertise," Raymond said as they sat on the rocks. He felt embarrassed and humbled by the incident.

"It was really funny," Jimmy said. "The look on your face was priceless."

"You could have been a Jap. I could be dead." Raymond tried to keep his voice steady so his frustration wouldn't show. He didn't like that Jimmy thought the whole thing was funny. But he wished he could take back what he had just said. He'd been dramatic to cover up how stupid he'd felt.

Jimmy laughed again. "You were trying to do too many things at the same time. All that concentration. You were glowing in the dark, like a firefly."

A firefly! Raymond felt angry and tried to think of a retort. But his fury passed and he exhaled wearily.

Over the last couple of weeks he'd lost his perspicacity and it now occurred to him that he was becoming a narcissist. He'd suggested to his fellow trainees that before his arrival at Toyon Bay he'd been involved in a dangerous espionage mission, while in fact the only real danger he'd faced was falling overboard after seeing Vera in her red bra and panties. It was a bit funny, he had to agree with Jimmy, and he decided to take it in stride.

"Next time, I'll be sure to bring a flashlight. So I don't mistake you for a tree. I'll never be a scout."

"Nonsense," Jimmy said. "You're the only guy who knew what I meant about becoming a part of the surroundings. You understand the concept perfectly. Now you must learn to apply it."

"It's impossible," Raymond asserted. He meant it broadly to encompass his ability to be a clandestine operative. What good was understanding something if he was so inept? Maybe he could transfer to a code-breaking assignment. He was a boy and this was a man's work, he thought. The narcissism was gone.

"You're discouraged," Jimmy said.

Raymond realized he'd sounded cynical. "I suppose so," he said.

"What you must do, Raymond, is relax."

"How's that work?"

"Let's listen to the sounds around us. You think you learn by experience–but by that you mean you must practice. It's not so, in this case. If you want to disappear into the mountainside, you must learn what the mountainside is, what an ironwood tree is, and what the darkness is. You can't practice being those things. So we'll sit for a while and feel them. We'll become like them after a while–so much like them, we'll be indistinguishable. It doesn't happen right away. It won't happen in one night. And don't close your eyes and strain at it."

Jimmy became quiet. Raymond watched him. It did seem that Jimmy was the same as the rocks and bushes around them, and he appeared not even to be breathing. Soon, Raymond stopped watching Jimmy and his thoughts slipped away, to the night air, the stars, and the long view of the Pacific. An hour later, or maybe it was two hours–it didn't matter–they stood up and went down the mountain. The descent seemed effortless, although later, when he was in his bunk, Raymond thought it might have seemed that way just because he was following Jimmy. But he couldn't remember whether he or Jimmy had led the way.

Over the next two months Raymond became a master of the Apache arts. He could track and kill a wild boar without making a sound, and traverse the mountainside as easily in darkness as in daylight. During night exercises, other trainees would walk within a few feet of him without the slightest knowledge of his presence. At the beginning of March, Jimmy Nearwell departed. No one saw him leave, which was unnerving to the commanding officer because the only way to leave Toyon Bay was by boat, and no boat had come or gone in a week.

A few days later, the trainees were divided into teams of three and assigned a final graduation exercise. Raymond and his teammates were tasked with infiltrating the waterfront defenses at Avalon in order to "liberate" as many pies as they could carry out of O'Shea's Bakery, one of the few civilian establishments remaining in Avalon. When Catalina had been sequestered by the military after Pearl Harbor, Jack O'Shea had convinced the authorities that his bakery should remain to serve the men who would be stationed on the island.

In the very early morning of March 6, 1944, Raymond's team left the Toyon Bay beach in a black rubber boat. The team included Ensign Walt Stoppard, a lumberjack from Maine, and Ensign Louie Barlow, an easy-going surfer from San Diego, California, whom Raymond thought had good instincts and a sharp mind. They quietly paddled southeast along the coastline to a spot just north of Avalon Harbor, where they stowed the boat and swam quietly through the harbor entrance. After they crept ashore, Raymond, who had studied a map, guided them through several back streets to O'Shea's Bakery.

A problem arose. A light was on inside the bakery. Raymond crept forward to the small window in the back door. The sole occupant was a young woman, who was mixing something in a large bowl. In their planning they'd failed to foresee that the bakery would be in operation in the early-morning hours. It was a stupid mistake. Raymond thought they should abort their mission, but then he looked at the baker more closely. She had shoulder-length auburn hair and a freckled face that captivated him. He crept back to the others.

"We'll have to take a hostage," he said calmly.

The others looked at him, dumbfounded.

"Are you crazy?" Walt asked.

Raymond had anticipated this response. The capture of the pies would make them heroes back at Toyon, but to encounter the baker would violate a strict order not to reveal that the OSS had a base on Catalina. So, Walt was right–they should back away. But Raymond had already decided to ignore him. Louie took it in stride. He said, "Cool," and secured the waterproof duffel he carried under his arm.

"We'll threaten her," Raymond said. Then he saw the incredulous look on Walt's face and quickly explained, "We'll tell her that if she tells anyone about us, we'll come back and smash her ovens." Due to the mobilization of factories and the military use of steel, he believed that replacing the ovens quickly would be almost impossible.

"Her?"

"The baker is a woman."

"Young, no doubt?" Walt had figured it out.

"Look," Raymond said, glancing back at the bakery so that the others couldn't read his face, "we've been taught to consider all our options in hostile situations. We can pull this off."

"And this is certainly a hostile situation," Walt said dryly.

Before he went in, Raymond studied the girl. She stood at the counter in front of the bowl of batter she had just mixed. Her face was centered around a small, distinguished nose. Her complexion was dotted with specks of the flour she had poured into the bowl. It made her freckles look uneven. The door squeaked when he opened it, but he thought she didn't hear it because she continued to spoon batter onto a cookie sheet. He proceeded toward her.

"Brendan," she called, "grab another cookie sheet on your way."

Raymond froze. Brendan? He had not seen another person in the bakery. He turned around. Louie stood behind him. Walt had remained at the door. Raymond looked at them in their black wet suits and the scene struck him as comical. Then the girl whirled around. He saw from the expression on her face that she was startled and afraid.

"Don't scream," he said quickly. "We're not going to hurt you." His statement was meant to be a command, but his voice sounded hesitant to him. And his stance felt awkward. He watched the look on her face change from fear to amusement, and he worried that he was not appearing serious.

"And what would I have to scream about?" she asked.

Raymond didn't know what to say. He watched her hands move to her hips as she glared at him. For a couple of moments he was speechless, and then he thought he saw her eyes flash with impatience.

"We're sorry, miss," Louie spoke up from behind Raymond, "but we're here to liberate some pies."

Raymond saw a quizzical look on her face. "We're on a classified mission. We have to take your pies," he said. He watched her glance at each of them in turn. Then she laughed.

"This is a pie heist? You must be kidding!"

Again Raymond was speechless, but this time it was because he thought she was the most beautiful girl he had ever seen. She was disheveled and had flour on her face, but he was mesmerized by the way she laughed. The aroma of oatmeal cookies made her even more enticing.

"I have to take the cookies out," she said.

When she opened the oven, hot air billowed out and swirled around her. He walked over to close the oven door when she brought the hot cookie sheet back to the counter. In order to remain next to her, he looked at the cookies.

"We could take some cookies as well," Louie said.

She looked at Raymond, not Louie, and pointed to the sheet of unbaked cookies she had been assembling when they arrived. "Will you want those baked, then, or do you want them just as they are?"

"Look," Raymond said, "we'll just take what's already baked and be on our way."

"Suppose I refuse?" she said, standing up straight.

She's flirting, he said to himself, and I can handle this. The look on her face was meant to be hostile, he thought, but to him it appeared mischievous. To keep himself from laughing, he picked up the sheet with the unbaked cookies and put it in the oven. When he turned back to her, she had picked up a rolling pin. I can be mischievous too, he thought.

"I'm afraid we'll have to kill you if you don't cooperate miss," he said.

What he really wanted to do was put his arms around her and kiss her passionately. He watched her slap the rolling pin against her palm a number of times. When she put it on the counter, he said, "Perhaps we should start from the beginning, Miss . . . I'm sorry, I've forgotten your name."

"You've not been told my name."

"Okay. How about if I go first. My name is William," Raymond said. "But please call me Bill."

After a moment she said, "I'm Megan O'Shea."

"Well, nice to meet you, Meg."

"Sorry, it's Megan to you."

"Okay. Nice to meet you, Megan." But he so wanted to call her Meg, to be the only one who would be permitted to use the endearment.

"Can't say I can say the same," she said.

Raymond was sure she didn't mean it. Her face looked too animated to be hostile. "Perhaps I can explain why we're here," he said.

"That would be lovely, Bill."

He heard the emphasis on the word lovely and he felt good. "You see, we're from a submarine that's been submerged for months," he said.

"Let me guess. You have no ovens aboard and your craving for pie overcame you."

"Something like that. It's been hard work looking for Japanese invaders of California. Our skipper thought some pies would give our crew a morale boost."

"Oh, and you saw our bakery through your periscope."

"Actually, it was on our charts."

"With a notation, I'm sure, that we make the best pies of all the islands on the coast."

"Exactly."

"Did it show the prices? We're probably not the cheapest, I must tell you."

"Well, now that you mention it, we weren't planning to pay for them."

"No kidding! No room for any money in those wet suits?"

"We're hoping you'll give us the pies to support the war effort."

He saw her look at the oven. Had it been that long since he'd put them in? Time was racing by. When he guessed she was about to walk to the oven, he grabbed the mitts and took the cookies out for her.

"Could you see your way to stealing yesterday's baked goods?" she asked, pointing at a case in the front of the store. "If you get caught, that would make the sentence lighter." Her attitude was no longer petulant and her voice no longer sarcastic, he noted.

Raymond agreed immediately and his team quickly loaded up the duffel. He thought Megan was pretending to be busy with the next batch of cookies. He lagged behind when Walt and Louie departed. She followed him to the door.

"You won't tell anyone about our visit," Raymond said.

"And what if I did? Oh, I forgot. You'd murder me!"

"Never." He put his hand on her arm and looked into her eyes. He was afraid he was being too bold, but she didn't draw back. "I won't be able to come back if you tell," he said. Then, he left her standing in the doorway and joined the others. Before they disappeared into the night, he took a quick look over his shoulder. She still stood there.

A week later, around the same time of morning, Raymond again stood outside the bakery, watching Megan. This time he'd made his way to Avalon by a trail he'd blazed through canyons and gullies, following a maze of goat paths where possible and otherwise bushwhacking around thickets. He'd made practice runs for several nights to be sure he could make it back to his bunk before reveille.

On his first practice trip, he'd lost his footing a couple of times and had to climb back up to a path. Later, he'd almost been spotted by an MP in a jeep while walking down an old dirt road that wound down a hillside close to town. Luckily, he'd heard the jeep, which had its headlights blacked out, and had been able to dive into a patch of high brush next to the road. None of these incidents made him reconsider his endeavor. He had to see her again, no matter what the risk.

While he stood at the door, he watched her tip over a container of spatulas and spoons, and then bump her head when she bent down to pick them up off the floor. Her head scarf slipped around her neck, and wet batter from her hands got into her hair when she pulled the scarf back up.

When he finally walked in, she was clutching a big wooden spatula and had a wild look in her eyes. He got ready to duck, but then she tossed the spatula aside and skipped into his arms.

Time stopped.

After she sighed, he dropped his arms to her waist and leaned back. He saw that her eyes were hazel. They were warm. He was sure she'd expected him to return. As if to confirm his thoughts, she said, "I figured you'd be back after your fellow submariners finished off the stuff you confiscated."

"Submariners?" he asked, confused until he recalled his earlier story. "Oh yes. The pies were well received."

"I don't believe you were on a submarine," she said.

He loved how she smiled.

"No?"

"No. And I don't believe your name is Bill."

"My name is Raymond."

"So, Raymond, what pastry were you hoping for this time?"

"No pastry this time." He kissed her.

It wasn't easy to extricate himself from her arms. He knew she had baking to do. More than likely, her father would be there soon. But she made no effort to release him, and each time he tried to back away, she hugged him tighter. As good as it felt, he became anxious: he had to traverse all those goat lanes before reveille. Finally, the batter in her hair gave him an idea. "You're a mess," he said, while gently pulling away to retrieve a wet cloth. He cleaned the batter off, then tucked the loose strands of her hair back under her scarf. At the door, he made no pledge to come back. He didn't think it was necessary.

When Raymond returned a few nights later, the place was orderly and she was a whirlwind of activity. Her scarf was perfectly tied and positioned and it looked to him that her clothes had been ironed. She broke their embrace quickly.

"I have to stay on schedule," she said. "Last time everything was awry when my dad got here, and he was a little suspicious. It's not like me."

"So, you didn't explain your romantic shenanigans with a mysterious sailor?" He had always liked the word shenanigans. His mother had often asked him what shenanigans he was up to. And it now seemed appropriate because he was in an Irish bakery.

"They'll be no shenanigans here, mister," she said, brandishing a whisk that was dripping with egg. "And I thought you wanted me to keep you secret?"

His heart soared. What an extraordinary girl she was! She seemed to glide from counter to counter. Blobs of batter miraculously appeared on the pans. He made himself useful by opening the ovens now and then.

"So, there is no submarine," he said.

"Of course not."

"But I can't tell you where my base is."

"It's okay," she said. A few strands of hair came loose when she bent over a bowl. They fell across her forehead. He tucked them back. She looked into his eyes. "I don't need to know where you come from, as long as you keep showing up." Then she turned back to mixing the dough.

"I think it's best that I don't come every night. It increases the risk of capture."

She smiled. "Oh, we certainly don't want you captured! You'd be court-martialed for trying to sabotage a bakery."

He laughed. "And you'd be exhausted."

"Well, every night does seem impractical in a lot of ways."

"I knew you were a practical girl."

She laughed. "My dad calls me his 'sensible girl.' I can be obsessive about things, I should warn you."

The bread loaves were ready for the oven. He thought they were beautiful, some of them round, some oval, and several rectangular. Even the way they were arranged on the pans was pleasing. He watched her hands as she made final adjustments. She would occasionally make a swirl on the top of a loaf with her finger. A small smile would form on her lips whenever she did this.

"Do you have particular designs you draw on the loaves?" he asked.

"What, these? They're not designs. I like for each one to have its own character. And then it's fun to hear how a customer describes it when she tells me which loaf she wants."

He loved her intensely after he heard that.

6

THE COMMANDER AT TOYON BAY found Raymond in the mess hall at breakfast. He said, "Lieutenant Hatcher, there's a boat here to take you to the mainland." Raymond was startled. The commander did not ordinarily allow boats to depart for the mainland during daylight hours.

"This is a joke," Raymond said. "But you're two days late for April Fool's."

"No joke, Lieutenant. Get your ass down to the dock," the commander said as he handed Raymond his orders.

Raymond read the orders while the launch sped across the channel. He would hitch a ride on a navy transport plane from the marine airfield at Pendleton to San Francisco. In San Francisco he was to report to the Mark Hopkins Hotel and ask for Ned Putzell. Further orders would be given to him there. But he didn't arrive at the Mark Hopkins until late evening, due to engine repairs on the plane at Pendleton. When he inquired about Putzell, a desk clerk handed him a room key and a note that read, "Breakfast at 0700 in Suite H."

After dropping off his bag, Raymond went down to the bar and ordered a gin and tonic. He watched the bartender's expression to see if he would need his well-rehearsed story about leaving his credentials in his room. He didn't know what the drinking age in California was. But his lieutenant's stripes were good enough and the gin and tonic appeared on the bar in front of him.

"First one is on the house, sir," the bartender said. "After that, you're on your own."

Raymond sipped his drink as he sat on a stool at the end of the bar. In his training he had learned how to position himself in different venues, as well as to estimate the number of steps to the exits and to examine the behavior of the people around him.

It seemed to him that the Mark Hopkins was the favored place of noncommissioned officers and reservists, at least those with money to pay for a room rather than go to a military billet. Most of them were navy men on their way to Hawaii, he guessed. Each of them had a girl on his arm, which made him think of Megan. She had hummed a song and they'd danced during his last visit to the bakery.

Raymond showed up at Suite H to find General Donovan eating breakfast. Next to Donovan was a young, wiry man with very large ears. Raymond suspected he was a lawyer.

"Lieutenant Hatcher," Donovan said briskly. "Glad you could get up here on short notice. Sit down and meet Ned Putzell, my aide."

"Thank you, sir," Raymond said as he sat, and then he nodded to Ned.

"We have a new assignment for you, Raymond," Donovan said.

Raymond waited for him to say what the assignment was. But when Donovan next spoke, it was chitchat about Raymond's parents. The general had come across them at a dinner party in Lisbon. "Your mother was as charming and vivacious as always," he said, "and your father is doing quite well. He's now the head of cultural affairs for Portugal." He winked at Raymond. "Of course, we both know he has certain other duties."

The general went on for several more minutes about the Russian front and the difficulties in Italy. Raymond thought Donovan might be about to disclose to him where the invasion of Europe would take place. He had the language skills appropriate for a landing on the Mediterranean coast.

"None of that has a thing to do with your assignment," Donovan said finally, looking at Raymond over the top of his coffee cup. "You're going west. I've made a little deal with Admiral Nimitz. You're joining a navy team going to support Macarthur's retaking of the Philippines. Nimitz was very impressed to learn that we train our officers for hand-to-hand combat on land as well as in the water. According to him, all of his underwater-demolition specialists can do only that–blow things up under water. Don't misunderstand me. These are brave men, very accomplished navy officers. But you put them on land and they turn into green foot soldiers. By god, they'd kill themselves going overland in the middle of the night from Toyon Bay to Avalon."

Raymond felt his face redden. How did Donovan know that?

The general laughed. "What? You thought Jimmy had left, didn't you?"

"Yes, sir. I guess I did."

"I promised your mother I'd keep my eye on you. Your father thought her asking me to do that wasn't appropriate. But you know her. She's very hard to say no to." Rose Crowley of Saint Paul had graduated from Bryn Mawr College in 1922 and taken what she'd thought was a glamorous position at the United States embassy in London. The work was dull and her British colleagues duller. Desperate for a conversation with someone from home, she pushed her way into a circle of guests surrounding the ambassador and introduced herself to the first one who spoke with an American accent, who was Leland Hatcher.

They were married in 1923, and in April 1925, their only child, Raymond Lansing Hatcher, was born in Saint Paul, Minnesota.

"I don't know what to say." Raymond had thought his night-time movements on Catalina had been entirely clandestine. And what now? Was he going to be reported to his mother for sneaking off to see a girl? He almost laughed.

"It was a good call to send Jimmy to Catalina," Donovan said. "He thinks you're the finest officer in the unit. And then he stayed around to observe you in his own way as others could not. His reports of how you carried out those excursions to Avalon with no one being the wiser convinced me he's right. And this is the OSS. We applaud initiative."

"Thank you, sir," Raymond said, still feeling uncomfortable that he'd been under surveillance.

"So, Admiral Nimitz thinks that pairing a couple of OSS men with one of his crack officers on a maritime team could work to both our benefits. You can choose one other candidate from Catalina to go with you. Someone you have confidence in. You'll be assigned to an operation in the Pacific that's being planned as we speak. Of course, if MacArthur finds out you're OSS, he may have both of you thrown overboard."

"Sir?"

"A joke. Mac and I served together in the First World War and we have some differences we can't find our way around. Neither Nimitz nor I want to deal with him, so we're going to keep the fact that you're OSS to ourselves. Got that?"

"Yes, sir."

"And if all goes well, we can get you to make a little side trip to Indochina. It's the same damn thing as what was going on in Yugoslavia. No one can figure out who the enemy is."

"Sir?"

"We'll get back to you on that."

Donovan pushed back his chair and stood, which prompted Raymond and Ned to do the same. He walked around the table and grasped Raymond's hand, then put his other hand on Raymond's shoulder.

"I will report to your mother when I see her that you're well and successful. I'll let you tell her about the baker's daughter."

Raymond thought he detected a glint in Donovan's eye. "Thank you, sir."

"Any questions, or anything else I can do, young man?"

"No, sir," he said, but before Donovan turned away, he blurted, "Sir, there is one thing. Would it be possible for me to go to Avalon in the daytime?"

Donovan laughed. "I don't see why not. What do you think, Putzell?"

"I think it can be arranged, General."

"Then let's take care of it. Ned will give Admiral Barlow a call and arrange for you to stay over in Avalon for the Easter weekend. We'll get word to your commanding officer to transport you to Avalon, and you can begin your Pacific passage from there."

"Admiral Barlow?" Raymond asked hesitantly.

The general laughed again. "The world is not as large a place as you might think, Raymond. And, never assume you know the whole story."

"But I'd planned to request Ensign Barlow."

"I expected you would," Donovan said. "And I'm happy because Admiral Barlow will be happy. Surprised, perhaps, but happy. Now, if you'll excuse me, Ned will give you your orders." He left the room.

"Lieutenant Hatcher, here are your orders." Putzell handed Raymond an envelope.

"It's Lieutenant, Junior Grade," Raymond said, after glancing at the orders.

Putzell laughed. "You've been promoted. He does that some-times. You're no doubt the youngest lieutenant in the navy."

"How does he get these things done, Ned? It takes a requisi-tion and a week just to get your boots repaired."

"He has his methods. In your case, it only took a card game with Secretary Knox and Admiral King."

On the flight to Pendleton, Raymond studied his orders. On Easter Monday he was to return to San Francisco, where he would await passage to Pearl Harbor. There, he would receive more-specific orders upon reporting to the chief of staff for Admiral Richmond K. Turner.

When he returned to Toyon Bay, Raymond found that his commanding officer wasn't very happy. "This makes no sense," the officer said. "I just got orders from Washington that the rest of us are to beat it back to the Bahamas to prepare for the invasion of Europe. And here you are going off for R and R in Avalon?"

Raymond tried not to grimace. "I was told to report to the navy office in Avalon, sir. No one told me it was R and R."

"Oh, right. You're going to study navy codes or something?"

Raymond thought the officer's tone was sarcastic and crabby, but he didn't know why and didn't think he should ask. "I wasn't told, sir."

"Okay, Lieutenant. Get your things together and I'll have the launch take you just before dawn. I'm not going to relax our security, and you shouldn't be telling people in Avalon where you came from."

"Yes, sir."

When Raymond got to his bunk, he found Louie there, his own set of orders in his hand. "Did my father have anything to do with this?"

"Nope. I specifically asked for you. There are only two of us going to Hawaii."

Louie had told Raymond, soon after the bakery caper, that he had washed out of Annapolis and that his father, Admiral Barlow, had been very upset. But Raymond thought Louie had conducted himself well during training and would be a good man to team up with.

"Yes, sir," Louie said. Raymond saw that he was looking at the new lieutenant bars.

"Cut it out with the 'sir' stuff, Louie."

"Right."

"So," Raymond said casually, "you didn't mention that Admiral Barlow is the commanding navy officer for all the California islands."

"You met him?"

Raymond laughed. "Oh no, but it appears he's acquainted with General Donovan, and he knows about our OSS base."

"Yeah. Of course, he's never come to Toyon Bay."

"Would his coming here be awkward for you?"

"You can never tell with him. Chances are he wouldn't acknowledge me, which would be okay. I'd rather not have any of the guys think I had any special privileges. Just as well if none of them know about Admiral Barlow."

Raymond decided to let it go at that. "Did you tell me you were a paramedic?" he asked.

"Yeah. I needed to do something while I was going to State. The less money I took from my father, the less opportunity he'd have to lecture me about going into a naval officer-training program, which I ended up doing anyway to avoid the draft." He laughed. "It set him back a little when I volunteered for the OSS detachment. I told him the same thing I told the OSS: I like being in the water, not on it."

7

RAYMOND WENT BY LAUNCH TO Avalon, where he walked around while waiting for someone to show up at the navy office. He felt awkward in his dress uniform and was disconcerted at first by salutes from enlisted men who hurried by. It hadn't been the convention at Toyon Bay. It also felt strange not to be using alleyways and avoiding people. O'Shea's Bakery would be serving coffee and doughnuts by now, but he wanted to save that for later, after he'd presented his orders. Finally, a light was on in the navy office.

"You must be Lieutenant Hatcher," said the ensign behind the desk.

"I am. I'm here to present these and be assigned a billet." He held out the orders.

"Those you present to Admiral Barlow," the ensign said and led him down the hall to an office.

Admiral Barlow stood behind a desk, his hands clasped behind his back. Raymond noted that he was an imposing man. He had bristly hair, steel-blue eyes, and broad shoulders that appeared to be chiseled out of a block of granite. Raymond saw a resemblance to Louie but only in the sense that a pencil drawing would create a likeness. The man's features were a stern rendition of Louie's face.

"Lieutenant Raymond Hatcher," he said, looking at the orders Raymond had presented him.

"Yes, sir."

"You're taking my son to the Mariana Islands."

Raymond said nothing. All he knew was that he was going to Pearl Harbor. Donovan had not mentioned any specific Pacific island.

Admiral Barlow chuckled. "Of course you wouldn't know that yet. You're assigned to a team under the command of Admiral Turner. I know Turner quite well–he's part of a Fifth Fleet task force under Admiral Spruance, striking the Caroline Islands. Maybe I'm being optimistic thinking they'll be in the Marianas soon."

"Yes, sir. I guess I should get a map to orient myself."

The admiral went to a nearby file cabinet and pulled out a map of the Pacific. In ten minutes Raymond learned how the navy had attacked the Gilbert Islands the preceding November, the Marshall Islands in January, and was now in the western Carolines.

"I probably shouldn't have mentioned the Marianas. You should forget that for now," Admiral Barlow said.

Raymond wasn't worried. The OSS had taught him the importance of secrecy. He felt complimented, as if the admiral instinctively trusted him. After a few more polite questions about Raymond's family, the admiral guided him to the door.

"I assume you didn't know Louis was my son."

"Oh no. Louie told me."

"You never can tell. I'd have guessed he wouldn't mention that I'm an admiral. He likes to be inconspicuous. And I'm not sure how he feels about the navy."

"I'm pretty sure he's happy doing what he's doing," Raymond said. It sounded a little stupid, but he couldn't think what else to say.

The admiral laughed. "You're very tactful. Our relationship has been strained the last couple of years. If he hasn't yet,

I'm sure he'll tell you. He's a good man. Donovan told me you requested him. You won't regret it."

"Yes, sir."

Admiral Barlow looked directly into Raymond's eyes for a moment, with only a few feet of space separating them. His eyes were not as cold as Raymond had first thought, and his countenance was softer. He grasped Raymond's shoulders. "I want you boys to take care of yourselves," he said. "You'll be in harm's way, no doubt, but I'm giving you both an order to return to California for dinner with me and Mrs. Barlow. Pass along that order to Louis."

Raymond left the admiral's office and walked up Catalina Avenue to the bakery, which was off Third Street. All the people he saw walked quickly, in contrast to Saint Paul, where everyone strolled. Catalina was a beautiful place, but he missed walking on Summit Avenue, one of his favorite places to think. No one he passed seemed contemplative.

When he entered the bakery, Megan had her back to him, and an older man with a ruddy complexion stood behind the counter. This was his first encounter with her father, and he didn't want to screw it up. The man looked welcoming and unburdened by wartime and the military takeover of his town.

"What can I get you, lad?" he asked, his voice cheerful, almost booming in the storefront. His eyebrows were slightly bushy and they quivered when he talked.

"I've got it, Dad," Megan said, wiping her hands on a towel and turning back to the counter.

Raymond stood straight in his uniform, his hat in his hand. He forced himself not to smile when Megan saw him. The atmosphere in the bakery became electric. It was better than he had visualized it. "Good morning, Megan," he said. He felt relaxed, as if it were an everyday occurrence for him to be there.

"Raymond!" she exclaimed. "What are you doing here?"

"I understand you make pretty good doughnuts." He paused for a moment. "I thought I'd have one for breakfast."

She stood staring at him and didn't speak. He felt like a movie star delivering his lines in a big scene. "And a cup of coffee would be good too." He watched her regain her composure.

"Doughnuts are rationed," she said. "A junior lieutenant doesn't have the rank to purchase one."

He saw her father look at her in astonishment and then at him. "But I have full lieutenant bars now," he said. "That should qualify me for at least one doughnut."

"As long as you don't insist that it be glazed—"

Raymond watched her raise her eyebrows and tilt her head to one side. He wanted to jump over the counter and take her in his arms.

"What in heaven is going on here?" Megan's father asked just as she came out from behind the counter and wrapped her arms around Raymond.

"It's okay, Dad," she said. "I know this guy."

While Megan attended to customers during the morning, Raymond sat with her father at one of the little tables. He made up a good story: He was a navy intelligence officer who occasionally came to the island for all-day meetings with Admiral Barlow's staff. One early morning when he couldn't sleep, he'd seen the light on and knocked at the door. Megan had given him a coffee and on later trips he'd come by in the early mornings and helped her in the bakery.

After only a few hours of talking to her father and watching her serve customers, Raymond was sure he wanted his relationship with Megan to continue for a long time. He knew he could be killed in action in the Pacific, but otherwise he would return.

Of that he was certain. What worried Raymond more was how Megan felt. She had told him that she was all her father had. Her brother, Brendan, was not dependable, and in any case had enlisted. How would Raymond fit in to that situation?

For the remainder of the week, Raymond began his mornings at the navy office, studying manuals for the new fast boats used to deploy divers before an invasion of an island. Megan worked mornings, until her father shooed her out to meet Raymond. The island's civilian community was small, and Raymond knew he and Megan were a hot topic among them.

In the afternoons, he and Megan walked. He showed her some of the closer goat trails he had taken to visit her. It seemed silly, but he was careful not to disclose that he'd been at Toyon Bay. After the war he'd tell her. One day they went to a bluff overlooking a cove where the seaplanes used to land, and then bushwhacked down a hillside to a ridge that offered views of Avalon. She pointed out the town's landmarks. He listened, but not very carefully because he was mesmerized by the expressions on her face when she spoke.

On the Friday before Easter, they climbed the mountain near McGee Lake. The distant view of the Pacific was extraordinary. It made him philosophic. "It's amazing how a distant ocean looks the same wherever you are," he said.

"I wouldn't know," Megan said. "I've only seen this one."

He put his arms around her then. She leaned her head against his shoulder and sighed. Normally, he thought, her sighs were signs of contentment, but this one struck him as an expression of melancholy. "One day we'll go together to see them all," he said. Then he realized it was the first time he had spoken of a future together.

"That would be very nice," she said.

He wished she had used the word will. But then he remembered that her father called her his sensible girl. Of course she would be cautious about future promises. It was a good thing, he thought; he was comfortable with there being no promises between them for now. He certainly wasn't in a position to make one.

On Saturday afternoon, they hiked east to a deserted sandy area nestled among the rocks on the shore. Before long they were almost naked and embracing passionately. He thought her body was beautiful, but, having never seen a woman naked before, he had no point of reference. It seemed to him that her breasts were perfectly proportioned, extending gracefully from her chest in the same kind of soft contour that flowed from her waist to her hips. But Raymond became uncomfortable. He was a virgin and he thought Megan was, too. The breeze and the waves, pounding on the rocks just a few yards away, were an aphrodisiac, he thought. Should he ask her to consummate their relationship? The desire in him was intense, and he thought she'd say yes. Then he thought it was no more appropriate for them to make love than to make plans for the future. He was going off to Hawaii the day after next, so they shouldn't do this, he decided. He didn't know whether he was too sensitive or too scared.

He looked into her eyes. "Have you ever watched a butterfly land?"

"Nope."

"How about the top of pastry in the oven just before it rises?"

"Ah, now you're speaking my language."

"Somehow the butterfly knows just the right time to land on a flower." When he saw her puzzled look, he said, "Just pretend a butterfly landing is the same as a pastry rising."

She laughed and they sat up to gaze at the ocean. What I just said makes absolutely no sense, he realized. Butterfly? Pastry? He hadn't got his point across that something miraculous can happen in an instant. But he didn't care. Their bodies glistened with sweat. He wanted to tell her that he loved her and would return to her, but he decided the moment was perfect without the words. She leaned against him until the sun began to set and they were cast in shadow.

The next day, Megan's father made an Easter ham. The islanders brought side dishes as well as curiosity about Raymond, who made a point to talk to everyone. He and Megan slipped away in the evening to walk up Crescent Avenue.

"If I could own that one," he said, pointing to a house with a red turret, "living here would be grand." He had a vision of a great library in the house with a large writing desk. He would read and write while looking out over the harbor.

"That's the Look Out Cottage," she said. "You'd be bored up there."

And then they parted in front of the Metropole. He watched her walk away. He'd never before felt such emptiness.

Louie and Raymond were in San Francisco only a single night, which Raymond spent in his room, thinking about what would happen to him next. There wasn't much to think about, because he only knew he was to be one of a three person secret OSS team imbedded in a Navy underwater demolitions unit going to the South Pacific. The third member of the team was not OSS. He was a US Navy Lieutenant Commander named Bradley Wright. Commander Wright was also the son of an Admiral, but he had graduated from the Academy and was a career officer. Raymond didn't know how that would play out with Louie. He'd find out soon enough, he thought, and make the best of it. The OSS was all about making the best of it.

Before he went to bed, Raymond wrote letters to his aunt and his mother. Since he could tell them neither where he'd been nor where he was going, the letters were hard to write, and so he confined himself to chatty depictions of people he'd met, using some hyperbole to keep the information from being painfully boring. He imagined his mother smiling when she read his jejune prose; he suspected that by now she had received a more dramatic rendition of his life from Donovan.

After he finished his letter to his aunt, he walked over to the mirror. The man he saw was very different from the boy he'd seen reflected from the glass of his aunt's door in Saint Paul. He'd been taught to kill and to lie, although he'd not yet been required to do either. He knew that would come soon. And he'd also discovered the difference between love and infatuation. He didn't know what would come of that. Back at the desk, he tried to write to Megan. After sitting for an hour in front of a blank page, he went to bed. He couldn't tolerate the idea of a navy censor reading what he wanted to write to her.

8

LIEUTENANT COMMANDER BRADLEY JAMES WRIGHT was assigned to the USS Augusta when he graduated from the United States Naval Academy in 1938. The ship was in China when he went aboard and he thought it was exciting. But it was deployed to the east coast of the United States early in 1941. After Pearl Harbor he became unhappy that he was doing North Atlantic convoy duty while his twin brother, Harold, was seeing action on an aircraft carrier in the Pacific. Bradley tried to get transferred to a warship in the Pacific, but his request was refused. He blamed his father, who was a retired, but still influential, admiral; he thought his father wanted to keep him out of the Pacific because Harold had barely survived the sinking of his ship at Midway. Finally, Bradley managed to get himself assigned to underwater-demolition training at Fort Pierce. There, in April 1944, on the same day Raymond met in San Francisco with General Donovan, Bradley received orders to go to Pearl Harbor.

Bradley had a week's leave before reporting to Hawaii. After visiting his father and Harold, he took a train to Springfield, Massachusetts to say goodbye to his girlfriend, Adelaide Clements. He'd debated whether to see her because he wasn't sure how he felt about her. But he decided it would be a loose end if he didn't go, and he hated loose ends.

When he got to Springfield, he found Adelaide and her twin sister, Betsy, packing a car to drive to Cape Cod. He knew that the Clements family had owned a summer home in Chatham for generations, until the recession of 1938, when the girls' father had sold the house to an old friend for cash to keep his machine-parts business operating. The sisters told him they were going to the Cape to try to purchase the house back from their father's friend. The man had his own family house on the Cape and had let the Clements' sisters continue to use their old house every year.

They asked Bradley to ride in the backseat so they could hear each other over the road noise. He didn't want to but he thought he had no choice. As he'd expected, they chattered most of the way about things that had nothing to do with him. Every now and then, Betsy would look over her shoulder and explain what they were talking about. She was trying to be inclusive, he thought, but it only perturbed him. He wasn't interested in the details of the Cape Cod house, which was called The Narrows. When they were crossing the canal to the Cape, Adelaide mentioned how hard it must be for Harold to get over the trauma of his ship, the USS Yorktown, being sunk by the Japanese. Harold had been pitched overboard by the explosions from several torpedoes; he'd witnessed the gruesome death of his captain and many of his shipmates. Bradley was tired of hearing everyone talk about Harold's anguish–it had been going on for a year and a half now. Bradley wanted to talk about what he'd been doing at Fort Pierce. By the time they turned onto the long, sandy road that led to The Narrows, he was fuming. Adelaide then made his aggravation worse: after giving him a tour of the house and showing him the view of Pleasant Bay, she insisted that he spend the night at the Cranberry Inn in Chatham. Betsy said it was silly–The Narrows had eight bedrooms. But Adelaide insisted it wouldn't be proper, and she drove him into town.

The next morning he waited for Adelaide in a booth at Oscar's. The mood in the diner seemed strained to him, and he saw that whenever he looked around at the other patrons, they quickly looked away. The only one who didn't appear to notice him was an elderly man sitting at the counter. The man's hand shook when he raised his coffee cup to his lips. It looked like such an arduous task for a sip of coffee. Bradley was sure his hands would never shake, no matter how old he was.

"So, I think today will be as nice as yesterday," he said when Adelaide joined him. He generally didn't make small talk about the weather, but he was worried she might be in a bad mood if her meeting with her father's friend, the current owner of The Narrows, hadn't gone well. He knew the house meant a lot to her.

"We've come to an arrangement," she said directly. He noted the excitement in her voice. "There's nothing on paper yet, and we can't count on anything until there is. He may be an old friend of my father, but he's mercurial."

Before Bradley could launch into the string of questions in his head, he was struck by a change in the diner's atmosphere. The other people no longer paid any attention to him. They all knew who Adelaide was, of course, and he surmised that her sitting at his booth made him ordinary, like the old man at the counter. He didn't like it, and he sat up as straight as he could in order to advertise with his officer's bars that he wasn't just an ordinary swabbie boyfriend. Then he realized that his distraction had led to an awkward few moments while Adelaide awaited his reaction to her news. She leaned forward to peer at his chin.

"What are you doing?" he asked.

"I was just checking to be sure you weren't Harold. By now you'd normally have asked me a dozen questions."

He laughed to hide his anger. She didn't need to look for the scar on his twin brother's chin. All she had to do was look at his collar to see that he was a lieutenant commander, while Harold was only a lieutenant. He recalled that his father had told Adelaide how one summer when Bradley and Harold were kids, Bradley had bullied Harold into standing in the bow of their sailboat on a fast approach to the dock. Bradley had planned to make a last-minute turn into the wind, which would stop the boat, and Harold would make an elegant leap to shore. But Bradley had initiated the turn a second too late. The boat had rammed the dock and Harold had sailed headfirst onto the wood planks, leaving him with a small scar on his chin. "When they're not speaking, that's how you tell who's who," his father had told her.

"So you're going to Hawaii?" she asked.

He presumed she'd noticed his irritation and so had deliberately changed the subject. "That's right," he responded. He no longer wanted to talk about himself, as he suspected that whatever he said would be met with thinly disguised indifference. He felt out-of-sorts and regretted that he had come to the Cape with her.

"Do you have a ship assignment?"

"Not yet. Probably when I get there." He didn't want to explain that he wasn't going to be assigned to a ship's crew because he was part of an underwater demolition team. They sat in silence for a few minutes.

"So, as I was saying, the owner agreed to sell the house to Betsy and me," she said.

"Can you raise the cash?"

"Yes. The owner said he'd sell the house to us for exactly what he paid Dad for it. But Dad doesn't like that. He believes we'd be taking advantage of his friend. A deal was a deal, and all that stuff."

"I understand how he feels."

"Really? I don't get you men. Anyway, Dad finally said he'll loan us the money. But he insists we pay a fair price, which in his mind is more than what he sold it for."

"I suppose you could buy a less expensive place. It's a pretty big house, after all." He saw her eyes narrow. Now what have I said? he wondered.

"You're not at all sentimental, are you?" she asked.

"Well, it would accomplish the same thing with less trouble, wouldn't it?"

"My great-grandfather built that house! Betsy and I have spent every summer of our lives there. Do you think we could just throw it off for something new?"

"A new place might be better," he persisted, even though he knew he should back down. He was being obstinate because he still felt the sting of her refusal to let him stay at the house the night before.

"It's like your father selling the Stonington house while you were at Annapolis. That didn't bother you? I know it bothered Harold."

Here we go, comparing me with Harold again, he thought. Harold had struggled with their father's sale of their home so soon after their mother's death, which occurred in their first year at Annapolis. Harold had become furious when Bradley said that it was no big deal because they would never live there again. And how does Adelaide know about that? he wondered. He could not remember telling her. In fact, he had forgotten the whole thing. "The Rhode Island house is pretty nice," he persisted. "And it's better for him."

In a tone he interpreted as dismissive, she said, "Well, no matter. The Narrows is very important to me and Betsy. You'll see."

"So, what happens next?" he asked, trying not to sound as sullen as he felt.

"We'll sign all the papers next week. With some luck we can have the place all gussied up by August. You and Harold can come up. Maybe even for a week? I still have a month to go in

Bermuda, training a new crew. Did you hear Betsy got a job in Washington?"

Bradley had not been inquiring about the house; he'd been asking what the two of them would do until their late-afternoon return to Boston. He was dumbfounded that she was thinking about August. He wanted to shake her. Maybe it was her way of pushing the war into the background–by focusing on something tangible and permanent, like buying back and fixing up The Narrows. Betsy was the opposite, he thought. For her, the war was very real and he remembered how she coped by filling her days going to Bermuda's pink-sand beaches, learning how to dance the Bermuda Gombey, meeting friends for lunch at out-of-the-way joints in the parishes, and exploring the old town of Saint George's.

"I'm sorry," Adelaide said. "You were probably just asking where we might go after breakfast. I know you have no idea where you might be in August."

"I'm still thinking about breakfast, to tell you the truth." He felt better now that she was focusing on him, not on his brother or on The Narrows. "Let's order something."

The waitress shuffled over when he raised his hand. He asked her if the eggs were real or powdered. From the corner of his eye he saw Adelaide wink at her. He figured she'd say to the woman later, "What can you do about these navy guys?" He was so distracted that only after the waitress had walked away he realized that she hadn't taken Adelaide's order.

"She knows what I want," Adelaide explained.

"Oh?"

"It's a small town."

They sat quietly for a while, not talking. He noticed there were no other conversations going on, either. Everyone seemed to be studying the coffee in their cups.

"So, tell me about Betsy's new job," he said.

"She'll be working for a General Donovan, who runs something called the OSS. I think it means Office of Strategic Services or maybe it's Special Services. I can't remember."

"It means 'Oh So Secret,'" he said.

Bradley wasn't surprised that Betsy was going to work for Donovan. The Clements sisters had been working in Bermuda since early 1941 for the British Strategic Operations Executive, or SOE. Harold had met Betsy when the Yorktown first docked there in April of that year, and Bradley had been introduced to Adelaide by them in May, when the Augusta had also visited the port. The girls would never say what they did in their basement office at the Princess Hotel, but Bradley suspected they had been opening mail bound for Europe, looking for German spies back in the United States.

"Are you making fun of me, Bradley?"

"No. Sorry. I was making a joke. The OSS is often maligned by the ONI, which is the Office of Navy Intelligence, by the way."

"You boys are all troubled with acronyms," she said. "Betsy told me the OSS has a whole book of them, but she can't tell me what they mean or else they'll shoot her."

"What I've heard is that the OSS is a bunch of Ivy League men playing at being spies. But it's all gossip, I'm sure. What's Betsy going to do for them?"

"That's so secret, even I don't know. But she'll be well paid, I can tell you that. And she'll fit in with the Ivy Leaguers, even though she's not a man."

"Won't you miss her? Have you two ever been apart?"

"Of course I'll miss her. Actually, the OSS offered me a job, too. Donovan is pretty chummy with the head of the SOE."

"And you're not going to take it?"

"No. I'm tired of Betsy always wanting me to go to parties with her. I'm a homebody, I guess."

"So you can go to Washington and not go out when she asks."

"It doesn't make sense to her, and she can't accept that I don't want to go anywhere. She'd be dragging me all over Washington."

"That might be exciting."

"No. I need a break."

Breakfast arrived. She took tiny bites of her toast and talked about looking for a job near home. He tried to be sympathetic, but it was hard. Washington was an exciting place, and working with General Donovan would put her right in the middle of the war effort. She'll end up working for her father.

Bradley watched her as she spoke about her plans for The Narrows. She and Betsy were identical twins, just as he and Harold were. Bradley told them apart by their clothes and their demeanor. Adelaide always stood still, while Betsy was always in motion, like a leaf on a tree in a breeze. They both had red hair, but he thought Betsy's was brighter. He thought Betsy the prettier of the two, because Adelaide always had an intense look on her face, and he sometimes felt nervous when she looked at him. Betsy was always smiling, and her eyes flashed when she talked about things that interested her. He liked to watch her. Sometimes he thought it was unfortunate that Harold had met Betsy first. After the sinking of the Yorktown, Harold had become very serious about life, and Bradley thought his twin was now much more like Adelaide than Betsy.

After breakfast, Bradley and Adelaide went back to The Narrows. The day was very clear, and the three of them took a walk on the beach. Betsy was in high spirits, as always. Just being next to her made Bradley feel better. Adelaide's hair was pulled tightly into a pony tail, but Betsy's fanned out behind her in the wind, unencumbered. The sun on it made it look like it was radiating red flashes. At one point Betsy slipped her hand into his and the three walked together, holding hands.

The girls wanted to get back to spend the Easter weekend with their father and younger sisters. So they drove Bradley to South Station in Boston, where he spent the night before catching a train to San Francisco by way of Chicago. He slept badly, which was unusual for him. The next night wasn't any better. He had a berth, but he still didn't sleep. When passing through Chicago on Easter Sunday, he imagined he felt Betsy's hand in his. The warm contour of her hand remained palpable all the way to San Francisco.

9

A WEEK LATER, ON THE day Commander Wright arrived in Hawaii, Raymond leaned against the bar in the officers' club at the Pearl Harbor base. Several groups of ensigns occasionally burst into raucous laughter and then looked around quickly to be sure they weren't bothering any senior officers. He watched them look him over carefully and he smiled at them to put them at ease. Louie was next to him.

"You wouldn't necessarily know this," Louie said, "but Lieutenant Commander Wright is a legend."

Raymond was anxious about Commander Wright, who had arrived an hour earlier. After a perfunctory greeting, Raymond had gone to meet Louie. Wright seemed to Raymond a hard-nosed navy man, wound up like a spring.

"Did I tell you he just arrived?"

"Nope. But every ensign from the Academy in the place knows it by now."

"So, how's he a legend?"

"At the Academy, plebes called him BJ."

"Meaning?"

"Big Jerk."

Raymond laughed. His first impression of Wright hadn't been that bad.

"You knew him?"

"Not really. I washed out after my first year, when he was a midshipman, but I remember that his demeanor was very intimidating to the plebes. He has a twin brother, who is a nice guy. The contrast probably added to his reputation."

"Perhaps he's mellowed with age," Raymond said. He didn't like what he was hearing. He and Louie had settled into a comfortable rapport. The new man could really mess things up by insisting on strict naval formality.

"Maybe. But the scuttlebutt is he volunteered for the underwater-demolition training program at Fort Pierce. Evidently he was an officer on a great ship that did antisubmarine convoy duty in the North Atlantic, but also had quite a bit of shore time on the East Coast. Most officers would kill for that assignment, and the word is that he was in a short line to be the exec. Then, he asked to go to the Pacific! Doesn't sound mellow to me."

"Maybe he was bored." Raymond remembered a navy guy he'd met on his way home from Bari. He'd said convoy duty was like baseball: you got tired of standing around watching the pitcher and the batter eye each other.

Louie snorted. "If you're bored, you go see a movie. You pretend you're Gary Cooper in the Spanish mountains with Ingrid Bergman in your arms."

They stood quietly for a while. The club wasn't very big, but it had two sets of double doors to a deck shaded by two large breadfruit trees. Beyond the shaded area were several walls of kou with orange flowers. Blue ginger clung to the deck railings.

"I suppose you're right," Louie said. "I'm a little bored too. All we've done is train. I'll probably miss the boredom the minute I get shot at. There's a rumor that we're going to be dropped off on the beaches by barges." He shook his head. "Why bus us to the beach? We're swimmers, after all. And all the other swimmers—they're calling them frogmen—are over at Maui, which is supposed to be secret, by the way. Of course, this is the U.S. Navy. They don't know secret. They could learn a thing or two from the OSS."

Raymond laughed. He'd just read a newly published book-let on amphibious operations. Copies hadn't yet made it down to the ensign ranks. "Evidently, the marines were massacred at Tarawa when their landing craft got hung up on coral reefs and underwater barriers put in by the Japs, like stakes and mines," he said. "Our job will be to survey the reefs and find the under-water defenses before the invasion occurs."

"You mean before the marines go in?" Louie asked. "How do we get in there?"

"I don't know, but I guess we go in the night before. It's probably going to be the same as we practiced sneaking ashore in Catalina."

"And if we find something–what then?"

Raymond laughed. "Hey, it's the navy. We'll make something up."

Raymond had told Commander Wright where he was going but was surprised when he showed up. Louie saluted. Raymond was about to, but Wright waved him off. "If it's okay with you guys, let's dispense with formalities." He looked at Louie. "You were at the Academy, I remember," he said, and Louie nodded. "How about you call me Bradley, rather than BJ, if that's okay."

At dinner, Raymond observed Bradley. The man was solid navy, he could see, and he listened to Bradley and Louie talk about growing up in a navy household. It seemed to make no difference that Louie had washed out of Annapolis. Bradley was rude to the restaurant staff, Raymond noticed, and seemed always on the edge of anger over minor infractions, like failing to refill a water glass.

In Maui the next day, Raymond was optimistic. Bradley had not been as rigid as he'd feared. As part of Operation Forager, they were assigned to Underwater Demolition Team Five, which was headed by Bradley's commander from Fort Pierce, a man named Kauffman. Where they were going was secret, except that it was an island in the Pacific Ocean.

Raymond was frustrated because they were not told the name of the island, nor were they given any maps. He liked to study maps; it comforted him to have a mental picture of where he was going. When he asked Bradley about it, he got another variation on the typical navy explanation: "The navy doesn't tell you anything until just before you get there. And sometimes they forget to tell you when you're there."

Kauffman held a one-mile swim in the ocean off a Maui beach. The UDT Five members were in good shape, but they had not spent months swimming in the ocean as Raymond and Louie had in Catalina. So, Raymond wasn't surprised when he and Louie finished before the others.

When Bradley climbed into the boat a few minutes later, Raymond saw right away that something was wrong. Bradley's breathing was strained and he had an angry look on his face, like he'd just lost a race. Raymond wasn't sure what to do. He hadn't considered the swim a race, but apparently Bradley had expected to win—on occasion he'd boasted about his prowess on the sports teams at Annapolis. Raymond thought he should inquire whether Bradley had a cramp or something. "You doing okay there?" he asked, trying to sound just casually concerned.

"You OSS guys probably think you're pretty tough shit," Bradley said.

It was the first acknowledgement that Bradley knew they were OSS, but Raymond wasn't surprised. Nimitz had surely given him the same briefing Raymond had received from Donovan. He saw Louie wince. The tone in Bradley's voice was more hostile than simple bad sportsmanship. He felt he had to say something. "I'm sorry, Bradley, but I'm not sure I understand."

"Sure you do," Bradley claimed. "You were showing off, making the Navy look bad. You people think you're superior, a bunch of haughty Ivy Leaguers." The anger in Bradley's eyes was startling.

Raymond was confused. He'd heard the stories about OSS being a club of Yale men, but he and Louie certainly didn't fit that mold. And Kauffman had said they were competing against themselves, the goal being only to finish. Raymond didn't think much of competition; the only time he'd felt competitive was when he was engaged in gutter fighting taught by Fearless Dan, and there it was life or death, not glory, that was at stake. "Hey, we weren't trying to make anyone look bad," he said. "We just happened to have done a lot of swimming over the last six months. I didn't think anyone was supposed to be a winner at the end."

He made himself look straight at Bradley and hold his position, no matter how much he feared what might happen. They stared at each other for a minute. Then Bradley waved his hand. "Forget it," he said. "It's no big deal."

Raymond thought about the incident later. He hoped it was just a case of Bradley's being unaccustomed to placing second. That was a disappointment one got over easily. But it could be more than that, he worried. It might be an obstinacy that could pop up in any situation; he was reminded of a friend he'd had in school who went berserk whenever someone chewed with his mouth open. The swim had been no big deal. No one except Bradley had thought it was a race. It was troubling to think that Bradley might lose control in a dangerous situation. Raymond took some comfort in the fact that Bradley had been promoted quickly during his tenure onboard the Augusta. But that was in a very controlled environment, much different from combat in open water.

Finally, Kauffman told the team some details about Operation Forager. Evidently, Terrible Turner, as the admiral was known, planned for them to conduct a reconnaissance of beaches during the daylight hours. Raymond was very anxious after he heard that; all their training had presumed a night operation. We'll be ducks on a pond during hunting season, he thought. Kauffman had objected, Bradley told Raymond, but Turner's response had been that "you can't see at night what you can see during the daytime." It was a good point, Raymond thought. Bradley told him it would be okay because the battleships and destroyers would lay down a barrage of artillery fire along the beach to discourage the Japanese from shooting at the frogmen.

On May 21, 1944, they learned that Operation Forager would be an invasion of Saipan, in the Marianas, and UDT Five would embark in a few days on the USS Gilmer. So, Admiral Barlow had been right, Raymond thought. Kauffman sent Bradley and Raymond to Pearl to pick up copies of the attack order, which included maps, to Raymond's delight.

The two of them stood on the deck of the USS Rocky Mount that afternoon, thumbing through the orders while waiting to be picked up by a launch for their return to Maui. A tremendous explosion came from the direction of West Loch, where all the beach-landing ships were mustered. They were watching clouds of smoke billow over the harbor when Terrible Turner came running on deck. He was known for being decisive and personally jumping into dangerous situations. The conflagration over West Loch clearly required men to help him. When he looked around he saw Bradley and Raymond standing a few feet away.

"Are you Lieutenant Commander Wright?" he demanded.

"Yes, sir," Bradley said.

"You two drop those damn books and come with me. I need your help now."

They sped across the harbor in Turner's launch. As they approached the area, several additional explosions occurred and a fireball flashed out from the center of the swirling smoke. The boatswain's mate piloting the boat slowed the craft and began to veer to one side of the conflagration rather than maintain course to the portion of a dock that was still visible.

Terrible Turner leaped to his feet. "Where the hell are you going?" he demanded.

"Sir, there's lots of ammunition exploding on that dock!" the mate said.

"You take this launch into that dock, son, or so help me God I will throw you over the side!"

At the dock, Raymond followed Bradley out of the boat. While securing the line, Raymond saw Bradley offer a hand to Turner. The admiral ignored it. "Get out of my way, dammit!" he said, and then he pointed at the boatswain's mate. "If he leaves this dock, shoot him."

Raymond wasn't sure what to do. Even if he'd a gun, he wouldn't have shot the man. Then Bradley motioned to him to follow him and Turner and leave the boatswain's mate behind. They came upon crews of men manning fire hoses and frantically relocating piles of ammunition away from the fires. Raymond watched Terrible Turner stride among them and shout orders over the noise of nearby explosions. The admiral ordered a group of men to push some crates of artillery shells into the water. The men hesitated and Raymond presumed that they were worried, as he was, that the seawater would ruin the ammunition. Turner yelled, "They're sure as hell not going to blow us up down there!"

Raymond saw that Bradley was calm and decisive while burning metal rained down around them. By the time they returned to the launch, all of Raymond's concerns about how Bradley would perform under pressure were forgotten. The boatswain's mate was covered with soot and part of his shirt had been ripped away. Raymond thought the man looked comical when he saluted the admiral. "The hell with that," Turner said. "Take us back to my ship." A couple of minutes later he said gruffly to the mate, "Good job, son." When back onboard the Rocky Mount, Turner said to Bradley and Raymond, "I would have been pissed if that sailor hadn't been waiting for us."

10

THE WEEKS OF PASSAGE TO Saipan were uneventful. During the days Raymond, Bradley, and Louie sat on deck making recon reels, which were large, empty bean cans around which they wrapped several hundred feet of line, every ten feet marked with a knot. "Enough practice already," Bradley said one day. "Time for the game to start."

Dog Day was set for June 15, 1944, and the frogmen began their reconnaissance operation the day before along the beaches at Charan Kanoa. Kauffman divided UDT Five into several divisions and made Bradley the leader of one of them. Raymond and Louie were in Bradley's division but they were on separate two-man teams. Their division was assigned the underwater reef off the beach called Green Two, which curved out to Afentna Point. Raymond and his teammate were given the part of the reef closest to the point.

The day did not start well. As they were disembarking from the Gilmer and boarding the fast boats that would deliver them to a point about a thousand yards from the beach, one of the battleships escorting their attack force, the USS California, was hit by artillery fire from Japanese positions onshore. The damage wasn't significant but it required the ship to make an evasive maneuver. So, when the frogmen got to their drop-off positions, the California's artillery fire was off its mark: it was landing more than a thousand yards beyond the beach. Japanese soldiers were standing in their bunkers watching the frogmen arrive.

Raymond and Kyle, his teammate, jumped out of the boat and swam toward the reef, holding on to an inflated rubber rectangle called a flying mattress because it had a small electric motor for propulsion. Kyle proved not to be a good swimmer under combat conditions. He couldn't get his breath. After ten yards, Raymond put him on the flying mattress and swam along beside it. When they got to the reef, Raymond realized the flying-mattress concept was a bad idea. It stuck out of the water and made a good target for the Japanese riflemen on the beach. Bullets were zinging into the water around them.

"Get the hell off that thing. Now!" he ordered. But Kyle only gripped the sides tighter and started to shake.

Raymond was about to upend the mattress when a bullet thumped into the side of it and a whoosh of air was released as it started to deflate. Kyle screamed and rolled off.

"Are you hit?" Raymond asked.

"Don't know," Kyle said, his teeth chattering.

"Can you swim?"

"Don't know."

The mattress remained buoyant enough to stay just below the surface, and their recon reels were still attached to it. The two buoys meant to mark their position had come loose and were floating several yards away. Raymond managed to maneuver the mattress and Kyle over the reef, where he found a large coral boulder in about five feet of water. He presumed Kyle had not been hit by a bullet because he saw no blood in the water.

"Listen," he said. "There's a large coral rock just below us. Find it with the bottom of your feet, the part your fins cover, so you don't cut yourself. Can you do that?"

Kyle flailed for a few seconds, until Raymond pushed his face into the water so he could see the boulder.

The Japs were shooting at the loose buoys; the waves were making Raymond and Kyle less noticeable. "We're easy targets out here. You'll have to keep submerging so they can't get a bead on you," Raymond said. When Kyle gave no indication he had heard him, Raymond slapped his face and shouted, "You'll need to stay below the surface as much as possible. Just squat down on the coral, until you get your swimming legs back." Kyle nodded, but Raymond saw terror, not comprehension, in his eyes. Japanese mortar shells were hitting other parts of the reef. Time was racing, and Raymond knew he needed to get going on their task, which he now had to do alone.

"I'm going to anchor a recon line right here where you're standing, and then swim in to measure the reef and see how deep the lagoon is. You stay right here and I'll follow the line back out to you. Then we'll swim out together for the pickup. You got that?"

Raymond dived down and anchored the recon line around the boulder that Kyle stood on. After returning to the surface to take a bearing on the beach, he swam under water as much as possible as he unwound the reel.

The reef was very ragged; the depth of the water varied between five feet and three feet. This was going to be a problem for landing craft. The curve of the beach toward Afentna Point added an additional complication: it allowed the Japanese to fire on the area from two sides. At one point, when he came to the surface for a breath, he saw soldiers at the waterline.

Raymond went no closer than the beach side of the reef where the surf was breaking, about three hundred yards out. He looked at his watch. The air cover should be strafing the beach right now, but it wasn't happening. He saw a group of soldiers setting up a mortar out in the open on a dune. The shells from the California were still falling far behind them, and the men's activity was not impeded. He decided he would not go into the lagoon, which from his underwater view looked like the inside of a washing machine with clouds of sand swirling around. It was impossible for him to see whether there were any stakes or mines.

He secured the recon reel on a coral boulder below him and swam in a zigzag pattern along its line toward Kyle. Halfway back he found a relatively smooth path across the reef, running at an angle toward the other end of Green Two beach. It was almost time for them to head back out from the reef for the pickup, but he thought that after he checked on Kyle he might still have time to deploy a buoy to mark the path through the reef.

Raymond came up for air and saw Kyle's head bobbing at the surface about ten yards away. The sound of mortar explosions seemed to be moving toward him, and he guessed the Japanese were synchronizing their bombardment in a pattern along the reef. Just after he submerged for his final swim to Kyle, a mortar shell exploded behind him when it hit a protrusion of coral. The concussive force was immense: it propelled Raymond completely out of the water. He slapped down hard on the surface.

He did not entirely lose consciousness, but the environment blurred around him. The explosions from the reef now sounded like distant thunder. Although he saw that he had miraculously landed on his back on the half-sunk carcass of the flying mattress, he started to think he was lying on a raft in a lagoon. He was faceup and could breathe, but he couldn't move his arms or legs. His surroundings were now on the periphery of his consciousness; he thought he was on the edge of sleep and was too lethargic to move. It occurred to him he could be dying. Perhaps his limbs weren't moving because they had been blown off. He remembered Megan watching the seals at the Catalina beach. If he died he would never hold her again. He was bothered not so much by that as by the notion that he would never know her intimately, he would never be able to use the endearment "Meg." It occurred to him to laugh out loud at such a stupid notion, but the thought drifted away from him.

When Bradley climbed into the recovery boat, he immediately counted heads. They were three short. He instructed the cox-swain to move the boat out beyond the mortar fire and hover there. The three missing were Raymond, Louie, and Louie's partner, a young man named Trent, who was from Texas. He spotted Kyle hunched inside the railing, hugging himself and shivering. This is not good, he thought, and his mind raced for alternatives.

"Where's Raymond?" he asked Kyle.

When he got no response, he moved closer and repeated the question. When he heard nothing, he slapped Kyle's face hard, grabbed his shoulders, and pulled him nose-to-nose.

"Listen to me, sailor! Where's Lieutenant Hatcher?"

"I think he's dead," Kyle said. "He was blown out of the water."

"You think! Did you check his pulse?"

"No, no, no . . . I just swam back."

When Kyle began to sob, Bradley knew that Raymond had been abandoned. He could be alive. All the men in the boat were quiet, watching to see what Bradley would do. Besides the one at the helm, there was another coxswain onboard; they were sailors from the Gilmer, not UDT Five members, and he saw that they were anxious to get the craft back to the ship. He picked up the radio. It sounded like there were a hundred voices talking at once. He hurled it overboard in a rage.

Think clear and fast, he said to himself, repeating the advice of one of his instructors at the Academy. He looked around. Trailing the boat was a rubber dinghy with a small outboard attached to it. Bradley pointed to it and then to the second coxswain.

"Unlash that dinghy and take me into the reef," he ordered.

The two coxswains look at each other with startled expressions. "Sir, our orders are only to bring you back to the ship," said the one Bradley had pointed to.

Bradley looked at them with a ferocity that made everyone onboard hold his breath. "Sailor, your orders are what I tell you. You will follow them or you will go over the side," he yelled, imitating Terrible Turner at West Loch.

At that point, two of the frogmen straightened to show they were ready at Bradley's command to put the coxswain over the side.

"Do you understand?" Bradley asked.

"Yes, sir," the man said, looking warily at the UDT men. Then he got into the rubber boat and started the outboard.

"You take these men back to the ship and then come back for us," Bradley said to the helmsman, after climbing aboard. He then addressed the UDT men in the boat: "Get your measurements to Commander Kauffman as soon as you get back."

There was a chorus of "aye, aye, sir" as the dinghy and the fast boat separated. At Bradley's direction, the coxswain zigzagged the dinghy toward the section of the reef Raymond and Louie had been assigned. They soon came upon Louie and Trent, about two hundred yards off the reef, just beyond the mortar and rifle fire.

"Sorry," Louie said when he was in the dinghy. "We were delayed a bit. Thanks for coming for us."

"Raymond is hurt," Bradley said. "We're going to find him."

They were now near the ocean edge of the reef and the mortar shells were very close, in several instances close enough to create waves, which rocked the small boat. Bradley saw soldiers with rifles scrambling out toward Afentna Point. From there they would be able to hit the dinghy when it was still outside the reef. Then he saw Raymond floating on his back about ten yards into the reef. He was too flat in the water for snipers to see him, but the waves were pushing him toward the lagoon, where he'd be an easy target.

"There he is, at ten o'clock!" Bradley yelled. He was careful not to point, as he didn't want the soldiers on shore to figure out what they were doing. "I'll have to swim in to get him. If we stop in there to pick him up, we'll get blasted. You hover out here and I'll tow him out."

"Well, y'all, I got a better idea," Trent said, picking up an extra roll of mooring line and starting to fashion a loop. "Why, we can just go bombin' in there with this boat, and I can snag him. Won't even have to slow down."

Bradley looked at him in disbelief. "Are you kidding? You can do that?"

Trent was now expertly twirling the loop around his head, its reach expanding with each circle. He said, "Hell, he ain't even movin'. I can snag a runnin' calf from horseback. This'll be a cinch."

Bradley looked at him and made up his mind. "Get out of the way," he yelled at the coxswain and put himself at the helm. He gunned the engine to full throttle and made a big circle seaward before he started to zigzag at high speed toward Raymond. "All right!" he yelled over the noise of the screaming outboard motor. "Here we go."

The captain of the Gilmer stood on the bridge, scanning the Green Two reef with his binoculars. Kauffman had told him that Lieutenant Commander Wright was in a dinghy going back to the reef to find some missing team members. It was a violation of orders. All recovery craft were required to return before

1100. In one minute the California would terminate its cover fire. Then the captain was told by his executive officer that one of the missing team members was Ensign Barlow.

"Oh, for the love of God!" the captain shouted to no one in particular, and then he commenced a babble of swearing about the navy and having to deal with admirals' sons. "Get me the California," he instructed.

He explained the situation to the captain of the California, who expressed his concern about moving his firing range closer to the beach: he feared shells could fall on the men approaching the reef. The two captains finally agreed that it wouldn't make the odds against Wright and Barlow any worse. As the guns were repositioned, and just before he issued the order to fire, the captain looked through his binoculars. He saw the dinghy speeding toward the shoreline with a man standing in its bow, swinging a lasso.

Bradley was amazed at how well Trent kept his footing in the bow while he swerved the boat in evasive maneuvers. Bullets were making lines of white bubbles in the water around them. They came around in a small arc so as to approach Raymond head-on. Trent released the lasso, which fell into the water just in front of Raymond's head. As soon as the roped slipped around his shoulders, Trent pulled it tight. At this point the dinghy unexpectedly lurched and swerved. Bradley saw that the lasso had also attached itself to the flying mattress below the waterline and the weight was more than the boat could handle. It was like they were going in a circle around an anchor. They were in trouble. His mind raced. He would need to get into the water to haul Raymond in, or all of them would have to abandon the dinghy. But Louie went over the side before Bradley could order someone to take the helm. He watched Louie swim along the lasso line toward Raymond. Good that he didn't ask permission, Bradley thought. Every second counts.

At that moment, all of Green Two, from the point to around the curve, exploded under a torrent of artillery shells fired by the California. The crescendo was deafening and huge amounts of smoke billowed up along the shoreline, flashing white as shells continued to fall. The Japanese mortar fire and the bullets that had been zinging around them ceased.

Bradley followed Louie with the dinghy. After Louie detached Raymond from the flying mattress, Trent pulled the two onboard. Just as the smoke started to envelop them, Bradley headed for open ocean.

On the ships, several minutes of silence went by as everyone watched the wall of explosions spread along the shoreline. Then a cheer went up from those who had binoculars as the dinghy roared out of the clouds of smoke, headed for open water.

In the recovery launch on their way to the Gilmer, Bradley noticed Raymond looking around in a disoriented way. The look on Raymond's face reminded him of Harold after the incident on the dock that had left the scar on his chin. "So, Raymond. You ran into a little trouble, did you?" he asked.

"Yeah," Raymond said. "I guess something snuck up on me."

Bradley nodded; he would learn more later. His mind was racing. He planned to find Kyle when he got back and deck him, after which he would turn in the papers to kick his ass off UDT Five. But he stopped his planning when Raymond spoke again.

"Say," Raymond said, "there is some good news."

"What?"

"My toes!" Raymond exclaimed, looking down at his legs. "I've still got them. I can wriggle them." He demonstrated. It made them all laugh.

Then Bradley heard Raymond say in a very soft voice just before he passed out, "Can I call you Meg now?" He'd have to ask him later what that meant.

11

RAYMOND WAS BACK TO HIS old self a couple of days after Green Two, but Bradley was cautious, so he benched Raymond for the remainder of the Marianas swims. It worked out to be a long break for Raymond because UDT Five went back to Maui in August, 1944. They sailed on the USS Humphreys to the Philippines in September, where they conducted reconnaissance of the Leyte Gulf beaches. In October, they moved to Noumea, where UDT Five was scheduled to wait for their next assignment. He and Raymond knew that Nimitz and Donovan planned to send them into Indochina, but they didn't know when or how. So Bradley asked Raymond to teach him and Louie some basic French and Vietnamese expressions during their wait. He regretted his request after Raymond and Louie began to tease him for his torturously deliberate manner of speaking. They claimed he had a navy accent.

On Christmas Eve the Humphreys was in Hollandia. Bradley received three letters. The one from his father was a short, obligatory paragraph informing him that he had come out of retirement on account of the war and that he and Harold were well and spending the winter in Washington, D.C. The one from Adelaide was a dry report about her job reorganizing the customer accounts for her father's company. He felt some satisfaction over his prediction that she'd do that. The third letter was from Betsy.

⟩ *Dear Bradley,*   ⟩

You most likely have forgotten that I went off to Washington to become a "secret strategist." Perhaps the censor will block out those two words, but in no event can I tell you what I do. When I'm not doing what I can't tell you, I'm trying to get your brother to ask me what I'm doing, which, of course, he will not do, being the muddy stick that he is. Oh, he is a dear. You know I think so. But he can be awfully solemn at times. Did you somehow inherit all the wit? I so miss your tongue-in-cheek observations, and the blank faces they often elicit from Adelaide and Harold. Occasionally I wonder whether we sisters got the brothers mixed up. Maybe you have thought that. I would ask, but I don't want to put you on the spot. Actually, I will put you on the spot and tell you I've been thinking about you quite often, perhaps more so than one should think about her sister's boyfriend. In any case, I wanted to tell someone who would appreciate it that I am so exhilarated with my job that some nights I can hardly sleep, so anxious for it to be morning so that I can go back to my office to do what I can't tell you about. I find it so wonderful that my life has a purpose beyond going to parties and on trips. My sister told me she thought Harold has been good for me, suggesting it is his influence that is making me grounded. It made me angry because, to tell you the truth, I think it was you, not Harold, who influenced me to look at my life more carefully. I love how you are so passionate about your career, but still able to enjoy and see the humor in everyday things. It may sound silly to you, but I think this all came clear to me when you held my hand while we walked on the shore at The Narrows. My chatter that day was only a disguise for what I was really feeling. Bradley, I worry for your safety every day and try in subtle ways to get information about you out of Admiral Wright, when I see him. Perhaps he is perplexed that I am waiting more anxiously for news about you than Adelaide is. Okay. If I have the courage to mail this letter and you receive it, and if you don't feel the same way about the two of us, I hope you will forget it entirely. I wish you a safe return.

Fondly, Betsy

Bradley replaced the letter in its envelope and put it on top of the two other letters. After a few minutes he picked it up and read it again, and then a third time. In the past, he'd generally avoided any analysis of his feelings. He saw himself as a pragmatic man and he thought contemplation was a waste of time. But after the third reading he became pensive. He wanted to organize his conflicting emotions into orderly piles, but he couldn't find a place to start. Soon he became frustrated and consigned the three letters to the bottom of his duffel.

During the first month of 1945, the team undertook several small reconnaissance missions. They had little information about what was happening with Macarthur's push into the Philippines. Many thought the next big action they saw would be an invasion of the Japanese home islands. Bradley dug Betsy's letter out of the duffel again and again, and soon knew he would tell her he loved her, if he ever got back home. He felt good with the decision even though he knew it would be difficult with Harold and Adelaide. In late February, Bradley was summoned by the new commander of UDT Five, who looked somber, and

Bradley's first reaction was to worry that something had happened to his father.

"Commander Wright, I'm not happy about this, but I've been given orders. You, Lieutenant Hatcher, and Ensign Barlow have been detached from UDT Five and will transfer to the USS Burrfish at 0200 tomorrow."

"I don't know that ship," Bradley observed. "What team are we joining?"

"It's a submarine. There are no frogmen aboard her as far as I know."

Bradley remembered Nimitz's plan to send them to Indochina. "Okay. Is there any information about our destination?"

"My orders only say you're assigned to the sub. You'll get specific orders from the sub captain. They're on their way here from Pearl to pick you up."

"We'll be ready."

"I was surprised when I got this command instead of you," the commander continued. "Everyone thought you'd replace Commander Kauffman. I suppose this detachment was planned all along."

The commander's statement might have been a question–Bradley couldn't decide. But it didn't matter. He couldn't acknowledge it. "I couldn't say. But the three of us were honored to be a part of the team and under your command, sir."

Over the next week, the Burrfish took them across the South China Sea to the Vietnam east coast near Cam Pha, north of Haiphong. It was a tedious trip because most of the time they were under water. On the only day the sub surfaced a destroyer noticed them and the captain ordered an emergency dive, after which the sub straddled the bottom and rocked while depth charges exploded above it. It was not the outdoors work the OSS team had trained for. And the confinement was made worse by the crew's truculence. Their mission was to torpedo Jap ships, not run a ferry service for a few navy officers.

On his knees and grasping a short stanchion on the deck, Bradley felt as if he were kneeling on a huge log that was rolling from side to side, up and down the ocean swells marching toward the coastline. Not a good beginning, he thought. The sliver of a new moon slipped in and out of streaming clouds and a stiff wind blew toward the land. All these conditions were good in some respects but bad in many others. Bradley thought it was incredible that Louie was on his feet. "This is awesome," Louie said. "It's like a giant board."

The crew inflated a rubber dinghy and strapped the team's gear into it. The captain stood next to Louie and motioned for Bradley, Raymond, and Louie to get in the vessel. "It's easy," he shouted over the noise of the waves. "You hold on tight. We unlash the dinghy and it'll slide off the deck when we maneuver the sub up over the crest of one of these rollers." Bradley shook his head. He wanted to say to the captain, Are you out of your mind? But he had no chance. "No matter what, don't let go of the dinghy if it turns over," the captain said just before he ran back to the bridge and the crew released the lines. The sub climbed a wave and the dinghy shot off into the sea. It was thrilling, Bradley had to admit. When he looked behind him, the Burrfish was gone, the only trace of her being a ribbon of roiling ocean water flickering in the dim moonlight.

"They lost no time beating it out of here," Louie remarked.

"Right," Bradley said, "they were happy to be rid of us."

The large waves created an easy-to-follow course between the scattered islands. They found a small, sandy patch of shore just below a row of limestone cliffs. When they reached the surf line, Louie guided the dinghy into position. They paddled with all their strength and rode a wave all the way to the beach. There was a protected gap under a limestone cliff and they set the raft against it at an angle. They huddled together beneath the raft, facing the only direction by which someone could approach them. Despite the roar of the waves only yards away, they managed a few hours of sleep.

Before dawn they deflated and then buried the raft. Bradley was aggravated because it had U.S. NAVY stenciled on it and the Japs would search for them if they found it. He grew more annoyed when they climbed a hillside to their rendezvous point and no one was there. By nightfall he was in a state. He'd thought they would be pretty far inland by now, and he didn't like it when schedules weren't met. Also, he was bothered by their orders. They were short and vague, nothing like what he was accustomed to, and they stated without any explanation that Bradley and his team were to claim they were League of Red Cross Societies, or Red Crescent, workers to everyone, even other U.S. military personnel they might encounter. Louie and Raymond kept speculating what that was about. It irked Bradley that the ambiguousness of their mission didn't bother them.

"It's now an OSS mission," Raymond said. "At the OSS, we keep secrets from everybody, including ourselves."

It seemed to Bradley that Raymond and Louie thought the whole situation was comical. He wanted to tell them how stupid the OSS was. You guys don't take anything seriously, he wanted to say to them, and it's going to get us killed. But he kept it in.

No one appeared the next day. A steady drizzle kept them damp and cold. Bradley's joints ached from sitting on the wet ground. At dusk he saw lights out beyond the hundreds of small islands in the bay, which he assumed were from ships traversing the gulf. Due to the contour of the hills along the coast, it wasn't possible to see any villages along the shore. Mountains and forests rose to the west and looked threatening and impregnable as the setting sun clothed them in darkness. They positioned themselves so that they made a triangle with their backs, shoulders leaning against shoulders. The configuration gave them a collective 360-degree view of their surroundings and made anything more than a doze impossible. They had taken turns sleeping in the daylight hours.

"I wish we had a campfire," Louie said. "We used to have them on the beach after surfing. It made everyone mellow."

"Right," Raymond said. "And we could roast the marshmallows I have in my pack."

"You have marshmallows!" Louie exclaimed. "I've got chocolate."

Bradley knew they were only joking about the marshmallows and chocolate, but he still wanted to slap them into seriousness. He hated the word mellow. Mellow meant lazy. He worried that the situation was becoming desperate. If their contact didn't show, they'd have to head overland on their own. Without an introduction from someone local, he doubted their Red Crescent credentials would do much good.

"We may need to head west on our own," he said.

"I'm sure our guide will show up soon," Raymond responded.

"Something is wrong. Maybe he left us when we didn't come up from the beach right away."

"Or he had some other things to take care of. I suspect he's not on military time," Raymond said.

"Okay, so I'm a goddamn navy officer and I like to be punctual. It's how I was trained," Bradley said defensively, his voice rising.

"Do we have a code word?" Louie broke in.

"What difference does that make?" Bradley demanded, exasperated.

"I was just thinking," Louie said. "How will we know we've got the right guy?"

"I suppose we'll know him when we see him," Raymond said.

After another of hour of fuming, Bradley's impatience with Raymond and Louie ebbed, though he remained nervous and agitated. The rain had stopped and the night sky was clear. He abandoned the triangle strategy and had them take turns on watch so he wouldn't have to sit still. After his watch he managed to fall into a restless slumber.

Raymond was excited by their circumstances. He liked the anticipation of the arrival of their mysterious contact. The surroundings interested him. He noted the texture of the ground, which was a bed of moss, and studied how the surrounding shrubbery looked under the new moon. This could be my last night alive, he thought, and I shouldn't miss a thing. The air on his skin felt like a gossamer blanket and the heavens were ablaze with stars.

The next day, Raymond saw that Bradley's agitation was more intense. He'd noticed it the day before and hoped it would pass. Now, he wasn't sure what to do. He'd figured Bradley for being strong and decisive, as he had been during their surveillance operations. But Bradley appeared to be unraveling, and Raymond couldn't see why. Another problem was that Raymond was afraid to challenge Bradley directly. So far, he had managed the tension with finesse. He wasn't sure what he might do if the situation forced a confrontation.

Bradley had started to talk more frequently about departing on their own. It wasn't a good idea, Raymond thought, so he suggested in the early afternoon that Bradley get some sleep because they should travel without a guide only under cover of darkness. It was a short time ploy, Raymond knew, but it was all he had.

The strategy worked. Bradley was still napping late in the afternoon when Raymond sensed a presence near a bush just downhill from them. It could have been a small animal, but he knew it wasn't. He leaned over and poked Bradley, who rolled quickly onto his knees, slapping his hand onto the pistol on the ground next to him.

"What?" Bradley asked in a whisper.

"Easy, boy. And let go of that thing before you shoot one of us."

"You poked me. You could've just said something."

Louie was awakened by the commotion "Is it cocktail time?" he asked.

"What time is it?" Bradley asked.

"We have a visitor," Raymond said.

He tilted his head toward some shrubbery in a dusky shadow. They watched a child emerge on his hands and knees. When clear of the branches, he stood up, but he did not approach them. A round straw hat partially covered his face until he pushed it back, revealing a small smile.

"Hatch," he said.

"Who are you?'" Bradley demanded. He was still holding the gun, but Raymond didn't think the boy was bothered by it.

"You Hatch. I Tu," the boy said, pointing first at Bradley and then at himself.

Raymond saw what the boy meant. He bowed to him, pointed to his own chest, and said, "Hatch." The boy's smile broadened and he launched a torrent of Annamese. It was too fast to follow, so Raymond held up his hand. He started with a few rudimentary phrases and soon had an idea what the boy was saying.

"We're to follow him to meet someone," Raymond said to Bradley and Louie. "I'm not sure I understood everything, but his name is Tu, he herds goats on these hillsides, and he's going to take us inland as soon as it gets dark."

An hour later, Tu led them off the hillside and into a forest at the base of the mountains to the west. It was very dark in the forest, and the path wound around trees and rocks. The ground was slick in places. Raymond and Louie followed the boy easily because they had trained for this kind of trek. But they were slowed down by Bradley, who was repeatedly whacked by obstacles and sometimes slid around the turns. Early the next morning, they came to a small house in a clearing. A man wearing khaki pants and a tan cotton shirt greeted them.

"I'm Charles," the man said. "I hope you don't mind if we use only first names. It's what everyone does in country. And we don't want to be conspicuous. We also need to bury your firearms, your packs, and the clothes you're wearing. We have clothes like mine for you to wear, and you can use these for your other gear." He held out several canvas bags with a red crescent and LORCS stenciled on them.

"I won't bury my sidearm," Bradley said. He and Charles stared at each other for a moment.

"It's a bad idea," Charles said. "Aid workers don't carry pistols. If the Japs see it, they'll shoot you without asking questions."

"I don't care," Bradley said. "It stays with me."

Raymond knew Bradley wasn't going to change his mind, and he didn't want to get him any more ruffled than he already was. "He'll keep it very well hidden," Raymond said to Charles. He was planning to keep his own OSS knives strapped to his body. They'd been a gift from Fearless Dan.

Charles relented, and over the next ten days led them overland around Hanoi and into Cao Bang province, close to the border of China. They were greeted warmly at an encampment near Pac Bo and were assigned a hut of their own. When Raymond saw that the other huts were crowded, he told Charles they didn't require special accommodations.

"They have specific orders to give you that hut," Charles said.

"Who gave the orders?"

"Uncle Ho. He's in Kunming, China at the moment. Last week he took a man name Shaw there. I think he was an American pilot whose plane was shot down near here."

"Who's Uncle Ho?"

"'Uncle' is a moniker of high regard here. Ho Chi Minh is the leader of the Vietnamese resistance, which is called the Viet Minh. The westerners in China are suspicious of the Viet Minh because it opposes both the Japanese and the French. I also think that it's communist. You'll find out soon enough."

Charles seemed nervous speaking about the topic, so Raymond decided to let some time pass before he asked any more questions. But Charles departed the next day, before he had a chance.

A week passed. Uncle Ho did not return. The three ventured out a little more each day. Raymond felt the Annamese culture seeping into him. He couldn't explain it, but living among the local inhabitants began to seem normal. He picked up the Annamese language quickly and soon spoke French the way the native people spoke it.

Life in Tonkin, Raymond learned quickly, was not represented in their camp. The food at the camp was simple—rice, root vegetables, and, often, pork—but Tonkin generally was suffering from a famine, brought on by flooding during the prior monsoon season and the confiscation of rice by the Japanese and the French. The ditches along the road were littered with corpses; the able-bodied men who would otherwise have buried them had been conscripted into the French military forces, except for the men hiding out with the Viet Minh. Raymond was upset to see the arrogant, cold-hearted treatment accorded the farmers by the French. He had happy memories of living in France; the French colonials here were different from the people he had known in Paris.

He interpreted the lack of guidance in their orders to mean they were under no restrictions, except for maintaining their cover. It was the same rationalization he had used to sneak over to the bakery on Catalina. But he knew that for Bradley, "no orders" meant "take no action." It was a quandary at first, but eventually he nudged Bradley forward, and in a couple of weeks the team began to engage in Viet Minh activities.

At first they did little things. Louie set up an infirmary of sorts. He'd worked on ambulances as a medic in San Diego and he had a rudimentary knowledge of how to treat wounds and infections. But his biggest contribution was getting all the medical supplies into one place and properly storing them. Bradley and Raymond worked in the rice fields alongside the Annamese farmers, most of whom were old men. At the end of one day, Bradley put together a small bag of rice he planned to bring back to the camp for the children. He was confronted by a Frenchman.

"Where do you think you're going with that?" the Frenchman inquired.

"We're Red Crescent workers from Pac Bo," Bradley said to the man. "The children there are starving."

"That's all my rice!" The man pointed at the large stack of bags Bradley had just helped harvest.

"It's only a small bag. It will do a lot of good."

"Fuck you, Mr. Red Crescent. That's my rice, every grain of it, and none of it is going to ungrateful peasants." The man put his hand on a pistol strapped to his side.

Bradley stood rigid for a moment. Raymond had seen the look in his eyes before. If the Frenchman had an ounce of sense he'd back down; Bradley would have his big hand wrapped around the man's scrawny neck before he'd get the gun's strap loose. Raymond noted several other Frenchmen nearby watching.

"Come on, Bradley. It's not worth it. Leave the rice," Raymond said as calmly as he could manage. He put his hand on Bradley's arm. It was as hard as iron.

"I don't want to see you in my fields again," the man said. "Take your good deeds someplace else."

Raymond tried to make chitchat on the way back but Bradley didn't talk. It had been a fine day before the confrontation with the Frenchman. The altercation had been a setback because Bradley's earlier funk had almost disappeared, and he had been making wisecracks about how he had joined the navy so he wouldn't have to be a farmer. Raymond had watched him be friendly to local men, even joking with them at times in a mix of jargon that Raymond suspected Bradley was making up on the spot. Now, back in the village, Bradley was brooding. When Raymond went to sleep, Bradley was still seated on the floor of the hut, legs crossed, his face an iron mask.

The brooding continued for a few days, and Raymond began to worry that he would soon face a situation similar to the one he'd faced when they were waiting for Tu. He could see that Bradley was restless, and he worried that he would have to confront an angry Bradley set on returning for a confrontation with the Frenchman. Then, one morning he couldn't find Bradley and just when he'd decided to head to the rice fields to look for him he found him squatting behind a hut next to an Annamese man who was drawing a diagram in the dirt with a stick. The man spoke a mishmash of French and English, but he and Bradley seemed to understand each other perfectly. They stood up when Raymond approached.

"I asked the guy nicely," Bradley said.

Raymond looked at the man. "Asked him what?"

"Not him! That frog from last week. I asked him nicely for some rice for the kids."

"That's true. You were polite."

"And he was rude."

"Yes, he was."

"So next time I won't ask him first."

Raymond figured it out. He was surprised. For Bradley it was very unconventional.

"I know our orders are vague, Bradley, but I suspect that acting in a Red Crescent capacity doesn't include engaging the enemy."

"What enemy? I don't plan to bother the Japanese. They can keep their rice. That pissant frog isn't the enemy. He's just an asshole."

"Still."

"We're going to raid the place at 0200 hundred hours. Meet here!" Bradley commanded before marching off across the camp.

The raid came off without a hitch. The French guards were so drunk they weren't even aware that the storage hut was being robbed. It was amazing to Raymond how easily Bradley got the Viet Minh men to perform. And Raymond saw that Bradley had given a lot of thought to the operation. Bradley's plan was clever. The French were too lazy to keep inventory, so Bradley and his men didn't take all the rice from any one location. They took only small quantities from a lot of different storage huts, and no one was the wiser.

Before long, Raymond noticed that Bradley had taken on the role of guerrilla strategist. He worked on maps and often talked late into the night about Japanese and French army movements with a man named Giap. Raymond was happy because Bradley's enthusiasm appeared to ward off the irritations that sometimes distracted him. As long as Bradley was so engaged, Raymond was confident that Bradley would not be troubled because no word had arrived from Donovan or Nimitz.

Since Bradley was in good spirits, Raymond disguised himself as a peasant and slipped away to Hanoi for a couple of days.

It was remarkably easy for him. He saw many Frenchmen in bars, celebrating the fall of the Vichy government in France. They were also bragging openly that the Americans would soon arrive in Vietnam to help them liberate their colony. The Japanese had been deferential to the French, allowing them to maintain their colonial army and to continue to run Indochina's government. Raymond thought the French braggarts would only make the Japanese suspicious.

On March 9, 1945, there was a great deal of commotion in the village. At first there was talk that the French colonial army was going to raid their camp. The Viet Minh soldiers were gathering their weapons. Then the word was that the Japanese were attacking the French army. Raymond and Bradley went to see what they could find out from Giap.

Before Raymond could ask a question, Giap said, "You had a nice visit to Hanoi."

Raymond was stunned. He had thought he'd slipped away without anyone's noticing. He saw Giap smiling at his reaction. "How did you know?"

"Some men were assigned to watch out for you, to make sure you didn't run into trouble. You did very well as a peasant. Quite impressive."

"Then they saw what I saw?

"Yes. It was very troubling, but now we know."

"The Japanese have taken over, then?"

"Yes. The timing of the Japanese coup was very good luck for us because the French army had been planning to raid our camps in the north. Now they're on the run toward China."

"Will the French departure be bad for you?"

"It's good. The Japanese aren't as bad as the French administration. And now they'll be the only enemy. But we're helping the French soldiers escape when we can."

"Why would you do that?"

"The Japanese are brutal. They'll murder them instead of taking them prisoner. And once we get them to the border, we confiscate their weapons."

During the following weeks Raymond dressed himself in peasant garb and walked around the countryside. At first he was awkward and many people he met were polite and dismissive, suspecting he was a French spy but fearing repercussions from rudeness. Others shunned him completely, turning and walking away the minute he tried to approach them. But he learned from each brush-off, keenly observant of what conduct or speech had tipped them off. Another person would have become frustrated and quit. The Annamese language, culture and terrain were all very foreign to a westerner. But the frequent relocation of his family during his formative years had often put Raymond in new surroundings and taught him how to insert himself subtly into new social environments. He loved to observe the intricacies of a culture, and he quickly understood the prevalent manners, diet and garb. His ear for languages was extraordinary, and he quickly picked up accents and slang. Raymond's observation skills were so prodigious that he could soon mimic facial expressions and body carriage that accompanied common conversations, and the emotions accompanying them. Soon the local people in villages he had not before visited welcomed him without suspicion, assuming he was a man from another part of Tonkin. And Raymond began to feel at home in the villages, sometimes forgetting for days the young college student he'd been in Saint Paul. Up until that time he'd thought frequently about Megan on Catalina, remembering how her hair would come loose from the head scarf she'd worn in the bakery. But Tonkin might as well have been another planet when compared with Catalina. The jungle paths were covered by dense canopies, causing Raymond to feel like he was passing through a tunnel.

They were nothing like the goat trails between Toyon Bay and Avalon where the only thing over his head was a canopy of stars.

When Raymond returned to camp one afternoon, he found that Bradley had joined the Viet Minh raiding parties and Louie was hard at work caring for seriously wounded Frenchmen the Viet Minh had rescued from the Japanese. So much for our orders, Raymond thought when he listened to Bradley describe how the Viet Minh took advantage of the Japanese pursuit of the French. The Japanese would leave behind very small squads of men at the forts abandoned by the French. Then the Viet Minh would overpower them and make off with all their weapons and food.

They moved south to Tan Trao in April. Raymond began spending nights in the countryside. He would sometimes sleep on the ground and find food at small farms and villages. He liked that he could walk openly among French colons and Japanese, all of them thinking he was a peasant. By the end of the month, he no longer thought of himself as Raymond Hatcher; the local people called him by an Annamese name that sounded like *Hatch*.

12

UNCLE HO CAME FROM CHINA in early May, 1945. The three of them were introduced to him as Red Crescent workers, but Bradley suspected Ho knew who they really were. Ho, a diminutive man, was very sick when he arrived. Louie said Ho had malaria, and treated him with quinine the Viet Minh had liberated from the forts.

In the middle of July, an OSS contingent of six called the Deer Team parachuted into the area. Bradley waited for their leader, Major Thomas, to say something, but it soon became clear that he didn't know the three were anything but Red Crescent workers. It worried Bradley. When he heard in early August that Japan had capitulated, he wondered if Nimitz and Donovan had forgotten them in all the commotion surrounding the end of the war. A few days later, Raymond didn't return from one of his journeys. Bradley grew very concerned about Raymond, but he was reluctant to say anything to Major Thomas for fear that their true identities would be compromised. His orders were specific and the jungle had not taken the academy out of him. Eventually, fast-moving events distracted him and, as hard as it was, he decided he had to let Raymond take care of himself. He had no other choice.

Bradley and Louie followed Ho to Hanoi, where, on August 19, 1945, a massive demonstration for independence occurred. Thousands of peasants from the surrounding countryside came into the city, many of them wearing their best clothes and all of them exhibiting their best manners. With no bloodshed, the Viet Minh took over the government. Captain Archimedes Patti landed on August 22 as a part of the OSS Mercy Mission, tasked with assuring the safety of POWs. Bradley and Louie were ushered into his office at Maison Gautier on August 24.

Patti sat behind a huge antique desk. He asked them immediately, "Where's Hatcher?"

"In country, sir," Bradley said.

After so many months of living in the mountain jungles, he found standing at attention very awkward and uncomfortable. Annapolis was long ago and far away. But at least someone knew who he was. He watched Patti study them. They were not in uniform. They were not even in western clothes; their pants were baggy and their shirts short-sleeved.

"In country, you say. That would be this country, I assume."

"Yes, sir."

"And would you know what he's doing 'in country'?"

"I'm not positive, sir, but I think he may be tagging along with Deer Team." It was a lie. Bradley had no idea where Raymond was, but he had no intention of saying anything to Patti, even if ordered.

"With Deer Team? That would be Colonel Thomas? Who you've met?"

"Yes, sir. We were at Tan Trao."

"And did you tell Thomas who you were?"

"We told him we were Red Crescent, sir."

"Why did you do that?"

"Our orders, sir, are not to tell anyone, including Americans, who we are."

"And what have you been doing while you've been here? How long have you been here?"

Bradley looked at Patti for a long moment. This was not going to be pleasant. He thought about how he would react if he were in Patti's place. The man was a captain. There was nothing to do about it. Orders were orders.

"With all due respect, sir, we wouldn't have told you who we were if you didn't indicate that you specifically knew our identities. As we haven't independently received any new orders, I'm not sure how much more I can say."

"I believe you're a navy man. Annapolis, right? Your father is Admiral Wright?"

"Yes, sir."

"And if I were to order you to tell me what I want?"

"I'd refuse, and expect you to lock me up, sir."

Bradley forced himself not to look at Louie, who he was sure was as anxious as he was. Life was easier in the jungle, he thought. Patti focused on Louie, as Bradley had expected.

"And you're also an admiral's son?"

"Yes, sir."

"And I'm going to guess your answer is the same?"

"Yes, sir."

Patti shook his head. Then he threw a sealed envelope across the desk at Bradley. He sat back in his chair, folded his arms across his chest, and watched Bradley open the envelope and read the orders inside. Bradley put the orders back in the envelope, then looked up and nodded at Patti.

"We came ashore north of Haiphong at the beginning of February," Bradley recounted. "Our orders were to meet a guide and proceed with him into northern Tonkin. He took us to a camp near Pac Bo. We stayed there several months and then moved to Tan Trao, where we lived until a couple of days ago, when we came here."

"You've been here since February! What the hell have you been doing?"

"We were watching and waiting to be contacted with further instructions. We received no further instructions, not even an acknowledgment. So, we became aid workers. Louie has some medical training, so he set up an infirmary of sorts. He had to work with medicines the Viet Minh captured, until an American named Frankie Tan showed up and arranged for a supply drop. Hatcher has an affinity for languages, and he now speaks Annamese like he was born here, not to mention French and some rudimentary Japanese. He's been teaching reading and writing. And I've been doing construction."

Bradley looked directly at Patti and waited, all the while trying to ignore the sense of confrontation swirling between them. He wondered whether Patti could tell he was holding back information. At this point he thought there was no reason why he should tell Patti, or anyone else, about his teaching combat techniques, his giving arms training, and his discussing guerrilla tactics. He'd helped Giap plan numerous assaults. And he'd purposely never asked Raymond what he did when he went off to the countryside. So he wasn't exactly lying. He was simply omitting. It was a rationalization, he knew. A year ago he wouldn't have done such a thing. But Tonkin had changed him.

"Just a busy Red Crescent team then? What do you know about that. You guys were forgotten completely. And then about a week ago Donovan announced that an OSS team composed of navy guys was here. There was somewhat of a kerfuffle back in Kunming, and a lot of suspicion. While you were down here, everything in the China theater was reorganized under General Wedemeyer, and nothing is to be done without his approval. You guys were not approved. Hell, no one knew about you! It wasn't even clear who sent you, Donovan or Nimitz."

"It was both, actually," Bradley said.

"Right. You'll be answering questions back home for a long time. At the moment, I'm too busy to care what you've been up to." Patti stood up, walked around the desk, and held out his hand. When Bradley took it, Patti held it for a moment, then added, "Look, I'm supposed to dispatch the three of you back to China right away. If you agree, I'm going to delay that a bit. You've been living with the Viet Minh for a while. I could use some advice."

"You've got it," Bradley said.

"And when Hatcher appears, send him to see me."

Raymond had still not appeared by the first of September, and Bradley decided he would ask Patti the next day for permission to travel back to Tan Trao to look for him. But Patti was unavailable on the morning of September 2, 1945, so Bradley went to Ba Dinh Square to hear Ho Chi Minh proclaim the day Vietnam's Independence Day. After the speeches, he was walking back to the Maison Gautier when he came face-to-face with Raymond, who was in peasant clothes and hat. For a moment they looked into each other's eyes. Then Raymond gave a nod and slipped away into the crowd. It was clear he didn't want to be found. Bradley saw that Raymond was in full control of his faculties, but he still struggled not to report the meeting to Patti, even after it became clear that he and Louie would have to leave Vietnam without him. There had been a determined look in Raymond's eyes, and without understanding why Bradley knew he had to let him go.

On September 4, Bradley, Louie, and Patti went to Kunming. Patti gave the OSS officers there the Red Crescent explanation that Bradley had given him, which they accepted without question. It was just like the navy, Bradley thought. No one wanted to be the one to tell Wedemeyer anything. On September 9, Bradley and Louie left China for the United States, and Patti returned to Hanoi.

After he saw Bradley in Ba Dinh Square, Raymond drifted south into Cochinchina, following the railroad along the coast through

Tourane. The coastline was very different from Catalina in that it often had jungle, not rocky hillsides, extending right down to the beaches. At night the sound of the waves would sometimes infiltrate his dreams, and he would be back in Megan's arms on a beach, watched over by seals. He would wake up with his heart pounding, and wonder why on earth he hadn't gone home with Bradley and Louie. But he'd seen and heard too much concerning the Annamese struggle for freedom from the French. He couldn't go home yet.

During the August Revolution there had been no Americans in the south, and no one suspected Raymond was an American as his appearance and manners were completely Annamese. As Raymond passed through Nha Trang and other towns he learned that the uprisings had not been as peaceful as in the north. When he got to Saigon, everyone he saw wore a hostile expression. He gathered information in the marketplaces and cafés. Viet Minh followers told him the British general Douglas Gracey planned to restore the colony to France. After a week passed, Raymond identified himself to Lieutenant Colonel Peter Dewey, who led Detachment 404, the OSS presence in Saigon.

"So, you're Hatcher," Dewey interrupted, after Raymond started to explain himself in vague terms. "I know all about you."

"Really?"

"Yes. I know Donovan sent you here and that you've been up north. I thought you might wander south. Wright and Barlow have departed for Washington. Transport is bad so they're probably not there yet. You should've gone with them. Patti is still in Hanoi. You'll have to trust me on this. I have no written orders for you. Patti has them."

"Okay." Raymond no longer cared about orders. At times he cared about nothing except the air he was breathing. Washington and Catalina were very far away. He thought frequently that he might never return to his old life.

"I want to know everything you know about what's going on in Saigon," Dewey said. "Then I want you to go back to Hanoi to find Patti. I don't want to tell the British about you because they'd tell the French, and the French are very suspicious of the OSS."

So Raymond told him what he knew: how the British were planning to arm the French and how the French were waiting to exact vengeance on the Vietnamese. Dewey said he wasn't surprised. He helped Raymond hitch a ride up the coast, away from Saigon.

Just as he was passing into Tonkin on September 29, in a small village he'd been to numerous times, Raymond learned that Dewey had been killed. Gracey blamed the Viet Minh, but the Viet Minh had a different story. A French colon had stolen the jeep's American flag when it was parked earlier in the day at the airport, so it wasn't apparent who was in it. Several Vietnamese who turned out to be French collaborators had told the Viet Minh patrol that the jeep's occupants were armed French Army officers. It had been a clever French plan to discredit the Viet Minh and to exact retribution against the Americans for their anticolonial attitude.

Raymond delayed his journey north for a night. He sat cross-legged in a small hut, sharpening his knife. He considered returning to Saigon to assassinate Gracey, which he was sure he could do. It was strange to him that he could think about murdering someone without an ounce of trepidation. His blood ran cold as he envisioned the deed, and the satisfaction he would feel when his blade slipped up through the back of the lower skull into the brain. He'd practiced the move many times on melons. Fearless Dan had taught him the exact entry point on the skull. The last thing Gracey would hear would be Raymond's voice saying, This is for Dewey. All of his senses focused on an overwhelming desire for revenge, not just for Dewey but for all the Vietnamese people. But he dreamed about Megan again that night and he went the next morning to Hanoi and found Patti.

"Well, the wandering agent returns," Patti said.

Raymond nodded. There was no reason for him to say anything. He was ashamed that America was doing nothing to stop the wrongs being committed by Gracey and the French. But he thought it wouldn't do any good to bring it up.

"You can join Ho and me for dinner here," Patti said. "Tomorrow you and I fly to Kunming. Ho will never say you were here or recount anything you tell us."

Patti then held out the copy of the orders he had shown Bradley. Raymond gazed at Patti's outstretched hand. He didn't care what the orders said, so he shook his head. When they arrived in Kunming the next day, they learned that Truman had disbanded the OSS and they were to return immediately to Washington.

13

RAYMOND EXPECTED TO BE JAILED when he got to Washington for his failure to report to Patti with Bradley and Louie. But he wasn't. It seemed to him that no one had planned what to do with the OSS after it was disbanded. From the first question asked of him, he knew his debriefing was a political exercise, so he was carefully vague and in some cases lied. It was easy. He told them he'd wandered in the jungle, that he'd been sick, and that he'd spent weeks hiding from the Japanese. It was imprudent, he knew, to tell them that he'd also hidden from the French, who were worse than the Japanese, but he couldn't help himself. His debriefing became hostile at that point and he thought he might end up in jail after all. But they let it go and sent him back to the hotel where returning OSS officers were being housed.

He kicked around Washington during November, 1945, while most of the other OSS officers were discharged and sent home. He didn't mind that he wasn't discharged with them, because he didn't think he could face his family in Saint Paul anytime soon. He was no longer that boy in the coffee shop who'd watched the waitress every morning. Finally he was summoned by General Magruder at the newly formed Strategic Services Unit at the War Department. The SSU was located in the old OSS space.

"Commander Hatcher," Magruder said, "it's good to meet you."

"It's Lieutenant Hatcher," Raymond said. He was disgusted with everything at that point, and he struggled not to appear surly. Washington seemed to him a mountain of incompetence.

"No, Raymond. It's Lieutenant Commander Hatcher now. I'm not Bill Donovan, but I have some influence. I got you promoted yesterday because I want to convince you to join me at the SSU."

"Really?" He'd thought he was going to be discharged, perhaps dishonorably.

"Yeah. No kidding. Unless you have some other plan, I could really use your talent here."

"What's the SSU?"

"You could call it a polite OSS. For now, we still gather intelligence but we don't do clandestine work. You're not very popular with the Truman guys, as you probably know. But I told them I need you because of your language skills. I emphasized the French and Croatian. You know what I mean?"

"I think so."

"And I promised you wouldn't be bad-mouthing the French."

Raymond shrugged. He had no other opportunity for employment and no enthusiasm for looking for one. Sitting around Washington translating things and looking at maps would be okay. "I could do that," he said.

"Excellent! Welcome aboard. Your first assignment is to take the rest of the year off. It will take me that long to get organized."

Raymond didn't go to St. Paul for Thanksgiving. He wasn't ready to answer questions. Wandering around a quiet and empty Washington, he tried to assimilate himself back into the American culture. It was not as easy as he'd done in Tonkin. What he saw often repulsed him. The Monday after Thanksgiving, Raymond went to see Bradley. He'd known the whole time where Bradley was—at the Office of Naval Intelligence—but he hadn't felt like explaining anything to anybody. Bradley at first didn't ask many questions–he talked only about his own feelings. It was a good strategy, Raymond thought. Bradley had come a long way from the abrupt, demanding navy man in Maui. He'd also been promoted to captain.

"I had a hard time when I came back," Bradley said. "I was really upset by what was going on in Vietnam. There was an arrogant French prick in Hanoi named Sainteny, who referred to the Vietnamese as 'ungrateful natives.' I wanted to punch him out. He was hell-bent on restoring the colony. Then I got back here and found that the hat peddler in the White House had betrayed Roosevelt's legacy and was giving in to de Gaulle's demands. God, I hate the French. Remember that asshole who gave me grief about taking a small bag of rice? I said some stuff in my debriefing that almost landed me in the brig."

"Yeah. I did the same."

"Anyway, I calmed down after a while. I figured I'd find something to do with myself and maybe even make some difference in this stupid postwar world. I really believed in what Roosevelt envisioned, and now it's all gone to crap. But the navy surprised me with my promotion to captain and an assignment to the ONI. It's like the OSS. I can't tell anyone anything about what I'm doing. But it's nothing secret. It's just stupid."

"All sounds familiar."

"And I see you've been promoted. You must be the youngest commander in navy history."

"Why do you say that?" For a second, Raymond felt the old worry about his age. But it made no difference anymore. Nothing made a difference to him anymore.

"I always knew how old you were. My father told me before I met you."

"It hardly matters now. It seems so long ago that we were in Maui. It's like a decade has passed."

"I never expected to be so disillusioned with the navy. I'm not thinking it's a career anymore. I have to bite my tongue when I see my father and my brother."

"What else would you do?"

"Believe it or not, I want to go back to Indochina to help the Vietnamese. I have no illusions that they'll keep their independence. But the French colonials will be no help to them, as we witnessed over and over."

Raymond remembered that Bradley had written every night in a notebook Giap had procured for him soon after they got to Tonkin. He'd always been careful to hide the notebook. "Did you manage to get your journal out with you and keep it away from the navy?"

"Oh yes. It's at home under my mattress. No one ever asked if I'd kept a diary. They only wanted to know if I'd written any reports."

"Got a plan for getting back there?"

"Nope. I'm just going to hang around ONI for a while and wait for an idea. How about you?"

"I accepted a position with something called SSU."

"That's Magruder's group. I've heard of them. It's the last vestige of the OSS."

"For what that's worth. What's up with Adelaide?"

"Oh, that's a long story. She's up in Springfield, and I've broken off our relationship. Actually, I've become involved with her sister Betsy. It's a touchy situation right now, because she was my brother's girl first. I can't explain why it all happened. But Betsy and I have become very close. It's very serious, although I've told no one else that."

Raymond thought the change in Bradley was quite remarkable. That pissant French farmer in Vietnam had been the catalyst to such a dramatic change in Bradley's approach to life. He was questioning everything now, and throwing himself open to crossing boundaries he might not have crossed before, like throwing over Adelaide for her sister Betsy. "I guess the world is a new place, Bradley. I can't say whether for me that's exciting or not."

"Hell, Raymond. It's exciting. You're still getting your feet wet. What about Megan?"

"I've written some letters. She's written back. It's been hard for me to reconcile my life in Tonkin with who I was back then." His voice cracked. He hadn't voiced this thought before, or his worry that going back to Megan might not be possible. He feared he'd lost the bright, positive man he'd been, and was now a man consumed with hatred and the desire for revenge and murder. If he went back to Vietnam now, it wouldn't be to help, like Bradley. It would be to kill. He saw Bradley studying him.

"Raymond," Bradley said, "you get your ass to the West Coast now. That's an order. I still outrank you."

Raymond stood erect on a pier in Long Beach, his shoes as shinny as black mirrors and his hat held at his side. Four years before he'd been a boy slouched over a table in a diner in Saint Paul, in a reverie about the waitress. What had happened to her? Today, he wore his dress uniform, thinking it would help him get a spot on the daily transport to Catalina. To his surprise, Admiral Barlow's launch motored up to the dock, the same ensign at the helm. The ensign told him that an Admiral Wright in Washington had sent word to Admiral Barlow.

Megan was at Steamer Pier, her hair uncharacteristically combed and held off her forehead by a barrette. Raymond guessed Admiral Barlow was behind her knowing the exact time he would get there. Raymond and she maneuvered through an awkward hug; the whole town had shown up to witness the event.

"Well, look at you," she said, standing back to admire his uniform and the new stars on his collar, "a big-shot navy man."

He looked around at all the spectators. "And you must be the famous baker's daughter!"

"The place is loaded with gawkers, as you can see. My father can't keep his mouth shut."

"They look like the seals at Seal Rocks," he said as he took her arm and started toward town.

They roamed farther down the island than on his last visit because the military security was relaxed, except for Camp Cactus, where there was a super-secret installation. One day they went to Isthmus and Bird Rock and then walked south to Catalina Harbor. Another day they sat for several hours at Seal Rocks, where, under the curious gaze of a squad of seals, Raymond told her cautiously about how dark he'd felt since his return from Vietnam. He was vague about it; he couldn't bring himself to tell her how he had wanted–how he still wanted– to plunge his knife into Gracey's skull. It seemed so impossible to him, that his entire disposition had flipped from positive to cynical. He couldn't think how to explain it to this beautiful girl. Her bright eyes and messy hair, the way she laughed, and her contentment with simply standing on a bluff and looking at the sea seemed to slap his face and say, You fool! Not everything is wrong with the world.

Over the next weeks leading up to Christmas, he began to feel like himself again. He wasn't the old Raymond; that person was gone for good. But it was a solid Raymond, ready to step forward, albeit cautiously, into a confusing world. Now he gave thought to Megan, and he knew that he wanted to spend the rest of his life with her. It was not the impetuous love of the year before, and perhaps that made it all the more exhilarating. There were obstacles, he knew. He couldn't ask her to leave the island and her father. But it was manageable. He would find something to do.

After dinner on Christmas he told her, "I'm going to cable Magruder to renege on my commitment."

"Now why would you do that?"

"I'm going to stay right here."

"And do what?"

"I don't know. I could raise goats."

She laughed. "Don't be silly. You'd be bored here soon enough. Trust me on that."

"I'd rather be bored than miserable, which is what life will be like for me without you."

"There's a solution to that, Raymond," she said softly.

He looked at her for a moment, noted how color had risen in her face, and struggled to understand. Then it dawned on him. He felt very stupid, but quickly recovered. "It'd be an honor," he said, "if you would agree to marry me."

"It is an honor for me to accept," she said, and he saw tears in her eyes. He'd worried while in the Pacific that Megan was only an infatuation, like the one with the diner waitress in Saint Paul. Now, he saw he'd worried for nothing. He'd matured in the Vietnam jungles and his feelings for her had grown with him. Looking into her eyes was like looking into the ocean, where so much was beneath the surface at great depth. He would be swept along in her currents of wisdom and strength for the rest of his life.

The crowd was back several days later to see Megan put her new fiancé on Admiral Barlow's launch. "As soon as I can get my father and my brother organized, I'll come to you in Washington," she told him.

I'm back on course, he said to himself as the island receded behind him. But he also felt embarrassed over the despair he'd struggled with. His desire for vengeance had been ameliorated by his future plans, but it hadn't gone away.

Raymond was best man when Bradley and Betsy were married in early January 1946. They had certainly moved quickly, Raymond thought, but he could see that Bradley and Betsy were clearly meant for each other. While he waited for Megan to arrive, he became enthusiastically engaged at the SSU in matters regarding the reconstruction of Europe. Bradley was best man when Raymond and Megan were married in April 1946. Thanks to Admiral Wright, the ceremony took place at the Annapolis chapel, complete with an Arch of Swords, which made Raymond feel awkward. But the reception was spectacular, he thought, when he observed his family and hers standing together and chatting like old friends.

Raymond threw himself into his work and his life with Megan. They visited the monuments and explored the Smithsonian. When they'd seen everything to see in Washington, they took weekend trips to civil war battlegrounds. They spent New Year's Eve in Times Square and a week during the summer of 1947 they vacationed with Bradley, Betsy and their son Herrick, who'd been born in October 1946. The SSU became the Central Intelligence Group and finally the Central Intelligence Agency during that time, and Raymond was exhilarated with its nascent clandestine operations program. He had been disappointed that Truman had appointed Admiral Souers, and not Magruder, as Director of Central Intelligence in January 1946, and then Vanderberg as DCI six months later. He thought both men were political hacks at Truman's beck and call. But Magruder and James Forrestal, the new Secretary of Defense, continued to guide the CIG and then the CIA in the background. Being a US

Navy officer, Raymond became an unofficial liaison between the two men and the agency.

In late summer of 1947 Raymond was deep into work on partition of Palestine issues when Bradley came to see him.

"I'm going to resign my commission," he said to Raymond.

"That may be a bit hasty," Raymond said. He'd become conventional since Megan and he had married, and he was enjoying how well they got along with Bradley and Betsy. Vietnam had been pushed down to a deep, dark place. So he had a hard time understanding why Bradley seemed so set to go back there. Besides, the exciting parts of the globe were the Middle East and Western Europe.

"It's the only way. Betsy and I are going to be missionaries in Tonkin. We already have a sponsor."

"Couldn't you just take a leave of absence to do that?"

"They don't do that in the navy. You know that. Besides, we need to be completely disassociated with the U.S. government, particularly an intelligence service like the ONI."

Raymond had heard some of the plan already, but had hoped it would never come to fruition. Magruder and Forrestal had been discussing the idea with Bradley. They couldn't actually run a clandestine operation in Vietnam through the CIA because the Truman administration was zealously keeping the new U.S. intelligence operations out of France's business. So, Bradley would be off the books, residing in a nether world somewhere between the CIA, the Department of Defense and the State Department. Raymond didn't care for it, admittedly mostly because he was prohibited from anything related to France's involvement in Vietnam.

"It bothers me," Raymond said. "I think it's very risky, and if you get in trouble, no one over here will do a damn thing to help you."

"What trouble? We're going to be teaching and providing health services, not sabotaging anything."

"Or raiding rice warehouses, either, I suppose." Raymond knew that the Forrestal's sole purpose for the mission was to gather information about what was going on in the country, not to help the local people.

"No, Raymond. We really are going to run a mission. It's my way of helping. I can't do anything about the French. Nothing I find out is going to cause the current administration to do anything about them."

"So, fine. You can go on over there and confirm that Uncle Ho is a communist and then come back home and make everyone feel better for turning our back on him."

"Come on, Raymond. Now you're being cynical."

Raymond couldn't help being cynical. He surmised that the CIA was about to become a giant bureaucracy, and he was worried his obligation to toe the political lines would go beyond staying out of France's business. US diplomatic and intelligence operations in his opinion must take account of cultural movements in the rest of the world, not just domestic political forces. It was bullshit to have foreign policy driven by the domestic-centric influences of pro-Israel and anti-communist groups in the US. But he knew he should be admiring Bradley for being one of the few who wanted to take positive action to make things better. Now that he thought about it, he was ashamed of his attitude. "You guys are doing a good thing," he said. "I'm sorry I've been negative. I'll want to read all about it someday, so make sure you write everything down in that journal of yours."

14

AFTER THE GERMANS SURRENDERED IN 1945, Georges Piquart returned to Paris, but he chose to forgo an army career because he feared his unsavory activities with the Moroccan Goumiers would come to light during his reviews. Re-entry into French life was easy. He slapped away introspection with quick bitter thoughts like he was swatting a bug flying around his head. The bitter thoughts would sometimes lead to rancor aimed at Bernard, but these hard feelings were easily assuaged by visits to nightclubs and brothels. His wealthy family provided him plenty of financial security, so he joined the French intelligence service, SDECE, which was at that time a club for the sons of the well to do who could pay their own way while they waited the requisite number of years to advance into higher offices in the diplomatic services or to government appointments. In the summer of 1947, he married Beatrice, a woman from a wealthy Normandy family. It was a good career move because the couple became well known in Paris social circles.

Beatrice was very attractive and outgoing, which made her popular at parties, but she was a prude at home and didn't allow Georges into her bed with any frequency. Even when she did acquiesce to an amorous moment, it wasn't for Georges the adventure he hoped for. She would allow him only one position and one orifice, neither of which were the ones he most wanted. What she would do didn't lend itself to his fantasies about Bernard. Then, despite their infrequent couplings, she bore their first child in 1949, after which their sexual relations occurred in the same manner as appointments with a dentist.

Georges couldn't risk the damage to his reputation that would come from his being seen at a brothel, but he discovered to his relief that his profession offered him an alternative. In the fall of 1950, at an informal gathering of intelligence professionals, he met Helene, an American analyst at the Paris office of the CIA. She mentioned that she had been a schoolgirl in Paris in the 1940s and remembered him as a boyfriend of Bernard de Lattre. The next night he seduced her and soon thereafter recruited her as a double agent for SDECE, demanding secret meetings in small hotel rooms in Paris. When her tour ended at the end of the year, she returned to Washington pregnant by Georges. But the affair had been noticed and early in 1951, with encouragement from his wife, Georges accepted a post in Hanoi as an undercover agent for SDECE, where the French Indochina War was raging. Georges was thrilled with the posting because he knew Bernard, who had made a career in the army, was detached there. Beatrice, of course, remained in France with the baby.

During that year Georges went back to France only once to see his wife and daughter. He told her he was very busy in Hanoi, but most of his time was spent hanging around the Metropole Bar and visiting brothels. Bernard was often in the field, and met Georges only in public for drinks with officers and foreign services personnel. Georges was sure Bernard's father had ordered this, but Bernard had laughed at this assertion, saying that the general was too busy to care what Bernard did in his spare time. Then, around Easter of the next year, Georges began to come across Bernard in the company of a young, attractive French woman.

At the end of May 1952, Bernard was killed near Ninh Binh in the Battle of the Day River. Although Bernard had treated him as merely an acquaintance in Hanoi when he'd introduced him to his girlfriend, the old flame in Georges's heart had still burned hot and Bernard's death hit him hard. General de Lattre treated Georges shabbily at the funeral Mass in Hanoi, barely acknowledging his presence.

Over the next month, Georges treated his despondency by concocting a theory that Bernard's death had been the result of a grand conspiracy between the United States and the Viet Minh. He frequented the Hotel Metropole bar, where he was known only by his alias, Jacques de Garde, an officer of a company that owned several large farms in the country. He would tell anyone who would listen that Americans were self-righteous, citing as evidence the State Department's program for literacy for peasants and the anticolonial rhetoric from the American press. At the end of the summer he told himself he had to stop the nonsense. Bernard was dead. Nothing could be done about that. He resolved to become conventional and conquer his secret desires–he'd been keeping them alive with the memory of Bernard and his conspiracy theory. Then he received a cable from Paris telling him Helene had reported to SDECE that the CIA was receiving information from two missionaries living in the Tuyen Quang province. It shattered his resolve to change.

He immediately went north under the pretext of visiting several colonial farming operations his company reputedly owned. It was sometimes dangerous to venture north of the de Lattre Line, so named on account of Bernard's father, but the Viet Minh was licking its wounds after its failure at the Day River, and there was a French garrison in Tuyen Quang. He also took along two SDECE agents for protection. They posed as business assistants, which was a thin disguise because the men were former legionnaires, mercenaries really, and looked like thugs.

Finding the missionaries was easy. It irritated Georges that many people in the valley, both French and Vietnamese, knew and liked them. He stayed a few days at the mansion of a prominent colonial landowner close to the small village where the mission was located. He intended to have the landowner introduce him to the missionaries, but first he sent his agents to reconnoiter. They reported back to him that the village was located in a forest clearing a few kilometers down an unpaved road.

The next morning, Georges set off alone to look at the village. He wanted to familiarize himself with the local surroundings so that he wouldn't be distracted when he went to meet and question the missionaries. He thought himself a master at detecting whether a suspect was hiding something.

He moved undetected around the perimeter of the village, just beyond where the clearing gave way to forest. He found the hut where the missionaries lived and saw that they had a young son. While he watched through his binoculars, the woman came out of the hut with a towel and walked around back, where there was an unenclosed outdoor shower, supplied with water from a large barrel on the hut's roof. The woman stepped beneath the stream of water and Georges was mesmerized by her lithe body. He adjusted the focus of the binoculars and studied her pert breasts and pubic hair, which was as red as the hair on her head. By the time she wrapped the towel around herself, he was sweating and his erection hurt him. He had to sit on the ground and unbutton his pants. Over the next hour, from different vantage points, he watched her flounce around the village, engaging merrily with the peasants. As he walked back to the colonial mansion, he pictured her naked over and over again. She was nothing but a sanctimonious American tart, he thought, and he became enraged that she had stirred up such lust in him.

The next day, Georges went back to the village and met the Wrights. The husband, whose name was Bradley, introduced his wife as Elisabeth, although Georges was told to call her Betsy.

It confirmed for Georges his conclusion that she was a tart, because no sophisticated woman named Elisabeth would allow herself to be addressed as Betsy. And she insulted him by excusing herself immediately to tend to activities with the peasants. He could hardly pay attention to his conversation with Bradley, he was so angry. In the end it made little difference. That night in his bed, thoughts of her in the shower made him erect again. She is making me besmirch the memory of Bernard, he concluded. Whether or not he could confirm the couple's connection with the CIA, he decided a reparation was due.

Bradley sat on the step of their hut, watching Herrick play tag with his nanny, whose name was Mai, although Herrick called her "My-My." He loved to watch Herrick at play. The boy was happy and shrugged off disappointments quickly. He was like Betsy in that respect, and often he reminded Bradley how untroubled Harold had been when they were kids.

Betsy came walking across the village from the infirmary. To him her gait always appeared carefree, even though she carefully scheduled her days. Her long red hair streamed behind her like a flag in the wind. She sat next to him. He sighed. While watching Herrick he'd been brooding a little.

"Oh no. Is there trouble?" she asked.

"I'm just so content sitting here watching Herrick run around. Look at him, will you. He's all you. A little ball of positive energy." It was a clever misdirection, he thought, but it probably wouldn't work. She was very observant, and eventually he'd let something slip and she would catch it.

"Hm. I see some Daddy there," she said. Herrick was doing a victory dance because he had just tagged My-My.

Bradley laughed. Now Herrick was hugging My-My. Bradley thought it was probably because Herrick was worried he'd hurt her feelings by winning. "Whatever he has of me, I hope has been cured by you."

"You've been ruminating again, haven't you?"

"Maybe a little."

"And you're thinking about what that navy doctor told you."

"There was logic to it. I could still be shuffling my anger under a rug."

"It was five years ago."

"But I'm so untroubled, I'm troubled."

She laughed. "You're too much! Herrick is a very happy little boy. And all you were before was impatient. One doesn't inherit impatience."

He was quiet for a while. It could be much more than that, he thought. Lately, he'd thought about his disposition more and more, and about his mother, whom he'd not thought of for more than a decade. "It may have been more than impatience," he said. "I have to tell you something I should have told you before, but couldn't. No one knows except my father." He paused for a moment to collect himself. "My mother killed herself. It wasn't a heart attack."

He couldn't look at her. Why have I chosen this particular time to tell her this? We were sitting here so happily, enjoying a respite from the rainy season. When his father had told him about his mother, he'd just accepted it and gone on with his life, as if it were no big deal. He'd been so wrapped up with his life at the Academy. And why had his father told him and not Harold? Because Harold would have blamed himself, Bradley had come to realize. Before, he'd thought only that his mother had been impatient, like he was. Then the navy doctor had said his impatience could be an early indicator of an impending nervous breakdown and had gently suggested that Bradley and his mother shared an emotional disposition that could prove troublesome; it could even be a mild form of schizophrenia. Bradley had dismissed it and thrown himself into his Vietnam planning. He kept telling himself that it was only impatience, nothing more. And how does one inherit an emotion? It wasn't like blue eyes. All the pieces had swirled around in his head for the last year, and recently it had worried him that it was more than impatience and that his son could turn out the same way.

"I know," Betsy said softly.

"You do? My father–he told you."

"He knew you hadn't, and he thought I should know."

Bradley was quiet. He was angry at his father, just like he'd been when he found out the navy doctor knew about his mother.

Betsy put her arm around him and leaned her head on his shoulder. "Hey, you're not your mother, Bradley. I'm not worried."

"It's complicated. And I can't make any sense of it."

"Oh, and of course you're very impatient with that, Mr. Have-an-answer-for-everything!"

They both laughed. Herrick was now kneeling behind a tree, holding his hands over his eyes and counting. My-My was running to hide.

"Maybe I've just lost my edge," Bradley said. He felt better now. "You know that guy Jacques who was here yesterday? I just welcomed him right in. He could have been here to kill us. The French don't care for American do-gooders."

"I didn't like him at all, but I don't think he's dangerous. He seemed like your run-of-the-mill French pervert to me. Yuck!"

They stood up and hugged. Bradley felt relieved, even though he had no more answers than he'd had when he first sat down on the step. He watched Betsy walk off to her next chore. After a few yards she looked back over her shoulder at him and smiled, as he knew she would. He loved her so much at that moment that his chest hurt. Herrick is one lucky boy to have a mommy like that, he said to himself, and walked back to their hut. He had journal entries to make.

Soon after Georges returned to Hanoi, he received a cable from Paris instructing him not to confront any Americans living in Vietnam. Negotiations regarding military aid were at a delicate stage. He ripped up the cable in disgust, indignant that the politicians in Paris were showing deference to the Americans. Have they no honor? he asked himself. In his mind, the Wrights were the embodiment of all Americans and they were no better than the peasants with whom they lived. He felt powerless to redress the slander of France by the Americans and he soon became paranoid, which led to a conviction that the Wrights had murdered Bernard.

He continued his search for something tangible to link the Wrights to the CIA. He could not present Helene's report to the politicians or the press; she was a double agent and it would blow her cover, not to mention that they might uncover his earlier liaison with Helene. His animosity increased with his nocturnal erections, which were now accompanied by imagined couplings between Bernard and the Wright woman. He made his usual rounds of Hanoi prostitutes, sometimes twice a night, but it didn't help.

After a week of this obsession, Georges decided to take action. It would mean the end of his SDECE career, he knew, but he didn't think that was so big a loss. He had come to hate all things associated with the French government. In Paris, the ministers were all calling Bernard's father, General de Lattre, a hero, and Georges hated him now as passionately as he had loved Bernard.

Georges knew the legionnaire henchmen working for him were ruthless and would enjoy an opportunity to get some

American blood on their hands. He gave them the assignment and admonished them that the killings must never be attributed to him or to France. After they murdered the couple and their little boy, they were to gather up all Wrights' papers and bring them to him. He would then dispatch the killers to a small garrison west of Hanoi near Hoa Binh under the guise of surveillance of traitorous activity by the Muong soldiers. They could hang around there until the whole thing blew over.

The operation did not go as well as he'd hoped. The henchmen were ruthless, but not particularly competent. They killed the parents but lost the boy when panic spread over the village after their gunshots. The papers they brought back contained only reports about the mission's literacy efforts and agricultural program and nothing that disparaged French colonial policy. His superiors at SDECE were suspicious that the Americans killed were those identified in the report from Helene. It was good luck that the initial report of the murders by the press in Hanoi suggested that the Viet Minh were the culprits. But he feared his good fortune wouldn't last. Several days later, Georges decided it was time to quit SDECE and his alias, Jacques de Garde, left Hanoi, telling his friends that he'd been promoted to a better job in Paris.

Raymond was in Cairo when he heard that Bradley and Betsy had been killed. His boss, Frank Wisner, had sent him there to confirm intelligence that the Egyptian government was about to disavow the Suez Canal treaty. When a man was needed to blend into a country's population and gather intelligence, Raymond was always the first one asked, unless it involved France. No one at the CIA actually knew where Raymond was in Egypt because he'd been wandering around the country the same way he'd once roamed through Vietnam. He was sure he'd be recalled to Washington the next time he made contact, and then he wouldn't be able to do what he intended to do. So he did what he'd done six years before: he disappeared.

He entered Indochina with fabricated credentials identifying him as a teacher going to help set up the State Department's reading room in Hanoi. It took him only a day to get local clothing and other gear, and one day after that to travel to the countryside north of the de Lattre Line, where he found Giap.

Immediately after a polite greeting, Giap said, "We didn't kill Bradley."

"Of course you didn't," Raymond said. "I know the story isn't true." He recalled the Dewey incident in Saigon, and he suspected a similar circumstance lurked here. "But I need to find out who and why."

"We've expected you," Giap said. "We have a little information. They were killed by two French legionnaires. We think the killers were working for French intelligence, but we're not sure of that. They were associated with a French businessman in Hanoi named Jacques de Garde. He has left the country."

"What kind of business?"

"His company owns interest in several colonial farm operations in the north."

"How would that have related to Bradley?"

"We don't know."

"Could he have known they were American intelligence?"

Giap smiled. "No one knew that. Not even me. Not until just now."

"Surely you suspected?"

"Bradley and his wife were doing very good things for the Vietnamese people. We watched them in the beginning. They showed no interest in anything but the villagers. There was no radio. They went to Hanoi now and then. They never had American visitors, only curious French colonials, to whom they were welcoming. Perhaps they were reporting to you on the French? We hoped they were, but we didn't know."

"There were reports. But I never saw one."

"We can take you to the village. The French Army investigators are gone. No Americans came."

Raymond, even as cynical as he was, was shocked. The State Department didn't know Bradley and Betsy were CIA. If they had known, Raymond thought, he might understand why they wouldn't take an active role in the matter. Anyplace else in the world, they would have played a prominent role in an investigation into the murder of American citizens. Raymond had no doubt they were bending over to be deferential to France. He struggled to keep the rage out of his voice. "What about the legionnaires?"

"They're at a garrison near Hoa Binh. But we have the little boy at one of our camps near here."

Raymond stared into the distance for a moment. Everything inside him felt hard, as if all his feelings and emotion had been sucked out. His skin was very cold and his muscles were unnaturally taut. Is this grief? he wondered. He'd never had to deal with grief before, so he didn't know. Below the hard, cold layers was probably turmoil, ready to rise to the surface. The hell with it, he thought. It doesn't matter. Nothing matters but what I'll do next.

He decided that Herrick was safe for now with Giap, and said, "I'll return in a few days to see the village and get the boy."

In Hoa Binh, as in every other garrison town in the country, there was a single drinking establishment run by an unsavory local Frenchman. The proprietor didn't care whom he served; he was more than likely a criminal who had fled France long ago. Raymond slouched in a corner with his straw hat obscuring his face. He listened to the two men talk. They were frustrated that they'd heard nothing from Jacques de Garde. Before the evening was over, he had heard enough to know their names and to know that Jacques de Garde was their boss at SDECE.

The next night, the men wandered off separately, each with a local prostitute. Raymond had no trouble with either of them. He surprised them with their pants down, their firearms out of reach, and their senses dull. In each case, he clenched the throat and slipped the long blade of his knife up into the brain, all in a matter of seconds. He'd considered interrogating one of them to learn more about Jacques and the motivation for the murders, but he couldn't stop the cold, blind momentum that had brought him to them. He didn't care what their reasons were. After he sent Herrick back to the United States, he intended to find Jacques de Garde. He wouldn't interrogate him, either.

When a cable arrived from the US mission in Hanoi, Frank Wisner instructed a team to pick up Herrick and bring him back to the United States, where he was delivered to a stunned Admiral Harold Wright and his wife Adelaide. They'd assumed along with the state department that Herrick had been killed with his parents. Raymond surfaced in Cairo a week later and, as he expected, was immediately recalled to Washington. Frank Wisner didn't ask Raymond where he'd been during the time he was out of touch in Egypt. And Raymond didn't offer to tell him. His debriefing was confined to information he'd gathered in Egypt.

Over the next decade Raymond was frequently out of the country, sometimes for long periods. His official employment moved to the US Department of State, where he continued to coordinate with Frank Wisner's Office of Policy Coordination. He was kept in the shadows during the 1950s by Wisner and the Dulles brothers, which allowed him to avoid an incident like the Carmel Offie one. Overt diplomatic missions gave him opportunities for covert operations. He was in Iran in 1953 for Operation Ajax and back in Egypt in 1954 when Nasser ousted Farouk. After the expulsion of Yugoslavia from COMINFORM in 1948, Raymond slowly began to build contacts in Croatia, starting with Vera and her new husband who both worked for the Yugoslavian intelligence service. They and Raymond secretly fought with the partisans in Hungary in 1956, barely escaping capture by crossing the frontier as refugees. It was an exciting time. But the early 1960s were a time of disillusionment for Raymond, in part because of Frank Wisner's failing health and because the Kennedy administration did not as he hoped lift the ban on his participation on matters involving the French, including the French Indochina War and its sad American aftermath.

Megan was a bright spot in his life throughout the time. Their relationship matured into a partnership, both amorous and intellectual, as she completed her higher education at Georgetown and worked her way up in the administration of the Smithsonian to be one of the directors in their section on cultures. Being as practical as she was, Megan accepted gracefully the news from Bethesda that she would never be able to conceive a child. She told Raymond they could fill their lives with each other and so many other things. It was nonsense, she said, to think that their lives could only be empty without a child. He thought she made sense, but he had to hide his disappointment, settling into the situation in the same manner he would settle into a covert role. He made frequent visits to Herrick and he was awarded the honorific of "Uncle Raymond."

In late 1963, he was visiting Herrick at Saint George's School in Newport when he heard that Diem had been assassinated. He thought it a start of an ominous chain of events, a feeling confirmed twenty days later when Kennedy was killed. In early 1964 Raymond thought his ban on operating in Vietnam would be lifted by the Johnson administration, but he was sent by the Director of Central Intelligence, Richard Helms, to Brazil.

Raymond wanted desperately to get back to Vietnam. He often thought that with his influence, Johnson wouldn't be in the muddle he faced. These were narcissistic thoughts, Raymond knew. And it wasn't typical for him to overestimate his abilities. What he really wanted, but couldn't admit to himself, was revenge, both for what happened in 1945 to Dewey and then later to Bradley and Betsy. Whenever he read briefings on Vietnam, whether classified or in the newspaper, there would always be a replay in his mind of Giap saying the name: Jacques de Garde. It was many years since Raymond had rescued the very scared little boy, who now, in the late summer of 1964, was about to go to college. It wasn't rational to think that he could return to Hanoi to find any evidence that would lead him to the man. He'd uncovered nothing from his discrete inquiries in France, although he was limited in what he could ask there, as he was still known to the French intelligence services as a Viet Minh collaborator. Still, he was unable to put it behind him, which would be the sensible thing, and he would awake sometimes in the early morning hours with the name being chanted from his emerging consciousness: *de Garde, de Garde, de Garde.*

PART 2
1964 to 2014

OLD SPIES

15

JAY JACKSON SAT ON HIS bed in the freshman dormitory at Princeton waiting for his roommate, Herrick Wright, to return. It was September, 1964 and they'd met for the first time two hours before, when Herrick and his family had descended upon the room. Herrick was now escorting his family to their car for the return trip to Boston.

Jay was anxious because he had never been away from home before without a passel of relatives tagging along. His home was a large ranch near San Saba, Texas, and his family was as a general rule suspicious of foreign places, which included New Jersey. His two older brothers, who were much older than he, had attended Texas A&M and then immediately returned to do their parts in the ranch operations. Neither they nor his father understood why he would choose to go to a place like Princeton. His mother had brought him up to New Jersey the day before.

One reason for his unease, he thought, might be that Herrick and his family were from Boston. All during high school Jay had harbored a secret wish that he had been raised in Boston, which to him was a place where everyone was worldly and sophisticated. He wasn't sure why he had wished for Boston in particular, because his concept of urbanity came primarily from fiction written by British novelists. Why the novels hadn't prompted him to attend Oxford or Saint Andrews he couldn't explain, except to say that those places were too far away. Now he worried that even Princeton was too far, as he had been intimidated by the Bostonians and was wishing he could saddle up his horse and ride out to one of the meadows to think. A minute later, Herrick returned and Jay thought he saw anxiety on his face as well.

"Did your parents get off okay?" he asked. But he flinched inside when he heard the word get sound like git and worried that get off was a Texanism for depart, which was the word he should've used. It was a bad start, the same as when he'd called Herrick's mother ma'am earlier. He intended to eliminate all of his Texas words and behaviors. His new roommate seemed not to notice.

"Oh, yes they did," Herrick said. "But look, you should know right from the start that they're not actually my parents. I know they introduced themselves that way, but they're really Uncle Harold and Aunt Adelaide–and Bradley, the kid they said was my younger brother, is really my cousin. My real parents are dead. I like for things to be out in the open."

"Sorry to hear about your parents."

"It happened a long time ago."

"What happened, if you don't mind my asking?"

"They were killed in Vietnam."

Jay wondered about this. He took a guess: "Were they both in the army?"

Herrick laughed. "No. They were missionaries, and it was in 1951, long before the war."

"Where were you? In Boston?"

"No. I was there, but they missed me."

"Who missed you?"

"They were murdered by Vietnamese rebels, and one of the villagers hid me so they wouldn't kill me."

This was not how Jay had expected his roommate from Boston to be. His life sounded both horrible and exciting, like one of Graham Greene's novels. "It sounds awful," he said, not able to think of anything else.

"I was very young and barely remember that day. I remember the village where we lived and how I played games with my nanny, but not much else. My uncle and aunt are good parents. I call them Mom and Dad. It's unusual. My real mother was my aunt's twin sister and my real father was my uncle's twin brother. How strange is that!"

"It's a little bizarre." Jay had a hard time putting all this together. The only twins he'd ever known were sisters from a neighboring ranch, and they had been very irritating.

"So enough about me. Where's your family?"

"My mom brought me yesterday but had to go home."

"And where's that?"

"Texas. We live on a ranch near Austin." Jay suspected Herrick had no concept of how big Texas was. Austin was a long way from San Saba, but it was the closest city. The ranch itself was bigger than the city of Princeton.

"Do you have horses?"

"Yes, but we also have a lot of cattle."

"That I want to see. We can make a trade. You take me to the ranch and I'll take you to an old house on Cape Cod called The Narrows. It's been in my aunt's family for generations."

Jay agreed, but what he really wanted was an invitation to Boston. He barely knew where Cape Cod was, so he thought he'd go to the library in the morning and look at an atlas. Herrick would easily find Austin in an atlas.

Jay and Herrick became close friends. Jay scaled back his plan to transform himself from Texan to Bostonian. In the end, the idea hadn't stood up to scrutiny, particularly from Herrick, who demanded that they be as candid about everything as he had been about the deaths of his parents. Many Princeton students seemed very sophisticated and Jay in his first year had often been anxious that he might be ostracized as a hick. It hadn't happened, but not because he had managed to act like a Bostonian. Jay was tall, blond, solidly built, and handsome. He was recruited to the rugby team, became a star player, and was quickly popular. It was what all the Princeton men wanted to be, and—what he would never have predicted—they were not put off by his Texas mannerisms. Still, he continued to be very mindful of his diction and the idioms he used.

During their second year, Herrick's uncle Raymond came to visit them. He wasn't Herrick's real uncle, Jay learned from Herrick, but he'd been a very close friend of Herrick's father in the navy during World War II and had stayed in touch with Herrick's uncle Harold and aunt Adelaide. It was 1966 and the Vietnam War was a dark cloud above them; they were going to lose their deferments upon graduation. Neither was in a position for draft dodging. Herrick's ancestors were pure navy, and Jay's Old Texas family would find him and shoot him if he refused to serve. So Jay was anxious until Raymond suggested that they consider the U.S. Navy Reserves Officer Training Corps, which he and Herrick's uncle Harold could easily arrange. It was what they did.

When they were about to graduate from Princeton in 1968 and begin their service in the navy, Uncle Raymond was back with another idea: Jay and Herrick could do their naval service in a program with the Central Intelligence Agency, which would offer an opportunity to begin a career at the CIA at the same time as they were fulfilling their service obligation. Raymond, who was a foreign-services officer at the State Department, had a connection at the CIA and could arrange it. Jay thought the connection was mysterious and was skeptical. He wanted to go to law school, and after two years of active duty he would be eligible for a navy program that would pay his tuition in exchange for an extended term of service in the Judge Advocate General's Corps. Raymond came back with a CIA alternative: they could go to law school after only one year of active duty in return for working in the CIA's Office of the General Counsel afterward.

They saw no combat during their year of active duty. They spent most of that time in San Diego, training aboard ships in the harbor there. Herrick had an uncle Louie who was a captain stationed there. Louie was also a doctor. And, like Uncle Raymond, he wasn't really an uncle.

"I don't get it," Jay said to Herrick one night. "Why do you have these uncles who aren't really your uncles?"

"They were friends of my father in World War Two."

"I know you've said that. But how does a friend become an uncle?"

Herrick didn't speak for a moment. Jay guessed he was arranging his response to make it orderly, something Herrick often did. "I've wondered that myself. I asked my grandfather once. He's a retired admiral. He told me that the three of them took part in some very dangerous missions in the Pacific during the war and became very close as a result. Then, after my father and mother were killed, Louie and Raymond started to come see me frequently when I was growing up, just like real uncles would. I'm not sure who anointed them as uncles. It was probably Uncle Louie. He's that way."

"What were the missions about? That might explain it."

"Nope. They were on a team of frogmen who surveyed the coastlines of islands about to be invaded, and I think they were in Indochina at one point. You know, I've never pressed anyone for details. I'm not sure why. I asked my grandfather if he could tell me what exactly they'd done, and he put me off. He said Uncle Raymond would tell me one day. Uncle Harold told me that what they'd done was still classified as secret by the navy. I dropped it after that."

"Maybe we can find out after we get our CIA clearances?"

"Maybe. To tell the truth, I'm not sure I want to know any more than I do. What I know fits into nice, orderly piles, and anything new right now would just raise many more questions. Someday I may get curious, but I like things as they stand at the moment."

Jay didn't question Herrick further after that, but he thought about it on several occasions during the rest of their stay in San Diego, particularly after visits with Uncle Louie, whose feelings for Herrick were clearly as strong as those for his own children. On one occasion Jay found himself sitting alone with Uncle Louie on some rocks near a breakwater at the end of a Torrey Pines trail. Herrick was down the beach with two of Uncle Louie's younger children.

"Raymond is a little mysterious," he said, meaning it to be more of a question than a statement.

Uncle Louie laughed. "Never heard it put that way before."

"I mean, he always seems to show up at the time a decision needs to be made."

"He does have a good sense of timing."

"So, what was he like in Vietnam? It's hard to picture him in the jungle."

Uncle Louie paused for a minute, and Jay worried that he may have overstepped his welcome.

"You know, Jay. Our little visit to Vietnam is still classified."

"Right. Sorry. I shouldn't have asked."

"I can tell you that what you call mysterious may just be curiosity. Raymond was always curious about everything and very attuned to the lives of people around him. So, keeping track of what you and Herrick are up to is probably just that. He's interested in what you're going through."

"Maybe. I don't know what he does at the State Department, but it must be more interesting than the two of us."

"Let me give you an example that I don't think is classified. When we were in Vietnam, we spent a lot of time in the jungle just waiting for something to happen. Raymond filled all that down time watching, no, a better description would be investigating, the local culture. I remember him going to the story telling time the village elders would conduct for the children. Raymond would sit right in the circle with the children, watching and listening, every bit as intent as the kids. He would do the same thing watching the cooking or the cleaning, listening intently to the everyday conversations people would have. I asked him about it once, and he said, 'you can learn more about their language and culture by watching this stuff than you can from a thousand books.' I suppose he was right, but I never had the patience he did. Never will."

Jay tried to picture Raymond in a Vietnamese village, but could only come up with memories of a group of ranch hands sitting around a fire. He'd liked to hang around and listen to them talk and watch their faces. It was probably similar, although not so exotic as the Vietnam jungle.

Later, Jay watched a conversation between Louie and Herrick. It was remarkable to see the fondness Louie had for Herrick. Raymond had shown the same thing. Yes, they'd been friends with Herrick's father, but the three hadn't spent that much time together after the war ended. The men in Jay's family were entirely different from Louie and Raymond. None of them would ever show as much emotion for their own children as Louie and Raymond demonstrated for Herrick. So, it was strange ground for Jay. He didn't understand it, but he found himself wishing that he had an uncle like Louie or Raymond. He also wondered what had happened in Vietnam that had forever intertwined the lives of the three men.

16

JAY AND HERRICK HAD ONLY sporadic contact with Raymond from 1969 to 1972 because their part time clerk positions at the Office of General Counsel (OGC) at CIA and their attendance at Georgetown Law School consumed their time. They saw him only on holidays, either at parties held by Herrick's family or small dinners that Raymond and Megan would invite them to. After graduation in 1972, they began their careers as first year lawyers in the OGC, working late nights and on weekends researching and writing memoranda. Richard Helms continued to keep Raymond away from Southeast Asia, telling Raymond he was far more valuable in the Middle East, Eastern Europe and Chile, where hostilities were below the surface. He thought it foolish to send an excellent agent into a country being bombed day and night by the US. Raymond was in Santiago in the month leading up to Allende's election and then back two years later when Pinochet's jets flew between the buildings and strafed the palace. He found himself in overt hostilities in the later stages of the Yom Kippur war, when he slipped into Egypt to meet with Anwar al-Sadat with whom he had over the previous decade developed a clandestine relationship. It was what he would have done with Giap had he been given the chance.

In late 1973, just back from Egypt, Raymond sat in a coffee shop in Georgetown, waiting for Herrick and Jay to join him. To meet at a coffee shop for a discussion like the one he had planned was unusual, but he didn't care much for offices, where everyone's presence was logged. He went to Langley to see Helms only when they could arrange for an official meeting that required the attendance of his cover as a foreign service office at the State Department. He thought how his father, were he still alive, would chuckle at the whole thing. Jay and Herrick were told only that Raymond collaborated with CIA on intelligence activities involving the State Department.

Raymond was at the coffee shop to persuade Herrick and Jay to move from the OGC to clandestine services and work on matters about which he was collaborating. They'd been writing memoranda regarding missions that Nixon and Kissinger wanted the CIA to undertake. Raymond thought the missions weren't going to turn out well and he didn't want Herrick and Jay to be associated with the whole mess when the finger-pointing started. Raymond hated the politics and the bureaucracy at the CIA. He was still around only because his overt career was in the foreign service. He traveled a great deal, often for weeks at a time and under other identities. So he wasn't present either at the CIA or the State Department often enough to get sucked into the politics. If they agreed to move to clandestine services, he would bring them in on the full extent of his collaboration, including his special relationship with Helms.

Raymond thought Jay was the better candidate for clandestine services, but he knew he wouldn't get him without taking Herrick. Also, he wanted to keep Herrick close to him because he'd come to think of Herrick as the child Megan hadn't been able to conceive. Herrick was like Bradley, his father, Raymond thought. He made his decisions too rigidly, and many times the process was much too slow. Raymond had never seen him express a hunch. In a tense undercover circumstance, a quick decision was better than a slow, perfect choice. Jay, on the other hand, had a natural instinct for quick decisions, and he would not get ruffled when adjustments needed to be made afterward.

He was also cool-headed and strong, like the cowboy who stands in the bow of a swerving dinghy and throws a lasso at an object bobbing in the waves. Raymond would move Herrick into the support side of clandestine ops, maybe even an analyst's position behind a desk. Jay would be taught what Fearless Dan and Jimmy Nearwell had taught him.

There was a complication. Raymond suspected that both boys were in love with the same woman. Genna was a young, talented operative in clandestine services who had started at the CIA the same year as Herrick and Jay. Raymond knew her assignments involved surveillance in Soviet Bloc countries and were sometimes dangerous. He guessed that Herrick, her actual suitor, was too naïve to see how Jay felt. Whether Genna had an inkling, Raymond couldn't be sure, but he suspected she did.

"I've got some news," Herrick said, immediately after he and Jay arrived at the coffee shop. "I've asked Genna to marry me and she's accepted."

Raymond didn't look at Jay because he knew it would give away what he suspected. He covered up his momentary hesitation with an excited tone. "That's really good news, Herrick. Congratulations. Tell her I wish her good luck. She'll be needing it."

Herrick laughed. "Will do."

"How about you, Jay?" Raymond asked. "Any good news from you?"

"Oh, no, Mr. Hatcher. I'm smart enough to keep from getting caught, I guess."

They all laughed. Raymond let the "Mr. Hatcher" go. He'd tried for years to get Jay to call him Raymond, but he hadn't been successful. Jay had told him once that it wasn't the cowboy way to address your boss by his first name. Raymond had remembered after that how Trent had called Louie by his first name but had always said "Lieutenant Hatcher" to Raymond.

"You saved my life. That certainly gives you the right to call me Raymond," he'd said to Trent. "Don't make no difference," Trent had said.

"I have my own proposal for you boys," Raymond said. "I'd like you to move over to clandestine services and work with me on some State Department projects." He saw Herrick's expression turn skeptical, as he'd known it would. Jay would wait for Herrick's reaction, as he always did.

"That's out of the blue," Herrick said. "Why would you want a couple of lawyers?"

"Nothing wrong with a lawyer if he's got good sense. In fact, you guys are very good at deciphering and deducing, which is what I look for in a candidate."

"I'm not much at fighting, Uncle Raymond, if that's what's involved. Jay will tell you that. I was dead last in the hand-to-hand combat course at navy camp. Worse, they made fun of me. And I'll be up front here: with getting married and all, I'm not sure how much danger I want."

Raymond remembered Herrick's father in the Tonkin jungle. He'd not been in the least intimidated by danger. In fact, he'd relished it at times. It was the other extreme, but it would have made Bradley just as bad a field operative as Herrick would be. And what about Genna? Raymond wondered. Doesn't it bother him that she's frequently in danger?

"He has a point," Jay said. "Why, Genna can whip his ass with no trouble."

It was a joke but also a sign of support, Raymond thought. Jay was very perceptive. And clever. He was being careful not to reveal his feelings about Raymond's offer. Raymond figured it was best to laugh with them.

"Guys, you've been reading too many novels. Who said anything about fighting? Very little clandestine-services work involves guns and knives. Do I look like a killer? The only armed confrontation you're likely to have is if you get mugged when I send you to a meeting in New York." All of that was untrue regarding Jay, but that would come later.

"Hell, writing memos to Kissinger is dangerous," Jay said. "I suppose this could be much safer." Raymond thought Jay was saying he was amenable to the offer.

"Does our boss know about this?" Herrick asked.

"He will when Mr. Helms tells him about it. I promise it won't hurt your careers."

Herrick peppered Raymond with questions after that. Almost an hour later, the two had agreed to the reassignment, subject, in Herrick's case, to his discussing it with Genna. Raymond wasn't worried about that. Genna was a very good agent and would assume that Herrick would never go into the field. She would ask Raymond right after Herrick told her, and Raymond would confirm it. It was a very good outcome, Raymond thought: Herrick would be insulated from the political fall-out at the CIA, if it came, and Raymond would have himself an excellent field operative in Jay.

As they were leaving, Raymond said, "One more thing, boys. From now on, you'll have to quit the 'Uncle Raymond' and 'Mr. Hatcher' stuff. We're all on a first-name basis at clandestine services."

17

IN SEPTEMBER 1952 GEORGES PIQUART was very close to going to prison. His handlers at SDECE thought it had been no coincidence that the Wrights had been murdered soon after Helene's report had come from Washington. They'd heard about Georges's proclivities and his hatred of Americans. He had professed his innocence, of course, stating that he'd immediately ceased his investigations after he'd received the cable instructing him to avoid confrontations with Americans. And the investigators at SDECE had no proof. It might have been different had the two legionnaire henchmen turned up, but they had disappeared. So Georges had been discharged from the intelligence service. He'd been instructed to stay out of Vietnam and away from any contacts with American intelligence agents, including Helene.

SDECE had no knowledge that Georges had an illegitimate daughter by Helene, and he hadn't told them that he'd no intention of cutting off his relationship with her. He was fond of his daughter and continued to be attracted to Helene, whose small breasts, narrow hips and blond hair, cut short above her ears, made her look boyish. When her pregnancy had been about to show she'd taken a leave of absence from CIA and gone to Belgium until she had the baby. Georges had found an excuse to travel there himself for a week during that time, and he'd had his way with her every day of his visit. In his passion he would look at her and see Bernard as he had looked in Paris when they were boys.

The Piquart family had a great deal of money and grand houses in the south of France and on the Normandy coast. When his father died in 1955, Georges inherited everything except for a large sum put into a trust for the benefit of his younger sister who had moved to Atlanta, Georgia the year before to marry a US Army officer. The inheritance only increased the wealth Georges controlled; he'd made himself rich after his discharge from SDECE by arranging a number of off-the-books transactions brought about by the US dollars that had flowed into Europe under the Marshall Plan. By the end of the decade Georges had established a confidential reputation among business executives and government officials around Europe as a man to call when discreet maneuvers were needed to influence a sensitive operation, such as a quiet movement of building materials and services to countries like Cuba and Thailand. He'd also spent some of his money on a restoration of his father's elegant chateau near Toulouse, which he'd renamed Chateau Bernard.

During the 1960s Georges continued to send money to Helene for their daughter, and both of them would visit him in Paris. The girl lived with Helene's mother and was sent to a boarding school in Switzerland as soon as she was old enough, at Georges' expense. Helene had informed the CIA about her daughter but the information had remained confidential in her employment file, and no one in the clandestine operations group, where she was a French language translator and analyst, knew about the girl. And Georges had never told Helene he was no longer in French intelligence. She was told that he was working undercover as a businessman in France, and she continued to provide him information from time to time. He thought her naïve. She had so easily believed his explanation that their collaboration had to remain secret because there were Russian moles working in both the US and the French intelligence services. The communist paranoia had worked for De Gaulle. Why not for him?

Helene met Herrick Wright in early 1974 when he began working in clandestine services. She mentioned him to Georges on a trip to Paris that summer. Herrick was a very nice young man, she told Georges, and it was too bad he'd just married because she'd wanted to match him with their daughter, who despite all the schooling in Switzerland was making a miserable start to her adult life. As Georges knew because he'd paid for it, the young woman had recently spent several months in an expensive addiction treatment facility. Georges didn't make a connection between Herrick and the Wrights he'd met in Vietnam until Helene casually mentioned during a trip to Paris the next summer how impressed she was that Herrick had overcome the trauma of seeing his missionary parents killed by the Viet Minh when he was a young boy. The discovery revived his long dormant hatred of the Wrights and America generally, but he put it aside quickly because he was so engaged in the new consulting business he'd recently started. He was preparing to go to Helsinki on behalf of a very prominent client and he had agents working in Morocco and Argentina who were beginning to send him reports. By Helene's description, Herrick was only an analyst at CIA. It was silly to waste any time on the man. He would just keep track of him by casually asking Helene about him when he saw her in the future.

The spring of 1977 didn't go well for Georges. He'd kept mistresses over the years but a recent one had caused him trouble. She'd said to him, "If you're only to fuck me in the ass every time, why not just find yourself a queer to keep." It was true, but it had enraged him and he'd beat her so badly he'd had to pay her and the French police substantial sums of money to keep the incident out of the papers. But the woman had sent

Beatrice graphic photographs of the bruises on her body with a salacious note describing the matter in detail. Beatrice moved to the Normandy chateau and, despite his entreaties, refused to see him and vowed never to set foot in the same house with him again. The episode had also distracted him from two very important operations he was running, one in Egypt relating to a rumor that Sadat was planning to engage with Jimmy Carter in some kind of peace initiative with Israel. If such were to occur, well placed contacts in Cairo would be well positioned to take advantage of business opportunities that were sure to follow. The second opportunity was for a French energy firm who wanted to bribe an East German official in order to influence the grant of a concession for the building of a pipeline system. Georges could have sent an agent to monitor a meeting the East German was attending in June near the Swiss border, but he decided to go himself. It would distract him from the uproar in his personal life and delay the confrontation with his children that he knew was coming, since Beatrice had recently confided in them why she refused to leave Normandy. It would be an easy assignment. All he would have to do was sit in a few cafés and see what he could find out about the people meeting with the East German. He would bring a couple of men with him in case a car needed to be followed.

Nothing went as expected. One person meeting the East German in Saint-Louis was an American woman. The snippets of conversation he'd managed to overhear suggested the woman knew a bidder was trying to influence the man's decision. And the car she was driving was owned by a company in Paris that Georges suspected had US intelligence connections. Perhaps he'd been hasty but he'd donned the uniform of a French policeman and pulled her over on her drive back toward Paris. She'd displayed the American attitude he detested and she had strawberry colored hair, both of which had reminded him of that Wright woman from Vietnam. So he'd taken her from her car and brought her to an out of the way house his men had found.

They sat in a small room. Georges watched her eyes. He thought they would flicker when she spoke if she was lying. They didn't, but he was sure she wasn't who she said she was.

"You've made a mistake," she said.

"Espionage is a serious offense, madam."

He was playing his role of French police official, and he'd alleged that she was in France on behalf of a foreign intelligence service—he hadn't said which one. She was handcuffed to a heavy chair.

"It's mademoiselle and I'm an American businesswoman. You have my passport. Call my embassy."

Her eyes remained glued to his. She's very good, he thought. He'd sent the information from her passport to Helene, who would reply soon. Then he would know.

"I will call," he said, and left the room.

The client had told Georges that an American woman was asking questions about bids being solicited by East Germany regarding the construction of a natural-gas pipeline. He knew that the client was paying bribes to an East German official. He also knew that a minister and a member of France's National Assembly were receiving secret payments. But he didn't care. It wasn't his business. His assignment was only to prevent interference by the American woman.

Georges planned to interrogate her and rough her up a bit. They would leave her in her car on a country road, after draining all the gasoline from the car's tank. Then he received a cable from Helene. The woman was a CIA agent and her passport was an alias. Her name was actually Genna Wright and she was the one married to Herrick Wright, the young man she had spoken about. According to Helene, the CIA planned to leak the information about the bribes to the press. The rage Georges felt after reading this was so strong that he had to sit for several minutes to regain his composure. It's another assault on the glory of France, he thought as he crumbled Helene's cable and threw it into the fireplace.

When he returned to the room, he said, "Madam Wright, your passport is an alias."

"You're mistaken. Did you call the embassy?"

He saw that her countenance was a perfect imitation of indignation at having her identity mistaken. But her eyes were cold. It made him smug. Your eyes give you away, he thought. But her stare bored into him, and his smugness unexpectedly changed to apprehension, which made him angry. He walked over and slapped her.

"Do you think me an amateur?" he shouted.

"You're mistaken," she repeated.

His slap had only messed up her hair. Her eyes continued to penetrate him. Why didn't she cry out? Why didn't she beg him to believe her? It rattled him, because he realized she'd correctly concluded that pleading with him would have no effect, while stolidity would frustrate him. He left the room and went to find his henchmen.

"Go in there and handcuff her wrists and ankles to the bedposts," he instructed.

"Should we take off her clothes?" one of them asked.

"No," Georges said gruffly. "Just handcuff her flat on the bed."

After the men came out, Georges went back into the room and stood over her. As he'd expected, her composure was the same.

"Now we stop playing games," he said. "We can call a truce on who you really are. But you must answer some questions about your activities in France."

"It's doubtful a policeman would strap me to a bed. Does the truce cover your identity as well?"

He detected a faint sarcasm in her voice, but he overcame the anger it caused. "Why were you meeting with the man from East Germany? What information did he give you or you give him?"

"I don't know any East German men."

"We observed you meeting him at the café yesterday in Saint-Louis."

"He is a Swiss banker. I am a businesswoman, as I've told you."

"We know the man isn't a Swiss banker."

"You're mistaken, again."

"I don't make such mistakes. I am a professional, like you."

She paused, and he thought she was considering whether to cooperate until she laughed. "All you are is a professional thug."

It was too much. His composure was swept away by a storm of indignation and rage. He was reminded again of the Wright woman in Tonkin. She'd had the same haughty expression on her face. He slapped her, back and forth, until his hand stung and her lips and nose bled. Then he ripped off her clothes, sure that he would find the same pert breasts and red pubic hair he'd seen on the Wright woman when she showered. His erection now pushed against his pants so hard that it caused his knees to bend. This time will be different, he thought as he hopped around the room in a frenzy, trying to get his pants off his ankles. He leaped onto her, like a raptor swooping onto a cardinal.

He kneeled above her when he was done, his chest heaving from the exertion. The hysteria of molesting her had distracted him from taking in what he now realized. She had neither cried out nor struggled, unlike the girl he'd raped in the Pyrenees after he'd killed the soldier. He knew before he looked down that her countenance would be phlegmatic, her cold stare digging into him again; she wasn't going to tell him a thing. Furious, he put all his weight into a punch to her head that knocked her unconscious. Then he dressed and left the room.

When he returned with a full syringe, he found his assistants standing over her, leering. She was still unconscious.

"One of us could fuck her while the other asks questions," one of them said. "That always works."

"No," Georges said, his voice so threatening that the two men backed away. He plunged the needle into her and emptied the syringe. She would never regain consciousness.

"Her clothes are torn," he said, pointing at the garments strewn around the room. "Dress her in clothes from her suitcase, put her into her car, and roll it into a tree so it looks like an accident. Then set the gas tank on fire."

During the hours it took him to drive back to Chateau Bernard, Georges turned the incident over in his mind. He'd lost control and been sloppy, he admitted to himself. Running the car into a tree and setting it ablaze wouldn't fool a careful investigator. A favor from a minister would be needed to make the investigation cursory. He didn't like to ask for favors because one day a quid pro quo would be required and he didn't like being beholden to anyone. "But it was definitely worth it," he said aloud in the empty car. The two imbeciles he'd hired in Vietnam shouldn't have allowed the boy, Herrick, to escape, and now he'd taken a step toward correcting that mistake. One day, he thought, he would have the opportunity to kill the woman's husband, the son of those missionary impostors. And then, finally, Bernard's death would be avenged. In the meantime, the husband could suffer over his wife's death the same way Georges had suffered after Bernard's death in the Battle of the Day River.

18

JAY LEFT HIS HOTEL IN East Berlin on a June evening in 1977, headed for a small restaurant where he thought he might come across a man he knew. The name on Jay's passport was François Aube, and he was in the city legally as a businessman from Paris. He sensed reconnaissance after a block and altered his direction, slowing to a stroll and stopping to look in a few shop windows. After almost an hour he was still unable to confirm that he was being followed, but his instinct told him he was. Then he glimpsed a shadow moving away from him beyond a pool of light from a streetlamp, and he immediately moved in the same direction at a quick pace, which was an unorthodox piece of tradecraft Raymond had taught him. He had been a clandestine operative for less than four years, but he was Raymond's protégé and he'd been offered opportunities no other young agent was given. In a few minutes, he turned quickly into an alley, which he'd noted when he passed it earlier, and hoped the shadow had made note of his move. He chose the alley because it was a dead end. The guy following him was very good and definitely not a Stasi or a KGB agent, who were notoriously sloppy when it came to tailing people; he would have identified one of them by now. He stood with his back against the old brick building on one side of the alley.

As apprehensive as he was about his tail, Jay struggled to keep a lid on his emotions. He had been in Argentina two days before, deep under cover, when he'd noticed a small blurb in a European newspaper about an American businesswoman, Genna Wright, having died in a car accident on the border between France and Germany. According to the report, she had lost control of the car she was driving back to Paris from a meeting in Wiesbaden. His mission in Argentina had made it impossible to confirm the report, but he had a hunch that Genna hadn't lost control of a car. Since his whereabouts were unknown, he left Argentina without anyone at Langley knowing and went to East Germany using credentials only Raymond knew he had. He hadn't cared for a moment whether he'd be fired or jailed.

Jay had fallen in love with Genna the day he met her, but he'd been too shy to tell her. He'd then watched the romance develop between her and Herrick. There had been nothing to do about it; he had too much honor to try to push Herrick aside. It wouldn't have been right. Genna and Herrick had once visited him at the ranch. His mother had seen immediately what was going on and taken him aside before they left. "I can see you love the girl," she'd said, "and I know it's difficult for you to understand, but she's not a good match for you. She wouldn't be happy with all the attention you would pay to her, and she'd never be happy here." Jay hadn't understood. He'd had no intention of ever returning to the ranch, but when he'd said so, his mother had only smiled and shaken her head. Just before Herrick had proposed to Genna, Jay had mustered up his courage and told Genna he loved her. He remembered how she had put her arms around him and said, "I know, Jay. It's been obvious to me. But the two of us aren't right for each other." He'd disagreed, but she'd laughed and said, "If you were the right man for me, Jay, you wouldn't be the man you are." He hadn't understood what she meant then, and he didn't understand now.

He watched the alley entrance, but no one came, and his thoughts drifted away again. What Herrick must be going through, he couldn't imagine. Their baby girl was only six months old. It was a nightmare. A rustle behind him made Jay's attention snap back, like a slap in the face. He whirled.

"Mr. Jackson, I presume," Raymond said.

Jay's heart banged in his chest. He'd let his guard slip, and he was embarrassed and angry.

"Shit, Raymond! What the hell are you doing?"

It flashed through his mind: The tail was so good because the tail was Raymond.

"That would be my question to you."

"You set me up. You knew I'd come into this alley."

"I did. I came in before you. Right after I let you get a glimpse of me so you'd turn in my direction."

This reminded Jay of how, during his training, Raymond would dissect what happened immediately afterward. It irked him.

"Someone did the same thing to me once," Raymond said.

But Jay had no time for it. "God damn, Raymond. What are you doing here?"

"Ah, you keep asking me the questions you should be answering. You're a very long way from Argentina."

"And you from Washington."

"I was in Prague, actually."

"Whatever. No one knows I'm here." Jay knew he wasn't making sense, and Raymond was going to banter until he did.

"It appears that I do."

"Have you heard about Genna?"

"I have, and if I were a betting man I'd wager that's why you're here, and not where you're supposed to be."

"Then it's why you're here also. The Agency is investigating." Jay felt good for a moment. His hunch had been right: it was no accident.

"Jay, both those statements are wrong. I'm here only because I knew you'd be here. The Agency isn't investigating. The French security service determined it was a car crash, and the Agency has deferred to them."

"What bullshit! She was investigating French dealings with an East German company. We know that!" Jay knew he was losing his cool and had to get it back. But his work had never been as personal as this was. He'd loved her when she walked down the aisle to Herrick, who had been standing next to him. He'd loved her when she gave birth to Samantha, for whom Herrick was now a single parent. He still loved her. Jay knew Raymond would be quiet until he spoke again, so he took several deep breaths and then addressed Raymond in a less emotional tone.

"Have you heard any news of Herrick?"

"No. As far as anyone knows, I'm still dark in Prague until the day after tomorrow. So you and I are both in the wind, you might say. Given the circumstances, and our relationship with Herrick and Genna, it might be best for both of us to stay dark on the schedule Langley assumes we're following."

"You must share my suspicions, or you wouldn't have assumed I'd go to East Berlin."

"Actually, no. I guessed you'd think it was East German involvement and come here to start, but I think your suspicion is wrong."

"Raymond, it wasn't a car crash. I just know it wasn't."

"I agree: it wasn't a car accident. We'll find out for sure when we go to Paris."

"Why Paris? They're the ones claiming it was an accident."

"I know. The autopsy report sent back to the State Department was sanitized. The real one is waiting for me in a hotel room in Paris. Someone in French intelligence owed me a favor." Raymond had learned from his source that the French police had found documents in Genna's hotel that suggested she was investigating whether a senior French government official had a stake in a company that was paying bribes to East German officials. It explained why the police had hurriedly determined that Genna's death had been an accident. "Before you get riled up, Jay, let's go to Paris and see what we find. It's unlikely that anyone in the French or East German governments ordered that Genna be murdered."

"I thought France was off-limits for you."

"France stopped paying for their membership in SEATO a couple of years ago, and Bush doesn't worry much about offending them. But I've been quiet about it, just making friends. And the old guys in their intelligence service from the Indochina days are mostly gone."

"Someone killed her, and they must know it. Why would they sweep murder under the rug?"

"Jay, I'm sorry. They're French. It's not in their culture to do the right thing in circumstances like this. It's hard to swallow, but there it is."

"You're sure about this?"

"Very. But if it'll make you feel better, go find your Stasi contact and see if you get a different story."

Jay thought for a moment. Perhaps the French wouldn't do the right thing, but he intended to. He'd never before felt murderous. It made him tremble.

"I want vengeance," he said, for no reason other than to hear it. He saw Raymond's forehead wrinkle, as if an old wound was hurting him. He hadn't noticed the lines in Raymond's face before, but there they were. The man was aging.

"I understand, Jay. I really do. But it would be good to get our facts straight first, don't you think?"

"Fine. Let's go to Paris."

"Perhaps you should go back to Argentina," Raymond said.

It was the Uncle Raymond voice Jay heard. When Raymond put his hand on his shoulder, Jay felt comforted. It made him able to reply calmly.

"No, Raymond. I need to stay with you and see this through."

19

ONE MIGHT ASSUME THAT A clandestine field operative lives a life of constant danger, his days and months a moving stream of intrigue and treachery. It isn't so. The time spent in harm's way may amount to no more than a few weeks during an entire decade. Everything else is planning and debriefing, or, particularly in Raymond's case, observing. What made Raymond so valuable at CIA was his ability to assimilate himself into a cultural environment, moving between places and among people like he had lived there his entire life. It was more than language skills and study. He had a sixth sense of how to act in the most unexpected situations. Of course, he could handle himself in a violent circumstance as well as any man ever trained by an instructor like Fearless Dan. But he was so good at not being detected that he seldom had to employ his physical prowess.

There were only a few men at CIA who knew about Raymond after 1977. He was never required to come into Langley because those men knew they would lose him if the bureaucracy were forced upon him, and he was too valuable to lose. So a few years before Casey became DCI in 1981 Raymond stopped going to Langley completely, and became a dark asset on their rolls, somewhat like a foreign born asset whose only link with Langley was through his handler. He maintained his cover identity in Washington as a demur and cerebral foreign services officer at the State Department. There he operated within a murky group of career officers who had maintained contacts and interests since the Allen Dulles days. They assigned him to mundane projects abroad, where he would have the opportunity to disappear into a foreign jurisdiction for a clandestine operation. In several cases he was more concerned with blowing his cover with his own government than a foreign one, as was the time Cyrus Vance demanded the identity of the operative inside Iran in 1979 who was claiming that a military action to rescue the hostages inside the embassy would fail. Luckily, Vance got so tied up in White House politics over the matter that he forgot about his request.

Jay continued his connection with Raymond and, as the 1980s progressed, they spent more time together. They were in Grenada before the invasion forces and in Poland soon after Gorbachev became the Soviet leader. When Raymond turned sixty in 1985, he knew he would need to rely on Jay in the future or he would have to leave the field. It wasn't something Raymond wanted to think about. Megan had raised the idea of retirement several times and he'd put her off. That year they bought a small farm in upstate New York and Megan suggested he might start planning his infiltration of the town of Hudson. Life among the cows, as he referred to it, was inconceivable to him. She'd thought he was referring to the cows in the pasture on the farm next to theirs, but he'd been thinking of some of the people he'd seen in the area.

A couple of years later, in early May 1987, Raymond sat across a small campfire from Jay. It was just after dawn and they were beside a large outcrop of rock in Ontario, equidistant between Akimiski Island and Thunder Bay. He watched Jay whittle a piece of wood Jay had extracted from the trunk of an old, fallen tree soon after they'd arrived two days before. Raymond thought it would be a star but he couldn't be sure because half of it was still ragged.

"What's that you're making?"

Jay held up his creation and turned it in his hand so Raymond could see it from every angle. "Why, it's a star, of course."

"What kind of star? A star of David?"

"Raymond, this one has but five sides, not six. It's the Lone Star of Texas, of course." He went back to his whittling.

Raymond laughed, as he always did when Jay spoke with his Texas drawl. But Jay's response also made him uneasy because it reminded him that Jay had been speaking with his drawl more frequently in recent months. It heightened Raymond's sense that something was up with Jay and Herrick. They'd also seemed remote recently. Raymond knew Herrick was thinking of leaving the Agency. His daughter, Sam, was almost twelve and Herrick planned to enroll her at St. George's School in Rhode Island, where Herrick, his father, and his grandfather had gone— Herrick often called it the kind and gentle alternative to Groton. Raymond knew Herrick wouldn't tolerate being as far away from her as Washington.

Raymond was sixty-two, which he knew was old for the spy business. He expected his cover job at the State Department to end soon because Shultz was shaking up the foreign service by replacing the old political types with professionals. This had made it more difficult for Raymond to stay under the radar; the new officers were examining everything, and most were unwilling to continue their old CIA relationships. Raymond suspected he'd be back at Langley in a desk job by the end of the decade unless he could make his way into the new Middle East group. He knew the region, having been in Tehran in 1979 and Beirut in 1983. But his CIA background would make it complicated. And without Jay it might be impossible. They'd been a team on all field operations which didn't involve difficult or long undercover activities in a country. Jay was the best sniper in the agency. For undercover work, Raymond always acted alone, something permitted by the agency only because he was one of the original covert operatives.

"What do you think?" Jay asked. "Will the honored guests show up this morning?"

"Don't know. But I hope so. My knees are bothering me."

About two hundred yards downhill from their location was a small lodge where they believed a meeting was going to take place among several important members of Maktab al-Khidamat, who were allegedly scheming to expand their jihadi activities outside Afghanistan, particularly into the United States. There was speculation that Abdullah Yusuf Azzam might be one of the attendees. Jay's sniper rifle was disguised in a pile of leaves at the base of the rock, from the top of which was a direct view of the lodge.

"Raymond, you just need to get some old-man liniment. When we get home, I'm going to call the ranch and have them send some of this stuff we use on the horses. Works like a charm on old men."

"I've tried liniment."

"Not this stuff. And how about stretches. They do wonders."

Raymond shook his head. "You can't teach an old horse new tricks."

Jay laughed. "So long as you brought up your old tricks, I've been meaning to ask you something, Raymond. Just what were you doing in Vietnam listening to children's stories?"

The question startled Raymond for a moment. It was so long ago. And Jay never asked questions just to make conversation. There was always a purpose. Raymond had taught him that. Then he made the connection.

"Louie tell you about that?"

"Long time ago. A cowboy never forgets. We were just swapping stories and he mentioned it in passing."

"Right. Just an offhand remark."

"Well, he said he didn't think it was classified. It just seems a bit strange to me, you sitting around with the kids listening to stuff when you couldn't understand what they were saying."

"But I did understand. It was how I learned the language. And not just that. It was how I learned to join in the culture. It's all in what they do and say in everyday life."

"So, it's how your disguises work so well."

"They work so well because they're not disguises. You make yourself as familiar as they are with everything around. I would walk into a shop or a café acting like a local. I believed myself to be a local."

Raymond had immersed himself in cultures to prepare for infiltrations. He would read fiction and poetry, not just newspapers. He'd watch movies. All of those things revealed elements of the lives of the people that no text book could explain. He thought Jay had some natural ability in the area. Jay was keenly observant. But as yet Raymond had not begun to teach him how to go about utilizing these skills. He needed to start the lessons soon.

A twig snapped ten yards away. Two burly men approached, one with a shotgun across his arm and the other with a pistol in his belt. Both had heavy beards. They looked like mountain men and were definitely not Middle Eastern. Raymond had watched them hanging around the lodge the last few days. If visitors were arriving today, he expected they would be scouting the perimeter. The small campfire had been the lure. Jay continued his whittling, looking up at them casually.

"What you boys doing up here?" one of them asked. "This be private property."

"Why, we thought this was a provincial park," Jay said in a thick drawl. "Maybe we got off course a bit."

The two men looked at each other and moved closer. Raymond saw their eyes scanning the area, looking for guns.

"You're miles away from Wabakimi," said the man with the shotgun. He was clearly the leader, and he now stood just a few feet from Jay. "You hunting?"

"Oh no," Raymond said. "Bird-watching. It's the migration back to Hudson Bay. Avocets and birds like that." He pointed to binoculars on the ground near him.

The man looked up at all the trees, as if he might see an avocet on a limb. Raymond suspected he wouldn't know an avocet from a warbler. "Bullshit," the man said. The other man moved closer to Raymond. Raymond thought it unlikely that the men planned to take them back to the lodge. What was going through the man's head at the moment, Raymond surmised, was how he could kill the two bird-watchers without the noise of the shotgun or the pistol.

"Now why would you fellas think we would be up to something else? That's not too friendly," Jay said.

The shotgun had slid only an inch down the man's arm before Jay threw his knife into the side of the man's neck. Blood spurted from the man's carotid artery. Raymond rolled to his feet, and the OSS knife he pulled from the sheath up his sleeve almost severed the wrist of the other man, who was in the process of pulling the pistol from his belt. Whirling around to the man's back, Raymond slid the knife into the man's brain. In only a few seconds, the two corpses collapsed side by side.

"A pity," Jay said. "They seemed like such nice folks."

"Right." Raymond was breathing harder than he liked. A twinge of pain shot through his lower back. For a moment it was hard to stand straight.

"You're sure quick for an old man," Jay said.

"Not as quick as I used to be."

Raymond suspected that Jay's comment was actually an inquiry whether he was okay. In fact, Raymond was a little distressed. He'd not been fast enough to get his knife to the man's skull before the pistol was out of his belt, so he'd had to slice the wrist. He was lucky the man had been momentarily stunned and hadn't screamed. Also, he'd missed the entrance to the brain on the first thrust, and had to extract and reinsert the knife. The worry about Jay leaving the Agency came upon him again, as he leaned forward with his hands on his knees. He'd not be able to work alone in the future, as he had in the past, and no one other than Jay would be willing to work in the field with a man his age.

"How about we mosey on up to our perch to await the guests," Jay said, then pulled the rifle out from the pile of leaves.

They climbed up the boulder and positioned themselves under a camouflage net. Jay deployed the rifle on a small tripod. A weak cold front had moved through the night before and the air was crisp and still. Raymond set up a camera with a long lens. He would snap pictures of the visitors and also give Jay corrections if his first shots missed. But the shots were right on target and the two Middle Eastern men who emerged from the car fell to the ground. Unfortunately, when the film was developed upon their return, it was determined that Yusuf Azzam was not one of them.

20

IT WAS THE BEGINNING OF 1990 and Raymond hadn't yet been sent back to a desk job at CIA, although he would soon turn sixty-five and the retirement police would be after him. Since the operation in Canada he'd only gone on clandestine mission's with Jay. During 1988 they spent time in the Middle East to assess the impact of the formation of Hamas and then later in the year the recognition of Israel by Arafat's PNC. The next year was a whirlwind tour of Eastern Europe, first to Poland, then Hungary and Romania, and finally Prague. In November they came across Vera in East Berlin during the festivities associated with the breach of the wall. Jay embarrassed Raymond by saying to Vera, "So you're Raymond's old flame. Why, I've been waiting years to meet you." How did Jay find out about the Bari adventure? He suspected Megan told him. He also thought Jay's brashness was a hint that a change was about to occur. They'd become very close, and Raymond knew Jay had grown tired of the Agency and its bureaucracy. Jay was too loyal to Herrick to tell him outright what they were planning, but the hint was enough to start Raymond's investigation. It didn't take long to find out the two of them were talking to law firms. Herrick was bad at covering his tracks.

So here I am again, Raymond said to himself a month later as he looked around the Georgetown coffee shop where, many years earlier, he had recruited Herrick and Jay to clandestine operations. This time they'd called the meeting. He'd arrived early because he liked to be comfortable in a place before discussing difficult business, whether that was the assassination of a terrorist or the receipt of bad news from his protégés. The waitress brought him bacon, fried eggs, and hash browns. Megan had noted the day before that he was "as skinny as a stick." He hadn't been interested in eating recently.

Raymond didn't like surprises, and recently he hadn't been too keen on changes. It wasn't that he feared change. The last time he could remember feeling afraid was just before he'd asked Megan to marry him, on Catalina Island. What bothered him was to have his equanimity disturbed. Megan had read him an article that suggested he was confronting his mortality, which was a common part of aging. Maybe so, he thought, but I've been confronting mortality for years in the field. Why would getting a few years older make a difference?

What was going to occur when they arrived wasn't a surprise, although he planned to appear shocked. Megan had warned him that they'd feel betrayed if they knew he'd meddled in their plans. They were going to tell him they were leaving the CIA to become partners in the international energy practice at the law firm Wanasas & Kindres. The managing partner of W&K was Raymond's old friend from his OSS days, John Wilde. He'd promised Raymond never to tell Herrick and Jay that Raymond had suggested he contact them, nor to indicate the second part of Raymond's plan.

He thought about Herrick for a time. When he'd gone to Tonkin to rescue him, he'd recovered Bradley's journals. The French thugs were stupid, and they'd been fooled by Bradley's dummy hiding place and papers. Over the years, he'd struggled with whether to give the journals to Herrick. After he'd first read them, he'd decided the time wasn't right. Now, after several more readings, he thought he would probably never give them to Herrick. It wasn't that the information in them had never been declassified. That was ridiculous. It was old and cold, he thought. The problem was the candid portrayal of Harold and Adelaide, and how Bradley had left Adelaide for Betsy. It wasn't pretty. Bradley had never been good at holding punches. Nothing good will come of it, Raymond thought.

There was more to the disclosure of the journals than Raymond was willing to admit to himself. Herrick would ask questions, very detailed questions, and it would require Raymond to relive the time. It wouldn't stop with the Vietnam operations, but extend out to the similar circumstances surrounding Genna's murder, like rainwater on a hillside moves away in numerous channels before it soaks into the ground or finds a pond. It would be too painful for Raymond. He'd deposited the murders into a locked box, pushing aside the fear that he'd failed his friend Bradley all those years ago by not preventing his and Betsy's Vietnam mission. He knew how ruthless the French could be. He'd seen it. They'd murdered Dewey. And then he he'd failed to find the man, Jacques de Garde, who'd ordered the murder of the Wrights.

The waitress came by and refilled his coffee cup without asking. He was picking at his food, putting small bits of egg and bacon into his mouth and trying to read his newspaper. He looked around the room, saw nothing interesting and fidgeted in his chair. When will they get here? he thought impatiently. He wanted to get this whole silly charade over with and go back to work, where he'd be able to think about what's next instead of what was.

By the time Herrick and Jay arrived, he'd eaten the eggs and bacon and pushed around the hash browns to make it look like there wasn't much left on the plate. He'd also mentally run through a script of how he expected they would inform him of their "shocking" news. Herrick was a very predictable person, like his father had been when he wasn't manic. Herrick would call him Uncle Raymond when they arrived and then say how difficult it was for them to do what they were going to do. Jay would let Herrick lead, as he always did.

"Thanks for meeting us here, Uncle Raymond," Herrick said after they'd sat down in the booth. "We know you like this place."

"Beats a government cafeteria."

"I suppose you're wondering why we're here."

"Something too touchy for a phone call, I suspect."

"We've thought long and hard about what we're going to tell you," Herrick said. "You've been like a father to me, and, well, it's always hard to leave home, if you know what I mean."

"Hey, I know you guys have been restless recently. You know I could rearrange things so you could have different responsibilities. Hell, I could get you positions over at State, which, much to my surprise, is working out well for me. Shultz is doing a good job."

Raymond was playing the game. He knew they were fed up with the government and would have no interest in the State Department. It was too bad. They were very good agents. Herrick was a master of planning. He'd perfectly coordinated their travel into and out of Quebec and had been exactly right on the location of the meeting. Somehow he'd found a safe lodge for them while they waited to go back across the border into Minnesota. He saw Herrick and Jay glance at each other.

"We appreciate that, Uncle Raymond. We really do. But we've decided to go to the private sector."

"Where?"

"New York City. We're going to be partners at a law firm. We'll be in their international energy-practice group."

Raymond nodded and paused for a few seconds to make it look like he was hearing this for the first time, even though John Wilde had told him all the details about W&K's opening an office in New York. "A law firm? That's a bit stodgy. How's that going to work for you, Jay?"

Jay laughed. "I went to Princeton, Raymond. I think I can handle a law firm."

"Right. But I wonder if they can handle you."

"It's been a very hard decision, Uncle Raymond," Herrick said. "But we think it's a good one."

"Okay. I'd admit you're probably right if I weren't going to miss you as much as I know I will. What does Sam think of this?"

Herrick brightened. "Oh, Sam is good with it. She's going to St. George's, so I'll be a lot closer."

Raymond nodded. It had gone well. "It's a big change, I'm sure you know. It doesn't make me happy, but I understand, and I wish you boys success. We'll stay in touch. Megan won't tolerate not seeing Sam frequently. And you never know, the three of us may cross paths again someday." It was hard for him to keep the emotion off his face. He was happy for them, but miserable for himself because he knew that without Jay he'd be driving a desk until the boys at the State Department made him retire. And he knew it would not be long before Jay became frustrated with law firm life. Then Raymond could implement the second part of his plan. That would make his desk job tolerable. And as he'd predicted, days, and then months, behind his desk shuffled by.

At the end of February 1991, Jay sat in the Star Deli on Lexington Avenue in Manhattan. What he'd just heard was so inconceivable that it was most likely true. And his frame of mind at the moment did not make him receptive to the matter. W&K wasn't what he'd expected; he often felt he was on a playground full of squabbling children, rather than a collegial organization composed of serious professionals. Recently he'd even been nostalgic for the old clandestine-operations team, which he'd been so happy to put behind him two years earlier. Raymond sat across the table from him with a smile that Jay thought looked a little smug. Somehow, he'd known the perfect time to deliver this news, Jay thought.

"Raymond, what you just said is really too fantastic for me to believe. You're the head of this club of dilettante spies that's so secret even the CIA doesn't know about it? And you actually run your own clandestine operations?" Jay spun his empty coffee cup on the table a couple of times. He couldn't keep still and it was hard for him to keep his voice low. His spy demeanor was rusty, and, worse, his own voice reminded him of a churlish partner at W&K.

"Take a breath, Jay," Raymond said calmly. "You've slanted what I said. None of us is a dilettante. We started off as a book club." Jay listened as Raymond described how he and his colleagues had swapped stories over at Frank Wisner's house and talked about novels by Cooper and Greene. "Yes, we were a little like The Room from Roosevelt's time. But there were no Vanderbilt types," Raymond said.

"Where'd that name Group come from?"

"Happenstance. Several of the book club members were in the Diplomatic Intelligence Compilation Group at State in 1953. It was disbanded in 1960 and we thought it would be interesting to keep gathering information on the side. We started calling ourselves the Group then."

"Dulles knew about the Group, of course."

Raymond's face was blank. Jay hadn't thought he would acknowledge this, just like he'd never acknowledged the rumor that Dulles and Acheson had moved him to the State Department for reasons other than interagency cooperation. The Group thing just muddied the water more.

"Okay, Raymond," Jay said. "Forget I asked that. But tell me how the Group manages to conduct an intelligence operation without all the back-office support and funding that the Agency has."

"Our operation is small and we have private funding."

"Come on! I know what kind of machinery it takes."

"You're ahead of me, Jay. I only told you about the Group's existence because I trust you and I want you to join us. Say you're in and I'll tell you everything."

"I'm happy being a lawyer. Why would I go back to the spy life, where someone on your own side is likely to betray you? I can't be a private assassin. That's over for me." He knew he was sounding melodramatic. But he'd suspected there'd been leaks at the Agency. And he didn't care how he sounded.

Raymond laughed.

"Jay, we're very compartmentalized at the Group. None of us knows what anyone else is doing, except for me because I'm the chairman. It's a pretty closed circle. Betrayal isn't a problem. As for assassination, we don't do that. And don't tell me you're happy being a lawyer. I know better. Besides, you won't have to quit your law job. The Group is like a hobby."

Jay put his head in his hands. He wondered whether Raymond could in fact read minds, as some at the CIA had joked. Jay was frustrated with his law-firm life. Recently he'd thought he should throw himself into a hobby of some kind to take his mind off all those imbeciles in the office. He'd also thought about moving back to the Jackson Ranch. His mother had died the year before and his father had lost his energy. Neither of his brothers had a son to move into the ranch management, and they were getting on in years. But he didn't think it was time yet to return. I can just be a private spy as a hobby, he thought.

"Okay, Raymond. You seem to know me better than I know me. What the hell. But don't ask me to dig out the sniper rifle. I'll just be a nonlethal private spook in my spare time."

"Wonderful."

"So give me a clue how you can be so well informed."

"First thing is that I'm the new chairman. My predecessor was Johnny Wilde."

Jay was stunned. "You have to be kidding!"

"Oh no. He was in the OSS in the old days, and then at the State Department and an early member of Wisner's book club. He ran the Group for twenty years."

"I can't believe it. You've had this planned from the start."

"Maybe. Johnny also had substantial family money, which helped us get off the ground. Now we're privately funded by men who have made their fortunes in business over the years. The private businesses also discreetly provide back-office help, and give us cover in foreign countries."

"So how many operations are you running?"

"One. We only run one at a time. We do intelligence-gathering on several fronts, but never more than one clandestine exercise. We're very selective."

They sat quietly for a couple of minutes. "Did the boys confine you to your State Department desk?" Jay asked.

"They did. Right after you left."

"I thought that would happen."

"I knew it would. But I still travel for diplomatic meetings and conferences. It's not too bad."

"And with this Group thing, I guess you look up old friends when you're in town."

Raymond didn't say anything. Jay knew he wouldn't. He pictured Raymond leaving his hotel, walking past members of the State Department entourage, but dressed and acting in a way that no one recognized him.

"And I guess my joining Group will make it easier for you."

"I've missed you Jay. We were a good team."

"No, Raymond. You were the mentor and I struggled to keep up."

"One learns from teaching. I learned a great deal. It was rewarding, which is why I've missed you."

Jay studied Raymond's face for a moment. The lines were deeper than they'd been the last time he'd seen him. But his eyes were crystal clear. The man was still on his game, and working with him again he knew would be exhilarating. "What about Herrick?"

"I'm on the fence there," Raymond replied. "I'd never use him in the field. You know that. But he was damn good at planning and coordination."

"I should've made my acceptance conditioned on your asking him."

Raymond laughed. "I should've known that. Okay. I'll talk to him. We've never had a member who doesn't go into the field. But it will work."

"And me?"

"What do you know about Kazakhstan?"

21

IN 2005, RAYMOND SAT ON the porch of his old farmhouse in Columbia County, New York. The porch wrapped around the house. He sat on the west side, looking out toward the town of Hudson, where Megan was at the moment. She'd started a bakery there three years before, the summer after the destruction of the Twin Towers, and she had gone to Hudson to prepare for the Memorial Day weekend, when New York City dwellers with country houses would arrive to kick off the summer season. A couple of miles down the rolling hills was the Taconic State Parkway. He thought it looked like a long, dark snake, only partially visible as it slithered through the landscape.

A decade earlier, he'd been forced to retire from the State Department. James Baker had delayed his forced retirement in 1992, when the bureaucratic machinery at State identified him as a retirement candidate. Then, Warren Christopher had given him a pass on account of how deep he was in the Haiti operation. But Raymond had turned seventy in 1995, and there had been no more extensions, just a nice retirement party. He'd then been a consultant to the CIA for a year on account of the Aldrich Ames matter, and the lawyers were nervous about several of his Cold War missions. He'd acted recalcitrantly, the same as he had in 1945, and they hadn't renewed his contract in 1996.

Megan had been happy to get out of Washington, and they'd fixed up the farmhouse with money Raymond had inherited. For several years, it had been easy to conduct his Group business from there. He'd driven to Poughkeepsie and taken the train into Grand Central, which was only a few blocks from a small office the Group provided him. Raymond had longed to accompany Jay on operations, but the management committee at Group had insisted it was too risky for their chairman to go into the field. And the year after the destruction of the Twin Towers, they'd asked him to retire. The new chairman, Ben Lufkin, had graciously said that Raymond would continue to be a trusted adviser.

Megan's car wound up the long road through their property, disappearing from time to time in the early-evening shadows cast by trees along the route. He could see someone in the car with her, and he hoped it wasn't the querulous woman Megan had hired to manage the bakery. The first thing he'd do when the woman got out of the car was go inside and pour himself a scotch. Then he would come back out with his Sibley Guide and his binoculars to look like he was engrossed in identifying some kind of woodpecker. He'd taken up birding the year before his eightieth birthday to keep himself busy. He wasn't finding it particularly rewarding, although he enjoyed using the binoculars and the camera with the long lens. It was just like the old days; only the quarry was different.

When Samantha Wright emerged from the car, Raymond was relieved. He loved visits from Sam, and hadn't seen her in months because she'd taken a clerkship with a federal judge in Texas right after her law-school graduation the year before. She reminded him of her mother and her grandmother. Like them, her hair was red, although a shade of color in between Betsy's brightness and Genna's strawberry. And there was Herrick's influence, Raymond thought, as he observed how her long bangs were pulled back from a perfect part down the middle and swept back to a clasp at the back of her head. The rest of her hair fell neatly to her shoulders. This symmetry was a sharp contrast to the chaos atop Megan's head, he thought. But he loved the bed-lam that accompanied Megan's appearance. No matter, it's only packaging, he thought.

"Look who walked into the bakery," Megan said as they climbed the porch steps. Raymond knew better. Megan loved to surprise him.

"Not too long after I walked to her car at the Poughkeepsie station," Sam added. "It's so good to see you, Uncle Raymond. I hear you just turned the big eight-zero, but you sure don't look that old."

"You're a wonderful surprise, Sam. Come over here and sit with me. I want you to tell me everything. Spare no details."

As the sun slipped toward the mountainous horizon beyond the Hudson River, Sam told him about her life in Houston. Megan went in and out of the house, which unsettled him. He liked being able to reach out and hold her hand for a moment whenever he liked. Sam reached the end of her account just as the sun disappeared behind the mountains.

"So what's up with your father?" he asked.

"Oh, just more of the same boring stuff. I told him yester-day that he's a stick-in-the-mud. He's never spontaneous. I don't remember him being so inhibited, but I was probably too wrapped up in what I was doing to notice."

Her choice of the idiom stick-in-the-mud made Raymond nostalgic. He remembered how Betsy had referred to Harold that way. It was referred to several times in Bradley's journal. Lately the old memories had been bubbling up to the surface. The details were often blurred, but Megan had a keen memory and would add the particulars when he asked her.

"He can't help it, Sam. He's a lawyer after all."

She laughed. "So it's what's in store for me then?"

"Oh no. I didn't mean that."

"There may be hope for him. He's left the law. Can you believe that?"

"Not really."

"Yes. He retired from the firm and became a partner at one of his clients', a private-equity firm."

"When?"

"Couple of months ago."

"Name?"

He watched her push her eyebrows together, as if the exertion would jar her memory.

"Can't remember. They invest in energy things, of course. I think it's transportation and terminals. Something like that."

"Branoble something?"

"That's it! How'd you know?"

"Just remembered him talking about them once."

He knew more than he told her. Branoble was run by Ben Lufkin. Herrick was an excellent intelligence analyst. Ben would want to keep him involved in Group matters.

"Did you see Uncle Jay?" he asked.

"Not this trip. He's in Doha, of all places, working on something about liquefied natural gas. But I saw him a couple of weeks ago in Houston."

Raymond suspected Jay was doing more in Qatar than an LNG project. He wondered if Jay was meeting with Omar. He missed the old days.

"And he was in good form, I hope," he said.

Sam laughed. "More Texan than ever. He's such a sweet and gentle cowboy. I've been to the ranch many times since I moved to Houston. Did you know his oldest brother died a few months ago? And the remaining one isn't looking good. I'm not sure what will happen when he dies."

Her comments about Jay made Raymond remember how they'd tracked Genna's murderers to a hideout near the Swiss border. He'd wanted to interrogate them, but the men had fool-ishly resisted. Killing a man in the course of an operation was just a part of work, but killing him in vengeance, as Jay had done, was wrenching. He wished it had never happened, either to him in Tonkin or to Jay in Switzerland. It was disturbing to remember how Jay had lost, if only for a moment, his sweet and gentle cowboy self.

Sam continued with more details about Jay–according to her father, Jay had adopted a cowboy persona in New York to the chagrin of his partners there but to the delight of the part-ners in the Houston office. Raymond's mind wandered to some funny instances when Jay had spoken French with a Texas-laden accent. It reminded him of his own interactions with Frenchmen over the years, particularly during the times he'd sought leads to the whereabouts of Jacques de Garde. "We have nothing in our files about a SDECE agent of that name in Hanoi during those years. You think he is connected to the murder of Mrs. Wright?" his acquaintance from the French sûreté had asked when Raymond was investigating Genna's murder. He should've dropped it–how could an agent in French colonial Vietnam pos-sibly be relevant–but this recent murder had brought back to him the horror of Bradley's murder in Tonkin. And, however tenuous, there was the connection that one victim was Herrick's father and the other Herrick's wife. "What about an alias?" he'd asked. "Monsieur," the Frenchman had said, "It was a bad time in Vietnam. The records are in a state you Americans would call full of holes. And, again, how is this connected? It's just history, no?" Reluctantly, he'd let it go, afraid that his questions would make the sûreté suspicious. They could turn up old files that showed he'd been restricted during that time from working in Vietnam and France, restrictions that had made his investiga-tion of the murder of the Wrights impossible when the evidence had been fresh.

The man is probably long dead, he thought as Sam's voice seemed to get farther and farther away. It was something he'd thought with more frequency in the last few years, probably because his failure to turn something up was so frustrating. There was a mention of de Garde in the final pages of Bradley's journals, but it was an incomplete reference to a businessman working for a company that owned neighboring farms. The names of French landowner businesses he'd found in Paris was incomplete and most of them had gone out of business after America had withdrawn and all French property in Vietnam was confiscated. He'd snuck back into Vietnam to look for local records, but the new regime had destroyed everything concerning French colonial activity. He remembered a Viet Minh acquaintance of his saying, "We burned everything we could to cleanse ourselves of the French plague." The man knew about Raymond's return to Vietnam to kill the men responsible for the deaths of the Wrights. "You found the assassins," the man had said. "It was long ago, my friend. This Frenchman only gave the order. You should let it go. Take care of yourself. Enjoy the rest of your life."

Yet, his gut went sour every time he thought he would put the whole thing behind him. How could he just let it go? Bradley had saved his life in the Pacific. He remembered drifting in the water on that stupid floating mattress and the surreal sight of that crazy Texan standing in the bow of the speeding boat, twirling a lasso. And after that he'd failed to save Bradley in Tonkin. Sometimes he would lay awake at night, his mind replaying all the investigations he'd made. Thinking about it now made his head hurt. Since he'd retired, he'd been able to push these kinds of thoughts aside. He'd worried they'd become an obsession. What had triggered it this time? The recollection of Jay's brutal reaction to Genna's killers? Whatever it was, the desire for an answer overwhelmed him. He could make one more series of calls, do one more Google search.

"Uncle Raymond, is everything okay?"

He felt her hand on his arm. He had slipped away from her into his thoughts. What was she talking about?

"Oh yes. Sorry. I was having a senior moment."

She laughed. "It happens. But there's another thing I want to tell you about. The partners in the W&K Houston office are recruiting me to join the firm next year when my clerkship ends. What do you think?"

"It's good news, no? You have your next job lined up before you're finished with the current one. What do your father and Uncle Jay think?"

"I haven't told my father. He'd drive me crazy with a list of pros and cons. Uncle Jay thinks I should look at some other firms. He said I'd have to stop calling him Uncle Jay if I joined W&K, and he wouldn't like that. But he's frustrated with the people in New York. The lawyers in the Houston office seem very nice. And it would save me the hassle of interviewing."

"I think there are good and bad people at every firm, and trying to guess what it'll be like is futile. But you shouldn't listen to me. I'm an old man. I look back over eighty years and feel silly I ever wrung my hands over a decision. Even if you're right about something at the time, it will inevitably change. Then you'll have to make adjustments, and all the pros and cons you thought about earlier are out the window."

"So I should accept their offer?"

He thought about how Herrick had struggled with all his decisions because he was so keen on making the perfect choice. But Raymond knew what Genna would do.

"I'd say, go with what feels best, and if it doesn't work, change it. What the hell."

She laughed again. He loved her laughter. It was more Betsy than Genna. "Sounds good," she said.

"If you tell your father what I said, he'll kill me."

Megan announced dinner. Raymond noticed that the crickets were making a racket. Either that or it was his tinnitus.

"It'll be our secret," Sam said quietly as they walked into the house.

Jay sat at a small table in a lounge in the Four Seasons Hotel in Doha. The hotel had opened a few months earlier and it was beautifully appointed. He had an expansive view of the Arabian Gulf. There were only a few people in the lounge and it was very quiet.

He had arrived in Doha the day before after several days of meetings with his client in Dubai, due west across the gulf. They'd been preparing for the meetings in Doha, scheduled to take place the next day. Qatar had huge reserves of natural gas, which it exported as LNG. The debottlenecking of the third train of Qatargas 1 had just been completed and a consortium of companies was scrambling to participate in a proposed Qatargas 2. Years ago he would've been excited by working on a huge project like this one. Today, he felt it was a burden. I don't give a shit about building a plant in the desert, he thought. I just want to go home. By home he meant San Saba, not New York, but he was reluctant to admit it to himself. He thought that Samantha was going to accept the job with W&K; he'd stick around a year or two to keep an eye on her. The Houston partners were flaky.

Two men dressed in elegantly tailored suits sat down a couple of tables away from Jay. He'd seen them the night before, when the lounge had been very crowded. One of them had gone to the bar and Jay had positioned himself next to him to hear the man's voice when he ordered his drink. He was French. Jay was troubled by them because they seemed uncomfortable in their clothes; one man's neck was so constrained by his shirt collar that he seemed near the point of asphyxiation. Jay wondered why the two men had shown up in an almost empty lounge with him in the middle of the day.

An hour later, Jay knew why. He was in one of the hotel's reading rooms when they appeared again. They sat down next to the newspaper rack, but neither took a paper. Fucking amateurs, he thought. It was a problem because he was waiting for a discreet meeting with Omar, an acquaintance who was part of Sheikh Hamad's inner circle. He would have to move out to the lobby and hope to run across Omar before he reached the reading room. But a disturbance occurred. The concierge came into the room and in a dramatic fashion requested the two men to accompany him to meet the hotel manager. The Frenchmen seemed perturbed at the interruption and at the fact that the concierge's French was very bad, which appeared to insult them. As the Frenchmen left, Jay saw Omar standing outside the doorway. He followed him down a hallway to a small room in the conference section of the hotel.

"No doubt you arranged for the concierge to distract those two," Jay said after they sat down. Jay had met Omar in 1996, when the CIA and the State Department had collaborated with Sheikh Hamad's foreign minister on the formation of Al Jazeera. It was something that the American public would never understand, if it ever was declassified.

"Of course. Those two bumblers were hard to miss, even by an amateur like me."

Jay laughed. Omar wasn't an amateur. He could appear and disappear in any venue as easily as Raymond had managed in earlier days. His job as an executive at Al Jazeera was a cover, and he was very close to Sheikh Hamad, something similar to a chief of staff. His relationship with the CIA had been strained recently, but he was on very good terms with the Group.

"I know you better than that, Omar. What do you know about them? Are they French intelligence?"

"Oh no. They work for a man named Georges Piquart, who is a consultant for French companies. I suspect his activities go a bit beyond giving advice, but I'm not sure. There's a French company that desperately wants to participate in Qatargas 2 and your client is their competitor. They're wasting their time, of course. Your client is favored. I'm sure you knew that."

"I didn't actually, but thanks for the tip and, I'm sure, for your influence in that matter."

"My friend, I have no influence in these business ventures. I only make sure they are reported correctly."

Jay laughed again. "Then I thank you for your reporting. Do you think the Frenchmen are dangerous?"

"They have weapons. Or so the housekeepers have told us. But I believe their interest in you is only on account of your client."

"Okay. Thanks. Now we can move on to our other business. What's happening with the Saudis?"

An hour later, Omar left the room. Ten minutes after that, Jay went out as well but he turned in the direction opposite the reading room. He'd studied the hotel map and knew he could follow the hallway to the conference-center lobby and then exit directly to the elevators, which couldn't be seen from the main section of the hotel, where he was sure the Frenchmen would be waiting. It was probably unnecessary, he thought, because he believed they were inconsequential, even if they had weapons.

He was wrong again. When he got off the elevator, the two men were standing in the hallway that led to his room. They moved together to block his passage as he approached them. I'm really too old for this, he thought, as every recent ache and pain in his body seemed to manifest itself suddenly.

"Howdy, fellas."

"You have something we want," the bigger one of them said belligerently.

"Why, boys," he drawled, "would this here be a mugging? In Doha? It may be a first."

"It's information we want," the other man said. "We can step into your room."

"Right out here is just fine with me, boys. What I know isn't much."

"Out here is no good," said the big one.

He took Jay's arm and pushed him toward the door to the room. There was a moment of hesitation as the small man stumbled aside and the big man released Jay's arm. It was all Jay needed. He whirled his elbow into the small man's chin and slid his other arm between the big man's arm and torso, employing his momentum to propel the man around a tight circle into the wall, face-first. A punch to the man's kidney immobilized him. Jay turned to deliver a blow to the small man's chest, but he found that two Arab men had rushed up. They immediately put handcuffs on the Frenchmen, who started cursing and claiming that Jay had attacked them.

One of the Arabs smiled and held a badge in the big Frenchman's face, saying in very bad French, "We have a hearing where you tell your story." Then he smiled and continued in English, "Of course, it may take some time to find someone to listen. Maybe a week or two." As his partner pushed the Frenchmen toward the elevator, the man with the badge said to Jay, "Omar sends his regards and asks that I tell you these men are staying in room 302."

Jay found two compact pistols with silencers in room 302. There were also papers showing the agenda and the names of the attendees for the project meetings with Qatargas that were beginning the next day. On a page by itself was a copy of Jay's picture and biographical sketch from the W&K web site. Nothing suggested they knew anything about Jay's other activities. Handwritten on the page was the name Parnell and a phone number. There was a young partner in the W&K Atlanta office named Will Parnell, but the phone number didn't begin with the Atlanta area code. It was odd, but a coincidence, he thought, because Parnell was feckless.

On the way back to his room, Jay deposited the unloaded pistols in a laundry chute behind one of the doors through which he had seen housekeepers enter and exit. He knew that corporate espionage had become prevalent in recent years, but this had been his first encounter with it. His elbow was very bruised and the muscles adjacent to his right shoulder blade were objecting when he turned to the left. I'm sure ranching would be much easier than this, he reflected. The long plane ride home wasn't going to be pleasant.

After a very busy summer at the bakery, Raymond and Megan took the train into New York City. For several years they'd gone in for the Labor Day weekend. They liked that the city dwellers left town during that time. Dinner reservations were easy to get. They stayed at The Four Seasons, on East Fifty-seventh Street; the older they grew, the more confident they became that they would not run out of money before they died.

That night they met Vera Stegineo and her granddaughter, Anna, for dinner. Over the decades Megan and Vera had developed a close friendship. The same was true with other old acquaintances; on his own, Raymond never thought to stay in touch.

Vera had worked in Tito's intelligence agency after the war and had married another operative. They'd had a son, who had joined a resistance movement in college, despite the fact that his parents were prominent members of the party and employed by the government. The son had been killed in a skirmish with Tito's security forces during the Croatian Spring and his young wife had fled to Paris, where she'd taken up with a group of artists and activists. Several years after that, she'd died from a drug overdose, leaving behind an illegitimate daughter. Vera and her husband, on account of their loyalty to Tito for so many years, had been permitted to bring Anna back and raise her.

Raymond made the dinner reservation at Giambelli, on East Fiftieth Street. He thought Vera would be comfortable with its traditional Italian style, and the place was right across the street from the New York Palace Hotel, where Vera was staying. Raymond remembered how Jay had referred to the hotel as the Texas Palace because back in the 1980s it was favored by his Texas clients. It was raining very hard, and the doorman at the hotel walked Vera and Anna across the street with his large umbrella.

The restaurant wasn't busy and they were shown to a good table in a corner. As soon as there was a break in the conversation between Megan and Vera, he asked, "So what brings you two to New York?" They looked at him like he'd just returned from "around the bend," as Jay often said, and had lost his memory completely. In the awkward silence he regretted his order of wine instead of scotch.

Anna came to his rescue. "Granny is here to visit. I've been living here for a few years."

Raymond strained to cover up that he couldn't recall a thing about Anna's living in New York. "Oh, of course," he said and smiled. Perhaps Megan had neglected to tell him? That was unlikely. The only thing he accomplished by trying to remember anything about Anna was to bring on a vivid flashback of Vera in 1943 on the deck of Plava Guska while the German plane buzzed them. And here Vera was being referred to as "Granny." He didn't like it when he tried to remember one thing and instead remembered something else. He'd had several such disjointed recollections recently.

"You remember, Raymond," Megan said. "Anna got a job at Goldman Sachs right after business school." He noted that Megan's reminder to him was gentle. But he was anxious that she was merely being kind to an old man in the dawn of senility. Anna was a beautiful girl, he saw. Her eyes and complexion were dark, unlike Vera's. The identity of her father was unknown, but his best guess was that he was French or Italian. Her features were sharp like Vera's, and she had the diminutive but strong, lithe carriage that he remembered in another flashback of Vera striding around Vis giving orders to the men building the staging area for provisions from Bari.

"Yes, I remember," he said.

"But I no longer work for Goldman," Anna said. "I've taken a job in the finance department at a company called IndoSun. You've probably not heard of it."

"No. Can't say I have," he said. The name sounded familiar but he wasn't going to take any chance of looking like an old fool. It was more believable, he thought, to claim ignorance. Megan looked at him suspiciously, like he was trying to hide something.

"Not sure why you would," Anna said. "It's not very glamorous. We own LNG tankers and terminals. The company was formed last year by a private-equity shop called Branoble Partners, so we don't get much press. Branoble rolled up a bunch of smaller companies to form IndoSun."

He had to struggle to keep his face from shouting that he knew about Branoble, and so he said the first thing he could think of: "It sounds like baking a cake. Right, Megan? Rolling up a batch of companies?"

"Raymond, I'm sure what Anna does is more sophisticated than baking a cake," Megan said.

"Certainly not one of your cakes, Megan." Anna laughed. "In any case, all the different financial records will need to be combined. Probably more tedious than sophisticated."

Megan asked Vera about her brother, Joe. They had shared an apartment since Vera's husband died. Joe must be ninety-something, Raymond thought. He didn't listen carefully. He didn't want to know what happened to you when you were ninety-something. Talking about IndoSun would have been dull, as well. Herrick had probably mentioned it the last time he'd visited them. Megan had remembered. She had a mind like a computer hard drive. She remembered everything, particularly those things he hoped never to think about again.

When the coffee arrived, Raymond looked up to find Vera's gaze fixed on him. He knew it signaled that she was about to tell him something she didn't want to but felt obliged to do so. His head hurt. Being ninety probably feels like this.

"Raymond, I keep up with several other old associates. Like us, none of them is in the game anymore, but they hear things. I went through Paris on my way here and saw an old friend there. She has good sources. I thought I wouldn't tell you what she told me, but now I'm going to tell you. It's about the murder of your friend in Vietnam in 1951. Sadly, it was ordered by a member of the French SDECE who was operating there, although he had no authorization from Paris. He was dismissed upon his return."

"I knew he was SDECE. His name was de Garde. I looked for him, but never found him."

"You didn't because de Garde was a cover identity. The French feared loss of U.S. military support, so SDECE was ordered to destroy all records about him. His real name is Georges Piquart. He's still alive."

"Where?"

"I don't know. He runs a consulting business called Le Cercle. My friend has contacts at the French General Intelligence Directorate. They investigated him about the death of a corporate executive last year. And they think he was also responsible for the murder of Genna Wright. But they don't have enough proof on either."

"I'll find him." His temples throbbed and the muscles in his hands readied themselves for action with the OSS knife that had gone everywhere in a sheathe strapped to him. It was stupid, he knew. There was no danger here at the table, or even in the city. These were reflexes born from a hatred he had thought was left behind at retirement, like the office supplies in his old desk. What he had left behind at retirement was his ability to subdue the emotions, to smile, and to make his face show a calm, complacent demeanor.

"I was worried you'd react this way. It's why I wasn't going to tell you. We're too old, Raymond, for ancient battles. The French will take care of this."

"Right. When we're all dead and buried, even him. Then they'll solve the case. I need to take care of it."

The sound of his own voice surprised him. It was bad to lose your composure, but much worse to vocalize it. The words sounded so murderous, so cold and harsh, full of venom. Now that he'd heard himself say them, he wished he could take them back. It was wishful thinking. He was somewhat light-headed. Too much wine.

Vera's eyes flashed. He hadn't seen that for a long time–not since Budapest in 1957. She'd hated the Russians. She'd wanted to kill a Red Army commander, but it would have blown their cover. It was still secret that the CIA had collaborated with Tito.

"Don't be foolish, Raymond," she said.

"I'm sorry," Anna interrupted. "What would you do if you found this man?"

Megan laughed. "Maybe a duel. They could slug it out with their canes."

It made him angry. Megan was thinking it wasn't serious. Maybe she was right. He had endeavored to forget about de Garde for many years. But to think that the same man had killed all three Wrights. His mind whirled. He'd have to look into it. It was so long ago. Suggesting he'd go to France was premature. Actually, it was grandiose. Megan's joke was meant to point this out. He got control of his anger.

"Megan knows one shouldn't mess with me and my cane," he said.

They put Anna in a cab and walked Vera across the street to the hotel. The rain had stopped but a mist swirled around them in the gusting wind. Vera held on to Megan's arm as she shuffled across the street. He had thought she was worried only that the road was slick, but then he noticed that her shuffle continued after she was in the lobby. It struck him: she's an old woman, even though she's a year younger than I am. Will I be shuffling that way soon? He vowed to himself he wouldn't, and quickened his pace up Madison Avenue toward The Four Seasons. It was too much for one evening, hearing about Piquart and witnessing Vera's shuffle. His mind raced and he walked faster. If only he had received this news a decade ago. He would have gone to France with his blade. It was what he had vowed in Vietnam after he'd killed the thugs.

At Fifth-sixth Street, Megan objected. "Raymond, if you had to pee you should have done that back at the Palace."

"I don't have to pee." It's one old-man thing after another tonight. Before long I'll be a shuffling geezer with a giant prostate. Both would prove a hindrance if he went after Piquart.

"Then why are we rushing?"

"Oh, sorry. Must be nervous energy from sitting in the restaurant all that time."

They crossed Fifty-seventh Street and turned right to the hotel. There was very little traffic and not many pedestrians. The city seemed deserted. They climbed the stairs in the lobby up to the elevators.

"Raymond, you should probably go do several laps around the block. If you get in bed now you'll fidget for hours and drive me crazy."

"Good idea."

Megan was not a good sleeper. In his state, he'd be wiggling around and cracking his toes. It wouldn't be long before she'd wake up and slug him.

He went out the Fifty-eighth Street side and turned west. After passing the Pierre Hotel, he crossed Fifth Avenue and walked north. The mist had turned to fog. It made glowing circles around the streetlamps and the headlights of the cars moving toward him. He thought about the dinner and it reminded him how he had recently come to realize that his spy career had more often than not been dull. Now and then there had been dangerous moments, but otherwise it had been tedious observation, always expecting things that didn't happen and never relaxing enough to enjoy a moment. Bird-watching was much more enjoyable. His life would make a boring biography. And no one would believe him. They'd think that the exciting parts were classified and he couldn't talk about them. And the hatred? He could never write about that.

At the Fifth Avenue entrance to the zoo in Central Park, a young couple came in his direction. They were the same height and dressed in rain slickers. He thought they looked like a strange animal with three legs because they walked side by side with their hips fused, their inside legs striding in unison.

As they passed, he heard them humming a tune together. He turned to watch them move away. Their unconcern with him was astounding. Never in his life had he been as unaware of his surroundings as that couple was of theirs.

22

JAY WAS RESTLESS. HERRICK HAD departed to join Branoble Partners two years earlier, in 2008, and Jay had little patience for law-firm culture. He wanted to retire early. When his last brother had died, he'd hired a manager for the ranch, but he longed to go back and run the place himself. Business there was good, and he didn't need his law firm compensation. It wasn't worth the aggravation. But Samantha had moved to New York to join the firm as an associate. She'd wanted to be close to her father, so she'd turned down the Houston office. And Jay was well acquainted with how the New York partners treated associates. So he'd decided to stick around a couple more years.

The clear October day streamed through the conference-room windows. Jay resented that he was in a partners' meeting. Mickey Pikels and Sunil Desai, private-equity partners, were talking about a new transaction. Warren Cook, head of the real estate team, sat next to Pikels. Cook's sharp features made him look like a fox. His forehead seemed to slant back away from his nose, and his front teeth and Adam's apple fell toward a bony chest, string-bean arms, and crooked fingers. Pikels was a burly, querulous man who was always gloomy and resentful. Desai was on the other side of Pikels. He was a small man with a flat nose, a flat forehead, and unruly eyebrows. His smile was too large and his teeth were unnaturally square. Tiny sprigs of hair protruding from his nostrils and ears quivered when he spoke. Desai perched on the edge of his chair like a weasel sitting on its hind legs. When Pikels's voice began to sound like an old refrigerator motor, Jay had to interrupt him to make it stop.

"So what's the hours' count on the project, Sonny? Just get to the point," Jay said. He liked to call Pikels that because the man reminded him of an old donkey at his ranch they'd named Sonny.

"Well, it's not about the hours after all," Pikels said. "This is a reputation-building matter for the firm."

When no one else said anything, Pikels returned to his eloquent puffery and Jay sighed. He wished he could vomit into the middle of the table. That would clear the room. He considered the BlackBerry ploy–acting as if he had received an important email that required him to step out of the meeting. But Norman Potter, the firm's chairman, cleared his throat to interrupt Pikels. Although it was meant to sound polite, it reminded Jay of how the cry of a hawk makes little varmints head for cover.

"Thank you for the report, Mickey, but we must adjourn for lunch. Before you go, I want to remind everyone not to comment to any reporters about the recent report on the web site Above the Law. Please refer inquiries to me."

Jay had read the story, which alleged that one of their young partners behaved inappropriately with a young woman associate. He didn't know who the woman was but he was pretty sure he knew the perpetrator. Potter would sweep the matter under the rug because the young partner was a favorite son from the Atlanta office. He had to say something.

"Oh hell, Norm, tell the whole story. Why, young Parnell tried to dip his bean in a place he shouldn't have and he got found out."

Jay regularly employed his Texas drawl. It always offended the prim Atlanta partners. He saw with satisfaction that Warren Cook rose imperiously from his seat.

"Sir, that's preposterous. Will comes from a prominent Atlanta family, and several of us at this table have known him since he was a child. He's a gentleman, and I'm sure you're simply repeating a rumor."

Jay liked to see Cook displeased. The man thought he was too good to eat beans. And Will Parnell was all hat and no cattle. He'd had to move to the New York office after he'd stripped naked and jumped into a pool at a party for summer associates. Not a lick of good sense in the boy, Jay thought.

"Why, I didn't know there was such a thing as pedigree immunity," Jay drawled. He knew he should let it go, but watching Cook's consternation was too much fun. "My daddy was from a good Texas family. He once told me that if you don't keep your eye on him, a blue-blooded shoat will roll in the mud on ribbon day."

It sounded good, but Jay suddenly lost the pleasure of it. He thought about the young woman. Here he was making a joke out of her misfortune.

Cook's face got red as he aimed his crooked finger at Jay. "In all my years as a partner in this firm, I have never been spoken to in this manner or heard anyone refer to another partner in such a way," he snarled, before he stormed out the door.

"Whoee," Jay said to no one in particular. "That man is all wax and no wick."

He returned to his office and gazed for a while over the Hudson River at the plains of New Jersey. The day was clear and the sun was shining, but he felt desolate after his encounter with Cook. The landscape looked one-dimensional to him. Samantha came into his office. Before she said a word, he knew: she was the young woman Parnell had been inappropriate with. He closed his door and sat next to her on his couch, same as he would if she were his daughter.

"I was so stupid," she said. "After the closing dinner for the Northern Industries transaction, Will Parnell asked me and the two other corporate associates out for a nightcap. I should have kept my mouth shut to see what the others said. After I said yes, they both said no, and I ended up with him alone at the bar. I had too many drinks and agreed to go to his place for a cup of coffee after he boasted about his brand-new fancy coffee machine. It cost, he said, a thousand dollars. It was dumb, I know–like agreeing to go up to see his etchings!

"Anyway, he was all over me the minute he closed the door. I pushed him away, saying it was a bad idea and I didn't want to. He backed off, but his eyes kept looking over me, leering, and I don't think he was paying any attention to the conversation I was desperately trying to make. Finally, he stumbled over to fiddle with his fancy coffee machine. I thought the threat was over, until he started to make lewd comments from the kitchen area, like 'you must know that your tits have been distracting me all night.' I knew I needed to get out of there, but I was worried he would ruin my career if I embarrassed or insulted him. And I didn't think I was in any real danger. You know how my dad made me take all those martial-arts classes during high school? I thought that, if necessary, I could deck him and walk out. He was pretty drunk, so I didn't think I'd have any trouble.

Boy, was I wrong! When I didn't respond to his lewd references he stumbled back to the couch, sat down and put his hand under my skirt. I pushed him away again and said, 'I told you no, Will. Just quit.' But this time he persisted and suddenly we were struggling. I couldn't believe it. He pushed his hand under my blouse and pulled at my bra. I shouted 'no' and rolled away from him. But he came at me again, and this time he pulled my panties to my ankles after he pinned me down. We had rolled onto the floor. He was too heavy. I couldn't get up. I was too drunk and lethargic to think clearly. My mind kept racing through a surreal puzzle about how I could do a karate move while laying on my back. It was so hard to keep fighting. Every part of my body hurt. Finally, he took his weight off me when he tried to unzip his pants and I managed to roll out from under him. I slapped his face as hard as I could when he came after me again. It stunned him for a moment and I was able to get to my feet when he sat back on his haunches. Then I kicked him in the stomach. It was just a girl kick—I couldn't think how to do a karate kick—but it knocked the wind out of him and gave me time to pull myself together and run out the door. I left behind my bag with my keys and had to go to my friend's place. Her boyfriend, who works for Above the Law, was there. I was hysterical but I shouldn't have talked to my friend in front of him."

Jay struggled to keep control of the rage exploding inside him. Yes, Parnell hadn't been successful, but he'd tried. He imagined scenes where Samantha wasn't lucky enough to slip away from Parnell's lecherous grasp. Jay knew how to kill. Parnell could be his next target.

She began to cry, and his unsettling image of what could have, but didn't, happen dissolved. It was replaced with a recollection of Samantha's visits to his family's ranch when she was a teenager. She could ride a horse like a cowhand, and they'd always had to stop and wait for Herrick to catch up to them. They'd camp out under the stars at Miriam's Meadow, so named for his grandmother, who had planted it with Mexican Hat. Ordinarily, such a memory would make him smile, but the circumstance prevented that. Instead, he put his arm around her. She wiped her tears away with her fingers.

"It was my fault as much as his. I drank too much and I should never have gone to his place. And maybe I acted like I was coming on to him. I keep thinking about everything I said or did in the bar. Some of it could have been interpreted wrongly."

"That's bullshit!" Jay said vehemently, trying to disguise his anger that she might be shouldering some blame for Parnell's attack. He listened to her sob for a few moments. "Sammy, there's no explaining some things, but this was not your fault," he said. He considered whether to add something like "Some men think with their dicks instead of their brains," or another old Texas saying about hogs like the one he had used earlier with Cook. It wouldn't help, he decided, and waited for her to speak next.

"I really fucked up by telling someone this happened. It would probably have just been forgotten. Now everyone knows." She paused for a moment, and then she laughed. "I suppose there's a silver lining: the firm can't fire me now for fear that I'll make a complaint against Parnell and sue the firm because he's a partner. So it was a great career move after all."

He laughed too, even though he didn't think it funny, and then he hugged her again before she left. There was nothing more he could think to do, except to find Parnell and thrash him. As good as that idea felt to him, he knew it would just make Parnell the victim and make her seem the one at fault. He stood at the window for a while. It was his spy training that told him to hold back when he felt the rage come over him. Raymond had taken him to New Mexico to see Jimmy Nearwell, and now he recalled the very old Indian saying that anger makes a man weak. Jay also knew that his anger could turn into a debilitating rage, like rain on the Edwards Plateau becomes a raging torrent of water in the Pedernales River. He was sick of the spy business and of law practice. There was nothing good or true in either of them. He thought the law firm was nothing but a breeding ground for despicable behavior like this. He missed Texas.

After an hour, he walked to her office. He planned to suggest they go to the Met, then stroll across the park for an early dinner at Rosa Mexicano and drink a margarita or two. Fuck the afternoon partners' meeting.

Parnell came around the corner and walked into Samantha's office while Jay was still down the hall. Jay reminded himself to keep his anger down. When he got to her doorway, he stood to the side, where he wouldn't be noticed. He saw that they stood face-to-face in front of her desk, and he could hear what they were saying.

"Seems you left this behind the other night," Parnell said, throwing her bag on her desk. "You left in a big hurry. I'd hoped you would spend the night."

"Thank you for bringing my bag back."

"I wish you hadn't run off. I think we would have had a good time."

"There wasn't going to be a good time."

"Oh, come on!"

"I told you to quit. And then you molested me."

"Not so. You were coming on to me."

"Are we on the same planet?" she asked, her voice shaking and increasing in volume. "What about slapping your face is coming on to you?"

"Hey, girls often say no when they mean yes. Let's just chalk it up to a misunderstanding. We can still be friends."

Parnell advanced toward her as if his offer to be friends authorized him hugging her. Samantha backed away quickly. Jay was through the door and on Parnell in an instant, twisting his arm behind him, turning him around and banging his forehead into the wall. Once. Twice. Parnell cried out. Jay stood back. He thought about the French thugs who'd killed Genna. That had been personal too.

Parnell turned toward them, but he had to lean forward with his hands on his knees for a moment. His face was red. When he straightened up, he focused only on Sam.

"You bitch!" he yelled. She said nothing. "You won't be working here next week. I promise you that." He turned to the door.

"Why, that's a coincidence, Parnell," Jay said, moving to block his exit. Parnell stopped, a look of fear on his face suggesting he thought Jay was going to hit him again. "I was about to say the very same thing to you."

"Fuck you, Jackson," Parnell said after a moment and walked toward the hallway.

Several Texas witticisms flashed through Jay's mind, but there was nothing funny about what this bastard had done. Images of Samantha squirming helplessly on the floor underneath Parnell flashed through Jay's mind suddenly, and his muscles tightened. In the end, he stepped aside and said nothing.

Jay went to Potter to demand that Parnell be fired, but he knew the firm wouldn't do it. A week later, Potter announced in a firm-wide memo that Parnell had graciously agreed to relocate to the Paris office for the firm's international corporate practice. Kiss my ass, Jay thought.

Samantha left the firm for a job with a law firm in Austin. Jay didn't try to talk her out of it. He knew it was a good way to put everything behind her. At the end of the year he retired and moved back to San Saba. He was done with W&K. Being a lawyer was the same as being a spy, he realized. You made a virtue of lying on the pretense it was for your client or the good of the firm. It was neither. For a law firm partner it was all ego, money and fame. At least for a spy, lying was an acknowledged part of the job, a part of one's patriotic duty. It wasn't much of a difference, he decided. He was done with the Group also.

23

MEGAN'S OSS BAKERY WAS ON Warren Street. On the wall behind the countertop and display cases was mounted a long piece of wood from an old barn wall; it was inscribed THE OH SO SWEET BAKERY. Raymond thought it was clever that Megan had used the OSS initials from his wartime years.

Raymond liked the tranquility of the bakery's back room during winter. There were few city dwellers in town and on weekdays he had the room to himself. There was an old leather couch along the interior wall. He imagined that the heat of the ovens radiated through the wall, even though he knew the wall was thick and solid. The building had once been a bank. Across the room, on the outside wall, was a fireplace and to one side of it were french doors leading out to a patio and garden. There were tables on the patio in summer and it was a popular spot.

Since Vera's visit several years before, Raymond had pursued two hobbies: bird-watching and Piquart. The bird-watching had gone well. Finding information about Piquart hadn't been successful. Many hours had been wasted on Google searches. He'd made contact with the few old intelligence friends who were still living. All he knew after so much effort was that Piquart was descended from old French wealth and ran a small consulting business. He lived on a huge estate in southern France, where he had state-of-the-art security. There were rumors and gossip, but nothing more. Raymond no longer brought his laptop to the bakery.

He sat on the old leather couch and put his feet up on the coffee table. From there he could look up from his reading and check out the bird activity on the patio. The headlines in The New York Times didn't appeal to Raymond that day. There was a typhoon in the Philippines, a strike in France, and Leon Panetta's lame explanation about a terrorist suicide bomber. He threw the paper unopened onto the coffee table and watched a group of blue jays on the patio enjoying leftover nuts and bread pieces Megan had thrown out there. He liked the way the jays hopped with both feet to get around. Sometimes there were a great many of them on the patio at the same time, and they would fly away in a swirling blue cloud when something spooked them. He knew that Megan didn't like them. She said they were bullies and were keeping the juncos from the nuts. But he could see juncos mixing in today, and a cardinal couple, he a bright red and she a dull rust with a bright orange beak. The cardinals always seemed mysterious to him. He didn't know why. Looking at the jays again, he had to admit that when several faced him, they looked like jihadists with black masks and white robes.

A young, pretty woman walked in and sat on the other end of the couch. She wore hiking boots and a dark green jacket with a brown corduroy collar that matched the color of her hair.

"You're Mr. Hatcher," she said.

"How'd you guess?"

"You're the only one in here."

"There's two of us now."

She paused. "The girl in the front told me you were back here."

"Nice to meet you, Ms. . . . ."

"Dumont."

"Then, welcome, Ms. Dumont."

"Oh, it's Helene Dumont. Just Helene is fine."

He thought she looked nervous. She rolled one hand in the other on her lap. He remembered another young woman who had done that in meetings at the CIA in the 1950s. But he didn't see a resemblance.

"It's funny," he said. "I knew a woman with the same name as yours a long time ago."

"My grandmother."

He looked at her again but still did not see a resemblance, nor did he remember that her grandmother had a family. The older Helene had been flighty. She'd been enamored with French culture and had been on the DCCI's staff on account of her fluency.

"I look like my father," she said.

It still made no sense. "I didn't know your grandmother had a son."

"She didn't. She had my mother. As far as I know, my father was a rumor who I looked like."

"I'm sorry, but your grandmother and I were only acquainted through work. I didn't know she had a child."

"No one at the CIA knew. My mother was illegitimate. It would've been scandalous then. So my grandmother took a leave of absence to do a sabbatical in France. Then she went to a hospital in Belgium to give birth. Her brother was a priest in a nearby town."

For a moment he watched a blue jay hop, then he looked at the girl again. She was very pretty and she sat quite properly, with her back straight and knees together, even though she was wearing jeans. He understood wanting to tie up loose ends and he wished he had something to tell her.

"I'm sorry, but I know nothing about your grandmother. She was on the staff, and came out for drinks a few times and seemed like a nice person."

"It's the other way around," she said. "I'm here to tell you about her. I found out about you when I went through her belongings. It's lucky I found you. The State Department gave me an address in Georgetown. My letter was returned by the current owner. The CIA wouldn't tell me a thing, except that you once were a consultant there. I looked for you for a couple of years. Then I found you mentioned on a web site about a reunion for old OSS agents who'd trained on Catalina Island. There was a blurb about how you'd married the baker's daughter. One day I was walking down Warren Street. I live near Rhinebeck. There it was, the OSS Bakery, right here in Hudson, with Megan Hatcher the proprietor. Too much a coincidence."

"Well, thank you for finding me."

He didn't know what else to say, and didn't want to hurt her feelings by wondering aloud why she thought he'd be interested in anything about Helene. Perhaps she had found something that suggested they'd had more contact than was actually the case, but he couldn't think how that would be. Also, he was skeptical about coincidences.

"I'm sure you're thinking I'm here to bother you with boring stuff about my grandmother. But that's not the case. She committed suicide when I was a teenager."

"I'm sorry."

"I'm not here for sympathy." She seemed perturbed at him, and they looked at each other quietly for a moment, until she added, "You'll see. Can I go on?"

"Okay."

"She raised me for the most part, because my mother was in and out of rehab facilities and would sometimes run off for months at a time. I was away at boarding school when my grandmother killed herself. It sobered up my mother for a while, until the year after I graduated from college. Then she went on a bender, crashed her car, and died. It was probably intentional, but the police let it go without an investigation."

"I'm sorry, again."

"Quit with the sorry stuff. It's just what happened. Okay?"

Raymond nodded. He didn't know what else to do. Suddenly, her face wasn't so pretty. It was hard. And her hands were clasped together tightly.

"There was a lot of money in my mother's accounts. She never had a career. When I looked into it, I found it had all come from my grandmother. I went back through old boxes of records I found in a closet. There were receipts for wire transfers of large amounts from a bank in Paris starting in 1951, the year my mother was born. Then I found an old trunk tucked away in the attic behind a false wall. In there was correspondence between her and a Frenchman named Georges Piquart. It was clear from the context he was my grandfather, even though my mother's Belgian birth record listed the father as Jacques de Garde."

The names stunned Raymond. This was more information about Piquart than he'd uncovered in three years. He fought to keep his composure. This girl did not need more burdens; she didn't need to know that her grandfather was a killer. She paused and was looking at his face.

"Not ringing a bell," he said.

"I can see that. Some of the letters from 1951 mention some missionaries in Vietnam named Wright, and then much later, around the time I was born, a CIA woman named Wright. My grandmother retired right after that and the letters from my grandfather became sporadic and much more formal. Your name was in a notebook that had hundreds of notes to herself and pages of strange, rambling thoughts. The note about you said, 'Ask Raymond Hatcher about de Garde.' I don't suppose she ever asked you."

"No. When would she have written that?"

"I don't know. The stuff in there made no sense to me. I couldn't find you but I found Piquart. He lives in the south of France. I went to Paris and sent him a formal letter that said I was Helene Dumont's granddaughter and asked if he would see me. It was a long shot, but it worked."

"Maybe he was worried about a scandal."

"Could be, but he spoke openly about my grandmother and my mother. I didn't know my mother had visited him. We were in his library for cocktails before dinner. His twin grandsons and his nephew were there and they all thought I didn't speak French. He had a conversation with the twins off to the side and he became angry. Do you know Herrick Wright?"

"No."

He had to lie. The girl had just walked in off the street. It could be a ruse. She could have been sent by Piquart.

"They were talking very fast, and my French isn't that good. I must have misunderstood because it sounded like they would have an opportunity to kill him soon. Ridiculous, right?"

"Definitely."

"But he had just been so charming to me, and then he was talking to the twins and it sounded so hateful. Then his nephew decided to hit on me after dinner. His name was Parnell. He was very aggressive. Lucky for me, Piquart's personal assistant–I think she's also his mistress–saw what was happening and arranged for a car to take me back to Paris right away so I didn't have to spend the night."

"I'm sorry."

She laughed. "I told you to quit with the sorry stuff."

"I know. But it must have been hard on you. Do you have any other family?"

"No. My grandmother's only sibling was a priest, so no cousins. Who knows who or where my father is? And I'll never have a husband or a child, that's for sure."

"Why would that be? Sorry if I'm being too personal. Don't answer if you don't want to."

"Oh no. I'm eccentric. I believe that once Fate gets her teeth into your ancestor, she follows the generations." She laughed again. "It's a dark way to describe a genetic predisposition that was probably why my grandmother and my mother killed themselves. I'm convinced I can't escape it and misery will come to any family I have. So I won't give Fate the satisfaction. The curse will die with me, one way or another."

He heard no emotion in her voice. It was strange. Her eyes were dry, but he was fighting back tears. It was tragic. He couldn't even say he was sorry again.

As if she had been sent for, Megan strolled into the room and offered the girl coffee. She'd always had a sixth sense for when to appear. In the past few years, it had become keener and he would often find her sitting next to him when he emerged from a dungeon of dark thoughts. She would never say anything, just put her hand on his arm and look at him with her deep compassionate eyes, after which he would tell her everything he'd been thinking. With her, he was never a spy.

"Oh, thank you, but I have to get going," the girl said. "Mr. Hatcher, if you walk me to my car, I have a box of things for you from my grandmother's trunk. They may make more sense to you than they have to me. It's just down the street."

He returned to the couch a few minutes later with the box. Megan stood in the doorway watching him as he began to take items out, handing each one of them as if it was an egg. A cloud had softened the sunlight coming through the french doors. It was still and quiet. The blue jays had gone.

24

GEORGES PIQUART, WHO HAD RECENTLY turned ninety years
old, sat on the terrace of Barry Silvers's mansion, which was on
a bluff several hundred yards back from Long Island Sound. The
October day was clear and the afternoon sun made the water
sparkle. He was perturbed nonetheless, because it was America
and not Chateau Bernard, which was in the foothills of the
Pyrenees near Argeles-sur-Mer.

He saw Sandrine appear as if by magic from a pair of hedges,
behind which was a door to the house, and walk toward him. She
wore a short skirt with frills that swirled around her thighs. He
liked her boyish look. She had shaggy brown hair that just covered the tops of her ears, and sharp features. When she leaned
over him to straighten the blanket over his legs, the jabot along
the button line of her blouse spread out, revealing perfectly
symmetrical breasts covered by a sheer undergarment through
which the outline of her nipples was discernible. He watched
her breasts swing forward and back when she stood.

"Ah, what an extravagant day it is!" she exclaimed in heavily
accented English.

He remembered that she'd promised not to speak a word
of French while they were in America. She'd claimed it was to
improve her English, but he was sure it was meant only to antag-
onize him. The night before, when saddled atop him, gyrating
so that her breasts had swung from side to side, she'd delivered her customary ribald exclamations in English, not French,

making it impossible for him to keep his erection. Convinced that she was taunting him again this morning, he became angry and considered slapping her. But when he'd hit her once before she'd screamed a litany about her college degree and two years at nursing school. Then she'd resigned and it had taken him a week to coax her back with a promise to double her pay. The recollection of how much he paid her made him resentful and he thought that for so exorbitant a sum she should speak French during sex.

After several minutes of his stony silence Sandrine pranced away, exaggerating the movement of her hips, which he interpreted as defiance. Soon, a detachment of servants scurried toward him with a tea service, a footrest, and a newspaper. The paper was The New York Times, not Le Monde, which he knew was inside. A headline announced the continuation of the general strikes in France about pension reform. He cursed, threw the paper on the ground, and stomped back to the house.

When he reached his room, he heard the shower running, so he lay down on the bed. He thought about the investment Parnell had arranged for him to make with Danna Partners. But that bored him and he soon fell asleep. When he awoke, Sandrine stood over him.

"The men are here. I was told to catch you," she said in English.

"Do you think I'm a fish?" he queried in French.

"You are very strange," she said. "But they wait for you."

He got up off the bed and checked his appearance in the mirror. A wizened face looked back at him and he quickly looked away. A newly pressed shirt and pants were called for, but he was still in a foul mood and decided only to comb his hair. He saw that Sandrine watched him, and he wondered whether she was making note of the lines on his forehead and around his mouth.

"While you were napping, I found the best chocolate shop in a town nearby," she said in English. "Better than our shop in Paris."

"Ridicule!" he exclaimed irritably.

"Perhaps I must go with you to this meeting to translate. You have forgotten your English. None of them will speak French, except your nephew, and you think him an idiot. No?"

"My English is perfect," he said, deliberately pronouncing each word slowly with no hint of a French accent.

"Ah, oui!" she replied flippantly, throwing herself into a chair and picking up a book. "Have an excruciatingly good time," she said in English, but then added, as he opened the door, "Bon chance!"

He walked into Barry's living room and found four men sitting on two couches. On a side table were a tea service, an ice bucket, and assorted bottles of liquor. Georges moved toward an armchair and hoped someone would offer him a cocktail immediately.

Parnell stood up. "Gentlemen, may I introduce Georges Piquart."

Piquart stood next to his chair for a moment, as each man got to his feet and shook his hand. He enjoyed that they stood up for him. When he sat, they sat.

"Mr. Silvers was just talking about our plans for Spain," Parnell said.

Georges thought Silvers would continue with what he'd been saying, but Sunil Desai, a man with unruly eyebrows, spoke instead.

"It's not just timing, but the perfect layering of actions taken," Desai said. "Nothing can look staged or contrived. The market has to worry that there's a design flaw in the terminal, and that the same is true for all of the company's terminals. It must be suggested by the media that governments in all the countries where there are terminals will commence safety investigations, and the investigations and studies will cause delays and cost the company millions of dollars."

The self-appointed master of ceremonies droned on with points on how to handle the media. Georges was in a slapping mood again and wished he could get up and whack the man's head. Silvers must have been feeling the same way, Georges thought, although Silvers seemed to him a model of patience, rotating a coffee cup in the socket of a saucer in his palm. In order to tune out Desai's irritating voice, Georges looked at the third man. He had chiseled features and steel-gray eyes. Georges thought he looked like a bodyguard and wished the man would take a pistol from inside his coat and put a slug between the little Indian's eyes.

Silvers put his cup and saucer on the table. He sat up straight and placed his hands on his knees. Desai stopped speaking in midsentence.

"Pardon me, Sunil," Silvers said. Georges didn't think his voice was apologetic. "I didn't ask Mr. Piquart to travel to America for a lecture on media relations." He turned to Georges. "I hope, Mr. Piquart, that you and your secretary have been made comfortable by the staff?"

"All is perfect, Mr. Silvers, but please, call me Georges. We French are not all so formal."

"Then you must call me Barry. Now, we're off to a good start. Our transaction is very simple, and we could have taken care of all but one matter without a meeting. As we explained to your nephew, that matter is sensitive and best handled in person."

"Yes, he told me. But maybe you should go over everything quickly."

"Of course."

Silvers spoke rapidly, describing how Meteor LNG Company had a contract to buy all of IndoSun Shipping Company's liquefied natural gas–shipping terminals around the world. Georges and Barry were to make a cash investment as part of the purchase price. It seemed to Georges that there were a dozen transaction steps and that every company had a subsidiary involved.

"My nephew is a lawyer and he bored me for hours with all the details you so astutely summarized."

"Well, good!" Barry exclaimed. "Then I'm not the only one being badgered by lawyers. But I tell Sunil it doesn't matter what the contract says."

Georges thought that was confusing. "In France, one is always bargaining," he said. "But I thought in America the contract was sacred."

"It's what the lawyers think, but there's always opportunity when one bends the rules."

"Of course."

Georges knew exactly what Barry was referring to. It was about uncovering secrets or causing the unexpected to happen. It was Georges's business.

"There are always ugly corporate secrets to disclose or the threat of hostile stockholder action," Barry continued. "My targets usually pay me to go away. In this case, we need to be a little more aggressive. That's why you're here."

Barry explained how the new enterprise would be a public company and some bad news would be needed, like an accident at the terminal facilities in Spain, where a ceremony was to be held after the transaction. Georges had originally balked at Barry's demand that Georges also invest. "Why should I do that?" he'd asked Parnell. And then Parnell had told him that Herrick Wright was a principal at IndoSun. An investment in the transaction could give him information and access to Wright. Parnell had already heard that Wright planned to attend the ceremony. But causing an accident detrimental to an investment didn't make sense.

"I'm sorry, Barry, but why do you want us to sabotage the entity we're investing in?"

Barry laughed. "We'll make only a small investment in the terminal subsidiary as a diversion. Meteor is a company with publicly traded stock. We'll sell the stock short in many unconnected trades. After the small accident at the terminal subsidiary, we'll use the rest of our investment to purchase the shares needed to cover the shorts at a fraction of our sales price. You'll triple your money."

"The market regulators won't detect this?"

"Nothing is in writing. We have many friends who'll make the trades. The SEC isn't so smart. And we have our investment in the terminal company. It will look like we're losers, not winners. And it's so small an accident. The market will recover eventually."

Georges nodded and smiled. His mind had leaped ahead to another opportunity, which Barry would never guess. He would make sure it wasn't a small accident, and he didn't care about the investment. It would be weeks before the fires would subside at the terminal in Spain. Wright would be incinerated and the accident would cover his tracks. That was his payoff.

"It's all good," he said. "What else?"

Desai was about to speak, but Barry cut him off. "Nothing, Georges. It's a fine day. Let's you and I take a walk."

They went across the lawn to a barrier of rocks abutting Long Island Sound. Barry's comportment had relaxed when they left the house. It reminded Georges of an actor who has just come off the stage. Le Cercle had looked into Barry's background. There wasn't much. His company, Danna Partners, was an activist hedge fund. He owned several houses, a yacht, and a jet. There was no mistress, and his marriage had lasted fifty years. Georges struggled to understand that. His own marriage had lasted until his wife died in 2006, but he'd fucked other women at least once a week since 1946. He was proud of it.

"I like to stand down here and look at the ocean," Barry said. "It's lovely."

They walked along the seawall. It's hardly an ocean, Georges thought as he observed tiny waves lap the sand. To him, it was an example of American banality, the same as their thin coffee and the lack of intonation in their speech. It was how he remembered that Wright woman's polite diction in Vietnam, as lightly contoured as her chest. How he'd hated her. He would invest whatever it cost to inflict the final blow on her progeny. Bernard's murder would be avenged. Barry could keep all the profit.

"You don't like Desai," Georges said when they started back across the lawn.

"He likes to hear himself talk."

"Lawyers are like that."

"Yes. But he's a twit and what he says is never important. What's more, he's a weasel and I don't trust him."

"But you're not worried about him knowing what you're doing."

"No. He's greedy and he loves prestige. My brother is on the management committee at Desai's law firm. Working for me makes Desai useful to them. I say something bad and he's gone. My brother is ruthless. The minute you don't serve his purpose, he has no tolerance for you."

"A tough guy."

"Not so much tough as remorseless. He's my brother and I shouldn't talk badly about him. But Steve is a bad guy, all the way through. If he does something he knows will hurt someone, he doesn't lose a second of sleep. I'm not always a good guy, but I suffer remorse."

Georges didn't understand that. He never felt remorse. If he was kind to someone, it was for no other reason than expediency. It was why he'd sent money to Helene all those years. He'd felt no remorse for getting her pregnant. It meant nothing to him that hundreds of innocent people would die when he blew up the terminal in Spain.

"Anyway," Barry continued, "Desai does everything I ask."

"That's useful."

"Perhaps, but I have no respect for him."

Georges had never needed money, and prestige had come with his name. When someone didn't show him respect, as had been the case with Bernard's father, he thought they were arrogant. The recollection of General de Lattre irked him. After killing Wright, he would never think about General de Lattre again.

The dinner guests were assembled on the terrace when Barry and Georges returned from their walk. Georges saw Sandrine talking to a man who resembled Barry but was as disheveled in appearance as Barry was elegant. She was being quite familiar, he thought. It disgusted him the way she kept saying "Oh, Steven" every time she addressed him. There were other guests. Parnell had latched on to a young woman in a tight skirt. Georges wished he could return to France immediately. He would sit in his comfortable chair in his study and read in Le Monde about the fireball in Spain.

25

A FEW DAYS LATER A provocative woman's voice said, "Make a U-turn at your next opportunity." Raymond was irritated. The agent at the rental-car company had included the navigation system for free. It had a tiny screen that he couldn't see without his reading glasses, which he couldn't wear while he was driving. It was the fifth time she'd demanded he turn onto a road where there was no road and then insisted he make a U-turn in order to go back to the road that wasn't there.

The Jackson Ranch was between San Saba and Goldthwaite. Raymond had been there once before, a couple of weeks following his meeting with Jay in East Berlin after Genna's murder. Jay and Herrick had decamped to the ranch and wouldn't answer the phone, so he'd flown in a CIA plane to the San Saba Municipal Airport. They'd been very upset over the Agency's handling of Genna's murder but had returned with him on the plane the next day. This time he'd taken a commercial flight to Austin and rented a car. It was now late afternoon and he was lost.

Before the woman could make her proclamation for the sixth time, he pulled over and turned off the engine. That shut her up. Then he pulled out his mobile phone, prayed for service, and tapped in the number.

The voice of the woman who answered was coarse and abrupt. "Unless you're calling the Jackson Ranch, you've got the wrong number," she said.

"Can I speak to Mr. Jackson, please."

The woman paused briefly. "If you knew him, you wouldn't be calling him Mr. Jackson. What can I do for you?"

"I'm can't find your place. I'm lost." He felt intimidated.

Another pause, then: "You must be that New York City fella comin' to visit."

"I am."

"You're late."

"That's because I'm lost."

"There's only but one way to get here."

"I can't seem to find it."

"What road you on?"

"Highway 16."

"Can't be far, then. Our road is at a big stand of live oaks. Only one between San Saba and Goldthwaite. Seen it?"

Raymond looked around. He'd pulled off the road not ten yards from the trees.

"Yes."

"Go back to where you saw 'em. There's a big sign next to a big gate, says 'Jackson Ranch' in blue letters. Can't miss it."

The sign was a little obscured by the low-hanging limbs of the live oaks, but it was big.

"I guess I'm right in front of it."

He heard a burst of laughter and the woman saying to someone nearby in Spanish, "This crazy Yankee is sitting in front of the gate and doesn't notice it." She didn't know that he understood Spanish, he realized. He heard the phone being passed to someone else.

"Uncle Raymond, where have you been?" It was Samantha.

"Hi, Sam. Driving around looking at the countryside."

She laughed. "I've been worried. And we've started cocktails without you."

The Jackson Ranch road snaked around hills and over several creeks that flowed into the Colorado River. It was a long road and it took him fifteen minutes to drive it. The last half mile was straight along the side of a meadow that had been cut short after the summer growing season. He saw the ranch buildings from a distance nestled together on a rise. They looked like a postcard, with the early-evening sky red behind them.

There were half a dozen people on a giant deck off the west side of the main house. Sam came up and hugged him as soon as he got to the top step. It was different from her visit to his farmhouse. Her hair was pulled back into a ponytail and she wore jeans and a blouse under a vest. The jeans were tucked into beautiful cowgirl boots that had intricate blue and red designs on the shaft and stitching on the vamp. He remembered how good her mother had been at fitting in to foreign places.

Jay walked up and shook Raymond's hand. "Rosie tells me you were lost, old man. See any birds while you were wandering around the countryside?"

"No. Lots of cows and prairie. It all blended together."

"Those would be steers."

The others came over and Raymond was introduced. There were three men and another woman, who appeared to be married to one of the men. Jay used only first names, so Raymond couldn't tell. It looked to him that the men were smitten with Samantha; they watched her carefully whenever she spoke. He remembered how men used to gather around Betsy, and the recollection distracted him for a moment. Then a Mexican woman put a scotch in his hand, though he hadn't asked for it. Her hair was very thick and black and shone as if she were under a spotlight.

They gathered around him and asked him about himself. He thought they were just being polite to an old man, but their interest didn't wane. They thought he really was Samantha's uncle, and she'd told them he'd been in the foreign service and traveled a great deal. The things I could tell them . . . But they were as interested in his farmhouse in upstate New York as they were in Budapest. The Mexican woman announced dinner, and he was relieved to get out of the limelight. Sam sat next to him.

"Did you bring your Sibley's?" she asked.

"No."

"It's a good time for birds in this part of Texas. Uncle Jay probably has a copy. Just ask Rosie."

"I hadn't expected a party," he said. He'd intentionally not told Herrick he was going to Texas.

"It's a good thing I called Uncle Jay yesterday and found out. My friends and I had plans to go to dinner in Austin tonight. I solved that problem by bringing them with me. It's hardly a party."

"It's just a quick visit."

"You never come to Texas. Did you think you were going to sneak in and out?"

"I wasn't sneaking."

"So why are you here?"

He couldn't tell her why and he hadn't prepared an explanation. Her suspicious look made him uncomfortable. He hadn't lied to anyone after he'd left the CIA. Then, he'd lied to Helene at the bakery, and now he would lie to Samantha. It was necessary, but he knew he would feel bad about it later.

"I hadn't seen Jay in a while," he said. "He doesn't come to New York. It's hard to explain. I've gotten older, and I worry about putting off anything for later. So here I am."

She laughed. "So, you've become an impetuous old man with a bucket list."

"Something like that." In truth, the only thing in his bucket was to sit on the porch with Megan. He'd seen all the places he wanted to see.

Across the table, one of the young men was telling a Cajun joke about a brain transplant. His accent and timing were very good, Raymond thought. He liked Samantha's friends. They were lighthearted and whimsical, even when talking about politics, and none of them seemed to be hiding anything. All his life he'd hidden things, and here he was hiding from her that he'd found the person who had killed her mother and her grandparents. It was hard for him to make conversation, with all these thoughts in his head.

Samantha and her friends departed for Austin after dinner. He stood on the porch and watched the taillights fade as their SUV moved down the road along the meadow. Jay came out and they sat on cushioned deck chairs next to a teak table that had turned gray with age. Rosie appeared with two glasses of brandy. She stood over them for a minute with her hands on her hips.

"The kitchen is closed," she said in Spanish.

"Thanks, Rosie," Jay said. "In the morning I'm going to town for an errand. Could you get Señor Hatcher some breakfast?"

"As long as the señor doesn't expect breakfast at lunchtime," she replied.

"It's no problem," Raymond said in Spanish. "I wake up early." The only time he'd slept past dawn was when they'd drugged him after the flying-mattress incident.

He thought his speaking Spanish would surprise her but he saw no indication of that on her face. She only shook her head and walked back into the house.

"I called Megan," Jay said. "I don't like surprises. She told me you were coming down here to look at birds. It's what I told Sam, but I know it's bullshit."

"Why?"

"Listen, Grandpa, your brain may be going but mine's as sharp as ever. No way you'd come here for birds. Megan told me that story to avoid telling me the real reason for your trip. So spit it out!"

Raymond had planned to ease into his revelation, but now he wasn't sure where to begin. He wasn't as nimble as he once had been.

"I suppose I could've just telephoned you. But that didn't seem right."

"Okay."

"It's about a man named Jacques de Garde. It was a long time ago."

"Never heard of him."

"He murdered Herrick's father."

"I thought it was the Viet Minh."

"No. There was a State Department cover-up. They were worried about the relationship with de Gaulle."

"When did you find this out?'

"In 1951."

"How?"

"I went to Vietnam right after. I talked to the Viet Minh. There were two French assassins. I killed them, but the mastermind had left the country."

The way he said it sounded so matter-of-fact, as if nothing had really happened to him, like a report in a newspaper. He paused and watched Jay's face. He thought he saw the connections clicking into place.

"So history repeats itself with the French," Jay said. "At least in Genna's case we didn't let the bastards get away."

"But we did, Jay. That's why I'm here."

The next part spilled out easily: how de Garde was an alias for Piquart, and that Helene Dumont had been a double agent. Then, the connection to Genna's murder.

"Did those bastards at the CIA know about Helene Dumont?"

Jay was furious. Raymond understood. He'd dammed up the memories of the murders for decades, but his recent discoveries about Georges Piquart had opened the flood gates. It had made him more angry than he'd even been, more angry than he was in the jungle before he'd killed the henchmen, and he knew now that he had denied all these years how strongly the murders of Bradley and Betsy had affected him.

"No, as far as I know."

"How'd you find out?'

He told Jay about Helene Dumont's granddaughter walking into the OSS Bakery and what he had discovered in the box she'd left him. Jay's shoulders slumped. He walked into the house and returned quickly with the bottle of brandy.

"You were right not to phone me, Raymond. I appreciate that you came down here."

"It was necessary."

"But as much as I'd enjoy it, I can't go to France and kill this evil frog. I just don't have it in me anymore, Raymond. You see, all I care about nowadays is being an old, retired cowboy."

The next part was hard, but Raymond knew he had to do it. He described what Helene had overheard in France. When he said Parnell's name, Jay sat up straight.

"You know Will Parnell?" Raymond asked.

"He was once a partner at W&K, but so much a womanizer they exiled him to Paris, until they finally kicked his sorry ass out. You think he's Piquart's nephew?"

"I looked online. His mother's maiden name is Piquart and I think she's the old man's kid sister."

"Why would Piquart murder Herrick?"

"Why Genna?"

"A coincidence, maybe. Or he couldn't resist the opportunity. I don't know."

"Maybe," Raymond said. "But I'm suspicious of coincidences."

"It could be nothing more than the old man is sore about how W&K treated his nephew. The girl probably just overheard some expression, not a real threat."

"More from Google," Raymond said and spilled out the last part: IndoSun was selling its LNG terminal company to Meteor; Piquart and a hedge-fund guy were providing some of the money; a closing ceremony was to be held at their facility in Bilbao, Spain. Jay shook his head and sighed.

"We're too old for this, Raymond."

"True."

"I thought we'd put it all behind us."

"So did I," Raymond replied, but he knew he had not really done so.

"You've told Herrick about this?"

"No. This stuff was all in the newspaper so I just asked him casually about it."

"And?"

"He's going to the ceremony in Spain and he's taking Samantha."

Jay sighed again and Raymond thought, He's right. We're too old. We can't manage this.

"What about Lufkin?" Jay asked. "IndoSun is his company."

"I'm worried about talking to him. There may be someone inside who's giving Piquart information. How'd he get into the deal?"

"The world is fucking crazy."

"Does Parnell have a connection?"

Jay's forehead wrinkled. His hand went limp and he had to put his glass on the table.

"It's that weasel Sunil Desai. Has to be. He was buddies with Parnell and he's done a lot of the work for IndoSun since I left."

Raymond laughed. He couldn't help it. Jay's face was so contorted and he'd picked up the brandy bottle but his hand was trembling.

"Jay, law-firm partners don't kill people."

"I did."

"That was different."

"You don't know Desai. He'd give an assassin directions to his mother's house if you paid him enough."

They sat quietly for a while and drank the brandy. The crickets were making a racket. They're gone for the season back at the farmhouse, Raymond thought. After a while, he thought he had to say something. "Jay, I thought all of this was over with. I really did. I was starting to enjoy my bird watching. It was like my early days, when I would study a language and a culture. The more you watched, the more you learned."

Jay laughed and shook his head.

"I didn't mean to be funny," Raymond said.

"Old man, you're something else. I just had an image of you sitting on a limb chirping, or squawking, or whatever."

"I sit on my porch mostly. Never in a tree. Megan won't let me do that."

Jay leaned back and put his hands on his head, eyes closed. Raymond suspected he was struggling with a memory of his anger in France that had accompanied his killing of the thugs who had murdered Genna. Jay had been asked at dinner whether he was bored at the ranch after all the excitement of living in New York City. He'd said, "Not a chance. What you see here when you look at something is exactly what it is. No one talking in code. No one trying to kill you." They'd all laughed, most likely assuming he'd been referring to other lawyers, muggers and taxi drivers.

Jay stood up. "Okay. Maybe we have no choice. Let's talk in the morning. I have to think."

The next morning, Raymond was awake early. The sun was just up, but the sky was already blue. Rosie had a place set on the table inside because it was cold on the porch. She brought him coffee, scrambled eggs, sausage, and a biscuit the size of a small loaf of bread.

"Señor Jackson says you were in the navy and fought the Japanese," she said.

"That's right," he said, and her abruptness made him smile.

"My father was out there too," she said and went back to the kitchen.

He wasn't hungry, but he made himself eat so he wouldn't hurt her feelings. The sun rose higher and the meadow turned gold. It would be nice to live here, he thought, and not have to shovel snow off the porch.

An old man appeared in the doorway to the kitchen and looked at Raymond. He wore an old cowboy hat that was worn along its edges but well cared for. The man came closer. The wrinkles in the leather on his boots looked like the lines in his face, and the recollection leaped at Raymond.

"Excuse my intrusion," Trent said and removed his hat. "Might you be Lieutenant Hatcher?"

"A long time ago."

"Well, I'll be damned! The last time I saw you, you was going off in a sub. Tried to look you up after the war, but damn navy don't tell you nothing."

"You saved my life." It was the only thing Raymond could think to say.

"Ah, bunk. All I did was throw a rope, like my daddy taught me to do. It was the commander who was drivin' the boat. Where's he now?"

"Sorry to say, he was killed."

"Well, that's a real shame." A couple of tears rolled down Trent's old face. "Not a day goes by when I don't thank my lucky stars I made it outa that mess."

"Me too."

"Well, Rosie told me someone named Hatcher was sittin' out here, so I had to check. She's my daughter, you know."

"I didn't."

"Yep. All hell broke loose when I courted her mother, a Mexican girl, but Mrs. Jackson stood up for us. She was a fine lady."

"I know."

The man was quiet for a moment and Raymond stood up. He didn't want to talk more and he thought Trent didn't, either. It was best to leave all the decades between them undisturbed. The bond they shared was so good and true that Raymond could not belittle it with a remark about how small a world it was. They clasped hands.

"Guess I'll leave you to your breakfast," he said. "I hope we'll be seeing each other again."

"Me too."

Rosie came out and took the dishes away. Not long after that, Jay returned. He told Raymond he'd decided they had to go to Spain. There wasn't much more to talk about, except to divide up the preparations. Once they knew the date of the ceremony, they'd meet in Bilbao.

Raymond got lost on his drive back to Austin, missed his plane, and had to spend several hours in the airport waiting for the next one. He wondered if he could find a recent photograph of Piquart. By the time he landed at Stewart Airport, he'd decided a picture wasn't necessary. Piquart wouldn't show up in Spain. He would send people to do it. And Raymond didn't need to picture his face. After so many years, he didn't care what the man looked like. Was his vengeance gone? Probably not, but it seemed like such an effort to set it burning again, which is all a picture would do. His recent outpouring of anger and acknowledgement of his decades of denial had been cleansing in a strange way. He was realistic. Georges Piquart and he now were two old spies. Dueling each other was absurd, like something from a novel. No, this mission, which would surely Raymond's last one, was only to prevent Piquart from striking again. Putting his blade in the man's skull, as good as he'd once thought that would feel, would be too much trouble.

26

AFTER RAYMOND LEFT, JAY SADDLED his horse and galloped across Julia's Meadow, named for his mother. The groundcover looked like clover now, but it was actually lupinus texensis, which in the spring bloomed into the bluest of all the bluebonnets. He picked a clutch when they bloomed every year and put them on Julia's grave. It was against the law in Texas to pick bluebonnets, but he didn't care and nobody bothered him.

There was a rise at the end of the meadow, a gully behind its crest, and then a rocky incline to higher ground. He made the horse climb carefully on a path that snaked around mesquite thickets, patches of shinnery oak, and outcroppings of rock. At another rise he came under a stand of live oaks, its canopy as big as a circus tent. There was a boulder with a large, bald cypress tree just beyond it. He got off the horse and climbed to the top of the boulder to look down on Miriam's Meadow. In the middle of the meadow was a large, flat piece of granite that was used as a table for picnics in the summer, when the Mexican Hat in the meadow glowed orange and yellow.

He lay on his back on the boulder. A red-shouldered hawk glided above him, its black-and-white-barred tail and wings very distinct. A blue norther had come through the night before and the air had a chill in it. He thought he should get back on the horse and go down the back side of the rise, then gallop across the pastures to the Colorado River. It would be an hour of hard riding and when he reached the river he'd enjoy the heat the gallop would stir up in him and the horse. But he didn't feel like moving. The rock beneath him was warm from the sun. That was good enough.

Raymond had looked awfully old yesterday, he thought. He remembered how much the old man loved his OSS knife. It didn't matter, because fighting with Piquart's men was not an option. There would be no drawing them into a confrontation. They'd have to figure out something else. Either that or they'd be killed. Then, Piquart would have gotten them all. No. Jay wasn't going to let that happen. He tried to summon the rage he'd felt in France when he'd hunted Genna's murderers. But it didn't come. He wouldn't let that filthy old man's henchmen kill Herrick and Samantha, but he didn't think he had it in him to go to France and kill the buzzard. The sun went behind a cloud and it was suddenly very cold on the rock, so he went down to the horse and headed back to the house.

The next day, Jay drove to the W&K office in Austin. His former partner from the Houston office was working there a couple of days a week, and she set him up in a conference room with a laptop to do some research. The firm's client files were on the other side of a firewall, but he hacked through that easily enough. He knew that she knew what he was doing. Why would he drive all the way to Austin for simple access to the Internet? They had worked together and been close friends for many years.

It didn't take long for him to go through the IndoSun documents about the Meteor transaction. It was complex because Meteor was doing a public offering to raise funds to pay part of the purchase price to IndoSun. Additional funds were being invested by a group led by Danna Partners. Piquart was not named, but a French company, Le Cercle, was named as one of the Danna Group members. The name Le Cercle was familiar to him, but he couldn't remember where he'd heard it. He didn't think Raymond had mentioned it the night before. Had it been a Group mission? An energy transaction? He'd done too good a job of washing all those times out of his mind.

She came back to the conference room late in the day, when he was loading up his backpack with his notes. Her eyes always sparkled and she was perpetually upbeat. It was why she was still at W&K and he was not.

"Let's go get a cocktail," he said.

She loved Grey Goose vodka and she always had her martini on the rocks with olives. He didn't care one way or the other, but he did the same because they'd done so for decades. Once he'd thought he was in love with her, but he'd done nothing about it. It would've been too complicated. And his romantic relationships always ended badly. One lover inevitably got bored with the other. Or worse, he'd love her and she'd die, like Genna had. It was better this way. The unrequited spark between them was good enough.

"I saw you worked on Meteor," he said.

She laughed. "Did you?"

"It was a good guess. You do IndoSun work."

"Herrick is a pain-in-the-ass client. But you know that."

"He's a little uptight."

"That's an understatement. Anyway, Meteor priced the offering today, so the closing is next Monday and I'll be done with him for a while."

"Don't you think it's strange that Danna Partners is in the deal?"

"Very. It gave us a lot of heartburn in the beginning, but it's really Meteor's problem, not ours, once the closing happens."

"But IndoSun will still own some Meteor stock."

"True. And so will Danna. Lufkin was willing to take the risk."

"What do you know about Danna?"

"They're creeps, like most activist hedge funds. But Barry Silvers is worse than most. He's taken positions in a couple of our other clients, and he's always an asshole at the meetings."

"Nothing illegal about being an asshole."

"Maybe there should be. Silvers was investigated for short-selling stock of a company that he knew was about to release bad news. But the SEC couldn't tie the trades to him."

Jay didn't think that was relevant. Piquart was rich. Why would he go to the trouble of insider trading? In fact, why would he even invest in a specialty deal like this? There had to be a reason.

"Did Desai work on the deal with you?"

She laughed. "Yes, speaking of assholes. And as long as we're talking about creeps, so did Will Parnell. He represented the French investors. It was the deal from hell."

"Sounds like it."

"Good thing you're retired, which leads to the question of why you're so interested."

"Just heard Herrick talking about it and was curious."

"Right. Don't tell me if you don't want to."

"I worry about him."

"You should. He's going to have a heart attack if he doesn't lighten up."

"I've offered him a piece of land at the ranch. He can build a house."

"Good luck with that. Why don't I have an offer like that?"

He watched her pop an olive into her mouth, and he motioned to the bartender that they'd have a second round. If she built a house for herself on the ranch, drinking martinis on her porch would be very nice. But she was always in motion, and he didn't know if he could deal with that. Still, she'd kept her good looks all these years. She was quite handsome. He wondered how she would react if he told her he'd once considered asking her to sleep with him. It was probably not a good idea.

"Say the word and it's yours. Lots of nice meadows to choose from."

"You don't think I would. That's why you've offered. And you're probably right. I can't figure out why you're not bored. A girl's got to get out and about."

"You must be going to the closing dinner in Spain."

"You really are well informed!"

"Herrick told me."

"It's not a closing dinner for the deal. That's in New York next week. This is a big ceremony to show off to the media Meteor's upgraded terminal and IndoSun's new state-of-the-art LNG carrier, which will be there to off-load LNG. It'll be next month. Only bigwigs invited. Not peons like me."

They had a third drink and he knew he wouldn't drive back to the ranch that night. They went to dinner. She was staying at one of the new hotels close to Lady Bird Lake. The nighttime view of the Texas State Capitol from her room was spectacular. He switched off the light. The city lights twinkled in her eyes.

27

RAYMOND SAT ON HIS PORCH. Nothing made sense to him. Why would Piquart carry out an assassination in Bilbao? There was no political motivation to warrant taking that kind of complexity and risk, and it was not Piquart's style. Piquart's investment in Meteor was also puzzling. At best, it might have allowed one of his men to gain access to the ceremony in Bilbao, where he could murder Herrick in close contact. It was a storyline from a movie, not a risky operation that would be taken by a veteran like Piquart. Raymond had always tried to allow some time to pass before an assassination could be discovered by the police, so the trail would be cold. He thought killing Herrick and Samantha on a visit to the Jackson Ranch would make much more sense, although getting access for such an opportunity would be difficult. The next day he called Jay to say he was stumped.

"The Meteor closing is tomorrow. The ceremony in Bilbao is in a week, the Wednesday after Thanksgiving," Jay said.

"How do you know this?"

"I talked to someone at W&K."

"Can he be trusted?"

"She can be trusted, but it doesn't matter. I haven't told her anything."

"Okay. Still, the whole scheme isn't making sense to me."

"That's because you're focused on Herrick. It's the terminal. Danna Partners is going to create bad news in order to manipulate the Meteor stock. I believe Piquart's role involves corporate espionage. Silvers has retained him to cause a small accident at the terminal during the ceremony. It will make headlines. The stock will plummet. Silvers and Piquart will make a fortune on short sales the day before."

"It still makes no sense. That will cause even more scrutiny. It will make killing Herrick more risky."

"Raymond, slow down a second. I believe Piquart is using the Silvers scheme for his own purpose. He'll get what he wants by causing a much bigger accident–much more than Silvers intends. It'll be a fireball that kills everyone at the ceremony, including Herrick."

Of course! Raymond thought. It's so obvious and I missed it. It was the same as with Genna. Piquart's client in that case probably had not wanted her dead.

"I'm so stupid."

"Come on, old man," Jay said. "You knew you were too close. That's why you came to see me. And I could be wrong. We're just getting started."

"What's next?"

Jay's planning felt odd to Raymond. They'd switched roles. Now, Jay was leading the mission. It was as it should be.

"We'll meet in Bilbao on Saturday. Piquart has very good sources, so use an alias. Still have one?"

"Ronald Burns."

"Okay, Ronnie. The Meteor people are all staying at the Hotel Carlton in Bilbao. We should stay closer to the terminal, somewhere in the Las Arenas area. I have an old friend in Spain helping me, and I'll let you know."

"How will we know if our theory is right?"

The was a pause for a few moments before Jay responded.

"If my former partner, Sunil Desai, shows up in Bilbao, we'll know we're wrong. He's a coward and will not show up there if he thinks there's any risk he might be hurt in an explosion."

28

THE LOBBY OF THE GRAN Hotel Puente Colgante was vacant except for a sleepy desk clerk and a bellman leaning back in a chair. In the off-season it rained and the air was cold and damp. It wasn't raining today, but the sun slid in and out of dark clouds. During the moments it shone, the surrounding buildings glowed and the Ria del Nervión sparkled.

"No rain?" Raymond asked the clerk.

"Tomorrow. You like the rain, Señor Burns?"

"Sometimes."

"It's no good for tourists. We only have businessmen this time of year."

"They pay just the same."

"Yes, but they're not fun. It's dull in the winter."

The terrace off the lobby faced upriver and overlooked El Solar Plaza. From his room he had a downriver view. The Vizcaya Zubia was in the foreground and the Bay of Biscay was in the distance. The LNG terminal wasn't visible because it was in the outer harbor to the west, behind a line of hills.

Later in the afternoon he walked out the Maria Diaz de Haro Kalea, where he had a good view of the inner-harbor marinas and some of the coastline to the north. There was the usual array of boats one would find in marinas: sloops, cutters and catamarans. Most were rigged for day sailing or, perhaps, short over-night trips to harbors along the coast, like San Sebastian. He stopped awhile across from a marina where larger yachts were docked, most of them larger than fifty feet but not so long as to require a mooring. One of them was a Nautor Swan ketch, the same as Plava Guska in Bari but a newer model. She was well-appointed and beautifully maintained, flying a French flag. He assumed she was rigged for ocean travel because there was an impressive array of radar and communications equipment on her mask and foredeck.

At the end of the walkway he watched the sun set behind the hills above the terminal. Looking at the ketch had made him pensive. Many, many years had slid by since he'd first boarded the Plava Guska. So many things had happened between that time and when Vera had held his arm recently as they crossed the street in New York. The harbor was quiet as the light faded. At his farmhouse there was enchanting birdsong at this time of day. He knew, but could not remember, what birds sang at dusk. It bothered him that he couldn't recall the names. He missed Megan.

Jay arrived very late that night and they met for breakfast the next day. The rain became very heavy and there were only a few patrons in the dining room. Raymond remembered how incessant the rain had been in Tonkin. It was a long time ago but many of his old memories from Vietnam had recently seemed to him like they had happened yesterday.

"Herrick and Samantha have gone up to San Sebastian," Jay said.

"Why?"

"I told Herrick in New York that I had learned about a plot to blow up the terminal. I had to do some fast talking to keep from telling him that it was actually a plot to kill him. He was suspicious, of course. He wanted to know why Lufkin wasn't handling this. I told him Ben suspected there was a spy inside Group and he'd asked me to handle this quietly."

"He believed that?"

"We're close friends. Why wouldn't he? And, in any case, what choice did he have?"

"Still, it's a stretch to think Lufkin would call us. We're retired. And we're old." Raymond was skeptical, but he could see how Herrick would believe Jay. Herrick was a smart guy but not someone who had good instincts when it came to deception. It was why Raymond had never sent him into the field.

"Hey, speak for yourself, old man. Besides I didn't tell him about you. I told him I'd learned about the scheme on my own and, because he had Samantha with him, I thought it would be a good idea for them to take a sight-seeing trip while I sorted things out."

"Will he tell Samantha?"

"No. I told him it was best not to. In fact, I told him not to even mention I was here."

"Isn't it risky? What if Piquart's men find out?"

"As far as anyone knows, it was a spur-of-the-moment decision this morning, so not enough time for Piquart to do anything."

"Still. It's like we're using them as bait."

"But that's exactly what we're doing."

"No," Raymond said. "It's a bad idea. They'll be unprotected up there. An assassination would be simple."

"Too little time for Piquart to plan that. I don't think it's risky. And there's a chance that the trip will confuse Piquart's men and cause them to make a mistake, reveal themselves in some way."

"I don't like it."

"And I have a hunch that Lufkin has a tail on them, no matter how convinced he is that we're just a couple of paranoid old men."

"Somehow, a hunch doesn't make me less nervous."

"I understand, Raymond. But we can't play it too safe or make Piquart abandon his attempt. He'll just try again another time. This has to end now. If we can expose him in this, the old investigations will be reopened and he'll be imprisoned until he croaks."

"Right. The French will finally do the right thing." His voice was sarcastic and bitter. He didn't for a minute think Herrick would ever be safe if they didn't eliminate Piquart. They'd kill his thugs for a third time, and Herrick and Samantha would continue to be in danger until Piquart died from old age.

"I know how you feel," Jay said. "But this time we at least have a chance to stop him, and not just clean up after the fact."

They were quiet for a short time. Jay was right. They had to keep their focus. If done correctly, Piquart could be exposed and the French authorities would have to do the right thing this time. But Raymond had never felt so helpless in his life. He was ashamed, suddenly. What he wanted was revenge, not just success. It would defeat him if he wasn't careful.

Jay put his hands on Raymond's shoulders. "We're a couple of old men, Raymond, with short attention spans. This is not the time to think about storming a fortress in France. How about we save that for later?"

Raymond knew he was being patronized. Jay was not an old man, he was. It was kind. He took a long breath and sighed. He missed the cardinals at his farmhouse. He loved to watch them in the winter, when there were fewer birds around. Watching them wasn't a bit complicated. No plots. No innuendo. The male's coloring was the same red as Betsy's hair. When this mission was over, he could go back to the cardinals. He would sit on the porch and smell whatever Megan was baking while he watched them, unless he and Jay failed and they were burned to crisp in a fireball at the wharf. He would think about going to

France later. "How will we get into the terminal and on the LNG tanker?" he asked.

"We only need access to the terminal. Think about it. If the accident occurs on the tanker it won't have the effect Silvers wants. It has to occur at the terminal and has to look like Meteor is at fault. Besides, Omar is on the job."

"Omar? How's he involved in this?"

Raymond hadn't seen Omar in many years. Was he still using his press credentials for cover or was he now a business executive for a Qatar energy company? Raymond had a faint recollection that Jay had been in Qatar on an energy project before he retired. Had Jay told him about that? Was Omar mentioned? He pushed some breakfast around on his plate, trying to remember. It was Samantha who'd mentioned it, he decided, but he couldn't remember when. He looked up and saw that Jay was watching him, a worried expression on his face.

"You okay there old man?" Jay asked.

"Fine. Fine. I was just remembering Omar and the old days."

"Right," Jay said. "I worked on a matter with him after you retired. Last week I remembered that he'd mentioned Piquart and his company, Le Cercle, at that time. So I called him. The LNG ship is owned by a joint venture between IndoSun and Qatargas. No one gets on that ship Omar doesn't know. And he's arranged for credentials for us to get into the terminal. We'll be inspecting the off-loading process for Qatargas."

"My god, what else have you thought of?"

"Your OSS knife. It's in a package waiting for you at the front desk."

The next morning, Jay sat in the hotel lobby behind a newspaper and watched Raymond emerge from the elevator looking like an elderly tourist stooped over a cane. He knew that Raymond was going into Bilbao to look around the Hotel Carlton. Raymond's shuffle to the cab was so impressive that the driver leaped out to open the door. The night before, Raymond had looked frail at dinner, and Jay was relieved to see that the frailty was part of a disguise–something Raymond was famous for.

Jay took a taxi to a café in Zierbena marina for the afternoon meal. It was as close as he could get to the terminal without having to show credentials. He knew he wouldn't see many terminal workers in the place because one had to drive in a circuitous route from there, either around the hills to the terminal entrance at La Arena or back toward Santurtzi for the main road into the harbor docks. After Zierbena he went to Santurtzi for a drink before returning to the hotel. There weren't many people around. The bay was peaceful and the sun, nearing the horizon, made the water sparkle. He struggled to recall Genna's face. It was so long ago. He'd like reparation, he knew. Was it necessary? Would Piquart pursue Herrick again if this attempt failed? Piquart was an old man. Was killing him the only way the evil could be extinguished? For now, he needed to set it aside. He thought about Austin, about how his friend's eyes sparked in the morning light after that night in her hotel room.

That evening, Omar surprised them at their table. Jay had expected that he would only send information, not show up.

"I couldn't help it. It sounded like too much fun," Omar said.

"And I'll guess you have some information," Jay said.

"Always. Information is my business. In this case I've learned that Technigaz, which constructed the terminal, has a team showing up tomorrow. It is customary when a ship as big as Mozah comes to port. And this time they are accompanied by several security advisers from Le Cercle."

"That's Piquart's company."

"It's perhaps a coincidence."

"I don't care for coincidences," Jay said.

"I remember. But you may think otherwise because by another coincidence I am here with my reporters. We'll leave Qatargas out of this." He slid Al Jazeera press credentials across the table to Raymond and Jay. "Tomorrow we have a very busy day with tours of the terminal and Mozah. Even if it's a false alarm, we'll have fun."

"It's not a false alarm," Raymond said.

"You sound quite certain," Omar said.

"I am. I asked at the front desk at the Hotel Carlton. The reservation for Sunil Desai was canceled."

Raymond sat at a table in the terminal's coffee room. Jay was on a tour with Omar, and Raymond had begged off on account of aching joints. He made small talk with several of the terminal's security guards who were on a break. They liked the fact that he was an interested old journalist and that his Spanish was so well spoken, in some instances including some Basque phrases. They talked too much and he quickly found out what he wanted to know: what part of the terminal was unpatrolled during their break. The area was a maze of pipes and machinery, where LNG vapor from the huge storage tank was either diverted in one line back to the ship if pressure was needed for off-loading or sent in another line to the recondenser. Igniting several leaks in those lines would cause the LNG in the main unloading line to warm quickly, while another breach would cause the heavier LNG to roll across the terminal in a fireball.

He also identified the Le Cercle men. They were thugs, the same as in Tonkin and in northeastern France. It amazed him. They spoke only French and made no effort to be friendly to the local security people.

Omar arrived late for dinner. He listened to Raymond's report, but his face was grave, not happy.

"We identified the men also," Omar said. "But they'd left the terminal by the time we found some evidence that the explosives had been set up. It was too dark to confirm. We'll go back tomorrow in the daylight."

"Why did they set them up so early?" Jay asked. "The ceremony isn't until the day after tomorrow."

"My guess is that they want to be far away when their accident occurs."

"How can you be sure?"

"They've checked out of their hotel near the terminal and we can't find them. One has a reservation on a flight tomorrow night to Paris and we will wait at the airport for him. But it will leave very little time to interrogate him about how to dismantle the bombs. We don't know travel plans for the other. If he is the trigger man, he is our bigger threat. He's probably hidden in a place where he can ascertain from a safe distance when the ceremony is about to start. My men are looking for such places, but it may be hard to cover them all."

"It shouldn't matter," Jay said. "We can dismantle their work at the terminal tomorrow."

Omar laughed. "My friends, you have been away from the business too long. Unless these two are imbeciles, we will not be able to tamper with their devices without blowing ourselves up. There will be a sophisticated radio-relay device. We will need the codes or we will have to find that device."

Later that night, Raymond went to Jay's room. He'd been overconfident about Piquart's thugs and he really just wanted to stay in his room, put his head in his hands, and weep. It's entirely futile, he thought. We'll never find the trigger man. And suppose the man's reservation to Paris is a ploy. The thug could be on a bus to San Sebastian right now. Outside Jay's door, a tear rolled down his cheek, which distressed him further. Megan said it was perfectly normal for old men to cry, no matter how stoic they'd been in younger years. But it humiliated him. He wiped his cheek before he went in.

"That frog may be on a bus to San Sebastian," Raymond said immediately.

"It's unlikely. Just as unlikely as that they know about us."

It upset Raymond that Jay seemed so sure. "But not impossible," he said.

"Ok. Not impossible," Jay said, but in a way that was distracted, not dismissive. He could tell from Jay's face that his mind was racing through scenarios and trying to make sense of what they'd just learned. It was bittersweet. His own mind was merely limping along, trying to keep up with what was happening. But Jay was manifesting all the training Raymond had given him through all the years since Princeton. All Raymond could think to do was tell Jay to make Herrick and Samantha come back immediately.

"Look," Jay said, before that suggestion could be made. "Let's call Herrick and tell him to come back. It's too risky to leave them out there. They have a better chance here with all the security Lufkin probably has around. And, it will make you feel better."

It didn't make Raymond feel much better. He had no idea what to do next. They'd all die together, he thought.

"Look, Raymond. We have to focus," Jay said. "It's all a contest at this point and we need to do whatever it takes to come out on top. There are many lives at stake, not just Herrick's and Samantha's. It's what you taught me: we take the best alternative and adjust as we go along. The solution that works will be the best one."

"Too optimistic for me," Raymond said. He was talking more to himself than to Jay. "If we can't win here, we should cut our losses and go to France and kill Piquart."

"You can't mean that."

"Why not? Herrick's father was optimistic. It made him think that ideals would always prevail over malevolence. It was why he went back to Vietnam, and in the end it got him killed. All his lofty principles didn't protect him." He'd never said it that way before. Did he really believe it? Have I become this cynical? he wondered.

"You'd have thought Herrick's father would have written down all those ideals," Jay said.

Raymond lost his composure for a moment when he heard that. He couldn't help it, and he knew Jay saw it. It was no use denying the existence of Bradley's journals anymore. "How'd you know?" he asked.

"It was a hunch. Now I know for sure," Jay said.

"Does Herrick know about your hunch?"

"Nope."

"Do you plan to tell him?"

"Do you plan to give them to him?"

"No."

"Then I won't be telling him. I'm with you about ideals, old man. They can get you in trouble. And Herrick is better off with the memories he has, as incomplete or rewritten as they may be."

Raymond didn't listen closely while Jay talked through their next moves. There was no point. Jay had the lead, and Raymond would go along. He was too old to spring an attack on Piquart by himself.

Raymond's doubts returned when he was back in his room, gazing out his window at the lights on the Maria Diaz de Haro Kalea. He tried to dispel them by repeating to himself his life-long mantra. Take life one step at a time, don't look back, don't think about the future. It sounded trite to him now, like a verse the coach of a sports team made his players chant. He was now an old spy whose disguise was disintegrating. Everyone is a spy, he thought. Each of us protects an inner self, using lies and diversions as a part of a subterfuge designed to enable us to live with the compromise of values and principles that society constantly demands. He was tired, exhausted by deceit and denial. No more, he decided, and thought again of the flight of the birds at his farmhouse and the smell of Megan's bread in the oven. "No more," he said aloud after he turned out the light.

It was easy to find the explosive devices the next day. They were cleverly disguised, but exactly where Raymond had predicted they'd be. And they were much bigger than was needed to create only an incident that would call into question the terminal's safety measures. As Omar had guessed, they were linked to wireless receivers and GPS mechanisms. If the wireless signal was interrupted or the devices were moved, they would detonate.

Later that afternoon, Raymond and Jay met Omar at a café near the Santurtzi Parkea. "We need to narrow down our search for the trigger mechanism," Omar said. His face looked strained to Raymond. Was the situation hopeless?

"How far will the signal carry?" Jay asked.

"That depends," Omar said. "If there's a line of sight, then the mechanism could work from as far away as a mile. Otherwise, it would have to be much closer, particularly if there are structures in between."

They walked from the café to a nearby pier. After looking around, Jay said, "The hills on the other side of the harbor may have a clear view, but they look too far away. Maybe if he walked over to the water's edge from a dock near the terminal, the signal would get through."

"Too close," Omar said. "All the nearby docks will go up in flames with the terminal. The triggerman needs an escape route. And I don't think the mechanism is just a small switch.

The receivers at the bombs are not cellular devices. The transmitter would at least be the size of a small suitcase. He would be conspicuous."

"So, a man will need to flip the switch? Those guys are still here?" Raymond asked. He worried they might be stalking Herrick and Samantha right now, while he and Jay were hanging around speculating about a suitcase.

"At least one of them," Omar said.

Raymond remembered how the terminal had been just out of sight at the end of the end of the Maria Diaz de Haro walkway. "How about a boat in one of the marinas?" he asked.

"It probably has the same proximity problem," Omar replied. "The fireball will spread out on the water through the marinas."

Raymond thought about how they'd stored the supplies on sailboats in Bari and then sailed them over to Vis in plain sight. The same idea would work here. "Suppose, the guy has the trigger onboard a sailboat and he sails it out of the harbor, where he maintains a line of sight and waits until he is far enough out to flip the switch safely?"

Omar and Jay looked at each other. "Old man!" Jay exclaimed. "That's brilliant. And there's no incriminating gear to leave behind for the investigators to find. Everything is on the boat."

"Of course we will have to search all the marinas around the harbor," Omar sighed. "Not just the close ones. It's a needle in a haystack."

The three men gazed in different directions at the sky. No one wants to speak, Raymond thought, because no one wants to admit how difficult it will be to find the boat. He took a deep breath and settled back in his chair. He'd watched Megan do it so many times. She'd told him that sometimes a quiet moment was needed to solve a riddle.

A late-afternoon sun emerged from the cloud bank to the west, and the tops of the trees in the park across the street turned bright red. It reminded Raymond again of his walk out to the end of the Maria Diaz de Haro walkway on Saturday at the same time of day. The masts of the sailboats in the nearby marina had lighted up the same way. He remembered the sailboat in the harbor with the fancy communications equipment.

"I think I know where it is," he announced.

Raymond and Jay went to the marina, while Omar went back to the terminal to check on whether his men had made any progress on the devices. Raymond pointed out the Nautor Swan, which was conspicuous because of the radio gear and the French flag on the mast. It didn't appear anyone was onboard, but they watched it for an hour, until they thought they couldn't wait any longer.

No one was aboard. They found a bank of communications equipment, and evidence that someone was staying there–an open suitcase was on the bed in the main stateroom. From the magazines and newspapers it was clear the occupant was a Frenchman, and as Raymond had thought, the radio equipment was very sophisticated. Looking under the papers on the counter he found a piece of Le Cercle stationery with a phone number written on it. Not very smart, Raymond thought, and then said to Jay, "We're definitely in the right place."

For a few minutes they rummaged through the cabin and found more evidence. Then, out a portal, Raymond saw a man approaching the boat. He alerted Jay and closed the stateroom door partway to hide himself.

"What the hell are you doing in here?" the man demanded in French when he saw Jay.

"Why, I must be on the wrong boat, pardner," Jay said in Texas French.

Raymond had to work hard to keep from laughing. It would piss off the Frenchman, he thought, as Jay probably intended. He was right. The man immediately lunged at Jay, who used the man's momentum to swing him around to the stateroom door, where Raymond stood, his OSS knife in his hand. The Frenchman crumpled to the floor.

"Sorry," Raymond said. "I guess we won't be asking him any questions."

"Why, Grandpa!" Jay exclaimed. "You're an old horse who can still gallop. I'll be damned."

"He didn't seem like the talkative type anyway," Raymond said. He was breathing hard. His wrist hurt from twisting the knife into the man's brain. He had been calm when he did it, but now rage welled inside him. It was a delayed reaction. I'm so old I can't kill and be angry at the same time, he thought. He saw that Jay was watching him.

"Go ahead, old man. Kick the bastard. Give 'im what-for!" Jay exclaimed.

Raymond nudged the man with his toe. For a moment he imagined himself jumping up and down on top of the body. If he kicked him, he would just hurt his leg. But the anger was gone, and he took a step back. Jay walked on the corpse on his way over to put his arm around Raymond's shoulders.

"I've stepped on a lot worse," Jay said. "At least he won't stick to my boot. Let's go topside and enjoy the evening."

They found a bottle of brandy and took it on deck. Raymond asked, "Do you ever think about Genna?"

"Now and then. But my memory has faded a bit."

"She's the reason you never married."

"Oh, I guess you could say that. But I can't say it was a conscious thing. For a while I'd compare her to every girl I met and, of course, it was impossible for anyone to compete. And then, getting married seemed too complicated."

Raymond thought about it for a few minutes. Megan was worth every bit of complication they'd ever had. "I'm sorry Megan and I didn't have a child."

"My mother once told me there was a reason for everything," Jay said after another pause. "Of course, you hardly ever know the damn reason." And a moment later, "Your reason could be Herrick."

Raymond nodded his head. "That would be a good reason."

Soon, Omar and his men came to clean up the mess. They figured out how to interrupt the relay of the codes to the devices, but they would need other codes to disarm them. Until then, they'd have to maintain the communications link between the boat and the terminal.

"I don't think you should ask Raymond to question the frog you capture at the airport," Jay said, winking at Raymond. When Omar looked at him inquisitively, Jay continued, "I'm just saying that old Raymond's interrogation skills are a bit rusty. He had no patience with that fella down below."

"I have arranged with my friends at CNI to interrogate our French friend who they picked up in San Sebastian this morning," Omar said. "Evidently his reservation on the flight to Paris was a deception and he took a bus instead. Perhaps the man on the boat was going to sail there. My guess is we'll have the disarm codes quickly."

"Why do you say that?" Jay asked.

"He's a Frenchmen, my friends. He'll choose the easy alternative. In any case, we'll keep this all to ourselves until the stock market in New York closes. Tomorrow I will announce at the ceremony that Qatargas has agreed to a joint venture with Meteor on several new terminals in the Middle East. It will be good news for Meteor, yes? And just in time for the stock market opening in New York."

"The Meteor stock will skyrocket."

"I'm glad I'm not holding short positions," Omar said, grinning. Raymond suspected it was the opposite, that Omar was, in fact, holding options. So it was a good day's work for him.

We were lucky, Raymond said to himself. He was happy that they'd stopped Piquart, but he didn't join in the celebration with Jay and Omar. Raymond knew that they'd somewhat stumbled into their victory. Their foe had not been clever, or at least his men had not been clever. And Piquart was still out there, even if he wasn't a big threat for the moment. Raymond tried to feel good, but he'd been a spy long enough to know that he should never underestimate his enemy.

"It's amazing," Jay said. "It was so brilliant a scheme, using a sailboat and radio device, but these guys made no effort to blend in. I mean, they were rude to everyone at the terminal, and there's a goddamn French flag up on the mast. The guy had written a phone number down. It will probably be linked to Piquart, as will ownership or a charter of the sailboat. A French prosecutor will have a field day with this stuff."

Raymond didn't find much comfort in those things. The French authorities had not come through for Bradley. The State Department would not want to dig up old files. Jay had evidently forgotten how the French had thwarted the investigation of Genna's murder. No doubt, Piquart still had friends in the right places.

Omar laughed. "Ah, these Frenchmen can't help themselves. They're more arrogant than clever. They never expect to get caught. Some of your American businessmen seem to have learned that from them. No? They think themselves the smartest men in the room."

Raymond saw a change of expression on Jay's face. What had he thought? Many of his former law partners were certainly as arrogant as Piquart. They weren't murderers, although to Raymond they were just as bad. Jay certainly knew this better than he did. But Raymond didn't care to know what Jay thought or to debate the amorality of lawyers. He only wanted to go home to his farmhouse and smell Megan's bread baking in the oven.

29

GEORGES PIQUART THOUGHT HIS TWIN grandsons were idiots. They were proficient at nothing except video games, with which they'd spent more time during their college years than books. After two years of sleeping during their days and going to clubs at night, their father had asked Georges if he would give them a chance at Le Cercle, which Georges thought plucky as his son and his other siblings had been very distant since Beatrice had moved to Normandy. She'd died a couple of years ago, but the children had barely been civil to him at the funeral. Still he took in the twins, thinking it might help his relationship with his own children. Over the last few years, he'd drifted toward the sentimental on occasion. It made him angry when he noticed it because it made him feel like an old man.

He'd been angry for two days, since the explosion at Bilbao hadn't occurred. The grandsons added to his irritation when he came across them sprawled on couches in the chateau. They'd been training at Le Cercle for more than a year, and they had yet to demonstrate any personal discipline unless one counted the punctuality with which they started cocktails every evening. They were lazy in all matters related to the intellectual side of business. The complicated explosive mechanisms that had been deployed in Bilbao hadn't interested them. The only thing they'd demonstrated any proficiency with was their sniper training. They were excellent marksmen.

Anger exasperated Georges's arthritis. Today his hip joints were on fire. He stomped around the chateau, banging his cane against the floor with every step and growling whenever he came upon a servant. His plan had been perfect and he believed the men he'd sent were competent. What had happened? He didn't care about the money he'd lost in the stock market, or that Barry was demanding to be made whole for his failure to create the incident. What could the man do? Make a claim for breach of a contract to blow up a terminal? And he wasn't concerned about the request for an interview he'd received that morning from the law enforcement officials in Paris. They would be bought off. What enraged him was the vision of Herrick Wright at the ceremony in Bilbao, standing next to his daughter who looked so much like the woman he'd watched in the shower in Vietnam.

Georges hadn't conjured up the vision of Herrick and Samantha. He'd sent a man to Bilbao to surreptitiously photograph the events. The man hadn't been told of the bomb plot, of course. He'd only been told to dispatch photos by email hourly, so Georges would be sure to get them before the man was incinerated. The photos now haunted Georges. He'd looked at them dozens of times until he'd had to sit back in a chair in his study, an ice bag on his head that was pounding from the hatred surging through his body.

Sandrine had left early that morning, but he'd been too distracted to listen to her explanation. The bitch did nothing to provide succor. She'd refused to fuck him the night before. "You are too angry," she'd said. "You want to fuck me like you kick a dog. There are many dogs outside in the kennel. Go fuck one of them."

Now, Sandrine returned with his nephew, Parnell, and a woman. And he saw it was cocktail time because his grandsons also showed up. He thought Parnell was a nitwit. It was Parnell's fault he'd become involved with Danna Partners. Georges was about to storm out of the room when he looked again at the woman. She was dressed in black slacks and a black vest over a dark blue blouse, an outfit that highlighted a long torso and long legs and made attractive the small, athletic breasts that were high on her chest. It was impossible, but he knew those long legs would assuage the pain in his hips.

The woman's name was Anna and Georges learned at dinner that Parnell had met her in the course of the deal with IndoSun, where she worked. She'd been in Bilbao, where Parnell had of course not gone. She'd gone to Paris to meet Parnell after the ceremony, and Sandrine had gone to pick them up. Perhaps, Georges thought, it was a bright side to the failure of his plan. She had mysterious dark eyes that flashed when she turned her slim, lithe body to address him.

Georges was in such high spirits after dinner that he decided to go back to his study for another look at the photos. Perhaps his change of mood would allow him to see something he'd missed. It did. In the background in several photos taken in the lobby of the hotel, there was an old man reclining in a chair. He looked familiar, and finally Georges remembered where he's seen the man. After his granddaughter had visited him several months before, he'd had her followed when she'd returned to New York. His man had taken several pictures of her giving a box from the trunk of her car to a man in Hudson. It was the same man.

He called Parnell into his study and together they made furious phone calls to old friends of Georges from French intelligence, sending the man's picture by email. At one in the morning, someone identified the man as Raymond Hatcher, a foreign services officer in the US State Department who French intelligence had thought was a CIA man. They were told of a rumor that Hatcher had been blacklisted from operating in France for many years because of his involvement in Indochina with the

OSS in 1945. Finally, a Google search turned up a photograph of Hatcher's wedding. There standing next to him was the Vietnam missionary, Bradley Wright.

The twins were summoned and told they were about to go to the United States on their first mission, one of them to New York and one of them to Texas. They would only have to do what they did best. They toasted with several glasses of brandy before Parnell went off to find Anna's room. Georges knew Parnell was going to fuck her if he could sober himself up a little. He envied him, but also hoped he would be able to keep his mouth shut.

30

AT HIS FARMHOUSE IN COLUMBIA County a week later, it wasn't too cold a day and the sun was shining, so Raymond went out to the porch. He liked to stand at the rail and listen to birds around the feeder he'd put up about ten yards to the north. Recently he'd started to write notes about them in a journal. The chickadees were extremely polite. They would swoop onto the feeder, take a seed, and then fly away to make room for others. The finches swarmed about, squabbling and pushing others off the sides. He had a birdbath nearby on a stand with a long electric cord from the house for a heater to keep it from freezing over.

He watched a blue jay hop a few times on the ground and then fly off in a burst of speed toward the big sugar-maple trees about fifty yards across a pasture. It reminded him of the German plane that had buzzed Plava Guska. In Bilbao, he'd gone to the Hotel Carlton lobby that night after they'd found the sailboat with the radio gear. Sitting in an easy chair behind a newspaper, he'd watched Herrick and Samantha return from dinner. He'd been surprised to see Anna Stegineo with them. She'd been wearing black pants and a well-tailored black jacket, exactly the kind he'd seen Genna wear when she was concealing a pistol in the small of her back. The manner in which she'd stridden across the lobby wasn't that of the mousy financial analyst he'd met at Giambelli. He suspected that she knew he was behind the newspaper.

He'd forgotten about Anna until now. His recollection of recent events was often muddled. He tried hard to remember what he'd done yesterday when he went to the OSS Bakery. All he could conjure up was how the milk, when added to a glass mug of coffee, swirled in an intricate pattern until it was stirred. Yet, he easily remembered every step on the trail between Toyon Bay and O'Shea's Bakery.

O'Shea's Bakery was still in operation. Brendan's son ran it now. He was a good man, with several children of his own. Raymond thought about Megan's good natured reaction when they learned it was impossible for them to have a child. She took it like the "Sensible Meg" she was. It was probably for the best, she'd said, since Raymond would often be gone for long stretches of time, she having no idea where he was but knowing he always faced danger. Had he been disappointed? He'd told her he wasn't, that life with her was as full as it could be for him. But it was a lie, another in his long history of deceptions.

It wasn't a lie that his life with her was as full as it could be. He loved her as he had that early morning he first saw her in the bakery making cookie dough. Of course he'd have made room for a child. In a way he'd done that with Herrick and Jay. He loved them like he would sons. Jay had taken control of the operation in Bilbao. It had bothered him at first because he thought it meant that he was too old to continue the work he'd been so good at. But now he was proud.

Raymond worried that Jay hadn't married, and wouldn't now have the fine companionship that Raymond and Megan shared. What he wanted for Jay, he thought, was what a father would want for his son. And then it struck him. Jay had Samantha for a companion. It was father daughter, not husband wife, but it worked the same way. It made Raymond smile. Life had a way of circling around for the good. He'd wasted too much time recently focused on the evil of Georges Piquart. He would talk to Megan. They would go down to the Jackson Ranch and spend some time sitting on Jay's porch. Megan will love Rosie.

Thinking about Jay reminded Raymond about Bradley's journals. It was another time and place, but he imagined Jay sitting in the camp in Vietnam with Bradley and Louie. They would be friends. He shook his head. It was absurd, a musing of an old man trying to tie his past and his present together. There was no purpose in it. He should let the present be what it is. Tonight he would build a fire in the fireplace and get the journals out from their hiding place under the floorboards in the back room.

Birdsong drifted to him from a bare peach tree close to the house, and he saw the bright red flash of a cardinal. Then all the birds on the feeder burst into a panicked retreat and it became very quiet. He thought it meant a raptor was in the vicinity, but he didn't see one. He scanned the line of sugar-maple trees.

Red flashed from a tree. He thought it was another cardinal, although he knew he was too far away to see something that small. Something slammed into his chest, propelling him against the house wall. As he began to slide down to a sitting position, he thought he heard the bullet passing through the wall and burrowing into the wood floor inside.

He'd gone on a safari once. It was when he was attached to an ambassador's entourage and he was there to collect information from an agent who was under cover as a hunting guide. He remembered the man talking about stalking a lion. If you didn't have a clean shot and you only wounded the lion, the lion would hide on his belly in tall grass, patiently harness his rage, and wait for an opportunity to charge.

Megan came running out onto the porch and stood over him. She fell to her knees in front of him and took his face in her hands, but he couldn't hear what she said. Then she stood up, faced the trees, and spread out her arms. It distressed him because she blocked his path to the steps. He intended to mount a ferocious charge on the assailant who had impersonated a cardinal. But he couldn't summon up any rage. Even though it was just past noon, he believed that the sun was slipping behind the mountain over the Hudson. It was getting dark and the temperature was dropping. He was going to ask his Meg what was in the oven, but she was shouting, and this time he heard her as clear as a bell: "Take me too." Her body fell to the porch floor in front of him. None of it made any sense to him.

31

WHEN RAYMOND HAD WALKED OUT onto his porch, it had been an hour earlier for Herrick and Samantha at the Jackson Ranch in Texas. It was a beautiful December day. The air was crystal clear and the sun was raising the cool morning temperature toward the sixties. Jay walked down to the stables with them. Rosie had packed them a saddlebag with her famous fried chicken, some honey biscuits, and a bottle of wine Jay had picked out.

"Uncle Jay," Samantha said as she was adjusting her saddle, "I would swear I saw you and Uncle Raymond sitting at a sidewalk café in Bilbao when Dad and I were there. At first I thought it was just some guys who looked like you two, but then I saw the boots. Those boots you're wearing right now. I remember they were custom-made for you."

"We were passing through. Real good bird-watching in Spain this time of year. Old Raymond needed some company. Megan wouldn't go with him."

"And you had no idea Dad and I were there, I suppose."

"I'd heard you might be there, but we didn't have an invitation to that fancy soiree you two were going to with all those bankers and lawyers."

"And you're 'just an old retired cowboy lawyer,' I'm guessing is your next statement."

"Exactly, Sammy."

He grinned at her. She wasn't buying it, he could tell from the look on her face. But that was okay. It was all behind them.

"Uncle Jay, you wouldn't be pissin' in my boots and telling me it's raining, would you?"

He thought she did a damn good imitation of his drawl. Texas had turned out to be a very good place for her. The hell with old Parnell, he thought. The hell with Piquart.

"Why, Sammy, I'd never be pissin' in your boots. You can count on that."

She hugged him. "That's a good thing."

Jay had to help Herrick get into his saddle. Sammy stepped on up into hers like she was getting into a car. Then he watched them ride out across Julia's Meadow. He thought the slab of granite out in Miriam's Meadow would be warm to sit on, a perfect place for their picnic.

He'd heard from his sources that Danna Partners had lost millions on their short positions in Meteor's stock. W&K had been tipped off that Desai was meeting with Barry Silvers at the same time he was representing IndoSun. There was an announcement that he'd be leaving the firm at the end of the year to pursue other interests. Omar had called to say that the French authorities had reopened their investigation into Le Cercle and were now also investigating Piquart.

None of it mattered to Jay. He had no sense of victory. And he was worried old Piquart wasn't done, as Raymond feared. Something was still amiss. He couldn't say what it was. It felt to him like a hunch, but it had no context. He thought through what had happened in Spain. That Piquart was being investigated made no difference to him. Genna was still dead. All he knew for certain was that Piquart and the devil drank through the same straw. Still, it was a long way from France, even for the devil.

He saddled his mare, put his Winchester in its saddle holder, and rode out toward the rise above Miriam's Meadow. If he bushwhacked through the thorn bushes beneath the bald cypress tree near the boulder, he could climb up and look down on the meadow without being detected. He didn't want to crash their picnic; he thought just watching them might make him feel better. There was no satisfaction for him in Barry Silvers's losing all that money or in Desai's being fired. But there was justice in that Herrick and Sam were still alive.

He gave the horse rein and let her keep her own pace up the winding trail to the circus tent of live oaks. She stopped when they neared the top of the rise and her ears went straight up. She'd been well trained and he knew something was ahead that shouldn't be. He slid his rifle out of its holder and dismounted. It was most likely a rattlesnake or a coyote. There had been some sightings of black bears recently, but he doubted that he would find one.

Nothing was under the live-oak canopy. As he walked quietly around the boulder, a flash caught his eye. It had come from the cypress. He squatted beside the boulder. A man with a sniper rifle was halfway up the tree. One more limb and he would have a direct shot at the granite table in the meadow below, where Herrick and Sam were enjoying their picnic. Here was what he'd sensed was amiss. Jay steadied his Winchester against the boulder. The man would step up onto the next limb and then straighten himself out in order to get his rifle in place and steady himself for the shot. At that point, he would be a big target for Jay.

When he had the man sighted, there was a rush of air that sounded to Jay like a quail being flushed from the brush. The sniper wavered for a moment on the limb and then fell to the ground. The thud was not loud enough to be heard in the meadow. Jay kept the rifle against his shoulder and moved its sight in a semicircle. There was movement just down the hill from the live oaks. He saw a woman dressed entirely in black carrying a bow and running to a horse. She leaped effortlessly into the saddle and galloped off in the direction of the Colorado River. He could tell she was a good rider and he wouldn't be able to catch her.

The sniper had an arrow through the back of his skull and protruding from his forehead. He'd seen an arrow like it before, when he was on a mission in the Balkans. The arrows were handmade and used for hunting by a group dedicated to maintaining an ancestral custom. It had been a perfect shot. Jay went through the man's pockets. He found a French passport along with a wad of money and a map. The man was young, probably in his twenties. The name didn't matter. He was sure it was a fake.

Jay sat down in a patch of sunlight. It was a fine day after all, he decided. A very fine day. He leaned back and pulled his hat down his forehead. Herrick and Samantha would be headed back soon enough. He thought about whether he should try to find out who the woman with the bow was. Tomorrow he could give Lufkin a call. And Raymond knew a lot about the Balkans. But he wasn't sure he wanted to tell Raymond about this. He would want to go to France to kill the old frog, and Jay had no intention of allowing Raymond to do that. Jay could get out his sniper rifle. Lufkin might offer logistical support, and Raymond would never be the wiser. Or he could just let it go for now. Maybe this would be the end. His instincts told him not, but he was tired and the sunlight felt good on his chest.

He decided he wouldn't call Raymond. He would leave him in peace, happy watching his birds and passing the time in Megan's OSS Bakery. In a month or so he would call them to invite them down to the ranch. It was sometimes cold in Central Texas in the winter, but not as cold as it would be in Columbia

County. They could drive down to North Padre Island for some bird watching. Rosie and Megan would become fast friends, he was sure. It was all a good plan, he thought. He would take care of old Piquart himself, and then have the Hatchers down to the ranch. They would tell old stories. Samantha would come out from Austin. Maybe he could get Raymond to talk about Vietnam and his time there with Herrick's father. It was still mysterious to Jay. He wondered whether Raymond had burned the journals, as he'd said he would. Jay hoped he hadn't. One day he would like to read them.

Raymond had never talked to Jay about Megan not being able to conceive a child, other than to say they were grateful to have each other. Jay doubted that there wasn't more. He'd said the same when someone occasionally asked him why he hadn't married, that his life was full with his work and now his ranch. It was a lie he told with all the finesse he employed when working under a false identity. But the question always stung him because it immediately made him recall his love for Genna. He knew he'd ameliorated his loneliness with his attention to Samantha, but he certainly couldn't say that.

A passing cloud made the light slipping in around his hat go dim, so he sat up to reconnoiter whether it was a brief change or the end to the sunny day. Several gray clouds were lined up from the north. There wouldn't be any more long periods of sunshine. The clouds on the horizon were promising the arrival of a blue norther. Tomorrow would be cold. It made him think about the cold emptiness that periodically swept over him. It had starting coming with more frequency, and he wasn't sure why. Working with the ranch hands was an antidote, but he knew that wouldn't work for long. Perhaps he should visit his former partner from Houston. Her name was Belinda, but she preferred to be called Lyn. She'd been warm all night long in Austin. If only she weren't so frenetic. Or he could continue traveling to the East after he went to France to take care of Piquart. If he had the journals, he could retrace the steps of Herrick's parents in Vietnam. But he couldn't think how he would get Raymond to hand them over. So he would return from France and buy himself a beach house down the coast of Baja. He'd often thought of that. No phone and no television would be inside. The sound of the waves would lull him to sleep at night. It deserved serious consideration. Dropping out of sight for a time could be just the thing to get rid of the emptiness. It would be the liniment rubbed into a sore muscle.

Too much thinking for an old cowboy, he said to himself. He got the horse and dragged the corpse down the hillside to some inhospitable terrain where he knew nobody went. Tomorrow he would return with a shovel and bury what the vultures left. Then he'd think some more about what to do next.

The End

Read on for a sneak peek of

I NOTICE THAT THE SEAT of Hal Green's pants is wet as I follow him out of the Venice Bar & Grill in Somerville, Massachusetts at almost 7:00 p.m. on a Friday in late October. The evening is in the waning moments of dusk, but the light isn't so bad that I can't see the wet spot.

"Hey, Hal. Your pants are wet," I say.

"Well, no kidding, Larry," he says, stopping so abruptly that I almost bump into the back of him. "You wouldn't be kidding, would you?"

He slaps both hands against his ass to emphasize just how wet he is, and then looks at me over his shoulder. It was I who had accidentally spilled the beer in his chair. I shrug my shoulders and walk around him toward the car.

"I'm not kidding," I say. "They're wet."

"Sweet Betsy," he says, pats the roof of his car, and throws himself into his seat. I always smile when he refers to his car as "Betsy" because Betsy is the name of one of my older sisters.

"Now the seat is wet, too," I mention to him as we roar out of the parking lot.

Hal and I have been good friends since September of 1965 when we met in our assigned dorm room as freshmen. One would never have guessed at the time that a friendship would develop. He was a jock and I was a book nerd. I still have a clear vision of him from that first day, standing in the doorway with a lacrosse stick in one hand, cleats tied together and slung over his shoulder, and other implements of sports warfare falling from his grasp onto the floor. Yet, we unexpectedly developed an appreciation for each other that transcended, and continues to transcend, our differences.

I suspect that the real glue of our friendship is a remarkable proclivity in each of us to be absolutely frank with each other. I don't have any idea how or why this practice developed, but it has been uncompromised and unwavering from its initial demonstration later that first day when I told him he reminded me of a gladiator and he responded that I should keep my books, which were piled three rows deep in the middle of the floor, on my side of the room. In those days I didn't go anywhere without my books; they were like the stuffed dog I had when I was younger. Actually, if the truth be told, I considered bringing that stuffed dog to college also, but at the last minute decided against it.

Frankness is not a quality one finds in any great abundance in most people. Actually, seldom in your life do you run across a person who is completely frank. I don't mean just an honest person, who may refrain from speaking his mind on occasion to spare your feelings. I mean someone who will step right up and tell you you're a dumb ass when you need him to. The problem is that most people, by their nature, are indirect. I don't know whether it's a matter of solicitude, by which I mean that people are generally reluctant to confront you with an observation that might distress you, or a matter of insecurity, by which I mean that when you make a frank, personal statement to someone, you often reveal as much about yourself as about the person you are addressing. The fact is that more often than not, even a close friend is reluctant to be completely candid with you, and you can waste a great deal of time beating around the bush just to get to a trusted intimacy that would have been best said at the beginning of your conversation.

Let me give an example. My cousin Herrick was in love with a girl who was a bitch of the worst sort. None of Herrick's or my siblings liked her, including my older sister Betsy, who has been a close friend of Herrick his whole life. In fact, as it later turned out, my aunt and uncle didn't care for her either. What was amazing was that none of us ever said a thing to Herrick about the girl. Of course, we would all talk about her in the worst way privately, but when they would come home together we'd be as nice as cherry pie. Finally, things went bad between them. The girl flipped out and broke up with him. I'm sure I heard an explanation at the time, but that's not important. About a month later, all of us were sitting on the lawn of the house on the Cape that our two families own and Betsy said to Herrick something to the effect that all of us had always thought the girl was a bitch. Well, Herrick became furious and demanded to know why we hadn't told him. None of us had an answer, of course, and we all just sat there with our fingers in our ears, so to speak. He didn't say a word to any of us for quite a while after that. It's hard to blame him. If just one of us had been candid with him about the girl, he might have been more cautious about getting as entangled as he did. And then, perspective is not always spawned by frankness. He could just as likely have ignored the observation.

My thoughts about Herrick dissipate when Hal swears at a guy in front of us who takes too long to make a turn. As he accelerates up the College Avenue hill, he nonchalantly proposes that we might just have one more beer over at George's Place, even though, as I point out, we're going in the wrong direction and we could have just stayed at the Venice. We were there for beer and pizza with several other faculty members from the school where we teach, the South Medford Junior High School. Hal teaches math and I teach English. We play volleyball with several other teachers in the school gym on Friday afternoons after the kids are gone, and then we all go to the Venice. I suspect Hal goes more on my account than because he enjoys hanging around with the other faculty. My suspicion grows out of my observation of his eyebrows while we're there. You have never seen eyebrows as thick as Hal's, although you don't notice them when you first meet him because he's such a big guy and the hair on his head is so bushy and unkempt. Anyway, at the Venice, usually about thirty minutes after we arrive, I always observe that his eyebrows appear to be moving toward the door. Of course, it could be I who am thinking about heading for the door. Whatever the case, he often suggests after we leave that we go to another place, and when we do he is noticeably more relaxed.

I tell Hal as we approach Veterans Circle that I think I am to meet Millie, my girlfriend, at my house, and he quizzes me about why I think I'm meeting her, as opposed to know I'm meeting her, somewhat in the manner that he would quiz one of his students about the basis for a solution to an algebra problem, although a bit more playfully. He knows me so well that he guesses that my meeting Millie at my house is actually wishful thinking on my part. As we drive along the side of the Medford College fields, I remember why she will not be meeting me, but I don't say anything to him. We turn onto Highland Street.

I live near the end of the street, up on the Medford Hillside. The three-story house is divided into three apartments, with one on each floor. Mine is in the middle. No lights illuminate my windows. He turns off the engine and we look at the dark house together.

"You want to go in and see if she left a note?" he asks.

"No. She hasn't been here," I say. "She's over at the Medford College Theater. She's in a show—*Guys and Dolls*."

He doesn't react for a minute, although even in the dusk I think I see his eyebrows rise. Then he glances sideways at me and suddenly twists his body to face me. He paints his face with an exaggerated look of dumbfoundedness.

"Of course," he exclaims, slapping his palm against his forehead. "Why didn't I think of that!" He looks out the driver-side window for a second, expels a breath noisily and asks, "Do you think you could have remembered this back at the Venice before we drove all the way up here?"

I'm not sure how to respond.

"She's one of the chorus girls," I say meekly.

"Oh, you're not kidding me, are you Larry?"

And then I remember.

"Oh, right," I say, feeling stupid. "You went with me last weekend to see the show."

He shakes his head, fires up the engine and turns the car around to drive back down the Hillside the way we came. It occurs to me that my forgetting he went to the show is not too surprising, as I spent most of the time in a dark funk, wishing I wasn't there. I'd like to tell him now, as we crawl through the traffic in Davis Square, how depressed the show made me the whole next week, but I can't. It seems that my propensity for frankness only applies to my being frank about his conduct, not about my own feelings. The chorus girls do a strip tease in the second act. I slouched down in my seat during the number. It drove me crazy to think about all those eyes on her body. It didn't bother her, though; her face broadcast a big, bright smile. "Look at me," the face said. "Look at my body." There were whistles from the audience. "More!" someone yelled. "Take it all off!" The smile became even brighter. "Anything you want," her face said. And Hal didn't see why her taking off her clothes up there should bother me, when I mentioned afterwards that it had made me a little uncomfortable. "It's just theater," he said. But he doesn't like Millie anyway, so I wasn't surprised. Perhaps he now remembers my remark, because he reaches over and slaps my shoulder.

"What you need," he says, "is a tall, cold brewski."

On Mass Ave the traffic is heavy. So we take a shortcut that avoids Harvard Square and will bring us up behind the Orson Welles Theater right around the corner from our destination. I start thinking again about old Herrick not seeing what a bitch his girlfriend was and that perhaps I could be doing the same thing. I admit, I sometimes struggle with perspective, and often I can't sort out whether my responses to self-questioning are arrived at objectively or only by way of rationalization. I frequently engage in narration and dialogue in my head as a self-perspective exercise, but the sorry truth is that I always hear what I want to hear. Perhaps that's not surprising. Think about how disturbing it is to realize something unpleasant about yourself from the words or actions of another person. How much worse would it be if you were the one conveying the message to yourself?

One easy way to demonstrate what I'm talking about is to pay attention the next time you hear someone describe you to another person, and then compare that description to your self-image. The dissimilarities should be remarkable. For example, I think of me as a tall skinny guy with somewhat baggy clothes and hair flopping over his ears. I'd also describe myself as a person who is always ready with a cynical observation and who believes that if in fact we are the creation of a god, then we are his idea of a joke. I am mostly serious about this; if Jonathan Swift were alive today, I could be a character of his. But other people describe me much differently. They say I am a reserved, polite young man who is scholarly and enthusiastic, like his father, who by the way, happens to be the Chairman of the English Department at Medford College. I do have in common with my father that we are both teachers, although his teaching post is certainly more lofty than mine. At the end of college I was somewhat ambivalent about choosing a career and I sent in my application to the Medford Public Schools because I could think of nothing else. And my getting hired was happenstance; an elderly teacher died over the summer and they were desperately looking for someone to replace her at the last minute. My guess is that my application just happened to be on the top of the pile. I suspect also that the school board lost my application photo, because I had not followed my father's advice to have a picture taken in a tweed sport coat. I don't even own a tweed sport coat. But that was five years ago, back in the Sixties.

My attention returns to Hal when he bangs his rear fender into a car in the parking space behind the one into which he has struggled to maneuver us. After he performs a perfunctory inspection for damage, we walk up the street and around the corner where there is a newspaper box that still has today's paper in the window. The headline says "Israeli Troops Advance." The first doorway we come to is George's Place, which is a big, square room with tables all around. The ceiling is painted black and covered with a spongy material. Pipes that hang from the ceiling are at eye level when you enter because the floor of the room is below street level. Hal goes through the door ahead of me, down the stairs and then takes off toward an empty table, but a big guy with a Celtics hat stops me on the landing inside the door. Hal thinks they always card me because I'm so skinny, my clothes are too big and my hair is never combed, none of which is completely accurate. "You're twenty-six and you look sixteen," he said last week when the same thing happened.

"Hold onto this table, Larry," Hal says, after I finally get in the place. "I'll be back in a flash." When he returns, he bangs down two mugs. Then he turns his chair around so its back is facing his abdomen.

"Larry, do you remember Winkle?" he asks.

"Yep. Randall Winkle. But I haven't seen him since graduation."

"I ran into him the other day," Hal says. "He owns a house on the Cape. He inherited it from his grandfather last year."

"You're kidding!" I say expressively, always interested in the Cape because my family owns a house in Orleans. "Where is it?"

"It's in Chatham Port," he says. "Isn't that near your family place?"

"It is," I say. "What's the name of the street? Do you know?"

"Oh, hell. I can't remember that," he says with a grimace. "It's out in the car. He invited me out for the weekend."

If my memory is accurate, Randall had a face like a little dog, and he was only about five foot five. So I was always looking at the top of his head when I was around him. And he sniffed his food just before he ate it. He held it right up to his nose and squinted his eyes. Then he'd wrinkle the top of his nose when he chewed.

"Wrinkle Winkle," I say, remembering also that Hal and Randall had been good friends in prep school but had drifted apart at Harvard, particularly after Hal dropped out. "You used to call him that."

"Yeah," Hal says. "But he's changed. I wouldn't call him that now. He's become pretty sophisticated."

"Oh, no!" I exclaim. "He was such a goof. He would drive down Mass Ave in that old red Porsche convertible like a bat out of hell."

"I remember! I remember!" Hal roars. "He'd put the top down in the winter and wear that old aviator's hat and goggles."

"That's right," I say, my eyes leaking a bit from laughing at my image of Randall and his goggles.

Thinking about Randall's car unfortunately reminds me of Richard Bevins and his red Corvette. I saw Millie and Richard standing on her porch last night, not that I was spying on her or anything. I just happened to be walking by on the other side of a row of hedges. His car was in front of her house for quite a long time. I have an image, suddenly, of Bevins speeding up the coast road to his family's estate in Rockport that Millie and her friends talk about all the time. In my image Millie sits beside him with a scarf covering her hair, holding her arms up against the wind, exclaiming how wonderful the feeling is.

"That was the spring I was learning to play golf," Hal laughs, assuming I remember some other incident with Randall that I don't remember.

"I remember," I say, happy to continue reminiscing without asking what incident he's referring to. "Your golf balls kept rolling around the room."

"There was a hole in my bag," he says, resting his chin on his hand. "It wasn't my fault."

"Well, I stepped on one in the morning once, and almost broke my neck," I say, feigning indignation.

"You should take it up, Larry. It's a great game."

"No thanks."

"In fact, that's what Winkle and I are doing this weekend. He belongs to the club right there in Chatham. Or is it Orleans? I can't remember."

"It must be Orleans," I say. "There's a course on the other side of Pleasant Bay from our house."

"God, that's a beautiful place," he says, his eyes unfocused in a way that suggests he is looking at Pleasant Bay as he speaks. I close my eyes for a second and can see the part of Pleasant Bay that abuts our house, the sun glinting off the water and Strong Island just across the channel. Beyond the island are the flats, which are just below the water line if the tide is in, and then the dunes rise up, shining white with spots of waving green beach grasses. On the other side of the dunes the surf is roaring ashore from the Atlantic. I imagine white foam and spray, although I know you can't see it from our side of Pleasant Bay on account of the dunes.

"Most of the leaves could be off the trees by now," I say. "My cousin Bradley and I would usually rake them up on Columbus Day."

"How is Bradley?" Hal asks, his eyes snapping back into focus.

"Okay, as far as I know," I say.

"I'd forgotten," Hal says. "You and Bradley used to hang around the Cape during the summer."

"Every summer of our lives, until just a couple of years ago."

"I know this," Hal says, hitting the side of his head with his knuckles. "Don't I know this?"

I've repeated the story to Hal on numerous occasions, how the Browns and the Wrights, related through our mothers, own an old house in Orleans on the top of Pleasant Bay, not far from the Cape Cod National Seashore. The property on which the house is situated juts out into Pleasant Bay and extends back toward the north along part of a narrow channel that connects Pleasant Bay with Little Pleasant Bay. On account of this channel we often refer to the house as "the Narrows." There are ten children between the two families. My twin sisters were born first. Betsy was third, about three years after the twins, and I'm the fourth, born a couple of years after her. Herrick is about the same age as Betsy. He's the son of my deceased aunt and uncle who were missionaries, killed when Herrick was a boy. His mother and Bradley's mother, my aunt Adelaide Wright, were twins, both of them a part of the four Clements sisters, who included my mother. Bradley Wright is my next cousin, a year older than I, and our cousin Sally, the daughter of another Clements sister, is a year younger than I. So, the three of us— Bradley, Sally and I—were the youngest children in the Cape

Cod household, until just about twelve years ago when Carla, my kid sister, was born.

All of those summers growing up, Bradley, Sally and I were inseparable friends, although in some of the grade school years I'm sure Sally suffered through the role of Bradley's tag-along little sister. As young teens we became particularly close, sharing complaints regarding our parents, our older siblings—who we believed were always mistreating us—and just the Establishment in general. College was the breaking point. One at a time we drifted away, led by Bradley going to college in California. We came together for shorter periods in the summer during the college years, until one summer Bradley didn't return from California and a couple of years later Sally went into the Peace Corps for two years.

"So what happened?" Hal asks, after I mention to him that I have not spent much time on the Cape recently. "Did everybody just stop going to the house or what?"

"No. Our parents still go. And Carla goes, of course. And some of the older children and their families go. Bradley, Sally and I just got involved in other things, like the Peace Corps."

"And Bradley's still on the West Coast?"

"I think so," I say. "I haven't heard from him in a while. At least, not directly."

"So what does that mean?" he asks, wrinkling his forehead at me. "Do you communicate by rumor or what?"

"No. Well, that's not far off, actually," I say slowly. "Every once in a while a girl will show up at my door, tell me Bradley gave her my address and ask to spend the night."

"Now that's unique," he says, his features animated. "Who are these chicks?"

"It's not how it sounds," I say quickly, "These girls have all been a little different."

"Oh?"

"They're into macrobiotics," I explain. "They bring their own rice to cook. I think they were all from a commune out there. I don't know. They don't talk much, either."

"Too bad," he says, shaking his head. "Anyway, it must have been nice, growing up with all those brothers and sisters and cousins. All I had was the chauffeur, the maid and the nanny. I was an only child, as you know."

"I remember. But having all those siblings isn't so great all the time, either."

"Nothing is perfect," he says, banging his fist on the table. "That's what I always say."

"You're right," I say, banging my fist also, mocking him.

"Larry," he says in a serious voice. "You should come with me to Winkle's. I can pick you up first thing in the morning. It will be good for you."

"Golf is such a stupid game," I say, disgustedly. "You spend five or six hours chasing a little white ball through the poison ivy. What's so thrilling about that?"

"Well, there's more to it than that," he says, a little defensively.

"It's bullshit," I say, feeling a little feisty from the beer I've been drinking. "It's just a bunch of grown men walking around with long sticks, acting affected."

"That's ridiculous," he sputters, but then composes himself. "So come along for the ride. Bring a book to read while we're out on the course. I bet Winkle's house is beautiful. And it would be great to see him. We can talk about old times. And you can look across the bay and remember all the good times at your house."

"I can't," I say, and then turn my gaze out over the crowd, hoping he will drop the subject.

But I have no such luck. He's all over me in a flash, wanting to know what I could possibly be doing that was better than going with him to the Cape. And in a way he's right, if the truth be told. Nothing could be better than going to the Cape. I think about how I could spend a morning drinking coffee down in Chatham, reading a book, and then later sitting on a dune at the National Sea Shore. An awkward fact comes out quickly from his questions: I am expecting to see Millie. It's also a fact, however, that there exists no actual arrangement to meet Millie. She has the closing performance of the show tomorrow night, and I know there is a cast party afterwards. She hasn't mentioned that to me, but surely she's just been too distracted and will call me tomorrow. Hal shakes his head in exasperation and put his palms to his forehead.

"You are such an idiot," he says very quietly.

I protest. Why would he think so? He starts counting reasons, which, I admit, sound plausible. She has stood me up before. Then I remember how I met Millie in the first place and I stop him to say that, regardless of whether she calls me, I have to be in town on Sunday afternoon for my father's annual professor-student mixer at my parent's house. That was where I first met Millie. And he knows that I enjoy going to my father's party to get some chuckles from all the freshmen trying to impress the professors.

"Oh. Well, I can see that," he says in a disappointed manner. "I just thought you could use a good time."

He's on his feet, suddenly, stretching his arms and back, and then he's off to the bar with both of our glasses. When he returns, he rotates the chair around to its conventional position. He bangs the glasses on the table again.

"Yours was warm," he says, good-naturedly. "Who can drink warm beer?"

"The British. They drink bitters warm."

"Well, then, here's to you, old chap," he says quickly as he polishes off half a glass.

"Cheers," I say, taking another tiny sip.

The roar of all the surrounding conversations suddenly ebbs, and I feel as if we are hearing the guttural inhalation of a retreating wave. When I look over at Hal to see if he notices, his countenance makes me think that he has willed the relative quiet for the purpose of making a point. I look around but no one is paying us the least bit of attention. He leans forward over the table. I brace myself.

"Oh, shit, Larry," he says quietly, his eyebrows moving closer together with what I suspect is an internal struggle over what he is to say next. "You're such a smart guy about so many things. I'm going to level with you. You don't know it, but that bitch is two-timing you."

"What? Do you say that she makes me a cuckold?" I ask, trying to use some levity to defuse the bomb he is arming.

"A what?"

"A cuckold."

"Is that something like a turkey?" he asks, looking puzzled.

"A turkey? Yeah, that's good," I laugh. "In a slangish sort of way, I guess it could mean that. It actually means the husband of an adulteress."

"God, I hope it never gets to that!" he exclaims.

"To what?"

"To the husband part. Anyway, this isn't a joke, goddamnit," he says, irritably. "Be serious with me, why don't you?"

"Okay," I relent.

"I think she's making it with that Sky King guy."

"That's Sky Masterson," I say.

"Well, whoever," he sputters, banging the table with his fist. "What difference does it make, goddamnit? That's not the point."

"Oh?"

"What's his real name, anyway?"

"Bevins. Richard Bevins."

"That's the guy," he says. "That's who I'm talking about."

"You're crazy," I say. "So they're in a show together. They're just friends."

"Oh, bullshit!" he roars, rolling his eyes around like an epileptic. "Just friends! I can't believe it."

"Besides, how do you know this?" I demand.

"I know," he says smugly, now that he has my attention.

"Just like that? You just know? Like you're some kind of psychic or what?"

"I have my sources," he says, leaning back in his chair and appearing to enjoy my agitation.

"What's that supposed to mean? Your sources? If you don't want to tell me, just say so."

"A little defensive, are you?"

"Maybe. What do you expect? You just told me my chorus girl was balling the leading man. Do you expect me to say, 'That's great news, Hal'?"

"Listen, nobody wants to hear shit like this, but it's something you have to know," he says, leaning forward in his chair. "She's taking you for a ride."

"I don't know," I say, shaking my head. "I think you're mistaken. People always jump to conclusions about things like this. They watch too many soap operas. That kind of stuff doesn't happen in real life."

"You're crazy. You know it? Do you think everyone in the world is as straight as you? Do me a favor. Leave your wallet with me when you go out from now on."

"So what do you want me to do—become a cynic overnight? It takes practice," I say.

"Just get real," he says, ignoring the slight. "That's all I'm saying."

"I'm as real as I can be. I just don't believe you're right."

"Clair," he says, almost in whisper. "The costume designer."

"Clair?"

"She's my source. And don't you go running to Millie and tell her this. Clair will kill me."

"She lives in Millie's house."

"That's the one."

"I didn't even know you knew her."

"I know her sister. What difference does that make?"

"Why didn't she tell me herself? I see her all the time."

"Are you crazy?" he says, rolling his eyeballs. "Girls don't do that kind of thing. Besides, what was she going to do? Walk up to you in the living room and say, 'Oh, Larry. Did you know that Sky King is poking old Millie when you're not around?'"

"So she told you."

"Right."

"And told you to tell me."

"No. She told me not to tell you."

"Why would she tell you if she didn't expect you to tell me?"

"She did expect me to tell you," he says, looking confused.

"But she told you not to tell me."

"That's the way that girls think," he says, exasperated. "What difference does it make?"

"Maybe she's lying," I say, desperately trying to discredit his information, although I know, perhaps better than he knows, that Clair is a credible source.

"Why would she do that?"

"Why would she tell you not to tell me?"

"Who the hell knows why a woman tells you anything," he says, and bangs the table with the bottom of his glass, which causes foam to rise on the top of the remaining beer. "Maybe I just caught her at a weak moment and it slipped out. Maybe she just wanted you to know, but she didn't want to be responsible. Who knows? I'm not a goddamn shrink. I'm a math teacher. And what difference does it make anyway?"

"I don't know," I say after a moment, trying to keep my voice steady. "I don't want to talk about it anymore."

He doesn't say anything, and looks around at the other tables. The noise from the room washes over me. But the image of waves rolling onto the shore leaves me. Now the sound is only a hundred voices speaking at once and sounding like a motor that needs a tune-up. My instinct is to look off into the distance in order to push the closeness of the moment away from me, separating myself at least by a theoretical gap. I can look no further than the wall across the room, unfortunately, because all of the windowpanes are painted black. You never know whether it's going to be raining when you go out.

The windowpanes were painted white on the back door of the house Millie lived in last year. I remember that because I studied them for a couple of hours one evening from the outside when an old boyfriend of hers from Hartford unexpectedly dropped in. She pushed me out the back door right after one of her roommates told her he was at the door. "He can't see you here. He's a caddie at the country club and he'll tell my father you were here," she said. The next day when I mentioned to her that I'd hung around on the lousy porch all that time she said, "Oh, I thought you'd gone home, Larry. I never thought you'd be standing on the porch. Why would anyone stand on the porch in the rain for that long?" It was as if it were my fault that she had forgotten me out there. Why would I leave when it was only supposed to be a minute, and she was going to get rid of him, and with the rain crashing down like it was! But I never asked her that. I just shrugged my shoulders and said something about it being a misunderstanding. Now I wish I had said something. Suddenly I regret all the times I never said anything, all those times when it inexplicably became my fault that she had done what she did to me. And I start to wonder whether, through some fantastic turn of logic, Bevins is my fault also. The thought is so preposterous that my attention snaps back to Hal.

"I can't believe it, Hal. She wouldn't do that."

"Sometimes truth is harder to believe than fiction," he says, drumming his fingers on the side of his glass.

I suspect he is demonstrating a gruff manner in order to keep himself from sympathetically agreeing with me and backing down in his determination that I face what he is sure is reality. And I feel for him suddenly. It is hard to stand your ground in the face of desperate denial.

"But it's not the truth," I insist, weakly. "It can't be."

"Suit yourself," he says and looks around the room again.

Just a few nights ago she held me in her arms and whispered in my ear, "You're the only one." The funny thing is that when I first met her, she said I was only the next of many before me. She was as matter of fact about all her prior sexual experiences as she was telling me her favorite ice cream flavor. Then, as I got to know her, I began to suspect that her stories were not true. Finally, I decided she had fabricated them, and after that it was as if she had never told them. Instead, she whispered in my ear, "You're the only one." It's as if time rubbed her stories smooth, like the sea takes the sharp edges off a piece of broken glass.

"Suppose you're wrong, Larry," Hal says, interrupting my thoughts. "Suppose it's true."

"Okay, Hal. Suppose it is."

"You wouldn't do anything, would you? If you found out for certain she'd been making it with Sky King," he says, intensely.

"What could I do?"

"Well. You could stop shining her damn shoes," he says, vehemently. "That would be a good start."

"How's that? If it's true, she's getting the shoes shined someplace else, to borrow your metaphor."

"Save the English stuff for your students, why don't you!" he yells.

"Sorry, but it was a metaphor," I say, leaning forward and almost whispering, in an attempt to quiet him down.

"So what?" he says with lower volume, as he realizes from my hint and the stares of the people at the table next to us that he's attracting attention. "Oh, for Christ sake, Larry," he says, now in a normal voice. "I'm trying to be serious and you're talking shop. How would you like it if I started doing algebra on the goddamn napkins while we were talking?"

"Okay, I'll rephrase. If she doesn't love me, she won't be coming around," I explain.

"Is that what you think?" he asks, his voice rising again momentarily. "That all this is about whether she loves you or not?"

"What else would I think?"

"You are out to lunch," he growls. "Love has nothing to do with this."

"Well, excuse me, Master Lewis," I say sarcastically. "What is it, then?"

"Trust me on this one," he says, ignoring my literary reference. "This is about a spoiled bitch who has one thing and wants everything."

"You know what, Hal? I don't want to talk about this anymore. I mean, you're entitled to your opinion and all. But I don't want to talk about it anymore."

"Fine," he says abruptly.

He turns in his chair a little, so he's not facing me, and looks across the room at the people filing in the door. The place is starting to get crowded.

I think about Millie being at my place last weekend. I remember Sunday morning like it was a photograph. She lay on her back and counted strands of her hair. She had her two hands up close to her face and her fingers gingerly separated the hair. Her eyes focused so close to her face that they almost crossed. Her body hardly made an indentation on the sheets. "I think I'll wear my yellow sweater today," she said. She's always speaking her thoughts out loud like that, like she's delivering a little running commentary for my benefit. "It's time to brush my hair now," she'll say, or "I wonder if I turned the tea kettle off." It's her way of being intimate. The image explodes in a rush of steam from the kettle when Hal leans across the table suddenly.

"You know what I think?" he says rhetorically. "It's not Millie you love, it's the idea of being in love with Millie that you love. Millie just happened to be around when you got the silly idea that you wanted to be in love with someone."

"That's crazy."

"Maybe. Maybe not."

"Why would I be doing that?"

"I'm not a psychologist, Larry."

"Okay."

"But why else would you continue to chase after this two-timing bitch like a lost puppy?"

"Assuming you're right," I say, my voice cracking a little.

"Well, I'm wrong or you're wrong," he says, pointing in an exaggerated way first at himself and then at me. "One of us is wrong. But I've got all the evidence on my side."

"So what? It's a mistake," I say, trying to be calm, trying to act as if this was so clearly a mistake that it's not worth discussing any longer. "She wouldn't do it."

"Why not? Give me an explanation," he presses, refusing to be put off.

"Because she's a good person," I say, regretting the words as they leave my lips.

"Oh, no. Not that!" he exclaims, slapping both hands to his cheeks with feigned theatrics.

"Cut it out, Hal," I say, trying not to look at him.

He's rolling his head around in an exaggerated manner, looking like I just hit him with a baseball bat.

"Not the 'good person' routine!" he says.

I shrug my shoulders. I'm not going to say it again so he can slobber all over the goddamn table.

"Spare me," he says.

"Get lost," I say.

"O Mighty Oberon!" he says. "This poor soul needs the service of your gentle Puck."

"Oh, for Christ sake, Hal. Give it a break, why don't you!"

"Post your Puck to pour a sweet liquor to reverse the foul magic that clouds the vision of our poor Demetrius."

"Cut it out, will you?"

"Did you like that? 'Post your Puck to pour.' What's that called?"

"Alliteration."

"Pretty goddamn good for a math teacher, if you ask me."

He stands and leans toward me, with both hands, palms flat, on the table. A girl with curly red hair and a lot of lipstick watches him, talking all the time to her tablemate. She's a couple of tables away and my line of vision is such that I'm looking at her in a diagonal across Hal's forearm, and she's looking right at his left rear pocket button. When she notices me watching her, she looks away. In a second she looks back quickly, then away again.

"I have an insight," Hal says.

"Won't it work from a seated position?"

He squints. He raises an eyebrow. Then he shifts his weight and gathers the mugs together by their handles. The glasses crack when they come together. I hate that sound, because I always think they're going to shatter into a million pieces. And that would be a pain in the ass. We'd have people all around us suddenly, trying to clean up, just like when I spilled the god-damn beer at the Venice earlier. And everyone in the place would be gawking at us. Whenever I do something like that, everyone develops a rubber neck.

"First, we'll have another," Hal says.

I toss a couple of ones on the table and he slaps his hand down on them while looking at me, probably wondering if he should refuse them, given his sympathies concerning what he's just told me. I rub my fingers on my pants. You can't rub away the feeling of money. It's just like talcum powder.

"If you insist," he says, crumpling up the currency like it's a used piece of Kleenex, and then walking away. The girl with red hair watches his swagger, glances back at me, then quickly turns her attention back to her companion. She reminds me of a lion, with the way her hair waves back against her shoulders. As she speaks to her companion she leans forward in an exagger-ated manner, trying to emphasize that she's concentrating on her conversation and is not distracted by us. Some things are so transparent.

Hal returns and starts up a banter that is playful in a way but, I suspect, a cleverly disguised strategy to come back around to his point about Millie. It's the same as when we were room-mates, he contends, my seeing the world through a filter com-posed of all the novels I had read. True, I did, and still do, read all the time. And perhaps I am influenced, I admit, through some vicarious connection with characters and plots. As I explain to him, however, I'm not substituting a novelist's plot for what's happening to me. At most, it's a case of applying experience to interpretation, a case of analyzing precedent. I got the prece-dent idea, by the way, from vicariously experiencing Herrick's law school travails.

"With real life, there is no plot," he says.

"Sure there is."

"No, there's not!" he insists. "Every minute you live is a beginning for which there is no end. There's no plot. There's no meaning. It just is what it is."

"How can you say that," I demand. "Just look back over the time since we met. There's a plot there. There's meaning to what's happened to us."

"But you see, that's it. That's it, exactly. You're looking back. We've already been there. When you're talking about life, you have to look forward."

"So, there's still a plot going on now. We just don't see it yet."

"No. That's the difference. There's no plot until it happens. Every word a novelist writes, every action one of his characters takes, comes about in the context of the conclusion he knows will occur. And that's not life. You can't see into the future. And you can't draw your conclusions and then live your life to fit them. That would be stupid, right?"

"I don't know."

"It's stupid. Just think about it. You expect Millie to be good to you because you're good to her. You expect that doing the 'right' thing always wins the reward. You look into the future and you see her acknowledging how great you've been to her. But you're living by a code that is given short shrift by real people. It's a code you got from your goddamn books."

"You mean like the Bible?"

"Yes, Mr. Sarcastic," he says, shaking his head in an exaggerated manner. "The Bible. And all the other goddamn books that have all the answers."

"People have values," I say. "That's all you're talking about."

"Sure they do," he says. "But you have to remember that in real life, it's the people who determine the outcome, not the values."

"What?"

"What I mean is that, generally speaking, people merely pay lip service to values, and when a situation is contrary to their desires, they mostly forget what they've said. Then they rationalize what they've done, or they beg forgiveness so they can have it both ways. In day-to-day life there's not a clear-cut ideology like you have in a novel. There's no fairy tale for every circumstance, Larry. You think that there's always a fairy tale ending ahead."

"You really think there isn't?"

"No," he says. "There isn't. There's only what you make yourself."

"You're depressing me."

"Not me, buddy boy," he says, leaning back in his chair. "You're depressing yourself with all the make-believe."

"I'm just trying to put a good slant on things, that's all," I say, sounding a little desperate suddenly. "I'm just a poor slob trying to get by. Your approach seems so cold, so empty and futile."

"Oh, boy. The poor slob trying to get by," he says, rolling his eyes around in his head. "Talk about putting a slant on things. And empty? Not a chance. My tank is full of reality. Yours has only the fumes of imagination and irrationality."

"That's pretty good," I say, smiling at his imagery. "The fumes of imagination and irrationality. Not bad for a math teacher."

"You like that?" he grins, and then shakes his head. "I've been hanging around with you too goddamn long."

The girl with red hair is watching us again. I look right at her, and she looks away quickly. I wonder if there is some twist to the plot starting here, with her clumsy observation of us. Perhaps she is a jilted girlfriend of Bevins and, hearing his name, is wondering at the connection, calculating whether there may be here some opportunity for recompense for the misery she has suffered. I look at her more closely. No, she is not pretty enough for that plot, unless he never actually paid her any attention in the first place and her believing herself to be jilted is a fantasy. That would certainly make her the one in this group with the least perspective, I think smugly.

I deflect Hal away from his questions about Millie to a conceptual conversation on reality. I have some good points of reference that I try on him, the best one, I think, is Shakespeare, with Hal being Theseus trying to set me straight about Hermia. Of course, the question from there is whether it is better to mistake a bear for a bush or to mistake a bush for a bear. He falls into the trap and answers that it is better to mistake a bush for a bear, as the consequences are not nearly so bad as the other way around. I pounce, observing that in reality, making such a mistake is preposterous, that only a mind heavy with imagination could come up with a circumstance where a bear is mistaken for a bush.

"It was a trick question," he yells.

"No, it wasn't," I say, calmly.

"You asked which was better, not which was possible."

"Do you often make value judgments about the impossible?"

"I'm confused," he says, shaking his head.

"True."

"How did we get to bears and bushes from Sky King and your two-timing girlfriend?"

"We were establishing, I think, that there is a delicate balance between reality and illusion, and, since you claim I live in the worlds of the fiction I read, between art and life."

"Look," he says, leaning forward. "You say she's a bush, I say she's a bear. If I'm right, you're going to get mauled."

I shrug my shoulders. The game is getting old and it's time to go home, I'd like to say.

The girl looks at us again, but just for a second before she stands up and stretches. She points her elbows by clasping her hands behind her head, and for an incredibly long time she stands like that with her eyes closed and her chest pushing against her sweater. The effect is appealing, I have to admit. Perhaps Bevins *was* attracted to her.

"Let's talk about something else," I say, hoping that he'll just suggest that we go home.

"Fine," he says. "Did you have your tenure visit?"

"Did you?" I ask, after shaking my head no.

"I sure did. And I got a haircut for it, in case you didn't notice," he says, grinning and turning his head from side to side.

"So you did," I say.

"You could use one yourself," he says.

"It's not going to make any difference, Hal."

"Sure it is," he says seriously. "And you could also consider teaching a conventional lesson when they come, not one of your weird things where everyone sits on his desk and chants."

"That was a good lesson, I'll have you know," I say, indignantly. "We were reading *Siddhartha*."

"Oh, give me a break, Larry. When they come, teach grammar or spelling or somebody like Mark Twain, if you have to teach literature."

"That would be intellectually dishonest, Hal."

"Oh my god," he says, going through his repertoire of eye rolls and facial contortions. "I can't believe it."

"You have no principles," I say, trying to look disgusted, but not exactly sure that he isn't right.

"Sure, Larry," he says. "And next year, you won't have a job."

"All on account of Hesse," I say, slapping the table and feeling a little ridiculous. "They're going to refuse me tenure on account of Hesse?"

"Oh, please, Larry. You make huge accommodations for Millie and for your tenure review, you're irredactable. Now that makes sense," he says, glaring at me with wide eyes.

"Oh, good word, Hal."

"You like that?"

"I do," I say, hoping I've broken his train of thought.

"I've always liked the sound of 'irredactable,'" he says. "It reminds me of gum you can't get off your shoe."

"You know what, Hal," I say after a moment. "I liked the Sixties better."

"Are you changing the topic, Larry?"

"No. Really. At least in the Sixties you felt good about yourself, no matter what you were doing. Now everybody is too busy getting ahead to worry about whether they feel good about themselves. It's a different culture, almost, and it happened in just a year or two. That's what is so incredible about it. Woodstock was a fluke, if you think about it."

"Maybe you're right," he says. "I've never thought about it."

There's a kid standing at the door showing his license to the bouncer. I notice him only because he looks a lot like Bradley, only younger. He has the same curly blond hair. I wonder if he'll get in.

Suddenly, the red-haired girl stands next to us.

"Hal?" she says. "Is it Hal Green?"

When he stands up, he towers over her.

"Sure is," he says.

"I'm Mary Ann McGuire."

"Mary Ann!" he says, enthusiastically. "How are you? Sorry I didn't recognize you, but it's been so long."

"Oh, don't apologize," she says, with a tiny laugh. "I've been sitting over there with a friend for an hour trying to remember where I knew you from."

"Well, sit down. And your friend. Where's your friend?" he says, looking around as he pulls out the chair to his left.

"Oh, he had to go," she says and sits down.

"Meet Larry Brown," he says. "We're teachers together at a public school in Medford."

"Nice to meet you," I say, feeling low suddenly with the evaporation of my hypothesis that Mary Ann had been cast off by Bevins.

"Likewise," she says.

Meeting old acquaintances always involves a ritual of establishing the circumstances by which you are acquainted. Hal and Mary Ann get right to it. They met at the Boston University School of Education. After graduation, he got his position in Medford and she became a guidance counselor in Roxbury.

The kid I saw at the door earlier sits down at the table next to us. He sits there by himself without a drink, staring at the wall. Some of the people at the neighboring tables gaze at him quizzically, as I do, but then my attention is diverted back to Mary Ann and Hal, whose conversation has moved on to Mary Ann's summer trip to England. I should keep my mouth shut, and just smile and nod. I know I should.

"Mary Ann," I say. "You didn't go to Oxford when you were in England?"

"No. I ran out of time. I really wanted to go. I wanted to go to the Cotswolds too."

"There's a great place near Oxford called Port Meadow," I say. "Have you heard of it?"

"No."

"It's this big meadow. Every year the Oxford sheriff is required by law to collect taxes from those who graze their animals in the meadow. So he nails up an announcement the day before, that he will collect the annual tax for all animals in the meadow the next day."

"Oh, that's smart," Hal says. "I bet half the cows are mysteriously missing the next day."

"Actually, all of them are. On annual tax day there's not a cow in the meadow."

"Really!" Mary Ann exclaims, her eyes so wide that I wonder, for a second, whether she is mocking me.

"No kidding," I say, deciding that she isn't. "In fact, most of the cows are standing right outside the fence in the road. And the whole town is there. The sheriff goes into the meadow, looks around and says, 'No tax this year,' or something like that, and the crowd cheers."

"Then what?"

"Then, they put all the cows back in the meadow and they all go to the Trout to celebrate."

"The Trout?"

"It's like a bar. It's down at one end of the meadow, next to the river. Of course, the sheriff doesn't pay for his own drinks."

"That is so incredible. I wish I'd made it to Oxford," Mary Ann says.

"You are so full of shit, Larry," Hal says.

"It's a true story. I swear to god. It happens every year."

"I'll never understand the English," Mary Ann says. "You'd think they'd just repeal the tax."

"You'd think so," I say, trying to duplicate the stupid look on her face, and finding it difficult. "Some people never want to change anything, do they?"

"It's so silly," she says.

"Even when it's completely stupid, they don't change."

"But you'd think someone would do something, anyway," she says.

"I suppose there's a moral to this story, Mr. Smart Guy," Hal says.

"I don't know. Maybe."

"You jerk."

"What? I don't get it," Mary Ann says.

"Well, maybe there's something to be said for tradition," I say.

"Oh," she says. "I see. I think."

Two guys walk up to the table next to us, where the kid is sitting by himself. I notice them right away because they look so straight. They're wearing perfectly ironed white shirts and their hair is really short. One of them actually has a crew cut. The other one reminds me of the Beaver's brother, Wally, from the television show. The kid just looks at the table in front of him, not acknowledging them. It occurs to me that he may have come into George's in the first place to evade them, figuring a bar would be an unlikely place to find him. None of them look like beer drinking types. The guy with the crew cut puts his hand on the kid's shoulder.

"Jeremy," he says, "we've been looking all over for you."

"I'm not going back," Jeremy says, pushing the hand away.

"Misha is disappointed," the guy who looks like Wally says.

"Fuck Misha," Jeremy says.

Old Wally and Mr. Crew Cut don't like that. I can see the displeasure in their faces. Jeremy clutches the end of the table, like he's afraid they're going to drag him away. He grips so hard that his knuckles turn white. He is clenching his teeth and still refuses to look up.

"You must come with us," Wally says softly, bending down close to Jeremy's face. "The devil is with us in this place."

"We must return to the Path," Mr. Crew Cut says, putting his hands on Jeremy's shoulder in a paternal fashion.

He tries to help Jeremy up, but Jeremy refuses to let go of the table.

"Oh, dear," Mary Ann says. "I'm afraid there's going to be trouble."

Hal leans over and taps Mr. Crew Cut's arm.

"Hey, Buddy," he says. "Why don't you leave the guy alone?"

"We are not here to make any trouble," Wally says quickly.

"Good," Hal says, "because we're all trying to have a good time here."

Wally and Mr. Crew Cut look at each other.

"Jeremy has lost his way," Wally says. "We're only trying to take him home to Misha."

"So what's the matter with him?" Hal says. "He can't find his own way?"

"You might say that."

"Come on home, Jeremy," Mr. Crew Cut says. "Come on home to Misha."

But Jeremy doesn't let go. His face is red and he grimaces.

"Oh, they're hurting him," Mary Ann whispers.

Mr. Crew Cut looks at her in a threatening manner. Hal pushes back his chair a little.

"Doesn't look to me like he wants to go see Mishy," Hal says in a loud voice. "What do you think, Larry?"

"Doesn't look that way to me," I say without looking at either of the men, wishing Hal would leave me out of this.

Hal looks at Mary Ann and raises his eyebrows. She shakes her head. Then he looks at a group at a nearby table.

"What about you guys? Does he want to go see Mishy?"

"Mishy fishy!" someone from another table yells.

Nervous laugher rocks the place. Mr. Crew Cut's neck turns red around his collar, and his lips press together, tight as a clam.

"That's Misha," he says, strictly.

"Okay," Hal shrugs. "Misha, then."

"Fuck Misha," Jeremy yells suddenly.

With the flash of his hand, too quick for the eye to follow, Mr. Crew Cut slaps Jeremy's face. Hal's body blurs across the distance between them, like the close passing of a speeding car. Chairs fall, a woman screams, several men yell, all amidst a general scramble to back away from our tables. Hal, with both hands about Mr. Crew Cut's throat, swings him in a circle.

The melee moves to the right, toward the wall. Hal's eyes are wild. He's going to hang Mr. Crew Cut on a hook like a coat, if no one stops him. The bouncer yells and pushes his way through the crowd.

Mary Ann screeches at me, like some kind of prehistoric bird. She pounds her fist on my shoulder. Wally advances toward Hal with a chair over his head.

"I should have gone home an hour ago," I say to no one in particular.

"Do something, Larry," she screams.

I never think clearly in situations like this. I just do the first thing that occurs to me. I have my hands on the table, so I give it a running push at Wally. It slides across the floor. I'm amazed by how easily it slides, almost like the floor is greased. I wonder if it's adrenaline, if this is one of those circumstances where I couldn't move the table to save my life if none of this commotion was going on.

The whole thing works better than I planned. I hadn't intended to push the table as hard as I did, and I didn't notice that the corner of the table was exactly groin-high on Wally. He falls to his knees and someone in the crowd grabs the chair that falls from his hands.

"Oh, I'm sorry," I say, sincerely. "I didn't realize."

Mr. Crew Cut's head hits the wall with a thud, like the sound of a basketball off a rim. Hal holds him in place, poised to give his head another slam. The bouncer is closer. I run over and tap Hal's shoulder.

"Sorry to interrupt, Hal," I say, as calmly as I can, "but I've got to get home."

"What?" he screams.

"For Christ sake, Hal. Let's go," I yell.

"Fine," he says and releases Mr. Crew Cut, who slides down to the floor.

People mill around now. Someone slaps Hal on the back. People in bars love this kind of thing.

Mary Ann stands aside, a bewildered look on her face. The bouncer leans over Wally. Hal pulls me by the arm.

"Nice to meet you," I say to her as we pass.

The air is so cold outside that it feels like water from a hose on a hot day flowing over my head. It's the same as when I was a kid and I got so hot playing baseball that I would put my head under the spigot.

"Are you going to stand out there all night, Larry? Let's go, already."

"Keep your pants on," I say, refusing to be hurried through my brief flashback of my childhood moment.

He gets the car moving before I even get the door closed.

"People park so goddamn close," he says. "How do they expect you to get out?"

He bumps a few fenders. Then we're out and driving down a dark side street, weaving our way home.

"Who were those guys, Larry?"

"Krishna people, maybe?"

"No," he says. "What makes you say that? They didn't have those little pony tails."

"Some other religious group, then," I say, just wanting to forget the whole thing. "There are lots of them."

"I don't remember them saying anything religious."

"Do you think someone named Misha is the leader of a motorcycle gang? Did they look like bikers?" I ask, sarcastically.

"Maybe it was a fraternity or something," he says, ignoring my insolence. "They were sort of dressed like fraternity guys."

"Fraternity guys don't dress like that anymore."

"Well, how would I know?" he asks, his voice showing his frustration.

"No, it was some weird religious thing," I say. "That guy was talking about the devil."

"You ever heard of Misha?"

"No."

"What about nonviolence? Don't all these guys preach non-violence?" he asks, his voice strained, almost to a shout.

"The violence was yours, Hal," I say quietly, knowing what I say will raise his hackles.

"Wait a minute," he yells, his eyes flashing at me. "He smacked the kid. What was I supposed to do?"

"Turn the other cheek," I say. "And you could watch the road also."

"It was his goddamn cheek, not mine," he rants.

"You're right. It surprised me too," I say in a conciliatory way.

"What about goddamn freedom of religion? What's hap-pened to that?"

"I don't know," I say, quietly, seeing that he's raving, all pumped up from his physical struggle.

"The kid didn't want to be in their club, did he?"

"Didn't look that way to me."

"Oh, never mind. What do I care."

"I'd forget it," I say, staring out the window and trying to appear disinterested.

"What happened to that other guy, anyway?"

"He bumped into the table."

"No, not him. The kid."

"Jeremy?"

"Right. Jeremy."

"I don't know. He disappeared, I guess, when the commotion started."

"Well, isn't that something!" he sputters.

"I'd forget it, Hal."

"Yeah. I'll forget it. In just a minute, I'll forget it. But here I stand up for this kid and he just beats it."

"What was he supposed to do, Hal? Hang around and kiss your ass?"

"Okay, Mr. Smart Guy. A simple thank-you would have been sufficient."

"Just forget it, Hal. That's my advice."

"You can't just forget it. What do you mean, forget it?"

"It was a fight in a bar," I say, a little irritably. "Aren't we too old for that?"

"Are you kidding? Speak for yourself."

"I'd forget it."

"It will make a great story on Monday."

"Looks like good weather on the Cape tomorrow, Hal."

"I'll say."

We drive along the soccer field, just after Veterans, and the moon is up over the tops of the houses on College Avenue. There's a starlit, clear sky, which is a harbinger for clear weather for the weekend.

It will be nice to have a crisp day for my father's party on Sunday. Professor O'Neill, an old friend of my parents, will make a big deal about it. He'll come banging into the house in his tweed coat and his pipe. Then he'll kiss my mother and yell "What about this fine weather!" And she'll say, "Luck of the Irish." That's what she'll say.

"Well, a good time was had by all," Hal says, as he pulls the car up in front of my house.

"I'd have had more fun sticking my head in an airplane propeller," I say grimly.

"Oh, come on, Larry," he says, punching my arm. "We had a good time."

"Just kidding," I say, giving him a weak smile.

"Okay, then, champ. Sure you don't want to come to the Cape? Last chance."

"Some other time."

"Your loss," he says.

"My loss."

He drives off. I don't feel like going inside, suddenly. The windows are dark. I think about how I'll describe my feelings in my journal later tonight, how I'm thinking that Millie, if she were upstairs, would have the lights on, how the windows would be aglow, her fear of being alone in an empty house in the dark all too strong, as I know from earlier occasions for which my way was lighted and my tardiness met with grave displeasure. My journal entry will sound like I'm old Leonard Bloom come home to look for his Molly.

I walk up my street to the top of the Medford Hillside and look back toward my house. The empty street reminds me of the strange visitor I had this morning. It was 6:00 a.m. and the early morning light was coming through the windows. A frail girl in old clothes and long, straight blond hair pounded on my door.

"Oh, you're not Bradley," she said, after I swung the door open.

"Who are you?"

"Is Bradley here?" she asked, trying to look around me.

"No, he's not."

"Are you Larry Brown by some chance?" she asked after she dug a wrinkled piece of paper out of her pocket.

"Yes."

"Bradley gave me your name, and, I'm sorry, I thought he might be here."

"He's in California. At least, that's where he was the last time I heard from him. And that was six months ago, or more."

"Oh."

"So, why don't you come in and sit down," I said, opening the door wider and standing aside.

"Oh, I can't," she said after she stared at me for a moment. "It's six in the morning!"

"Well, you knocked, didn't you?"

"I'm sorry. I thought he would be here."

"Why?"

"What?"

"Why would he be here? He's in California, like I said before."

She looked around, as if she'd forgotten where she was.

"You're right. I mean, I don't know. I'm sorry I bothered you."

She started down the stairs.

"Wait. What should I tell him?"

She stopped, suddenly, and turned around.

"But you said he wasn't here."

"He's not. But if he shows up, what's your name?"

"He probably won't," she said, waving her hand.

"But if he does, I should tell him you were here."

"I have to go," she said as she ran down the stairs.

"Wait," I called after her.

I paused because I didn't have my shoes on, but then I ran after her anyway.

"I'm sorry I woke you up," she yelled.

By the time I got to the porch, she was already a couple of houses away. I watched her run down the hill toward Highland, the same hill I'm now looking at. I remember wanting to yell to her to come back so she could tell me something, anything, about Bradley: what he's doing, how he's feeling. But I didn't know her name. So I couldn't.

Acknowledgements

This book was written during a time that included retirement, moving from our home in New York City to a foreign county, and bringing a puppy into the family. A better person than I may have been able to write in such circumstances without being querulous. Not so with me. So, here I express my gratitude for the patience and understanding of my wife, Nancy, our daughters Kate and Andie, whom we "abandoned" in New York City after selling their childhood home, our daughter Sarah, who had to tolerate us in her San Diego house while we dealt with the logistics of getting our Baja home in order, and, of course, our dog Finnegan, who took it all in stride as only a good dog can. All of them, except Finnegan, had tolerated for decades my wistful aspirations to write fiction instead of contracts and indentures. And, finally, I thank my editor and publisher, Ross Palmer, for taking a chance with me and patiently devoting so much time and effort to make my jumbled prose into something readable.

About the Author

MARK ZVONKOVIC IS A NOVELIST and recovering lawyer who lives in Baja, California with his wife Nancy and their two dogs, Finn and Cooper. When he's not writing, he and his dogs watch pelicans fly.

www.ingramcontent.com/pod-product-compliance
Lightning Source LLC
Chambersburg PA
CBHW030601180626
46816CB00005B/1628